A SILKEN THREAD

BRENDA JACKSON

A SILKEN THREAD

A SILKEN THREAD

ISBN-13: 978-0-373-53426-5

Recycling programs for this product may not exist in your area.

www.kimanipress.com

Printed in U.S.A.

Acknowledgments

To the love of my life, Gerald Jackson, Sr.

To everyone who loves to escape between the pages of a good book. This one is for you. Happy reading!

Dear Reader,

I was born and raised in the largest city in Florida—Jacksonville. I often wondered how it would be to live in a smaller town where most of the people knew each other and everyone had a secret they never wanted told. That curiosity propelled me to write about a fictitious town in the northwest called Hattersville, Ohio.

I officially want to welcome you to Hattersville, where over the next books you will get to meet some of its town folks. Each has a different story to tell, some of survival, of belonging and others of wanting some things you just can't have. Hattersville is being revitalized. New residents are moving in and in some areas, old residents who swore when they left they would never come back are returning. And it seems that love, sex, divorce and revenge are on some people's minds. A new generation is determined to put the city on the map, while the old want to keep things as they've always been.

A Silken Thread explores how love can survive when threatened by vengeful secrets from the past and how two couples refuse to be denied the happiness they deserve and are determined to share a love that has no boundaries. This story is a very special one and I hope you enjoy reading it as much as I enjoyed writing it.

Happy reading!

Brenda Jackson

Love endures long and is patient and kind…it takes no account of evil done to it—pays no attention to a suffered wrong.
—*I Corinthians* 13:4, 5

Chapter One

"So, tell me. Have wedding jitters taken a toll on you yet?"

Erica Sanders glanced across the table, thinking that only April, her close friend since junior high school, would have the nerve to ask her something like that with a straight face. April North knew her so well. She could tell Erica's anxiety and stress were mounting, only a couple of weeks from the engagement party at which the couple's families would officially meet. Erica was so not looking forward to that affair—unless her mother's attitude changed drastically.

"Yes, I'm a *little* stressed," she admitted. "My sanity is barely holding up. But it's to be expected of every bride, isn't it?" She figured if anyone should know, surely April would. After all, her best friend had walked down the aisle three times already.

"Umm, a *little* stress is to be expected of every bride. But in your situation…" April left the words unsaid.

Erica's mother was driving her crazy.

With one breath Karen Sanders would rant and rave about Brian Lawson not being good enough to marry her daughter, and with the next breath she'd give the wedding planner hell because she intended for Erica's wedding to be the social event of the year.

It would be a wedding befitting the great-great-granddaughter of one of the founding fathers of Hattersville, a small town of seven thousand, noted in the history books as one of the first cities for freed blacks in Ohio. Erica had lived in Hattersville all twenty-seven years of her life, except for her college years in Wisconsin. Living in another city those four years had opened her eyes to a lot of things, especially how closed-minded and snobbish some of the residents of her hometown were. But not all of the citizens were privileged. Her friend April had been born on the other side of the tracks, in the Fifth Ward—something Erica's mother liked to remind her of every chance she got. But to Erica, what side of the tracks someone was born on didn't matter, and her close friendship with April had always been special. Besides, April, who had always been a beautiful person, had gone from rags to riches and was now a world-famous model. That proved that anyone who put her heart and mind to it could become successful, despite her humble beginnings.

Needing to escape the oppressive atmosphere of the town even more than Erica did, April had traveled west to attend UCLA, where she'd met husbands one and two. Husband number three, whom she'd divorced a year ago, was someone she'd met in Great Britain.

"You know as well as I do," April continued to say while eating her salad, "that Ms. Karen's idea of a dream marriage is one between you and Griffin."

Erica knew that was true. Griffin Hayes's family, like hers, represented old money in Hattersville. Naturally some people, especially her mother, assumed she and Griffin would grow up and marry. There were those, again namely her mother, who figured that doing such a thing was not only politically correct, but would destroy some curse reputed to have been placed upon the two families that could only be broken by a marriage between them.

Unfortunately, nobody bothered to inform her and Griffin's hearts, since they just weren't feeling it. Their families had thrown them together so often when they were growing up that eventually they began thinking of themselves as sister and brother, rather than as a couple whose lives were destined to end in holy matrimony.

Although they'd tried dating while in high school, the fire was simply not there. Griffin had recognized it and so had she. That was when they'd made the decision to be nothing more than friends.

"Mom might as well get used to the idea that I will not be Mrs. Griffin Hayes," Erica said. "I most certainly have. Trust me. Brian is all the man I want and need." She doubted anyone, even April, knew just how much she meant that.

"Will he be flying in this weekend?"

A huge smile spread across Erica's lips and she held up two crossed fingers. "Let's hope. They've hired two more attorneys at his firm but he still has a large caseload."

She and Brian, an attorney at a prestigious law firm in Dallas, had met last summer while vacationing in Myrtle Beach. He had been out fishing on the pier one morning and she had been jogging along the shoreline. They had struck up a conversation, and he had invited her to breakfast the next day. A few weeks later, they had become lovers.

When the summer ended they decided to keep the affair going and, beating the odds, their long-distance romance had survived. Over the Christmas holidays Brian had asked her to marry him. She had accepted and now looked forward to her August wedding and her move to Texas.

Her mother had been in an uproar at the thought of her only child marrying someone other than a Hayes and moving away. Even now, months later, there were days Karen Sanders had problems coping with the inevitable.

"So how's your dad holding out?" April asked, breaking in on Erica's thoughts. "Has your mom convinced him to disown you yet?"

Erica thought about her dad, with his soft hazel eyes so filled with love and understanding. He had given her his full support—although he kept it low-key so as not to get her mother riled. But it was the little things he would say and do to let her know he admired the fact that she was doing the very thing he hadn't done, marrying for love instead of for the sake of preserving some legacy. It was no secret her parents' marriage had been arranged.

"You know as well as I that won't be happening," she replied. She and her father had a close relationship and things between them would always be that way.

A short while later she and April were walking to their parked cars, promising to get together several more times while April was in town visiting her grandmother. It was the first week of March and there was definitely an Ohio chill in the air, which made Erica tighten her shawl around her shoulders. The shawl, a Giorgio exclusive, had been a birthday gift last year from April.

Up ahead Erica saw the town's square, brightly lit and rimmed by a well-maintained lawn. The parks in the Fifth Ward might look deteriorated and in need of care, but here the statues of the city's forefathers were in perfect condition. It almost sickened her when she thought of the good citizens' priorities.

She glanced at her watch. It wasn't even eight o'clock and already the retail businesses had closed, leaving the area looking like a ghost town. The town had survived what would have been rough economic times when a few wealthy residents had come in and bought out the small, struggling businesses, which made the rich even richer and gave them tighter control and ownership of the town.

Even her job as head librarian and accountant at the town's historical library was nothing more than a cushy position created by her parents—mainly her mother—to assure the history of Hattersville was well preserved. Erica was constantly reminded that if it hadn't been for the forefathers—those free blacks who'd come from Canada—the town wouldn't exist.

For generations there had been a distinct line between the two groups of people living in Hattersville, the haves and the have-nots. Those that had money—the Hayeses, Delberts, Sanderses, Carters, Heards, Bakers, Cobbs and Stonewells—were those who owned major manufacturing corporations that employed thousands of people who drove into the city to work.

After giving April a good-bye hug, Erica slid into her car, a cherry-red Mercedes two-door that had been a birthday gift from her father a couple of years ago. After strapping on her seat belt, she was about to turn the key in the ignition when her cell phone rang. She smiled when she saw the caller was Brian. She wasted no time answering it. "Hi."

"Hi, sweetheart. Where are you?" he asked.

"About to leave Ryder's Steak House. April's in town so we did dinner." She paused a moment and then asked, "So, do you think you can get away for the weekend?"

She heard his chuckle and the sexiness of it carried through the phone. She immediately recalled the first time she'd seen him, shirtless and wearing a pair of cutoff jeans with a fishing pole in his hands. He had given her a flirty smile and she'd turned to mush. She had actually felt that smile in every part of her body, every pore and every single cell. That smile had transformed her into one hot and achy mass and on that day she'd discovered that the whole concept of lust was as real as real could get.

"Yes, I think I can get away," he said, interrupting her thoughts. "By the way, there's something waiting for you at your house."

A smile touched her lips. He had been known to send her thinking-of-you gifts through the mail. "There is?"

"Yes."

She wondered what he'd sent her this time. Last week it was a CD on which he'd recorded "Rock-a-bye Baby" in his deep voice like Barry White's as a way to lull her to sleep each night. "What is it?" she asked.

He gave her another sexy chuckle before simply saying, "Me. And now that you know, don't speed getting here."

How could she not, Erica thought after a quick gasp escaped her lips. They hadn't seen each other in over three weeks and she was filled with a deep longing that she knew would be getting satisfied in a big way when she saw him. Sensual shivers danced up her spine when she envisioned how that would be accomplished.

"Make yourself comfortable until I get there," she told him.

"I've done that already and I can't wait to see you, baby."

She couldn't wait to see him, either. "I'm on my way."

Before Brian could give her a hot response, one that would probably make her detonate, she clicked off the phone, started her engine and pulled out of the parking lot. With Brian in town her plans for the weekend had definitely changed. Everyone would understand.

Everyone but her mother.

Brian Lawson held his mobile phone in his hand a moment longer than necessary before putting it on the table. He released a satisfying breath at the same time that he felt flutters in the pit of his stomach. The same thing always happened to him whenever he heard Erica's voice.

If anyone had told him that falling in love with a woman would be this way, he would not have believed them. But he was convinced he had fallen in love with Erica the moment he'd seen her that day on the beach, and somehow he had known she was different from the other women he'd dated.

He had been a man comfortable with being single. A man who enjoyed dating when it suited him, with no plans to settle down anytime soon. However, after spending time with Erica that summer, he had known in a short period that she was a forever kind of girl. But the thought hadn't scared him off like it really should have. Instead, the more he'd gotten to know her, the more he'd wanted to become her forever kind of man.

Sighing deeply, he took another swallow of beer and glanced around his future wife's eat-in kitchen. It was large, spacious and it suited her since she enjoyed cooking. So did he. That was one of the first things they discovered they had in common.

The walls were painted a pale yellow and her appliances, all white, actually made the room appear larger. His stainless steel kitchen back in Dallas, although it might look more modern, seemed depressingly sterile compared to hers. And then there was that huge picture on the wall, the one of Myrtle Beach beneath a sunny South Carolina sky. It was nice to look at while sitting at the kitchen table, especially during a frosty Ohio winter. Even better, it was a drawing of the exact place they'd met that summer. Right down to the actual pier. When he'd seen it in a gallery in Texas, of all places, he couldn't miss the chance to get it for her. For them.

He sat down at the table to wait for Erica to come home. If he remembered correctly, Ryder's was twenty minutes away on the other side of town, and although he'd warned Erica not to rush, he knew that she would anyway. That meant she would be arriving in ten minutes or so.

He glanced around the kitchen again, and from where he sat he had a good view of her dining room and living room. His condo back in Dallas wasn't nearly as large. It was the perfect bachelor pad, but they had decided that they would move into a bigger place after they married, one closer to the office.

They had also decided to keep this condo so they would have a place to stay whenever they returned to Hattersville to visit her parents. Of course there were plenty of guest rooms in her parents' monstrosity of a house, which could easily be considered a mansion. But he appreciated Erica's intuitiveness in knowing he'd be uncomfortable spending even one night under Karen Sanders's roof. It was no big secret that he wasn't exactly her choice for a son-in-law.

Erica's mother was definitely nothing like his mother. Rita Lawson had to be one of the sweetest and most down-to-earth women to walk this earth. She had raised him after his father died of an aneurysm when Brian was fifteen. Putting him through college and law school hadn't been easy, but she had done it without any complaints. For that he was exceedingly grateful. And now he was proud that she was doing something she'd always wanted to do. She'd always loved the outdoors and was now a landscape architect for a major corporation. Her job entailed a lot of traveling, which was something she'd always dreamed of. Just last week she had returned from Beijing. It had been her first trip to China and he couldn't help but recall how excited she was when she'd shared the experience with him.

She had officially met Erica months ago and had immediately fallen in love with the woman who was to be her future daughter-in-law. He took another sip of his beer wishing Erica's mother had been that accepting of him.

He tried not to let the thought bother him, but every once in a while he couldn't help but dwell on it. Didn't the woman know that the time when parents selected spouses for their offspring was over? Erica had her own life and was old enough to determine just how she wanted to live it and with whom.

Brian heard the sound of a car door closing and knew Erica was home. He stood up and a feeling of anxiousness flooded him. Anxiousness and love.

He heard the rattling of the keys at the back door and knew within seconds he would be seeing the woman he'd chosen to spend the rest of his life with, the woman he wanted to have his babies, share his name, be by his side forever. He would honor her, love her and respect her for as long as he lived.

Trying to get a grip on all the emotions that began over-taking him, he drew in a deep breath the moment she opened the door. Their gazes immediately connected and the smile on her lips seemed to stroke every single inch of him.

She was wearing her hair down, and tonight it fell around her shoulders in fluid waves. Some of the dark strands seemed lighter underneath the brightness of her kitchen light. His gaze moved to her face. The first thing that had captivated him about her was her eyes. They were cat eyes, hazel in color and so captivating that a man could take one look in them and lose his senses. He definitely had that the first time. The next feature he noticed were her lips. They were per-fectly shaped, made exclusively for his. She'd once said she hadn't experienced a bona fide kiss until she'd kissed him.

His gaze traveled slowly from her face to her feet, admir-ing everything he saw in between, especially the curves that shaped her figure. She wasn't as tall as most women he'd dated, but he thought her five-four height perfectly com-plemented his six-three frame.

Yes, Erica was a strikingly beautiful woman, a creature

that sensual fantasies were made of. His chest tightened. She was so damn gorgeous that when he looked at her he couldn't think straight, and a fierce, primitive need rumbled through him. He felt himself take his first steps toward her at the same time she kicked the door closed with her sandaled foot and moved toward him.

The moment she was within arm's length he reached out for her, mumbled from deep in his throat, "Welcome home, sweetheart," just seconds before he captured her mouth beneath his. He felt her immediate response as she automatically plastered her body to his as if she had every right to do so.

And she did.

By asking her to marry him and putting that ring on her finger he'd given her rights he'd never given another woman. Rights he would continue to give her. She was his heart, the very epitome of his soul, and he loved her in a way he had thought he could never love a woman. In a way he truly hadn't wanted to love a woman.

At fifteen he had been old enough to remember the hurt and pain his mother had endured when they'd lost his father unexpectedly. Patrick Lawson had been there one day, a vital part of their lives, presumably in the best of health, working as a partner in a prestigious law firm—the same one where Brian was presently employed, but then the next he was gone. Neither Brian nor his mother had been prepared for the loss, and even now, nearly fifteen years later, he often wondered if his mother would ever recover, since she hadn't allowed another man in her life.

He pushed those thoughts aside and concentrated on the woman in his arms, the way her tongue was tangling with his, diligently determined to swipe any and every thought out of his mind except for one—making love to her with a need he felt all the way to his toes. For now that was all that mattered. She was all that mattered.

He'd been having erotic dreams of Erica every night since last seeing her. She hadn't helped the situation during their nightly talks. She had been better than any dial-up sex line any man could have called. During their late-night talks, she would deliberately make her voice even huskier in their sexually explicit conversations. She would whisper things she would do to him when they were together again that he was certain weren't found in any sex manual. They were promises that only fueled his sexual fantasies. No wonder he was fighting for control and trying not to succumb to the urge to strip her naked right now. Right here.

"Make love to me, Brian. Show me how much you've missed me."

She broke off the kiss and whispered the words against his moist lips. He smiled, thinking that would be easy. He needed to be inside her as much as she needed him. He'd had too many lonely nights without her and he intended to make up for them this weekend. With that thought in mind, he swept her off her feet and carried her toward the bedroom.

Erica buried her face in Brian's shirt as he effortlessly carried her toward her bedroom. From the moment his lips had touched hers, she became lost in the demands of her body, her mind and, most importantly, her heart.

Until that moment she hadn't known it was possible for any woman to love any man this much.

She inhaled deeply and drew Brian's scent into her nostrils. He smelled manly, with a tang of wild and reckless. She knew from experience that he could turn her bedroom into an adventureland that even Disney couldn't compete with. There was no doubt in her mind that tonight Brian would be bringing all of her erotic dreams to life, all those sexual urges to fruition and all those private thoughts to the forefront.

Tonight, this entire weekend, she would join him in letting

go and giving in to physical needs as well as emotional ones. And as he placed her on the bed, she knew the pleasure was just beginning. The moment the bedcovers touched her back she tipped her head up and met his gaze. The dark eyes staring back at her nearly took her breath away.

Not for the first time she thought Brian Lawson wasn't just classically handsome; he was heart-wrenchingly beautiful in a masculine way. From the deep darkness of his eyes that could hold her spellbound, all the way to the elegant bone structure of his cocoa-colored face, which would be flawless if not for that small dent on his nose. He'd said it had gotten broken when he had taken a fall off his skateboard as a child. But that minor imperfection only added to his looks, giving them an arrogance that was not a part of his demeanor. Not one iota. She doubted there was one conceited bone in his body.

The women might all pause when he walked into a room, but he didn't use his looks to get what he wanted. He was a charmer by nature, with a smile that could sweep a woman off her feet. With dimples in both cheeks and a cleft in the center of his chiseled jaw, he exuded a strong sense of manliness, while at the same time making her feel as if she was the most precious and feminine being on earth.

"We have on too many clothes, don't you think?"

His words intruded into her thoughts and she couldn't help but get turned on from the playful grin that touched his lips. Drawing in deep, steady breaths, she watched as he began removing some of his clothes. She enjoyed seeing him naked, watching him expose the most dynamite male body, from his head to his feet. But she definitely loved those areas in between. Those parts that could make her temperature spike while delivering pleasure beyond measure.

Fueled by a need she'd only discovered since knowing him, she felt an ache travel from the lower part of her stomach to the juncture of her thighs. Desire took on a life of its own when he eased his jeans, along with his briefs, down power-ful, masculine thighs and legs. When her gaze settled on his erection, she stifled a gasp. Although she doubted it was pos-sible, he seemed to have grown since the last time.

Fire flared through her veins and when he stood before her completely naked, love and lust dueled within her. She knew those feelings were totally acceptable. He'd taught her time and time again there was nothing wrong with having such a hot and heavy desire for the man she loved.

"Strip for me, Erica."

She eased up on the bed, knowing he liked seeing her take off her clothes, although she much preferred those times he took them off for her. But she would accommodate him, give him exactly what he wanted, since she knew he would be taking care of every one of her needs.

She whipped her blouse over her head and sent it sailing across the room, coming within inches of landing in the small wastepaper basket. She glanced over at Brian and when he lifted an amused brow, she could only throw her head back and laugh while reaching behind her to remove her bra.

His breathing changed when her breasts were freed. She heard it and as she studied the way his chest was moving, she saw it. She kicked off her sandals and seductively leaned back to make it easier to remove her slacks. She worked out often, so she was proud of her body.

She loved the way Brian was looking at her, letting her know he liked her body, as well. His gaze darkened and his erection grew, revealing, unashamedly, just how much he liked it.

When she was completely naked she sat back on her haunches in the middle of her bed and smiled at him. She flung her head back, tossing her hair wildly around her shoul-ders, met his gaze and asked, "Think you can handle this?"

He smiled. "I'm going to try." And then he reached for her, pulled her into his arms, lowered his head and covered her mouth with his.

Brian thought there was nothing like making love to a woman who was more than your other half. The woman who could make you fight reaching an orgasm just from her feminine scent alone. A woman who was driven with a need just as fierce as your own.

She was kissing him back with a passion he felt all the way to his toes, but he especially felt it around the head of his shaft, right there, that part that wanted to connect with her in the most primitive way. She could ignite feelings and emotions in him that were almost overwhelming. The first time he experienced it, he'd been tempted to haul ass as far away from her as he could get. He'd been completely convinced she'd cast a spell on him, used some sort of witchery to literally bring him to his knees.

But he didn't run as he'd been tempted to do. He'd been too intrigued, too determined to discover what it was about Erica that made her different from all the others. And after spending time with her he'd found the answer. She was just as alluring out of the bedroom as she was inside it. She didn't have a pretentious bone in her body. She was totally genuine and he loved her.

Amazing, how he loved her.

And with that thought embedded deep in his mind as well as in his heart, he continued to kiss her, enjoying the way she was kissing him back with a combination of heat and passion.

His hands roamed all over her body as he angled his head to kiss her even deeper, needing to touch her, reacquaint his hands with her heated skin and the parts of her he could never forget. Never intended to forget. There was an urgency within him that he felt and knew she felt, as well.

The phone on her nightstand began ringing and he pulled his mouth from hers. She was flat on her back as he loomed over her. "Do you need to get that?" he asked.

She blinked as if hearing the ringing phone for the first time and then she shook her head. "It's probably Mom. I'll call her back later."

And then she reached up, wrapped her arms around his neck and pulled his mouth back down to hers. A rush of profound desire filled him to capacity, made his entire manhood ache in a way that only she could. Made him feel like one greedy bastard with a need to get inside her, be enveloped in her hot heat, her inner muscles clenching him in a way that could make him growl.

Like he was doing now.

She recognized the sound, knew what it meant, and it seemed her body prepared for what was to come. Her response only fueled his need as he leaned back and flipped her on her belly, and then his mouth went to work. He needed to taste her all over, every inch of her skin, top to bottom, inside and out.

He felt her shiver when his tongue did a hot sweep up her spine, over her buttocks and thighs. And when he flipped her on her back and continued the torment with his mouth to her breasts, licking the dark nipples, before sucking the hard pebbles into his mouth, he couldn't help but feel the desperation that flamed his actions, fired his senses.

The next minutes consisted of seduction in its most sensuous form, both sweet and raw, and by the time his mouth settled between her legs, using his tongue to excite her even more, to make her squirm in sensual need beneath his mouth, something inside of him nearly broke.

Being here with her, loving her this way was the reason

he had nearly driven himself crazy reworking his schedule to make it here before the weekend. The flight had been torturous. All he could think about was what he would do to her when he saw her, how her body would react while he made love to her.

"Brian!"

He recognized the tone of her voice, knew what it meant, and he pulled his mouth from her and eased his body in position over hers, parting her thighs in the process. "I'm here, baby."

And with one smooth thrust, he was inside of her. For a minute he stayed still, needing to absorb the feel of being planted inside of her, feeling the way her inner muscles clenched him greedily as if trying to milk everything out of him.

Then he began moving, withdrawing and thrusting again, over and over, listening as her whimpers turned into murmurs and then groans. No woman knew how to take him in like she could.

She was with him all the way, never missing a beat as he made love to her the way he was driven to do, the way he knew she expected. The next time they would go slow, savor the moment. But for now it was fast and voracious. Hard. Relentless. No restrictions.

At that moment he couldn't imagine his life without her. He wondered how he'd made it before he'd met her, and knew it didn't matter now. She was here, in his life, in his arms, sharing his body while he rocked within her, and he knew at that moment August couldn't come fast enough to suit him.

He took her mouth again and she gasped the moment he did so, causing a firestorm of emotions to erupt within him. He thrust deeper, harder, and when she screamed his name, his senses shattered and his erection exploded. The hot release that shot from him into her, mixing with her juices, made him pull back his mouth to suck in a deep satisfying breath. He inhaled the scent of sex—raw, primitive and edgy.

One hell of an orgasm ripped through them, wrapped them in a cocoon of sensations, enveloped them in something so deep and absolute he knew she was an element in his life that he needed just as much as he needed his next breath.

And as they slowly began drifting back down to earth, he knew they would rest up a bit and then do this all over again. He was looking forward to it.

Chapter Two

"Erica isn't answering her phone, Wilson. I think I'll call Griffin and ask that he go over there and check on her," Karen Sanders said, tossing the words to her husband who stood on the other side of the living room about to pour a glass of scotch. For years this particular room served as the place the two of them would retire after dinner.

Lately, however, she couldn't help noticing their paths crossed increasingly infrequently, especially since Erica had moved out. There was less conversation between her and Wilson these days, although she would be the first to admit during the thirty years of their marriage there had never been much dialogue anyway.

Their marriage had not been one of love, but over the years they'd put up a good front and tried to make the best of it. Now without Erica there to motivate the pretense, such a charade was no longer needed...at least not in private. It was as it was. He'd been born a Sanders and she a Delbert. Their parents had planned their futures and they'd had no say in the matter. That's the way things had been and she fully understood the importance of preserving one's family heritage, especially when it was a distinguished one such as theirs.

Instead of hanging up the phone she immediately began dialing the number of the man she'd always assumed would one day be her son-in-law. As far as she was concerned, engaged or not, there was still hope that Erica would come to her senses.

"I wish you wouldn't do that, Karen."

She glanced across the room again and met Wilson's tired gaze. He had been working a lot of hours at the office lately, doing more business traveling in his role as CEO of a multimillion-dollar corporation, one that had been in the Sanders family for generations. He had good people working for him and, though he was turning sixty in November, he wouldn't hear of retiring.

"Excuse me, but why wouldn't you want me to call Griffin to go over and check on Erica?" she asked him. "He lives only a few miles from her so it shouldn't be a problem."

He frowned. "That has nothing to do with it and you know it. You think I don't know what you're doing? You're deliberately putting Griffin in Erica's face every chance you get. When are you going to accept the fact that our daughter has fallen in love and it isn't with the man you picked out?"

That statement hit a nerve that was completely raw. "She would have listened to me, possibly even considered my position, if you had backed me up on the matter, Wilson."

He all but slammed his tumbler down on the coffee table. "When are you going to realize it's not about you, Karen? Our daughter has fallen in love. That in itself should make you happy."

She waved off his words with an elegant hand. "Happy? The very thought makes me want to have a stiff drink. Spare me the spiel about love, Wilson. It has nothing to do with our daughter. We raised her to expect the finer things in life. Love won't keep those expectations coming her way. My ancestors, yours and the Hayes's have established their places in Ohio's history. We aren't regular people and everyone in this town knows it. They go out of their way to give us the respect we deserve. The respect our forefathers always intended for us to get. The notion of Erica leaving Hattersville is bad enough, but she plans to get a professional job, for crying out loud."

"A little hard work never killed anyone. That little glamour job as librarian you made sure was dropped in her lap is a joke and she knows it. She's always resented it and only took it to keep peace between you two."

She stared at him for a moment and then said, "A person born of both Sanders and Delbert blood should not have to work. There are enough people in the lower classes capable of handling the manual labor."

Wilson pressed his lips together to keep from coming right out and calling his wife a snob. She would probably take it as a compliment, anyway. Over the years he'd been tempted more than once to deliberately plunge the company into bankruptcy so that she could see how it felt to be one of those less fortunate souls, those same people she looked down her nose at. He knew she went to bed each night thinking she'd done her Christian duties by giving her time to make life just a little better for those she considered inferior.

"Whether you think I should call Griffin or not, Wilson, our daughter is missing."

He rolled his eyes. "Cut the drama, Karen. Erica is not missing. She probably went out for the evening. I talked to her earlier today and she mentioned April was in town. The two of them are probably together somewhere."

He saw in his wife's eyes the frown she couldn't hide. Erica's friendship with April North was another thorn in her side, something she'd always considered an evil. He'd always been proud of Erica for standing up to her mother on that particular issue, refusing to let Karen choose her friends, just as he was proud of Erica for refusing to let Karen manipulate her into marrying Griffin.

"Well, either we let Griffin verify she's all right or I'm calling Bob."

Bob Denison was the chief of police in Hattersville. Wilson was well aware that his wife had practically bankrolled the man's last couple of reelection campaigns, which put him in Karen' back pocket pretty damn deep.

"Don't involve Bob," he said, reaching for his jacket. "I'll go check on Erica myself."

He didn't add that he needed a reason to get out of the house, a reason to dismiss himself from her presence. Little did she know that, although she would badger him on occasion about the hours he put in at the firm, the main reason he did so was because he'd rather be there than here.

There was no need to pretend that he was in love with his wife, because he wasn't. And the sad thing about it was that he never had been. But then, she hadn't ever loved him, either, so any absence of emotions on his part didn't warrant a guilt trip. Their marriage had started off from day one as a business arrangement. At least that's how their parents had explained it to them. Now, thirty years later, nothing had changed other than their ages and the fact that during one of those rare times they'd made love they had produced a daughter.

He wondered if Karen had ever considered getting out of their farce of a marriage. Had she ever thought about wanting more or mulled over how it would be to really fall in love? Had she asked him for a divorce he would have gladly given her one. But she'd never asked, which meant she was satisfied with how things were between them. He was not. Never had been. And lately he was beginning to realize just how dissatisfied he was.

"When you find Erica, please let me know she's all right."

He worked the jacket over his shoulders. "Erica's not lost, Karen. When are you going to realize and accept she's a grown woman and not a child?"

Of course her response was one he didn't want to hear, and a weary sigh flowed from his lips as he left the room.

"Close your eyes and open your mouth, sweetheart."

Erica smiled and did what Brian asked. The moment she felt the spoon enter her mouth and tasted the chocolate concoction on her tongue she couldn't help but moan.

She opened her eyes. "It's delicious, Brian. Where did you get the recipe?"

They were standing in her kitchen. He was barefoot and shirtless and his jeans hung low on his hips. She was wearing his dress shirt and nothing else. After making love a second time he had dragged her out of bed and into the kitchen. They had ordered pizza and he had taken over her kitchen to make his favorite sweet treat. Brownies. And to top them off he'd made a mouthwatering chocolate sauce.

"It's one of Mom's. She uses it in her cake batter sometimes to make it moister."

She nodded as she licked her lips. She'd been serious when she'd said the sauce was delicious and she couldn't wait until the brownies cooled so they could layer it on top of them. The coffee had been brewing and she was anxious to pour a cup to go along with them.

"And how is your mom?" she asked.

He smiled as he turned back to the stove. "She's great. Her contract with the Hastings Corporation was renewed, which means even more international travels for her. But she loves it."

Erica leaned against the kitchen counter. She had met Brian's mother months ago, the first time she'd visited him in Dallas. At first she'd found it hard to believe that the woman was old enough to have given birth to him. She looked to be in her early forties instead of fifty-two. And upon their introduction, Erica had immediately felt a genuine warmth emanating from her. She hadn't known what to expect, since she'd figured out early in their relationship that Brian and his mother were rather close.

"Is she looking forward to the engagement party my parents are planning for us?" she decided to ask.

"Of course."

Erica's brows lifted in surprise. "She is?"

Brian chuckled. "Yes."

At her doubtful look, he leaned over and brushed a kiss across her lips. His eyes were gentle and held a depth of understanding that she couldn't help but appreciate. "I told you not to worry, Erica. Everything will be fine. Mom knows your mother doesn't think I'm good enough for you."

Hearing him put her mother's very thoughts into words made her shiver. "And knowing all of that, she hasn't talked you out of marrying me?"

His laughter filled the room and he pulled her into his arms. "Baby, no one can talk me out of marrying you. Besides, Mom wouldn't think of doing so anyway. She's gotten to know you and thinks I'm a lucky man, and I can't help but agree."

Erica shook her head. There were times when she felt she'd somehow found favor with the man upstairs. Surely no woman could be this lucky. Months before meeting Brian she'd been reading articles about how hard it was for women to find good men. And as far as she was concerned the cream of the crop had been dropped into her lap when she had least expected it.

She had needed to get away from her home for the summer and April suggested her place on the beach in South Carolina. Erica didn't hesitate to take her friend up on her offer. April was to join her for at least half of the time but an unexpected modeling gig had kept her in Paris longer than either of them anticipated.

The thought of spending her time alone did not bother Erica. She had packed up enough books to read and DVDs to watch. But loneliness was never an issue. She had met Brian during her first week there.

"I hope you know that I won't let what your mother thinks influence me in any way. You're her daughter, so she wants the best for you." A smile curved the corners of his lips when he added, "It's just taking her a little time to figure out what's best for you is me."

"Oh, you," she said, laughing, gently punching him in the arm and giving him a playful shove. "You're beginning to sound conceited."

"Am I?"

"A little."

Whatever else she was about to say died in her throat when he took a step closer, recovering the distance between them. Her gaze met his before it lowered slightly to his mouth. There lay the crux of a lot of their problems whenever they were alone. If she concentrated on his mouth for too long she would start remembering all the naughty things he could do with it.

She watched the corners of that same mouth curve into a seductive smile. "What are you thinking about, sweetheart?"

Like she really had to tell him. He already knew the answer, so why had he bothered to ask? But since he had she might as well respond. "Your taste." It couldn't get any plainer than that.

"Why think about it when you can sample it? Again." He

said the words in a deep rumbling voice with the casual ease of a man who was not only sure of himself but also of the woman he was with.

She wrapped her arms around his neck and melted against him. "Good question. Why should I waste my time thinking about it?"

She saw the intense look of desire in his eyes just moments before she leaned up on tiptoes and brought her mouth to his. His kisses were the foundation that pleasure was built on. A feeling of something totally right filled every part of her when he captured her tongue with his to give her the taste she wanted.

She closed her eyes and became lost in the intensity of the emotions flooding her. When he suddenly pulled back, breaking off the kiss, she opened her eyes and watched a smile touch his lips.

"Sounds like our pizza has arrived," he said.

When she just stared at him with a questioning look on her face, he added, "The doorbell sounded. Didn't you hear it?"

She shook her head and managed her own smile. She hadn't heard anything for feeling so deeply. "No. I think you'd better answer the door. I'm not dressed to be seen."

His gaze roamed the length of her. His shirt stopped above the knee and showed a generous amount of thigh. More thigh than she wanted anyone else to see.

"I agree. You can take the brownies out of the oven. They should be done now."

Brian couldn't help but smile as he walked out of the kitchen and headed toward the front door. They had ordered pizza from this particular restaurant before while he'd been in town and he knew their pizzas were totally delicious. But nothing, he thought, was as delicious as the kiss he'd just shared with Erica.

After pizza and brownies they would head back to bed.

He was definitely looking forward to more time beneath the covers with her. He had spent his days in Dallas working hard and his nights missing her like crazy. Their nightly phone calls had helped, except for those times when she would intentionally add a little steam into the mix. Then he would go to bed with a longing and a hard-on that couldn't be assuaged.

Brian opened the door expecting to find the deliveryman standing there with their pizza, but instead he met the gaze of Erica's father. It was obvious the man was as surprised to see Brian as Brian was to see him. He greeted Mr. Sanders with as much calm as he could muster as he stepped aside to let him enter. "Hello, Mr. Sanders."

The older man lifted a brow after taking note of Brian's bare chest and low-hanging jeans, which he hadn't bothered to snap. His gaze then returned to Brian's face. He looked thoughtfully at him for a moment and then said, "Brian. I didn't know you were coming to town."

Brian swallowed. From the way he was dressed it wouldn't take a rocket scientist to figure out what he and Erica had been doing earlier. To him it was no big deal, since they would be getting married in a few months, but he figured to her father it probably was a big deal.

"I wasn't sure I could get away until the last minute and I wanted to surprise Erica."

When Mr. Sanders didn't say anything, Brian then continued by adding an explanation of why he'd come to the door half-dressed. "I thought you were the pizza deliveryman."

"Did you?" Wilson asked mildly.

"Yes. You're out sort of late, aren't you?" Brian wished he could take back the words the moment he'd said them. The last thing he wanted to do was insinuate that the man could not visit his daughter whenever it suited him.

"Yes, it is rather late. Karen tried calling and when she

couldn't reach Erica she got worried. I volunteered to come over to make sure everything was all right."

Brian didn't know what to say to that, considering what they'd been doing when Erica hadn't answered the phone earlier. He was about to ask Mr. Sanders if he wanted something to drink, since he didn't seem to be the least little bit in a hurry to leave. Before they could exchange any further conversation, Erica's voice filled the room and she suddenly rounded the corner from the kitchen.

"Brian, what's taking you so long to bring the pizza in the—"

She stopped in her tracks, frozen in place when she saw her father standing in the middle of her living room. "Dad!"

Wilson's gaze alighted on his daughter and her skimpy attire. Brian immediately picked up on the fact that the older man was seeing Erica in a whole new light. He no longer saw her as Daddy's little girl, but as a woman who was obviously intimately involved with a man.

Brian had dated enough women to know some fathers could get weird when it came to discovering their daughters weren't the innocents they'd thought them to be. But in the man's defense, he could understand and even see himself becoming that kind of father one day if he ever had a daughter. Especially if she looked anything like Erica.

Wilson finally responded. "Erica." And then as if he'd made a decision to accept the situation, he smiled, winked and said, "Nice shirt."

Brian couldn't help but admire the man for how he was handling things. He didn't want to think how differently things would have been had it been Erica's mother who'd shown up unexpectedly.

He watched Erica's features and knew she was grateful for her father's acceptance of their relationship. She returned his smile. "Thanks."

And then her expression became serious when she asked, "Why did you drop by this late? Is something wrong?"

He shook his head. "No, nothing's wrong. Your mother tried calling you a few times and couldn't reach you and was worried."

"Oh."

Brian decided then to speak up. "Erica and I will be having a pizza when it's delivered, Mr. Sanders. You're welcome to stay and join us."

Wilson turned his attention to Brian. "No, thanks. Now that I know Erica is fine, I'll be leaving."

"Dad, you can stay for a while if you want. Like Brian said, we've ordered pizza and he's made brownies and—"

"No, sweetheart. You and Brian spend enough time away from each other as it is and I won't intrude."

"You won't be," Erica quickly said.

Wilson chuckled. "Yes, I will be." He glanced back at Brian. "We're looking forward to meeting your family in a few weeks."

"Thanks, sir, and my mother and grandparents are looking forward to meeting you and Mrs. Sanders, as well." That was no lie. His family adored Erica and couldn't wait to meet her family at the engagement dinner.

At that moment the doorbell sounded. "That's probably your pizza deliveryman," Wilson pointed out. "I'll leave now."

Before he could turn toward the door, Erica moved quickly across the room to her father and kissed him on his cheek. "'Bye, Dad. Thanks for caring enough to come by to check on me. I love you."

"Sweetheart, I'll always care and I love you, too." He then looked at Brian and unspoken communication passed between them. It was a message that Brian deciphered immediately.

I'm depending on you to make her happy. Please don't let either of us down.

It hit Brian just then what the magnitude of the man's thoughts meant. In a roundabout way, Wilson was bestowing his blessing on them. Brian nodded and then said, "I'll walk you to the door, Mr. Sanders."

He was grateful Erica hung back, allowing him time alone with her father. Before opening the door, he said, "I love Erica, Mr. Sanders, and I intend to spend the rest of my life making her happy."

Wilson nodded and then smiled. "And that's all the father of a future bride can ask for. Good night, Brian."

Chapter Three

April glanced down at the pooch that was walking beside her on the leash and decided this was one of the primary reasons she didn't own a pet. They required too much attention, which was why she was out here at eleven o'clock walking the dog instead of back inside her grandmother's house curled up in bed.

In a way, she couldn't get mad at Fluffy, the white Yorkie terrier she'd purchased for her grandmother as company when she'd landed her first modeling job. A few years later, after her career had soared to unprecedented heights and she'd married Mark, she'd purchased her grandmother a house in one of the most exclusive neighborhoods in Hattersville, along with furnishings and a live-in housekeeper.

Now both Fluffy and Melba were family to her grandmother, which meant a lot to April when she had to fly all over the world for work.

Fluffy stopped walking and April paused right along with her. Evidently this area was one of the dog's favorites to do his business. April loosened her hold on the leash and glanced around, thinking if anyone had told her she would be returning to her birthplace as often as she was now, she would not have believed them. She'd barely been able to wait until she'd finished high school to blow this town. But her grandmother, the one person she adored and loved in this life, hadn't wanted to move away with her.

Nana said Hattersville was her home. She had been born here and she wanted to die here. April hadn't known just how much her grandmother had meant those words until her senior year in college when her constant badgering to get Nana to move out west with her had led to Nana's heart attack.

While her grandmother was in the hospital April had tearfully promised not to broach the subject again.

Even if that meant the burden of travel would fall on April, since her grandmother refused to fly.

The one thing she'd been able to convince her grandmother to do years later was to move out of her shabby house in the Fifth Ward, and live in the house April had purchased for her on, of all places, Wellington Road. April recalled how Nana had made a living as the housekeeper and nanny for some of the homeowners on this very street. Now Nana had her own grand place with a live-in housekeeper of her own, and April didn't know of anyone more deserving.

Her grandmother had always been there for her. After giving birth to her at sixteen, her mother had left the state a few days later, leaving April with her grandmother to raise. No one knew the identity of her father; it was a secret her mother had taken to the grave with her. The year April turned ten, Latonia North had come home from living a wild life in Miami, just long enough to spend a few months with her mother and daughter before dying of lung cancer. April hadn't known the woman who had shown up, nothing but skin and bones, at her and Nana's house near the tracks. But now a part of April regretted not having known her and she wondered if her mother had died with the same regret.

She leaned against a tree and glanced at her watch before taking a quick peek over at Fluffy, and then wished she hadn't. It seemed the dog was just getting started. It was getting rather late and anyone in Hattersville with a lick of sense was in their bed getting a good night's sleep. She could have awakened Melba and had her take Fluffy out, but she knew that Nana and Melba had stayed up late playing cards and had just gotten into bed. They had gotten so involved in their game that neither remembered to walk the dog. Anyway, she herself was used to crazy hours and changes in time zones with her irregular work schedule as a model.

She shook her head, smiling while thinking that her grandmother had turned into a regular cardsharp. When April was a child the older woman wouldn't even let her play a game of old maid. Connie North had been convinced playing cards were tools from the devil's arsenal. Evidently over the years Melba had somehow changed Nana's mind about that.

"Out rather late tonight, aren't you?"

April swung around at the same time she threw her hand over her chest to calm her startled heart. She drew in a deep breath and glanced over at the man who stood almost towering over her. Hell, where had he come from? It was a good thing she recognized her late-night intruder.

"I could say the same about you, Griffin."

She had gotten her shocked heart to slow down, so now she could work on the desire fluttering around in her belly. Griffin had always managed to elicit that sort of a reaction from her even though she'd fought it.

"Yes, you could say the same," he said, smiling warmly. "But my folks are out of town and I promised to go over twice a day to let Pebbles out." He chuckled. "I went this morning but almost forgot to do so this evening. Luckily I remembered before I went in for the night."

April nodded and glanced down at the Saint Bernard on the leash. Fluffy had returned to her side and was staring over at Pebbles as if the dog was definitely an object of interest. Didn't big and little dogs usually get into barking matches? Surprisingly, the two seemed to like each other.

April returned her gaze to Griffin and then wished she hadn't. He was dressed casually, as if he'd been out on a date. She didn't want to think of him with another woman; in fact over the years she'd done a pretty good job of not thinking of him at all. A busy career and three husbands followed by three divorces had helped to keep her from pining over a lost love.

But seeing him now was reminding her of just how handsome he was and why she'd fallen head over heels for him back in high school. He'd been the guy all the girls had wanted, except for Erica.

In addition to loving him, April also liked him. Although he'd been born with a silver spoon planted firmly in his mouth, he hadn't acted obnoxious like some of the others guys around town. He'd always treated her with respect, and not with the mere tolerance some of the upper echelons had bestowed upon her as Erica's best friend.

"I guess remembering your duties to Pebbles before going home was a good thing," April decided to say. "I would hate to imagine what would have happened if you hadn't."

He chuckled. "Hey, come on now. Do you for one minute believe my parents didn't have a backup plan? It probably wouldn't surprise me if Pebbles knew how to get to the phone, use her paw and punch in nine-one-one."

April couldn't help but laugh. Another thing she'd always liked about Griffin was his sense of humor. Seldom was he a serious kind of guy. But she figured that was the norm when you were born to a life without a care in the world.

She would give him the benefit of the doubt since she knew he'd left town and attended college before returning home to take over running his family's rubber company. As long as there were tires on the road Hayes Rubber Plant would probably remain in business, which made her question the recent rumor her grandmother had shared with her that he was thinking about going into politics.

Fluffy tugged on his leash drawing April's attention and when Fluffy began trotting in the opposite way of home, April figured the dog wasn't ready to settle in for the night just yet and decided neither was she. Evidently Pebbles had the same notion and began trotting beside Fluffy, which made Griffin join April in what had to be a somewhat comical stroll.

"So when did you come home?" Griffin asked, glancing over at her.

She glanced back at him and wished she wasn't so hopelessly conscious of how handsome he looked tonight and how good he smelled. "A couple of days ago."

"Does Erica know you're in town?"

"Of course. We had dinner together at Ryder's tonight."

He laughed and the sound carried through the trees. "That means the two of you only had a salad."

She couldn't help but laugh as well, since his remark had been right on the money. She'd always been one to watch her figure, and over the years Erica had fallen in line right along with her. She was surprised that he would remember something like that.

"I saw your spread in *Sports Illustrated Swimsuit Edition* earlier this year. It was nice."

"Thanks."

The thought that he'd seen her in that skimpy swimwear

made her bite down on her lips. What had he thought when
he'd seen it? She really shouldn't care since modeling was her
life and she enjoyed what she did. She had been a Victoria's
Secret model for a few years before being asked to pose for
that issue of *Sports Illustrated*. She'd agreed without batting
an eye, so why was she suddenly feeling like she should have
added a wrap to the bikini she'd posed in?

She drew in a deep breath as she looked over Griffin
and decided to take the conversation off herself for a while.
"What's this I hear about you thinking about running for
mayor?"

He glanced over at her and smiled. "Yes, that's my plan.
Do I have your vote?"

She shrugged. "Not sure I'm still considered a legal resi-
dent."

"Sure you are. You own property in this town."

Yes, she certainly did. Although she'd bought her grandmother the house, the property was in April's name. And
the house where she'd been born still belonged to her, too,
although she had fixed it up and was renting it out. She'd
wanted to tear it down but Nana hadn't let her. "Well, we'll
see. Does Erica plan to vote for you?"

"By the time the election comes around she'll be married
and moved out of town."

April studied his reaction. Erica had always sworn she
and Griffin didn't love each other, but for some reason April
needed to know for certain. She had to know just how Griffin truly felt about Erica marrying another man.

"I know. It's hard to believe she's going to marry and move
to Texas," she said.

He went quiet, as if he was considering what she'd just
said. "Yes, it is hard to believe. I'm truly going to miss her,"
he finally responded.

For a moment April felt an uneasiness in the pit of her

stomach. And then Griffin added, "But maybe now the town will finally accept what Erica and I have been trying to tell everyone for years."

April swallowed. "Which is?"

"That the most we could ever be is friends. We love each other but we're not in love with each other. There's a big difference."

April didn't say anything as they continued walking. Yes, there was a big difference and she would be the first to agree on that point. How could she not? She'd been married three times. She hadn't loved Mark although she'd liked him. They had gotten along well but then Mark voiced regrets over their union less than a year into their marriage.

She'd married Campbell less than a year later because it had seemed the right thing to do at the time. He was her friend, gay and wasn't ready to come out of the closet. His parents and some of his so-called friends had begun getting suspicious and she'd agreed to marry him to keep the skeptics at bay. It had worked for a while until he'd fallen in love with someone and then hadn't cared who knew of his sexual preference.

Then there had been Green, whose brothers were actually named Red, Blue and Black. The four Englishmen were musicians in the well-known rock band Colors. She and Green had met at a concert when he'd practically plucked her out of the audience onto the stage to sit beside him while he beat mercilessly on his drums. They'd dated a few times after that, and then decided to be wild and reckless and marry when the tabloids figured they wouldn't. It took her less than a year to figure out that they really shouldn't have, when Green refused to give up the drugs.

"So do I have your vote?"

His question pulled her out of her reverie and she smiled up at him. "This is some shameless campaigning you're doing at eleven o'clock on the sidewalk, Griffin. But you haven't said what you plan on doing for the city."

He lifted a brow. "Do you really care?"

She chuckled. "No, but like you said, I own property here and for some reason my grandmother is determined to die here."

"And how is Ms. Connie?"

His question made her remember that Nana had been his first nanny and had worked for the Hayeses until Griffin had started school. When Nana spoke of him it was with fondness. "She's fine. She mentioned you've dropped by a few times."

In fact, according to Melba, Griffin was the only one who'd bothered to drop by to welcome her grandmother to the neighborhood when she'd moved in, and he still dropped by to see if they needed anything.

He shrugged. "Not as much as I'd like. The last time I saw her she and her companion were in the park and I happened to be jogging by. She mentioned your divorce."

April glanced up at him and grinned. "Which one?" When a woman had married three times for all the wrong reasons, she found it easy to make light of them.

"Your most recent...from that rocker guy in England."

"Oh, that one," she said, smiling.

He smiled back. "I take it you weren't left with a broken heart?"

"Good grief, no. I gave him an ultimatum. It was either me or the drugs. He chose the drugs so I walked."

"Good for you."

They'd stopped walking and she noticed they'd come to the end of the lane. As if they'd known what to do, Fluffy and Pebbles turned around and were trotting back in the direction they'd come. So she and Griffin did likewise. It was a beautiful night in March. Stars dotted the sky and a full moon was overhead. A chill was in the air and she pulled her jacket tighter around her.

As they strolled back toward their destinations, for the moment the chat between her and Griffin had come to a standstill. In a way she appreciated the absence of conversation. It gave her time to wonder if her breakup with Green was really good for her, as Griffin had said.

Here she was twenty-seven, a three-time divorcée, and the one man she'd ever loved was walking beside her and didn't have a clue.

Chapter Four

"I can't believe the outfit Brian's mother is wearing."

Wilson followed his wife's gaze and glanced across the room to look at Rita Lawson. He would be the first to admit that he'd been surprised when their maid had escorted Brian, and his mother and grandparents to the area of the house where the engagement party was being held. He wasn't sure what he'd expected but it wasn't the very attractive woman on her son's arm.

He glanced back to his wife, grateful they were alone, and hoped no one had overheard her thoughtless remark. "I see nothing wrong with what she's wearing." In fact, he thought the long flowing skirt and lace peasant blouse, belted to highlight the woman's small waistline looked pretty damn good on her. He would even go so far as to say that she exuded more grace, femininity and elegance in her outfit than his wife and her friends who were dressed to the nines in their designer attire.

Karen rolled her eyes. "Of course you wouldn't see anything wrong with it. You're a man."

He could only smile at that. Yes, he was a man. A man who could still admire a beautiful woman when he saw one.

"I can only imagine what she plans to wear to the wedding. It would be most embarrassing if she didn't show up dressed her age."

When Karen didn't get a response from him, she went on to add, "Even Marva had something to say about her outfit."

Wilson took a sip of his wine. He couldn't imagine Marva not having something to say about it. After all, Marva Hayes was Griffin's mother and, like Karen, she'd had high hopes for their only offspring to tie the knot. Both women had to be fit to be tied right now. Served them right that all their planning, prodding and manipulations over the years hadn't worked.

"I'm curious to know why you invited Marva. She's not family," he decided to point out, although he knew doing so would get a rise out of his wife.

She cut him the look he'd expected. "Marva is my dearest friend, so of course she and Herbert were invited. I'm just disappointed that Griffin refused to come."

Wilson shrugged. That showed him the boy had good sense even if his parents didn't. Why would he have come? Erica had made her choice. Still, he was sure Griffin wasn't heartbroken over the decision. Wilson had long ago seen what his wife had refused to see. What Griffin and Erica shared was a close friendship and nothing else.

Personally, he could tolerate the Hayeses most of the time, but he'd hoped like hell they wouldn't ever become his in-laws. He'd known Marva and Herbert all his life and they still ran around in the same social circles. But lately Wilson had felt that circle tightening, grating on his last nerve.

"Oh, my, the woman has started mingling, Wilson. Do something."

Wilson raised a brow. "And there's a problem with her mingling?"

Karen glanced over at him like he was daft. "Yes. The less she has to say to the family and my friends the better."

He took another sip of wine and then said, "I don't know why you feel that way. She's an educated woman, well versed in numerous topics. I had the pleasure of talking with her earlier and found her to be most refreshing."

Karen frowned. "Then please go across the room and take the refreshing widow off my hands. I haven't been able to mingle much myself. I've been too busy trying to make sure she doesn't make a fool of herself and of us. Look at her. She's staring at our aquarium like she's never seen one before."

He figured the woman probably hadn't—at least not one like that. The aquarium Karen had had built off the patio a few years ago was huge and gaudy. What Karen thought was a masterpiece was nothing but a waste of money. But then his wife didn't care about the cost of anything. The important thing was making sure she had something her friends didn't have.

"Well, will you do what I asked, Wilson, and go spend some time with the woman?"

He drew in a deep breath. "Is there any reason you can't display some of those Delbert–Sanders manners you think everyone else around you is lacking and go spend some time with her yourself?"

"Don't be an ass, Wilson. Just do what I ask."

He frowned down at her before glancing over to where Rita Lawson stood still staring at the aquarium. "Gladly," he said, while grabbing a glass of wine from the tray of a passing server.

He smiled as he moved across the room. No doubt he would appreciate Ms. Lawson's company more than his own wife's.

★ ★ ★

"It would be nice if everyone who told us how happy they are for us truly meant it," Brian whispered in Erica's ear.

She tilted her head up and was relieved to see he was smiling, which meant her family's phoniness was not getting next to him. But it was getting next to her. He had ignored the sugarcoated insults for the sake of peace but she wondered how long his tolerance would last.

"Doesn't matter," she said, turning and wrapping her arms around his neck. "They're just jealous."

"And I'm plain lucky."

She shook her head. "No, sweetheart, I'm the lucky one." She then raised on tiptoe and placed a kiss on his lips, not caring who saw and who didn't approve.

"Don't look now but your mother is glaring over at us."

Erica tilted back her head and laughed. "In that case..." She kissed him again.

He shook his head and smiled. "Hey, what are you doing? Trying to get me into trouble?"

"Who, me?" she asked innocently. "Not on your life. Just reminding whoever needs reminding that you're the only man I want. The only man I will ever love." She enjoyed telling him stuff like that because she meant every word of it.

"I wish I had you alone someplace," he leaned down to murmur in her ear.

She wished he had her alone someplace, too, but since that was not the case they needed to make the most of it. Besides, even with the hypocrites present, the engagement party had turned out to be a nice affair. At least Brian's family seemed to be enjoying themselves. His grandparents seemed amused by her mother's outlandish extravagance. It would probably surprise Karen to discover most people would feel the same.

"Did I tell you how beautiful you look?"

"Yes," she said, remembering when he'd done so. It had been when he'd arrived at her parents' home with his mother and grandparents. After introductions had been made he had eased to her side, slid his arms around her waist and whispered the words in her ear. He had also told her just what he intended to do when he got her alone later. She had looked up at him with a hopeful look in her eyes and smiled.

Trying to quell the heat she felt at the memory, she glanced around the room. Was that her father talking with Brian's mother? Well, at least one of her parents had the sense to display good manners.

"It seems your dad and my mom have a lot to talk about," Brian said, grinning and following her gaze across the room to the couple.

She smiled back at him. "Yes, it looks that way. It's good to know there's another Lawson and Sanders pair getting along besides us."

"So you enjoy traveling, Rita?"

Rita Lawson glanced up at the tall, refined and handsome man. Erica's father. She wasn't stupid. She was well aware that Erica's mother had sent him to keep her entertained. Karen Sanders had downed her snooty nose at her the moment they'd been introduced.

Brian had warned her about what to expect. She just hadn't expected his tip-off to be so darn accurate. There was definitely a distinct chill in the air. But Rita would be the first to admit she wasn't feeling any negative vibes from Wilson. He seemed to be a genuinely kind man with smiling eyes. He may have been drafted to keep her out of the way but she had no problem with his doing so. She enjoyed their conversations.

"So how often do you travel outside the United States?" he asked her.

They were outside strolling along the patio that overlooked a huge lake. Other guests were mulling around, and on occasion a number of people had come up and to introduce themselves and to assure her that Brian would be marrying a lovely girl. Rita was just as quick to inform them that Erica would be trying the knot with a kind and gentle man who loved her very much.

"I travel outside the States at least twice every month," Rita answered. "The company I work for provides landscaping for businesses abroad and I help design exactly what they need."

"That's sounds like an interesting profession."

She glanced over at him. There was a gentleness in the lines etching his eyes and the grin that marked his lips appeared unguarded. Genuine. Although she hadn't spent a lot of time in the company of Erica's mother, she couldn't imagine Karen and Wilson Sanders sharing a life together. He seemed so warmhearted and friendly. What could have brought two totally opposite people together in marriage?

Admonishing herself for conjecturing on a subject that didn't truly concern her, she turned around and steered Wilson back toward the house. For some reason her stomach had begun to tighten in knots. Wilson had gotten quiet and she felt he was no longer with her to merely take her off his wife's hands. No longer there to spy on her and report back to his wife.

To keep the conversation going, she asked, "What about you? Do you travel a lot?"

"Yes, every chance I get. I love international travels. I've gotten to the point where I have a good staff to run the company and my services are more valuable as an ambassador."

She nodded. She could definitely see him fulfilling that role. "Have you ever been to Dubai?"

"Yes, it's one of my favorite places in the Middle East."

Rita's face broke into a huge grin. "No kidding? It's also mine. I just love the Aiden. Have you ever eaten there?"

"Yes, several times. Not only is the food fantastic but it's housed right in the Cumja Gallery. The artwork there is exquisite."

"I agree. I was there last month and noted they've added a few new pieces by Terina, if you're into her work."

"I am and I'm going to have to check them out the next time I'm there."

"You won't be disappointed, Wilson."

He shot her a glittering smile that she felt down to her toes. "I'm sure I won't be."

"Brian's mother seems to be taking up quite a bit of Wilson's time, Karen. Is that wise?"

Karen cast an annoyed glance over at Aggie Pittman, a cousin on her mother's side who often got on her last dignified nerve. "It is wise if he's on a mission for me. I suggested he go keep her company to make sure she doesn't cause us any embarrassing moments...if you know what I mean. Just look at her outfit. It has department store written all over it."

"Yes, but it does look good on her. I wasn't aware a woman that age could still have a figure like that. Not everyone can pull such a style off and look so hot. My waistline certainly wouldn't let me." Aggie chuckled and added, "Neither would yours."

If Aggie's words were meant to amuse, they came up short. "I saw Jaye leaving the party. Is something wrong?" Aggie's youngest son, Jaye, was a private investigator living in New

York. Jaye came home almost every weekend to check on his father, who was confined to a wheelchair.

"No, he just needs to get back to New York to deal with some case he's working on. I wish he would go back to practicing law."

Aggie and her husband, Lester, had sent Jaye to law school. He'd practiced a few years, claimed he was bored and become a private investigator instead. His change in professions had been a big disappointment for Aggie. Karen could understand. Children could be so selfish at times.

She glanced across the room at her daughter. She fell within that category. Erica was everything Karen hadn't been at her age, namely defiant. Unfortunately Wilson hadn't been much help trying to get their daughter to obey.

Karen had once been young, pretty and vibrant like her daughter but she'd always known how far to take things. There was never a time that she hadn't felt the weight of the Delbert empire and legacy on her shoulders. Her father would have much preferred she had been born a male and had never let her forget it. She had tried so hard to please him, even going so far as to marry the man he'd picked out for her. The man whose blood was just as blue as hers.

But, Erica… Even as a child she'd been defiant and headstrong. Growing up, she'd wanted to be a normal kid like all the others. It had taken all Karen had to try and make Erica realize that she was of a unique class of people, with a heritage that set her apart and would always keep her that way.

And now Karen would give all she had to keep her daughter from making a fool of herself by marrying Brian instead of Griffin.

Karen tightened her hand on the wineglass she held and turned back to her cousin. "Aggie, please inform Jaye that I'd like to have a private meeting with him when he comes home again."

"I will."

If Aggie found her request irregular she didn't show it. Just as well, Karen thought. There were some things one was better off not knowing.

Chapter Five

April glanced around the restaurant where she was meeting her agent, Neil Burton. She had flown into New York a few hours ago, barely having time to check into her hotel room and freshen up.

She had spent the last couple of weeks in Hattersville with Nana and would only be in New York for the weekend before flying to Paris for a magazine shoot. She'd stopped here purposely just to meet with Neil. They had important business to discuss about her future.

Neil had been her agent since he'd discovered her one summer on the sandy beach in Corpus Christi, where she'd gone her first year out of college to decide what she really wanted to do with her life and her new degree. She had been ready for the business world but it seemed the business world wasn't ready for her. Job interviews had become synonymous with the word *rejection* and she had begun to feel she had gone to college for nothing.

When he'd first approached her she'd thought he was trying to hit on her. She'd soon discovered his sexual preference would not have made that possible. He had convinced her that her beauty—which she hadn't truly known she had—should grace the cover of every magazine and that he was just the man to make that happen.

Distrusting her own instincts she had taken him home to Nana. He survived her grandmother's interrogation and had won Nana's trust and respect when he'd promised to look after her as if she was his own child. Much to April's chagrin, he'd done just that. He thought Mark was too immature for marriage, had strong misgivings about Campbell, since Neil believed a gay person should never be in the closet anyway, and he outright detested Green. He'd warned her that the rocker was bad news from the start but she hadn't listened. She had promised Neil the next time she married it would be for love—which meant she would never marry, since unfortunately the man who had her heart would never know it.

Thinking of Griffin she couldn't help recall that night they had run into each other while out walking their pets. It had been nice sharing that stretch of concrete with him, walking beside him and indulging in lighthearted conversation. When they'd reached Nana's house he had said good-night, wished her well and continued on to his parents' home.

That night she had lain in bed, remembering the encounter, replaying every aspect of it over and over in her mind. Loving Griffin was something she had accepted as a part of her and over the years had schooled herself not to think about it. There was no point in doing so anyway, since their worlds were light-years apart. But on the very rare occasions when they had run into each other she savored the moments and thought of them often. She had remained in Hattersville for another two weeks but she hadn't seen him again. She had deliberately taken Fluffy out for a late-evening stroll a few times but hadn't run into Griffin and Pebbles.

"Sorry I'm late but traffic on the George Washington Bridge was a bitch."

The apologetic male voice pulled her out of her reverie. "No problem, Neil. I was just sitting here and enjoying the view."

In a way she had been. It was a beautiful day and the late-afternoon sun shining through the window was warm. She loved New York, and unfortunately didn't get here often enough. Most of her time was spent out of the country and when she did return back to the States it was to the West Coast. But she fondly remembered the three years she had lived in Manhattan during the early days of her modeling career. Those had been fun times, wild times, especially when Erica would visit her. But then it had also been the time she'd needed before finally settling down to become the responsible woman she was now. A woman who knew what she wanted to do with her life and was about to go after all her dreams and desires.

Except for one.

She dismissed thoughts of Griffin from her mind and gave her attention to Neil. With his blond hair, blue eyes and a too-handsome face, Neil was one gorgeous hunk. An older one—in his late forties—but gorgeous nonetheless. But women would be sorely disappointed to discover they wouldn't be his cup of tea. He and his partner, a lovable guy by the name of Aaron Crews, considered themselves married, although the laws of the land did not.

The waitress came to take their order and then April and Neil spent time chitchatting about Nana. It was only after the waitress delivered their food that Neil got down to business. "Now, what's this nonsense about you not wanting to expand your career into film?"

She smiled over at him. "No nonsense, Neil. I tried film

once. It was nice but I can't see myself doing something like that on a permanent basis."

They both knew that at twenty-seven her career as a model was coming to an end. Although she kept her body in shape and in most cases was still sought after for modeling gigs, younger women were coming on board and being discovered—some right out of high school—and were dominating the scene. It was time for her to prepare for life after modeling. Neil had agreed with her on that part; however, he was determined that she become Hollywood's next leading lady.

"You're the face of Maybelline now and that's a lot of exposure, April."

She knew that was true. The cosmetic giant took out ads in most major magazines and it seemed her face was plastered in all of them.

"James Cameron called me just last week asking about you."

She could tell by the excitement in Neil's voice that he was hoping the inquiry was going someplace. Deep down she was hoping that it didn't. "I don't mind doing films on occasion, Neil, but my primary focus is elsewhere. I want to open a modeling school here in New York. I need to find a vacant building or warehouse and transform the space."

"If you want to open a school, then do it later when you're my age. But you're still young, April. Too young not to continue to take advantage of your beauty."

She took a sip of her wine. "I don't see things that way, Neil and—"

"Excuse me. Hello, April."

The deep sexy voice compelled April to look up. At that moment her eyes connected with Griffin's. The moment they did, sensations she could only feel when she was around him flooded her insides.

"Griffin," she said with the surprise in her voice that she

couldn't hide. She hadn't seen the man for years and now she'd seen him twice in a four-week period. How uncanny was that? "What are you doing in New York?"

"I thought this would be the perfect weekend to get away and I picked New York because I have friends here."

That was when April finally noticed the woman plastered to his side, who was giving her a cool look. April ignored the woman, since Griffin hadn't bothered to introduce her, but then she realized she hadn't bothered to introduce Neil, either. "This is Neil. A friend," she said simply, deciding not to reveal that Neil was her agent, as well.

Neil stood and the two men shook hands.

"And this is Paulina. Paulina, April is a friend from Hattersville."

A friend? For some reason April had merely considered Griffin and herself as acquaintances rather than friends, April thought, extending her hand out to the woman. The woman barely touched it before leaning even closer to Griffin and whispering loud enough for all to hear, "I think we should find our table. I'm famished, sweetheart, and it's all your fault."

Something flickered inside of April. In an underhanded, strictly bitchy sort of way, Paulina had deliberately given April the impression the reason for her hunger was because she had spent long hours in bed with Griffin and was now in desperate need of something to eat. April was tempted to tell the woman to pull in her claws, since she was out of Griffin's league. Always had been and always would be.

"I'm surprised you're not in Hattersville this weekend," Griffin said, reclaiming her attention.

April figured since Erica was her best friend he'd assumed she would be at Erica and Brian's engagement party. "I figured that I would play the good girl and not give Mrs. Sanders another gray hair," she said honestly, knowing he would get her drift.

The twinkle in his eyes indicated that he did. "And I figured I wouldn't attend just to make sure my presence didn't give her the wrong impression."

Paulina eyed her, evidently annoyed at the fact she had no idea what they were discussing.

"They won't hold our table much longer, Griff," the woman said in an annoyed voice.

Griff? April lifted a brow. She recalled Griffin never liked that nickname back in the day and from the look in his eyes she could tell he still didn't. This woman might be his flavor for the hour—or the past hours—but little did she know she was skating on thin ice by using that nickname.

"I'll let you two get back to your meal and we can grab our table," Griffin said tightly. With a brief nod to Neil, he said, "Nice meeting you." And then to April he said, "Good seeing you again."

Unable to resist, she said, "Same here, *Griff.*"

He cut her a look that said he would get her for that the next time they ran into each other.

He gave her a smile before he and his bed partner turned and walked away.

"They're sleeping together, you know."

April turned to Neil and frowned. "And your point in telling me that?"

Neil chuckled. "Not the same point she wanted to make in dropping her hint, evidently. But there was something I detected, something in your reaction to seeing him with her, that gave me notice. Makes me think there's something there."

She picked up her wineglass to take a sip and laughed somewhat nervously. "You're imagining things."

"Am I?"

"Yes." Her response had been quick. It had sounded confident. But she knew that she hadn't fooled Neil.

She couldn't help glancing over to the table where Griffin and the woman were now sitting. Her gaze met Griffin's and she wasn't sure if she was imagining things or not, but she could swear there was an intense look in the dark depths of his eyes that she'd never seen before.

Chapter Six

"Do you have any idea how disastrous last weekend was?" Karen asked her daughter as she stared at her from across the kitchen table.

Erica looked up from the table, where she had several sheets of paper spread out in front of her, deciding not to be bothered by her mother's negative attitude and constant complaints. "No, I thought everything went fine. In fact, Brian and I are pleased with how things turned out," she said in a pleasant tone.

Karen rolled her eyes. "It's quite obvious the two families won't mesh."

Erica chuckled. "Mom, it doesn't matter if the two families mesh. Brian and I mesh and that's what counts. Now, are you going to help with this list or not? I don't want to offend anyone by not inviting them to the bridal shower April is giving me in a few weeks."

"I'm surprised she didn't come to your engagement party. She was invited."

"April had business to take care of in New York."

Karen gave a dignified snort. "Considering she is supposed to be your best friend, I would think your engagement party would have taken precedence over any business matters."

Erica leaned back in her chair and crossed her arms over her chest. Her mother was always trying to chomp away at her and April's friendship. "April didn't have to be here for me to know I have her support. Besides, I'm sure she figured she would make things easier on you by not showing up."

Other than rolling her eyes Karen didn't make a comment. Erica knew there was nothing her mother could truly say. At fifty-seven her mother would never change her way of thinking. It was an ingrained part of her. Erica's position was and would always be that her mother's opinion wasn't her own. Ninety-nine percent of the time it wasn't.

Erica gathered the papers together in front of her, slid them into her purse and stood up. "Since you don't seem to have anything nice to say today, Mom, I'd rather be somewhere else. Your negativity is draining and I'm still tired from this weekend."

"Before you go there is something we need to discuss."

"What?"

"Brian's mother and that outfit she wore. Makes me cringe to think what she might wear to the wedding."

Erica turned to leave thinking that holding a conversation with her mother was becoming excruciatingly difficult. For once she would like to visit without feeling resentful and wondering just how her father managed to put up with it.

Undaunted, her mother continued. "Do you think it would be out of line if I were to suggest that Harriet give her a call?"

Erica swung back around, her eyes full of anger. "Don't you dare, Mom." Harriet was her mother's personal clothes designer and for some reason her mother thought if Harriet hadn't made it then it shouldn't be worn.

Erica pulled in a deep breath thinking she'd had enough. She had tried being patient with her mother, even a little understanding. Now here it was just three months before her wedding to a wonderful man and her mother still hadn't accepted how things were going to be.

"Several people happened to like Ms. Lawson's outfit and thought it was very flattering. I was one of those people." And without giving her mother a chance to say anything, Erica opened the back door and walked out.

When she got to her car she just sat there for a moment as she gazed up at the house she had lived in most of her life. The Sanders Estate was a huge three-story mansion with dormer windows housed under a gambrel roof. She'd always been told that her great-great-grandfather had befriended a Dutchman who had built the house in 1915, which was the reason for its Dutch colonial design.

She had always loved everything about the house, especially the fireplaces in all the bedrooms. As a child she would lie on the shiny hardwood floors in front of her bedroom fireplace with a pillow and blanket while she read her favorite book.

The huge, welcoming structure had been her safe haven, and her secret "away place" beneath the stairs had been her private sanctuary. Even after returning home from college she hadn't thought of living anyplace else but here, especially since she'd had the entire third floor practically all to herself.

But things changed after that summer she'd met Brian. Once her mother began badgering her to break things off with him and focus on winning Griffin's heart, she'd made the decision to move out. It hadn't taken her long to turn her condo into a home and, when Brian had flown in one weekend to spend time with her, he had helped her christen the place in the most romantic and intimate way. Just thinking about that particular weekend always made her smile.

She had been upfront with Brian from the start, figuring it was best to level with him regarding her mother's attitude. He had accepted it all in stride and assured her he was the sort of guy who eventually grew on people.

So far he hadn't grown on her mother...and probably never would.

"Thanks for letting me sit in on your court case today, Brian."

Sitting across the table in the now empty conference room, Brian glanced up and smiled at one of the firm's new attorneys, Donna Hardy. "No problem. I hope you were able to learn something."

"I did. Never go into a courtroom to face Judge Meadows unprepared."

Brian laughed as he stood. "You figured that one out quickly, didn't you?"

"Yes. I admired the way you handled him."

"Or the way he handled me," he responded with a smooth grin. "I've been in his courtroom enough, and besides, my father was there before me. All the rumors you've probably heard about Judge Meadows are probably true, and to be downright frank, it's long past time he retired."

"I agree but I have a feeling he'll be around awhile." They began walking out of the conference room together when Donna asked, "So, your father was also an attorney?"

"Yes, and one of the best until an aneurysm cut his life short when I was fifteen."

"Did your mother remarry?"

He glanced over at her, wondering why she'd asked. "No."

She nodded. "My dad died when I was twelve and Mom

remarried within a year to a man who also had a daughter my age. I was lucky to acquire a sister and a best friend in one."

Yes, he thought she was lucky in that aspect. When he was younger he'd thought about his mother remarrying and having another child, but after a while he got used to it being just the two of them. He'd wondered how his mother would adjust once he left home for college and she'd made the transition just fine. It wasn't uncommon to get a call from her from just about anywhere in the world.

"I understand you live in the Vanity Oaks subdivision."

He nodded, wondering who'd told her that.

"I'm buying a home there, too. On Pecan Park Road."

He chuckled. "Hey, that's right around the corner from me. That means we'll be neighbors...at least for a while. My fiancée and I plan to live there for a couple of years before building elsewhere."

She lifted a brow, surprised. "You're engaged?"

A huge smile spread across his lips. "Yes, and I'm counting the days."

She tilted her head to stare at him fully. "It's nice to hear a man say that. Most are brought to the altar kicking and screaming."

Brian chuckled. "Not me. I've been single long enough," he said, remembering the time he'd thought women and their mutual attraction were all that mattered in his life. He would leave home Friday night and make his rounds and not return back to his bed until Monday morning. At the time he'd thought life was good.

But that was before Erica.

He glanced at his watch. "I have a meeting with Mr. Hughes at one, so I'd better grab something to eat first."

"Sure. And thanks again for letting me join you in court."

"Don't mention it." Then he walked off.

Donna continued to watch him until he turned the corner

toward the elevator. She wondered how it would be for a man to love her as much as Brian Lawson evidently loved the woman he planned to marry. She had been in and out of too many affairs that went nowhere. It was rather sad, actually. Good-looking brothers who had a decent job and weren't gay or on the down-low were hard to come by.

Here she was, thirty-three with no prospects in sight. All men wanted these days was a quick and easy lay on whatever day of the week that suited them. She drew in a deep breath and headed toward her office. She couldn't help remembering Brian's performance in the courtroom. He had been awesome. No wonder the other attorneys were whispering that they wouldn't be surprised if he were to make partner in the firm soon. To get your foot in the door at Brown and Samuels was a coup for any attorney. But to make partner was simply fantastic.

When she got to her office she closed and locked the door and leaned against it. Brian Lawson had a deep, sexy voice and a body that was a total turn-on. She could feel the tips of her breasts hardening and the heat between her thighs stirring just thinking how he'd looked standing in the courtroom addressing the people on the jury.

Moving across the room to the windows she pulled the blinds and darkened the room before removing her jacket and sliding her skirt up her hips. She needed help from Freddy today.

Going to her desk she used the key to open the bottom drawer and smiled when she pulled out her new toy. Well, it wasn't so new, since she'd been giving it one hell of a workout since buying it a few weeks ago. She kept Sam at home. Roger went on the road with her. And Freddy would stay at the office.

Sam. Roger. Freddy. Each toy named after a man who'd helped her move her career forward, in the direction she wanted it to go. Professor Sam Dinkins was the old fart who had helped her get her law degree. He'd made sure she'd gotten passing grades when she should have failed half the courses.

Then there was Roger Lewis, a colleague of the professor's who'd demanded daily blow jobs, among other things, when he'd learned the truth after snooping around Professor Dinkins's office one day and discovering all the exams she'd flunked. Although he'd been good in bed, she'd never appreciated the way she'd been at his beck and call. She hadn't felt an ounce of sympathy when she'd read in the paper a few years ago that he had gotten killed in a car accident. She had returned to Trenton, New Jersey, not to pay her last respects, but to verify for herself that the bastard was truly dead.

And lastly, there had been Fred Almay, the one man she'd enjoyed the most. He had hired her to work at his law firm right out of college, and she had slept with him of her own free will. They had spent two years together as lovers and he had taught her a lot. She would even admit to falling in love with him. He'd been a master at manipulation and had taught her all the key components of the game. But no matter how much she'd tried to please him, he had refused to leave his wife for her.

In the end Donna had decided it was in her best interest to move on when Mrs. Almay became suspicious of her role in Fred's life and her work at the firm. The one thing Fred had given her was the glowing recommendation that had helped her to land her job at Brown and Samuels.

She smiled as she curled into her chair. Her toys were okay when she needed a quick fix, but of course she much preferred the real thing. She licked her lips when she thought of Brian Lawson. He was an extremely good-looking man, well spoken and highly intelligent, and she knew he was going places.

He had charisma and charm and he radiated the confidence that only a natural-born leader could display. He was well liked by everyone at the firm and highly respected. And his knowledge of corporate law truly amazed her. She knew she could learn a lot from him, both in and out of the bedroom.

It meant nothing to her that he was engaged to be married. There was no such thing as a true-blue committed fiancé and she wondered how long it would take to tempt him mercilessly and get what she wanted.

There was only one way to find out.

The secretary smiled over at Brian. "Mr. Brown and Mr. Samuels would like to see you now, Mr. Lawson."

Brian returned her smile as he stood to his feet. He figured the two men had asked to meet with him because of his successful handling of the charity drive for children with leukemia. Every year one of the attorneys working for the firm would chair the event. This had been his year and he had helped raise over five hundred thousand dollars on the firm's behalf.

"Come on in, Brian," Talbert Brown called out to him the moment he opened the door. "Please come join me and Minor in a toast." It was then that he saw the bottle of champagne on ice and the glasses already filled with the bubbly drink.

Brian nodded and then accepted the glass of champagne that Mr. Brown handed to him. He figured the partners were going all out just for a good showing in the charity drive.

"Do you know why we invited you here today, Brian?"

He met Talbert Brown's deep blue eyes. "I assume it's to celebrate the money we raised for the Leukemia Foundation drive."

Minor Samuels chuckled. "There is a reason to celebrate that, too, but that's not why you're here."

Brian lifted a brow. "It's not?"

Talbert leaned against his desk. "Your father worked hard for this firm and it saddened us to remove his name as partner when he passed away."

Brian remembered his father working for the firm. According to his mother he'd become employed with them right after college. He'd been partner for five years when he died.

"Minor and I worked right alongside of him and the three of us made partners the same time under my father's leadership." A sad smile touched his lips before he added, "We went out to celebrate the following weekend and it was one of the last times we had a chance to really party together on the town. After that we spent every waking moment working our butts off."

Brian wondered why they were telling him all of this now. Evidently that question was reflected in his gaze, because Talbert then said, "You've been doing a fine job for us, Brian, one that we are proud of, one that your father would be proud of. So it seems right that you should take his place in this firm."

Brian wasn't sure he was hearing correctly. Were they saying what he thought they were saying?

"Yes, that's what we're saying," Talbert said, as if he was reading his mind again. "And it's not that we think we owe you anything because of your father, son. It's because you've earned a place here. Effective Monday, this firm will become Brown, Samuels and Lawson."

The words sent instant shudders through Brian and he stared at the two men in disbelief. He hadn't expected to be considered for partner for a couple more years down the road. There were others who'd been working at the firm longer than he had.

"That's not all, Brian."

He blinked. "It's not?"

"No. We have more good news to share," Talbert said, beaming.

Brian wasn't sure he could handle any more good news. "You do?"

"Yes. Your father became partner on your tenth birthday. I can remember it clearly because we couldn't celebrate that day because he had to leave to cohost your party. One of the perks of becoming partner is the firm's trust fund that can be set up for family members. Well, your father established one in your name with a twenty-year maturity date."

Minor then picked up the conversation. "Patrick was a smart man because it matured the year you decided to get married. Extra money will definitely come in handy now, don't you think?"

Brian nodded in agreement. "Yes, sir, it definitely will." He wasn't sure how much money they were talking about, but just the thought that his father had had the foresight to do something like that touched him deeply.

Over the years he'd enjoyed the finer things in life but had always looked out for his future, cultivating a really nice nest egg. He'd made several good investment choices and his money had been kept safe and secure even during the Wall Street fiasco. Many would be surprised to know just how solid his financial portfolio looked.

Minor reached behind him to retrieve an envelope off his desk. "Here you are."

Brian accepted the sealed envelope and nervously tore it open. He stared at it and then blinked, not believing what he saw. It took a minute to catch his breath and another minute to stop the erratic beating of his heart. He slowly glanced up at the two men in shock. "This is mine?" he asked in an incredulous tone.

"Yes, it's yours from your father and the continued success of this firm, which you've helped make possible. Every year that the company made a profit, a percentage of it was matched against the amount that was held in trust. "

Brian was speechless. Still standing—but barely—he stared down at the check. He glanced up and asked, "Did my mother know about this?"

"Yes, she knew, and as your guardian she could have taken the funds out at any time. However, she chose to let it remain in trust until maturity."

Brian drew in a deep breath and glanced back down at the check. Thanks to Mr. Brown and Mr. Samuels he had become a partner in the firm. And thanks to his father and his mother, he'd become a millionaire.

She quickly clicked over to the other line. "Brian?"

"Yes, baby?"

"You're calling early tonight. What's up?" she asked, sitting up in bed.

"Can you come out this weekend if I were to send for you?"

She pushed her hair behind her head. They hadn't seen each other since the engagement party two weeks ago. And then they had been surrounded by so much family they hadn't had a chance to spend a lot of time together alone.

She smiled as she eased back down in bed. "Are you missing me?"

"I'm always missing you, baby. I can't wait until you're here with me permanently."

She couldn't wait until she was there with him, too.

"But there's also another reason I want you here."

She lifted a brow. "And what reason is that?" It was then that she noticed something in his voice. It was still deep, husky and sexy, but she also detected something else. Excitement maybe?

"I made partner today."

Erica jerked upward, nearly dropping the phone out of her hand. "What? But you figured it would be another couple of years before you'd be considered for that. And that there were so many other attorneys ahead of you."

"Well, today Mr. Brown and Mr. Samuels informed me that I was their choice, and more than anything I want you here this weekend to celebrate with me."

Erica drew in a deep breath and fought back tears. She was so proud of him. From the time she'd met Brian she'd been aware of what a fantastic attorney he was. He worked hard and was deserving of whatever achievements came his way.

"I can't imagine being anywhere else this weekend other than there helping you celebrate. And you don't have to send for me. I can pay for my own ticket."

"I know, but I want to. I'll call you tomorrow with all the flight details."

"Okay."

As she cuddled in bed she knew when she saw him again, she would show him just how proud she was of him.

An hour or so later Brian hung up the phone from talking to Erica. He chuckled. She had fallen asleep on the phone after he'd sung her a lullaby. He headed for the study to read a few case files he'd brought home.

He had intentionally not mentioned anything to Erica about his trust fund after deciding he would share the news with her on what would be the most important day of his life—his wedding day.

He'd always felt capable of taking on a wife financially, which was one of the reasons he'd always found it rather amusing when Erica's mother insinuated that he was not. The woman knew nothing about him, and evidently she knew nothing about her daughter, either. Especially if she assumed a man's wealth was all Erica cared about.

One of the first things he'd discovered about his future wife was that even with her wealthy upbringing she didn't have a snobbish bone in her body. She was one of the last persons who would flaunt the fact that she'd been born with a silver spoon in her mouth. She was sweet and genuine, which was why he'd fallen hopelessly in love with her so easy and so quickly. Their love was solid and wasn't dictated by occupation or social status.

And he meant what he'd told her earlier. He couldn't wait until she joined him in Dallas permanently. Now that he knew he was even more capable of taking care of her, he felt wonderful and couldn't wait to see her again to celebrate all his good fortune.

"My mother indicated you wanted to meet with me, Mrs. Sanders."

Karen removed her reading glasses to glance up at the man her housekeeper had escorted into the study. Although they were distant relatives, she always encouraged him to address her in a formal fashion. She remembered the day Jaye Pittman was born, close to thirty-five years ago. There had been some who'd wondered if he was really Lester Pittman's son, but they figured even if he wasn't they could overlook that little transgression, since everyone knew just what a skirt chaser Lester had been both before and during his marriage to Aggie. It seemed hilariously fitting that his wife might have done to Lester what he'd done to her all those years. There were a number of Lester Pittman's bastards walking around Hattersville.

"Yes, Jaye, good seeing you and I'm glad you could drop by. How's your father?"

"He's doing well."

Lester was confined to a wheelchair these days after an auto accident had left him paralyzed. He had been drinking and lost control of the vehicle. The embarrassing thing about it was that he hadn't been alone. A woman, probably his flavor for the evening, had been killed instantly.

"That's good." Karen paused a moment and then said, "The reason I wanted to meet with you was to hire you. I need you to find out something for me. And it's information that I'd rather not use any of the local agencies to uncover."

"And what information is that?"

She was trying to get a feel for him and couldn't. She needed someone she could trust to keep her secrets, and who'd do what they were told without asking questions. She decided to take a chance since she was somewhat desperate at this point. Erica's wedding was in three months.

"As you know, Erica is getting married in August. I'm also sure you've heard that I am totally against the marriage. Although the man is a successful attorney in Texas, I don't think he is good enough for my daughter. It was always my dream that she find a good man here in Hattersville."

Jaye didn't say anything for a minute and then asked, "What is it that you want me to do for you?"

She lowered her guard somewhat. "It's my belief that most men have a past they prefer not revealing. I want you to find Brian Lawson's before the wedding."

"And you think there's something in his past that will be severe enough for Erica to call off the wedding?"

"I'm hoping so. It's obvious he might have once been a ladies' man. I'd like to find out about one or two of these ladies. See if they're really out of his life completely." She met his gaze and then added, "And even if they are, I want to know if—for a price—they are willing to return to stir up some trouble."

Jaye Pittman didn't say anything for a moment, but from the look in his eyes, she knew he had understood fully what she was asking of him. He leaned back in his chair as if to consider her business proposition. Then he asked, "And you're willing to go that far to make sure a wedding doesn't take place?"

She didn't hesitate in responding. "Yes."

He nodded his approval and smiled. "In that case, you have the right man for the job."

Chapter Seven

"Excuse me, but do you have any idea how much longer my flight will be delayed?" Rita Lawson asked the agent behind the customer service counter. She had been in Sweden for two weeks and had rushed to the airport for her flight home, only to be told of a delay.

"No, sorry," the woman said in a thick Swedish accent. "All the flights have been delayed as a result of the volcanic ash from Iceland."

Rita nodded. She recalled the same thing happening once before. Airlines couldn't risk the possibility of engine failure if they were to fly through the ash. "When will we know something?"

"Not sure, but we will keep you informed of any updates. Here is a courtesy coupon for the restaurant on the next floor."

Rita drew in a deep breath. She didn't want a courtesy coupon; she wanted to go home. Although she always enjoyed her business trips here, she couldn't wait to get home and see Brian's smile for herself now that he knew about the trust fund. She had heard it in his voice when he'd called her earlier in the week but she needed to see it.

After Patrick died, she had made Brian her entire life. It was only after he'd left home for college that she'd decided to get a life of her own and further her education. She'd gotten a bachelor's degree while attending Tuskegee University, where she'd met Patrick, and had decided to go to grad school when Brian left home for college. She used that master's degree to get her current position of landscape architect and she enjoyed traveling all over the world.

And now with Brian getting married in a few months, she was glad she wasn't one of those parents who built her life around her child. She loved him with every breath in her body, but had accepted he had his own life to live and she had hers.

She smiled thinking of the woman her son would marry. Brian loved Erica deeply and, after having met Erica and spent time with her, Rita knew in her heart that Erica Sanders was the woman who would make her son happy. And, she thought as she walked away from the customer service counter, although it might be a wee bit too early to think about, she was looking forward to the day when she would become a grandmother.

After stepping off the escalator, she glanced down at the meal voucher she'd been given and decided to get something to eat.

It seemed to take her forever to go through the line for her food order, but she occupied her mind. At some point she needed to let Brian know of the delay, since he would be picking her up from the airport. Normally, she would leave her car parked at the airport but she had decided to have the vehicle's yearly service-check performed during the two weeks she was away.

Finally she got her food and, holding her tray firmly in

her hand, she glanced around and saw an empty table. She quickly headed toward it. At least she had a good book to read while she waited.

She had settled at the table when she felt a presence next to her. She glanced up. Rita couldn't help the smile that touched her lips when she recognized the individual. "Wilson!"

He chuckled. "Yes, and I'm glad to see a familiar face among these bodies of disgruntled flyers. May I join you?"

"Of course." Rita couldn't contain her excitement at seeing him and didn't question why she felt good about it. He'd mentioned at the engagement party that, like her, he traveled internationally quite a bit, but what were the chances of them running into each other during one of those times?

"You've been in Sweden?" she asked, watching him pull out a chair to sit down. Although she knew it wasn't possible, he seemed taller today than the last time she'd seen him.

"I had business to take care of in Finland and for some reason I had a connecting flight here. What about you? Have you been in Sweden?"

"I've been here for two weeks. In fact I arrived here a week after the engagement party."

He nodded as his smile broadened. "I understand that Brian made partner at the law firm he works for. Erica called and told me. That's a wonderful accomplishment. You have to be proud of him."

Rita could feel herself beaming. "I am. He's worked hard and deserves it. Erica's going to Dallas this weekend to help him celebrate."

"Yes, that's what she told me."

She glanced over at his plate and saw the muffin that he would occasionally munch on while sipping his coffee. "That's all you're having?"

"Yes. I'm not a big eater."

"Yes, but there's no telling how much longer we'll be stuck here so you might as well endure it on a full stomach."

His smile deepened and she could see that he had dimples in the same place on his face as Erica. And she couldn't help noticing how totally masculine his facial features were. He was definitely a handsome man and his pleasant attitude and disposition made him even more so. If she were to guess she would say he was just a few years older than she, which would put him in his late fifties.

"I'm hoping it's not much longer, but even so, it's not going to be too bad now that I have such nice company."

She accepted his words as a compliment. Had it been any other man she would even go so far as to think that he was flirting with her. But she knew better. Wilson Sanders was a married man. The father of her son's fiancée. But still, as off-limits as he was, she still found him desirable and, for a woman who hadn't shown any real interest in a man since her husband's death fifteen years ago, that was a startling surprise.

But then, she was still a woman.

"Thanks for saying that. You know, in a few months our families will become connected through our children."

"Yes, that's true. I propose a toast," he said, holding up his coffee cup.

"And what are we toasting?" she asked, laughing, following suit and holding up hers.

"To your son and my daughter. May they have a wonderful marriage. One that's filled with love."

Rita couldn't help but smile in seeing that Wilson's attitude toward the upcoming nuptials was nothing like his wife's. "Yes, to Brian and Erica."

Their cups touched and then they smiled as they took sips of their coffee.

* * *

As much as he didn't want to be, Wilson knew at that moment he was attracted to Rita. And that wasn't a good thing.

He drew in a deep breath as he looked beyond her to study the landscape outside the window. At least he was pretending to study the landscape, when in all actuality his main focus was still on her.

She looked elegant in her own sort of way, and now he knew what it was about her that he admired. Style. He found it totally hilarious that he was drawn to her for the very thing Karen thought she lacked. As far as he was concerned, she didn't need to wear all those famous name brands and designer labels that Karen boasted about. Rita made a statement in a way that he found admirable.

Even now for traveling she was wearing jeans and a printed peasant blouse. Her hair was pinned up and a pair of hoop earrings dangled from her ears. Another thing he liked about her was her positive attitude. If he was a man interested in pursuing an affair with a woman he would definitely put her at the top of his list.

But he didn't have a list. He'd never had a list. He'd never had a choice of a mate, either, since one had been chosen for him before he could walk. Probably before he'd been born. It was only lately that he'd found himself reflecting over his life and realizing just how unhappy he was married to Karen. How unhappy he'd been for a long time. It wouldn't be so regrettable if there'd been any phase of their marriage he would say he'd found memorable. But sadly, he couldn't. The only good thing that had come from it was Erica. And he was determined to make sure she married for love even if he hadn't.

But with all those emotions he was now bringing forth and all the rights Karen had been denying him as a husband for years, he had not once been unfaithful to her. He had thought about it once or twice but could never go through with it. Things were as they were. He'd made his bed years ago when he'd allowed his parents to run his life and he'd been paying hell for it since. He rubbed a hand over his brow. The entire thought was depressing. He would be sixty at the end of the year and he'd spent all of his life trying to please someone. First his parents and now his wife. Erica was probably the only person that truly loved him unconditionally.

His gaze returned to Rita. She was sipping her coffee and appeared to be lost in her own thoughts. He couldn't help wondering what they were. And, since she seemed preoccupied as he had been earlier, he allowed his gaze to travel over her. He liked what he saw too much and forced an image of Karen in his mind but it refused to come to the forefront where it belonged.

The best thing to do would be to finish off his coffee, stand up, bid her a safe trip back home and then go somewhere where he couldn't see her, where he couldn't think about her, where he couldn't wonder…

"Was this a productive trip for you, Wilson?"

Her soft voice intruded into his thoughts and broke the silence surrounding them. Their gazes held, maybe for a second too long, because she then looked away, down into her coffee cup. And then it hit him. She had picked up on the same vibes that he had picked up on earlier. And like him she was trying to ignore them. Doing so made perfect sense, since they shouldn't be having these feelings anyway. He wasn't free to act on them. But she was a widow and free to do whatever she wanted with any other man, although not with him. He was taken. Why did that realization dampen his spirits?

He leaned back and forced his brain to formulate a response to her question. "Yes, I think it was productive, and my staff will agree since I clinched a million-dollar deal."

"Congratulations."

"Thanks. What about you? Was this trip productive for you?"

She laughed. "I didn't clinch a million-dollar deal or anything close to that, but I did get a few members of the royal family to agree to consider my company when they landscape the palace grounds."

For the next twenty minutes or so they continued talking, engaging in pleasant conversation about their work. He enjoyed being educated about something he didn't know a lot about. Plants. His only excuse was that the Sanders Estates always had a gardener who knew what he was doing, which meant that Wilson didn't necessarily have to learn.

The more Rita talked the more he kept thinking that it didn't seem possible that a woman like her—smart, stylish and classy—who had a lot going for her, had remained single after her husband died.

When there was a pause in the conversation, he heard himself asking, "Why didn't you ever remarry?"

She glanced up and looked stunned by his question. She could have said it wasn't any of his business, and it would have been within her rights to do so. Instead she said, "Patrick and I were college sweethearts and I took his death extremely hard, mainly because I hadn't seen it coming. He'd never been sick a day in his life."

She paused a moment when a waitress came by and refilled their coffee cups. "I figured he would be here forever," she then said. "I had assumed that he would always be my rock, my shining star, the man who was everything a husband and father should be. The pain of losing him was excruciating, but I had to endure it for Brian. Although I was hurting, I knew he was hurting just as much. He was very close to his father."

She took a sip of her coffee. "It was important to me not to bring another man into Brian's life that would take Patrick's place because I thought no one could. So I filled the role of both mom and dad and was satisfied with doing that."

Wilson nodded. "What about when Brian left for college?"

She shrugged what he thought were beautiful shoulders. "I dated but not often, and never let anyone think it was serious. Patrick's parents tried encouraging me to go on with my life, saying that's what he would have wanted, and I know that to be true, but I couldn't date anyone else. To fill the void of Brian leaving home I decided to go back to college for my master's degree."

She lowered her head and took another sip of her coffee as if reliving those times.

"Do you date now?"

She lifted her gaze, tilted her head and studied him for a second. "Why do you want to know that?"

That was a good question. Why did he want to know the answer to that? "Curious."

He waited a heartbeat for her to ask why. Instead she said, "I go out on occasion with friends—both males and females— but that's all I want right now. Friendship. Less cluttered and complicated that way."

He was saved from having to say anything when a voice came over the speaker system. "Attention, passengers. We regret to inform everyone that all flights have been cancelled for the next twenty-four hours. Please go to your respective airline's customer service counter for further details regarding obtaining a hotel voucher. We repeat, all flights..."

He watched as Rita stood. "I guess that means I need to go back upstairs. It was good seeing you and I hope that—"

"The announcer said we're stuck here for twenty-four hours. Would you like to join me for dinner somewhere?" he asked as he stood.

She began shaking her head even before he could get all the words out of his mouth. "Thanks, but no. I'm just going to stay in my room and relax. It was good seeing you again, and I hope you have a safe trip back home."

"You, too."

He watched her hurry across the floor toward the escalator as if fire was nipping at her heels. Evidently his line of questions had made her uncomfortable. Understandably so. He'd really had no right asking them. But it was something he wanted to know. Something he needed to know.

He walked to get information from his own airline, in the opposite direction from where she had gone. At least they had offered them a hotel room. He wished he could say he intended to relax, as Rita had indicated she was going to do, but he couldn't. After checking in to the hotel he planned on going out and finding the nearest bar to wash away these emotions, which he shouldn't be having in the first place.

As he stepped onto the escalator that would carry him down to his gate, he thought that a glass of scotch later sounded pretty damn nice.

Rita glanced around her hotel room a moment before tilting her head back, closing her eyes and drawing in a deep breath. She inhaled the scent of cinnamon and all but licked her lips at the thought of all the goodies in the bakery across the street. An image of her enjoying any sort of pastry with a cup of coffee made a silly grin form on her face. She immediately opened her eyes when images of something else flashed across her brain…or should she say someone else.

Wilson Sanders.

She could admit in private that she liked him a little too much. She had begun feeling things she should not be feeling. The man was married, for heaven's sake, and he was her son's future father-in-law. Then why did she—a woman known to be more interested in the positioning of yucca plants than men—find herself so attracted to him?

When he smiled, funny feelings would erupt in her mid-section. Even when he did something as simple as shrug his massive shoulders, she was consumed by emotions she hadn't felt in a long time. And that in itself wasn't good. She felt completely out of her element around him, while at the same time she felt like a real woman for the first time in years. A woman with primitive urges and true yearnings. That would be all well and good if the object of her attention wasn't who he was.

She closed her eyes and tilted her head back again, wishing the features of another man would pop into her head. She'd met several on her Sweden trip. No such luck.

She opened her eyes, deciding she had done the right thing in turning down Wilson's invitation to dinner. She'd never respected women who were involved with married men. Marriage vows were sacred and were meant to be forever. For the time being, until she could sort out in her mind why she was being pulled in a direction she would rather not go, she would keep a safe and comfortable distance from Wilson.

Her stomach made a growling sound and she remembered she hadn't eaten anything since the sandwich she'd had with coffee earlier. The meal she'd shared with Wilson. Not wanting to think of anything associated with Wilson at the moment, she decided to appease her stomach, while at the same time enjoying her extra night in Stockholm.

She remembered the receptionist at the front desk had mentioned that Stockholm's most popular restaurant/night club was in walking distance of the hotel. Maybe a night out on the town was what she needed. When was the last time she'd done such a thing? Probably last year when she and her best friend, Lori Spencer, had gone out for Lori's fiftieth birthday. She hoped there wouldn't be nude men dancing in front of her face tonight.

She smiled when she thought of Lori. Her best friend topped the list of those who felt she was wasting a lot of her years not having a man in her life. Of course that would be a natural assumption for Lori to make, since she seemed to breathe men. Divorced by choice, Lori thought men were put here for women to enjoy. But Rita knew that, even as open and brazen as Lori was, she'd never become involved with a married man.

But then, Rita wasn't talking about an involvement with Wilson. Things would never go that far. She was having issues with the fact that she was attracted to him in the first place— something she knew Lori would say was normal. Maybe Lori would be right. The attraction was harmless. In fact, when they saw each other again, which probably wouldn't be until the actual wedding, whatever vibes they'd felt earlier would probably be out of their systems. Gone and forever forgotten. She certainly hoped so. Otherwise, seeing him again could prove to be an uncomfortable situation.

A short while later, after she had showered and dressed, she checked herself in the mirror. She didn't look bad for a woman her age.

She grabbed her purse and headed out. The night was young and alive and she intended to enjoy it.

"What are we having tonight, sir?"

"Let's start with scotch on the rocks. You can bring a menu later."

"Yes, sir."

Wilson leaned back in his chair while watching members of the band he assumed would be performing for the evening set up their musical equipment onstage. He then glanced around at the club from his table in the back where the lights were dimmed.

This club had come recommended by the staff at the hotel where he was staying. After dealing with business all week, he needed to unwind and thought coming here would do the trick. Besides, he needed a drink.

It didn't take long for the waiter to return with Wilson's scotch. He wasted no time taking a swallow of it.

He needed the night alone and the drink to think about what had happened earlier with Rita. She had done the right thing in not accepting his invitation to dinner. Although he'd meant it sincerely, they both knew there was more between them than either of them wanted. It wasn't a good situation for either of them to be caught up in. They were adults, and expectedly, a lot wiser. Smart enough to ward off any circumstances that could lead to a mistake.

Rita was a beautiful woman, and as a man who could not only recognize beauty but appreciate it as well, he couldn't help finding her desirable. His being married had nothing to do with it. Beautiful women attracted normal men.

But in his case there was more to it than that. Sometimes he wondered just how "normal" he was. He'd been married for thirty years yet he hadn't made love to his wife in over twenty. She had turned him down each and every time he had made an attempt. He'd tried to romance her, entice her with getaways, and every time she had flatly refused him, saying she didn't need sex in her life.

He knew his wife was too selfish to care about the possibility that he did need sex and might go where he could to find it. But he had never given betraying her that way any thought, although he'd had had several opportunities to do so.

Last year his younger brother Marshall had asked him how long he would remain in a loveless marriage. Unlike him,

Marshall had married for love and it showed. It hadn't mattered to Marshall that the family had almost disowned him for marrying Swan Callahan, a woman whose family had been born on the other side of the tracks, as Karen liked to say. Marshall hadn't needed the Sanders' name or money to succeed, and today both he and Swan worked as doctors at Hattersville General and their twins were in college.

He hadn't had an answer for Marshall then and didn't have one now. However, being around Rita had made him realize that he was a man with needs. Needs he had locked away for a lifetime to be a good husband and father.

He picked up his scotch glass to take another sip when suddenly his senses became alert. Even a little edgy. The hand holding the glass tightened as he scanned the club.

And then he saw her.

Rita had entered the restaurant alone. She was looking sleek, stylish and sexy in a rather sophisticated dress that hit at the knees, showing her legs. This was the first time he'd actually seen her legs and he thought they should be on display all the time.

His eyes continued to glide over her as the waitress escorted her to a table. She hadn't looked his way, but then she had no reason to, since he was seated in a darkened area in the back. To his way of thinking, this gave him an advantage. An advantage he probably had no right to be taking. He was, after all, a married man, regardless of whether he wanted to be. But then, a part of his brain kept insinuating that, married or not, there was nothing wrong with a man appreciating a beautiful woman, as long as he didn't get out of line or act on that appreciation. And he had no intentions of ever doing anything like that.

As far as he was concerned, there was no reason they couldn't enjoy each other's company over dinner tonight.

However, since she had turned down his invitation to dinner earlier, he would let her dine now in peace.

Unless she looked over his way and saw him, she had no reason to know he was even here. Picking up his glass he settled back in his chair to enjoy the view.

Chapter Eight

By the time the band broke for intermission, Rita was on her third glass of wine after dinner. For the first time in a long time she felt at ease, calm and totally relaxed. She was sure the wine had something to do with it. Not that she'd taken leave of her senses. In fact somehow the wine made her feel more alert. More attuned. Warmed to the soul.

As the lights in the club became brighter, people began moving around. Some were leaving; others were arriving. Then, there appeared to be a sudden quietness, although she could still see people buzzing about. She slowly drew a deep breath and turned her head, not sure exactly what she was looking for or expected to find. And then she saw Wilson, sitting alone at a table in the back of the club.

Their eyes met and she felt her body tense at the same time she felt shivers in the pit of her stomach. When had he arrived? She was sitting in close proximity to the entrance so there was no way he could have walked in without her noticing him. That meant he had been there all the time.

As their gazes held, his lips moved and he gave her a smile

so sensual that it nearly stole her next breath. She swallowed, felt her throat getting dry and automatically took another sip of her wine.

Embarrassment nearly tinted her features. He had asked her to join him for dinner and she had turned him down, using the flimsy excuse that she wanted to hang out in her hotel room and chill. Well, although she might be chilling, this definitely wasn't her hotel room. But a woman did have the right to change her mind, didn't she? Would he see it as that or would he recognize it for what it had been? A way to put distance between them.

Her heart began beating furiously in her chest as their gazes continued to hold. As she watched, he finally stood and, without disconnecting his gaze from hers, he began walking over toward her table. She could feel herself tremble with every slow and methodical step that he took. He was staring at her with the same intensity that she was staring at him. What was she going to say to him? She had failed miserably at keeping him at bay.

She cleared her throat when he came to a stop in front of her table and she had to tilt her head back to look up at him.

"Rita."

She swallowed before she managed to say, "Wilson."

"You look lovely tonight."

"Thank you."

He jammed his hands into the pockets of his pants. "Did you enjoy dinner?"

She hesitated a moment before saying, "Yes. Did you?"

He chuckled. "Funny thing, I never got around to ordering anything. I guess I was fine with my drink."

The proper thing to do was to ask him to join her, since she felt bad being caught in a lie. "If you continue to stand I'm going to get a crook in my neck looking up at you," she said in a teasing tone, trying to make light of the situation she had backed herself into. "Would you like to join me?"

He nodded. "Yes," he said, pulling out a chair and taking it.

She leaned back and crossed her legs. "How long have you been in here?"

He seemed to have studied her movement and his gaze moved from her legs up to her face. "Awhile. I saw you when you walked in."

"Why didn't you let me know you were here?"

He shrugged. "I figured you would prefer it that way."

Because of what she'd said earlier when he'd invited her to dinner. There was nothing she could say...but that didn't mean she shouldn't try.

"Wilson, I—"

"There's no need to explain, Rita."

She was quiet for a long moment as she thought about what he'd said. No, there was no need to explain. But she felt she needed to anyway.

"You're married."

If he found that statement odd he didn't show it. "Yes, I am married."

She released a shuddering breath. Not that he needed to confirm such a thing, but for some reason she needed to make sure his marital status was out there, planted firmly in both of their minds.

"And I have never been unfaithful to my wife during the entire thirty years of our marriage."

She nodded. That was good to hear. Had he said that to let her know that—although there might be some crazy vibes still flowing between them, vibes that seemed more heated now than earlier—he was a happily married man? For some reason she doubted the happily married part. Her aunt Grace had once told her that being married meant more than sharing names on a marriage certificate. It meant being one with the other. As she had been with Patrick.

Remembering the man she had loved deeply made her take another sip of her wine and she couldn't help noticing her glass was almost empty. Her server had already noticed before she had and he was back refilling her glass. She should tell him she'd had enough, but decided not to do so.

The man then turned to Wilson. "Sir, would you like a refill?"

"Yes."

"And will you be joining the madam here?"

He gave her a quick glance before returning his attention back to the server and saying, "Yes."

The server then quickly moved away and they were alone again. Wilson's gaze reclaimed hers. "Now, you were saying..."

She managed a shrug, not sure she was capable of saying anything. She took a sip of her wine. "Nothing. I think you've said it all, Wilson."

He chuckled, and the rich, husky sound was something to be admired. Really it was. There was something so invigorating about him. She thought that Karen Sanders was a very lucky woman and wondered if she knew that.

"Have you been enjoying the music?" he asked her.

"Yes, very much so. I've always enjoyed good music and was trying to compare this club with one back home."

A smile touched his lips. "The music is somewhat different, although I've always been a fan of Lars Gullin and the Swedish jazz sound. The man was one hell of a saxophone player."

"Yes, I know."

At the slow lifting of his brow she smiled and said, "I was an army brat and traveled around the world a lot. Although

I never lived in Sweden, I did live for a while in Liverpool. The Swedish jazz sound was pretty big there."

Their conversation paused when the server returned with Wilson's drink. Moments later the musicians took the stage again and Rita became absorbed in her surroundings and the music. At least she tried to become absorbed in them. Neither could compete with the man sitting at her table. The man who—whether she wanted it or not—couldn't help but claim every bit of her attention.

"Do you think we'll get to fly out tomorrow?" she decided to ask, for lack of anything better to say at the moment.

"Yes. Are you getting homesick already?"

She smiled and was reminded of why she had liked him. He hadn't asked with ridicule in his tone. Although it was quite obvious that a man in his profession would be used to giving orders instead of taking them, she felt he could still reach down and converse genuinely on a personal level.

"Yes, I can admit I am homesick in a way. I talked to Brian earlier, to let him know my flight was being delayed, and he happened to be on his way to the airport to pick up Erica."

Wilson raised a surprised brow. "I thought she wasn't flying to Dallas until the weekend."

"I guess she changed her mind." Rita smiled. "She's a woman, she has a right to do that, you know."

He chuckled. "Trust me, I know."

She didn't say anything for a moment and then a question came to her mind. "What hotel did your airline put you up in?"

"The Hilton. What about you?"

Rita pulled in a deep breath. "The same one."

"Oh."

He'd spoken that one word and she couldn't tell if it was a good *oh,* or a bad *oh.*

As for her, either way, she needed to prepare herself for

the walk back to the hotel room, since she had a darn good feeling they would be sharing it.

Wilson glanced over at the woman walking by his side, grateful for the fresh night air. He needed to clear his head for more reasons than one. Although he wasn't drunk by any means, he still had imbibed more scotch tonight than he had in a long time. However, instead of it dulling his senses, he felt they were sharper than ever. And that had everything to do with Rita.

He glanced up at the sky, saw the stars and the full moon, and for a while he thought the piano music he'd heard tonight wasn't the only magical thing around here. The night held some wonders of its own and he felt good being here. Especially while walking beside Rita, sharing her space.

Tomorrow they would fly out, go their separate ways, and their paths wouldn't cross again until the day of their offspring's wedding. He smiled just thinking about it.

"What's the smile for?"

He glanced over at her. "I was just thinking about Brian and Erica's wedding."

She smiled, as well. "It won't be long now and I promise to look after her when she moves to Dallas."

He nodded. "I appreciate that. Karen still isn't happy about her moving away from Hattersville."

"But you don't have a problem with it?"

"No, not a one. I think Brian is a fine young man and it's her place to be with her husband." Just like he knew it was his place to be with his wife, although lately he had begun wondering why. He had called her earlier to let her know his flight was delayed and she hadn't even asked him why. She rushed him off the phone saying she was on her way out and didn't have time for idle chitchat. When it came to him she'd never had time for anything. And for years he'd let her get away with it. She had conveniently placed him on a shelf and he had stayed there. Tonight he realized how it would be to spend time with a woman, if for nothing more than to share a drink and some music. He and Karen did share after-dinner drinks, but it was only to give her a chance to unwind and talk about the people she felt were beneath her.

When they entered the hotel lobby Rita slowed her pace. "Thanks for the walk. I needed it."

"So did I."

She stopped walking. "This is where we need to say good-night and good-bye until August."

He leaned forward and smiled. "Do you honestly think I'll leave you on your own to get to your room?"

She decided not to argue. "Fine. I'm on the fifth floor," she said, and began walking toward the bank of elevators.

Other couples were around and got onto the elevator with them. The ride up to the fifth floor was short. Done in silence. There wasn't anything to say as they stood beside each other in the cramped quarters.

When they reached her floor and the doors swooshed open, they both stepped out. He glanced over at her thinking he didn't regret anything about tonight. He had enjoyed sitting at the table sharing drinks with her while they listened to the jazz, and he appreciated the conversation. He liked hearing her talk. She had a soft voice, the kind he could probably listen to for hours on end and not get tired of hearing.

And he had liked glancing across the table at her when she didn't know he was looking. When he should not have been looking. He didn't have the right, but he had done so anyway. And his chest had thumped deeply each time she had smiled with enjoyment when the band ended one number and began another.

He couldn't help but wonder if what his brother had claimed all these years was true. Did every living human being have a soul mate? A person so attuned to another person that loving them, wanting to be with them, was just as vital as eating and breathing? At the moment he didn't know. He truly couldn't imagine such a thing.

He began looking straight ahead down the long, seemingly endless hallway, counting the doors they passed on their way to hers. When they reached their destination, he would say good-bye, tell her that he hoped she had a safe flight home and then turn to leave. Simple. Yet for him, for some reason it would be hard. Whatever time they had shared over the past twelve hours would be just a memory. A memory she might eventually banish from her mind, though he doubted he ever would.

"Thank you for walking me to my door," she said when she came to a stop.

He halted his steps as well and glanced at her, saw her smile and at that moment his breath was nearly snatched right from his lungs. What was happening to him? Why was his heart beating so fast? What were these emotions that were surging inside of him and rapidly consuming him?

"Don't mention it," he heard himself say. "Have a safe flight back and hug that daughter of mine when you see her, will you?"

She chuckled as her face lit up, and the sound flitted through parts of his body. "Of course I will. You know, Wilson, you're a good father."

"I've always tried to be." He paused a moment then said, "Good-bye, Rita."

"Good-bye, Wilson." She then used her pass key to unlock the door and he began to walk off.

He told himself to keep walking and not look back, and could attribute a number of things to the reason he suddenly stopped. It could have been the absence of the sound of the door opening and closing shut behind her, or the need to

see her one last time even if it was just a glimpse of her flee-
ing back.

But when he turned, what he saw gave him pause. Had
him groaning silently. Rita was looking directly at him and
there was a need he saw in the depths of her eyes that probably matched his own. A need that was twenty years in the
making for him. The smile was gone and the intense look
shaping her mouth and the longing in the deep set of her gaze
almost froze him in place.

And when she whispered his name in a soundless plea, one
he would not have heard had he not seen her lips move, he
began slowly walking back to her, not sure what he would do
when he reached her.

That uncertainty was taken out of his hands and instinctively he pulled her into his arms and lowered his head.
Taking her mouth was probably the easiest thing he'd ever
done. And the tastiest. Their tongues tangled, dueled and intimately connected.

He leaned against the door and found it ajar, so without
breaking the kiss he eased them both inside and closed the
door behind them with his heel. Something flared through
him, something he hadn't felt in years, if ever. He was downright dizzy with passion. Hunger for her gnawed in the pit of
his stomach, cutting a quick path to his groin.

He was fifty-nine years old, for heaven's sake. Where did
all this greed and fire come from? All this animal lust? And
why was it coming out in full blast for this woman? He didn't
have time to dwell on those questions when he felt the back
of his legs touch the bed. It was only then that he pulled his
mouth from hers, so they could both breathe.

He needed to slow down, savor the moments, relish every
second he had with her, but a part of him didn't want to take
things slow. First thing he needed to do was speak words to
make her understand something and hope she believed him.

Wilson reached out and caressed her cheek with the back of his hand. Her skin was soft and smooth to the touch. His touch. "I never meant for this to happen, Rita. I tried to fight wanting you and it did no good. I need you." He heard the crackle in his voice and knew he was a man who'd been pushed over the edge. He had gone over twenty years without a woman, yet tonight, now, he felt he needed her with an intensity that had every part of him literally shaking inside.

And then he lowered his mouth to hers again, not wanting to give her the chance to think too deeply. Just to accept things as they were now. He decided not to question anything, just act on it. Pulsing heat began racing through his body when he began removing her clothes as well as his own, not stopping to think. As tension pricked at his nerve endings, he could tell she was pushed over the same edge as he was.

When they were both naked together they tumbled back on the bed. He had known the instant she'd opened her arms to him outside that door that they would end up here. He gazed down and saw the most gorgeous naked female body. A woman whose breasts could probably still rival a woman's half her age. Whose legs were slightly parted, open for him.

He couldn't contain himself when he shifted positions and lowered his head to her belly and placed a kiss there. Why he'd wanted to do that he wasn't sure but the moment he did so he felt a need to enjoy other parts of her below the waist.

So he did and kissed a trail down to the apex of her thighs. When he flicked a quick lick across her womanly folds before using his fingers to slide them open, he heard a moan from deep within her throat. He didn't need any other encouragement or approval to go further.

His hands slid down her thighs and lifted her hips to his mouth. He hadn't done this to a woman in over twenty years but his tongue seemed hot, greedy and ready for the opportunity to get back in circulation. And the instant it slid inside her feminine charms, he went after her with a voracity and need that he knew neither of them had been prepared for.

She continued to moan as she grabbed hold of his head to keep it in place, opening her legs wider and lifting her hips to his mouth for a more concentrated penetration of his tongue. Her hips began moving instinctively against his mouth and he continued to savor her with an all-consuming ardor.

"Wilson!"

His name became a whimpering moan off her lips and he felt the moment her body bucked into an orgasm. He kept his tongue planted inside of her and continued to feed his longing and enjoy this intimate time with her.

Moments later when he shifted upward and met her gaze he lowered his body in place over hers. She stared back at him through glazed eyes and he felt something besides lust jolt inside of him. Not wanting to question what it was, he leaned forward and kissed her mouth, needing the connection.

Sexual need, to a degree he hadn't known could exist until tonight, rushed through him and at that moment he needed her with a ferociousness that was overwhelming, near blinding. Without preamble he slid inside of her. The body enveloping him felt tight, incredibly feminine, and when he eased his mouth away from her to stare down at her, there was something else he felt. A sense of belonging.

And when her inner muscles began clenching him, he started to move, to thrust inside of her, stroke her with everything he had. He drove them to the edge then snapped them away before they could take a plunge.

The respite didn't last long. When he felt her legs tighten around him and she deeply moaned his name, he thrust one last time. They both exploded into a fiery ball of sensations that shook everything inside of him and had them both gasp-

ing for breath. They were overcome with unadulterated pleasure, intense heat and an obliteration of all thoughts but this
one. The one centered on them and their needs.

Wilson threw his head back and sucked into his nostrils a
scent that was uniquely hers. He released the deep breath and
drew her closer into his arms, as he remained inside her.

It was only later when he had no more strength left that he
managed to shift positions to hold her. Somehow he worked
their bodies beneath the covers and held her in his arms while
they slept.

The ringing of the telephone woke up Wilson. It took
him a few moments to remember he wasn't in his own hotel
room but was in Rita's. When she didn't answer the phone
he opened his eyes and glanced around. Sunlight was coming
through the window denoting another day.

The bed was empty. He picked up the phone, saw it was
a wake-up call and hung up. Thinking Rita had gone to the
bathroom he waited a while before realizing he was in the
room alone and she was gone and wouldn't be back.

Ah, hell. He had an idea what that meant. The reason she
had skipped out on him, why she'd left without saying good-
bye. Maybe he should be feeling some of that same remorse
about what they'd done last night, but he didn't. He could
truly say that his and Karen's marriage had ended years ago
and the connection they shared now was on paper only. Last
night had proven just how empty his marriage was, and how
it would feel to be with a woman he enjoyed spending time
with.

He slid out of bed. He didn't even have Rita's cell phone
number to call her. He must have been sleeping pretty damn
hard for her to get out of bed and pack without waking him.
But when a man had experienced the best lovemaking of his

life, after his mind, body and senses had exploded the way they had, it was a wonder he could still see straight.

He knew what he had to do when he returned to Hattersville. He would ask Karen for a divorce, which was something he should have done years ago. His daughter had taken control of her own life and now he needed to follow her example and take control of his.

Chapter Nine

Sunlight filtered through the window and hit Erica right in the face. She slowly opened her eyes and shifted in bed to snuggle closer to Brian, only to find the spot empty.

She drew in a deep breath and sat up in the huge bed. Her luggage was still where it had been left last night. They had barely made it inside the house before they'd begun tearing at each other's clothes. As far as they were concerned, two weeks was a long time not to be together.

It seemed that the closer they got to their wedding, the stronger their need and desire for each other was getting. She smiled thinking that last night it might have even gotten a little out of hand. She'd practically been on her back since she'd arrived, but had no complaints about it. Making love with Brian was the best, and more than once she'd pinched herself to make sure everything that was happening to her was truly real.

She frowned when she heard voices. At first she thought the sounds were being carried from downstairs, but then she realized they were coming in from the window.

Grabbing Brian's shirt she moved to the window. He was down below standing in the front yard. Since he had the newspaper in his hand she could only assume he'd gone out to get it. But Brian holding a newspaper wasn't what grabbed her attention. It was the jogger he was conversing with. A woman who looked liked she had walked off the cover of *Cosmopolitan*. She was gorgeous, although Erica doubted all that hair flowing over her shoulders had actually grown on her head.

Her jogging shorts should be outlawed, and who in the hell wore makeup to exercise? *Only a woman after a man,* a voice in the back of her head said loud and clear. And it wasn't her own voice; it was April's. If anyone should know it was April.

Erica frowned. She'd never been the jealous type and trusted Brian explicitly, but there was something about this barely dressed woman practically leaning all over him, almost in his face, that had the hairs standing up on her neck.

Evidently she was someone who lived in this neighborhood, but with the hours she knew he spent at work, when did he have time to socialize with neighbors? And what in the heck were they laughing and chatting about?

Okay, okay, maybe Erica was getting carried away with her thoughts and the woman was the mother of five and her husband was a clone of Idris Elba. Umm, for some reason Erica didn't think so, which meant she needed to protect what was hers. With the shortage of brothers a sistah had to be on her *p*'s and *q*'s for man snatchers, especially men already taken. There was no shame in some women's game.

Hopefully she wasn't blowing anything out of proportion, but she wouldn't take any chances. She backed away from the window and moved toward her luggage. There was a reason she'd come to Dallas early. And a reason Brian had taken a couple of days off work to spend with her while she was here. They were to celebrate and she was ready to let the party began.

"Good morning."

Brian turned away from the sink and smiled at the same time he felt heat rush through his groin. There stood the love of his life, looking sexier than any woman he knew. Some women liked flaunting their beauty. Erica didn't need to do so, since she exuded hers naturally.

The sundress she was wearing made her appear even more feminine and showcased her gorgeous legs. He could vividly remember those same legs wrapped around his waist last night, holding on tight while they made love. He inhaled sharply at the memory.

He threw the dish towel on the counter and moved toward her, feeling desire escalate through his body with every step he took. When he was in reaching distance of her, he pulled her to him and captured her mouth, hungrily, as a surge of longing poured all through him. When a man loved a woman this much, and when she loved him back, that was definitely a blessing from the man upstairs.

When he released her mouth she tilted her head and met his gaze. "And good morning to you, sweetheart," he said, leaning down and placing another kiss on her lips. He couldn't resist such a move.

"I woke up and you weren't there," she said, wrapping her arms around his neck.

He smiled. It felt good knowing he was missed. "I got up early. You were sleeping so soundly I didn't want to wake you. I wanted to grab the paper and drink a cup of coffee before preparing breakfast."

"I figured as much. I heard voices outside the window and glanced out and saw you."

"Did you?"

"Yes. I also saw your neighbor. She's pretty."

He chuckled. "Is she? I hadn't noticed."

She rolled her eyes. "Yeah, right. She got close enough for her scent to be practically all over you. She was wearing Allure."

He lifted his arm and took a sniff and smiled. "Umm, not bad."

When she frowned, he chuckled and pulled out a chair from the table, sat down and tugged her into his lap. He'd been around enough women to know when the green-eyed jealousy monster had invaded their genes. He never cared before because he hadn't placed a ring on any woman's finger. Until now. This was Erica, the one woman that mattered. The one wearing his ring. And it was important to him that she knew she had his heart totally. When it came to her there was no competition.

"Her name is Donna Hardy and she started working at the firm a few months ago."

Erica lifted a brow. "She works for you."

"Yes, and I guess you can say that now since I'm officially a partner. So far she's been holding her own and I think she's going to work out fine."

She nodded. "And what if I told you that I think she's trying to get next to you?"

Brian shook his head and laughed out loud. "You got that all wrong."

"No. I'm pretty sure I got it right. I'm a woman. My parents might think I was raised clueless about such things, but thanks to April I can pick up on stuff like that."

"Stuff like what?"

"A woman who is interested in a man."

He gave her a doubtful look. "And you figured all that by looking out the window and seeing us conversing?"

"Yes. The makeup, the hair and the way she got close, all in your face, gave her away."

"She was being friendly, Erica. Some people are just touchy-feely that way."

She rolled her eyes. "Men are so clueless." Then she said, "Trust me, I could tell, Brian."

He shook his head. "Then you have to trust me and believe that the only woman I want in my bed, my life and my heart is you."

He meant every word he'd just spoken and he intended to show her how true it was. She had never doubted his love before and he didn't intend for her to start doubting it now. And he knew she was wrong about Donna. The only reason she wanted to take up time with him was because she was trying to get acclimated to the office. But since he was now a partner, they would be spending less time together anyway, so Erica's concern was a moot point now.

He stood and began walking her up the stairs. "And just where are you taking me, Mr. Lawson?"

He smiled down at her. "Back to bed."

"But I thought we were meeting your mom later for lunch."

"We are, granted her plane didn't get delayed again. When I spoke with her yesterday she was hoping to get a flight out today."

He decided they had talked enough and before taking another step he leaned down and gave her the heated kiss they both needed and wanted.

"Here, drink this," Lori Spencer said, shoving the glass of vodka into Rita's hand. "You definitely seem to need it.

And then as calmly as you can, please tell me what the hell happened."

Rita took the glass and glanced up at the woman who was her dearest friend in the entire world. Always had been, even when the two of them were in grade school. They'd even attended the same college. The only time they'd really separated was when Lori had moved to Atlanta after college to attend law school.

Lori hadn't stayed away from Texas too long, returning to the city she loved and landing a job as part of the Dallas Cowboys legal counsel. The woman actually bled blue and silver, and during football season could get just as rowdy as any male. But there was no mistaking—Lori was all woman. She was a beauty who didn't look her age and had been a known cougar once or twice. In fact she was one now. Her current lover was eight years her junior.

Rita lifted the glass to her lips and then frowned. She glanced up at Lori. "It's straight."

Lori rolled her eyes as she took a chair at the table where Rita sat. "Is there a law against such a thing? Go ahead. It might grow some hair on your chest. But if you want to be a baby, just take a few sips."

In a way Rita wished she could go back to infancy, and then she wouldn't be in this mess. She took her first sip and the drink seemed to burn a hole in her lungs while going down.

"Now, tell me what happened that made you call asking that I pick you up from the airport instead of Brian, and then burst into tears as soon as you get into my car saying, 'I should not have done it.' What, pray tell, should you not have done?"

Rita swallowed, suddenly feeling as if her panties were too tight. Hell, that wasn't the crux of her problem. The problem had started last night when she'd taken them off...or had let someone else take them off.

"Well?"

She took a quick sip of her drink and met Lori's gaze. "I had an affair with a man."

Lori stared at her for a second and then a slow smile spread across her lips. "About time. Did he have to use pliers to snip away at the fasteners?"

"Lori!"

"Well, hell, what do you want me to say? It had been how long? Fifteen years? Even Patrick would not have wanted you to go that long without getting laid. I never understood why you locked your stuff up and threw away the key. I would have gone pure crazy by now."

Rita drew in a deep breath. "You haven't heard everything, Lori."

Lori raised a brow when she heard the tremble in Rita's voice. "Hell, what did he do? Handcuff you to the bed? Blindfold you? Share you with a friend? What? What could have been so bad to put a downer on your face instead of a smile after fifteen years?"

"He's married." She hadn't meant to blurt it out like that but once she had, she couldn't take it back.

"Oh." The surprised look on Lori's face would have been priceless if the situation wasn't so awful. Tears she couldn't hold back sprang into her eyes.

Lori was out of her chair in a second and leaned over and hugged her tight. "Hey, it's not so bad. Don't cry."

Rita pulled away. "You haven't heard the worst of it."

Lori reached out and grabbed hold of her hand. "Okay, so you slept with a married man. The bastard probably didn't tell you the truth and you found out and—"

"No, no," Rita interrupted, shaking her head while trying

to wipe her eyes. "That's what's so awful. I knew all along he was married, but I slept with him anyway."

Lori lifted a brow. "Were you drunk?"

"I don't think so. I'd had more wine than I needed to have, I will admit that, but I won't lie and say I was drunk. I was attracted to him and my hormones got the best of me."

"Well, was the toss between the sheets worth all this misery you're going through?"

Rita thought of everything she'd done with Wilson last night, every single thing. Even now she could feel his hands on her, touching her all over. And his mouth performing oral sex on her that had her practically blushing. But nothing could compare to the way he'd made love to her. It had been a long time for her, but he'd been gentle, sensual and thorough. She hadn't thought making love to a man could leave a woman breathless, panting for more and wishing the night would never end.

"Well? Was it good?"

Rita drew in a deep breath and said as if still in awe, "Yes, it was good. Very good. I felt things I'd never felt before. It was totally awesome."

Lori smiled and threw up her hands and looked heavenward. "Thank you, Jesus." She then returned her gaze to Rita. "Now you see what you've been missing. Forget about the fact he was a married man."

"I wish I could."

"I don't see why you can't, Rita. Chances are you'll never see him again and he'll never tell his wife what—"

"You don't understand, Lori. I know the guy."

Lori looked stunned. "You know him?"

"Yes."

Rita knew how Lori's mind worked and knew her best friend was trying to grasp all she was saying; trying to put it together, shove it all into that brilliant brain of hers. "And you also know his wife?"

"Yes."

Lori grabbed her head and pretended to pull out her hair. "Please. Please tell me it wasn't Fred."

Rita fought to keep from laughing. Fred McConnell and his wife were Lori's neighbors and he tried hitting on them behind his wife's back every chance he got. "No, it wasn't Fred."

"Thank God." She paused a moment and then asked, "So who is he? What's the name of this married man that you know?"

Rita met Lori's gaze and fought back more tears from her eyes when she thought of what she'd done and the ramifications of the mess she'd gotten herself into. She drew in a deep breath. "Wilson. Wilson Sanders."

Rita knew when Lori remembered where she'd heard the name before. A stunned look appeared on her face. "Wilson Sanders? Hey, isn't that...?"

Lori's words trailed off and she figured her best friend was probably too shocked to finish what she was about to say, so Rita finished for her. "Yes, Wilson Sanders is Erica's father."

Rita glanced down at her hands as she rubbed them nervously together. Her body began trembling in despair and gloom. "I slept with the man who in a few months will become my son's father-in-law."

Chapter Ten

"Is everything all right, Brian?" Erica asked, watching him hang up the phone with a concerned look on his face.

He glanced over at her and shrugged. "That was Mom. She can't meet us for lunch and doubts she can reschedule for dinner. She sounded pretty awful."

"Really, what's wrong?"

"I guess she's just tired from the delay in Sweden. She'll probably sleep the rest of the day. Get over all that jet lag."

"I talked to my mom a while ago and she said Dad's flight got delayed somewhere in Europe as well, all because of that volcanic ash in the air. I have to agree with the airlines in delaying flights instead of trying to fly through it."

"Same here," he agreed. "I'd rather have a tired mom than no mom."

She heard the love for his mother in his voice and couldn't help but admire him for it.

"So I guess it's just me and you for lunch, kid."

She met Brian's gaze and smiled. "I don't have a problem with that."

She crossed the kitchen to where he was standing and wrapped her arms around his neck. "Thank you."

He raised a brow. "For what?"

"For knowing I needed reassuring and taking the time to do it. For taking me upstairs and making me feel like I am loved deeply and that I am the most important woman in your life and that I am your life."

"You are."

Erica stared up at him. She believed him because he always went out of his way to make her believe. Their love was what storybook romances were made of. From day one their attraction had been magical.

Memories of the summer she'd met Brian flooded her mind. She'd needed to get away that summer because of her mother. Every day she'd concoct a reason to shove Griffin down her throat.

Things had been just as bad at Griffin's house. So the two had come up with a plan to deliberately go their separate ways for summer. Griffin had escaped to Paris and she had decided to take April up on her offer to spend the summer at her beach house in South Carolina. And the rest, as they say, was history.

She stood on tiptoes and brushed a kiss across Brian's lips. He hadn't shaved yet and the shadow on his jaw made him look sexy. She couldn't help but think of the sweetest chocolate as she looked into his brown eyes, and everyone knew that chocolate was a weakness of hers.

Brian looked down at her. "Hey, I think you can do better than that."

She met his gaze and could tell by the teasing glint in his eyes and the smile on his lips that he was ribbing her. "Yes, I *can* do better than that."

Erica stood on tiptoes again and pressed her mouth to his and, when she felt his arms wrap around her and his hand gently squeeze her backside, she parted her lips on a breathless sigh, giving him the opening he evidently needed.

His tongue delved into her mouth but she refused to let it take control. She was determined to show him just what she could do and how she could do it better than ever before. Passion began filling her bones, but she doubted it had left from the time he'd kissed her when she'd arrived at the airport.

She deepened the kiss and could immediately feel his erection pressed hard against her middle. The man was doomed and she intended for him to stay that way for a while. She always enjoyed assaulting his mouth this way, letting him know she enjoyed his taste and every aspect of their relationship, especially this.

When he pulled her closer, it seemed he had gotten even harder. Shivers raced through her when the hands resting on her backside pressed her even closer to him, letting her feel every hard inch of him.

She finally pulled back, breaking off the kiss and smiling when he gave her wet lips one last intimate swipe. "Was that better?" she asked, keeping a smile on her lips while leaning in closer.

"Yes, and you know what I think?"

"No, what do you think, sweetheart?" she asked.

"I need to go out and get some more condoms."

She tossed back her head, laughing. She had gone off the Pill last month when they'd both agreed to start a family right after the wedding, since they both wanted kids. It wouldn't bother her in the least if she were to get pregnant on her wedding night.

"That might not be such a bad idea." She leaned in for another quick kiss.

His dazzling smile reached his chocolate eyes. "I can't wait to introduce you to Minor and Talbert Saturday night. Once they meet you they will know what a lucky guy I am."

★ ★ ★

"So, you're back."

Wilson turned around and met Karen's gaze. She stood in the doorway of their bedroom. At least it used to be their bedroom. She had suggested once Erica had moved out that he find somewhere else in the house to sleep. He hadn't wanted to pull rank and remind her that technically the house and everything in it was his and had been in *his* family for years. Instead, he'd taken up residence in one of the guest bedrooms. However, for appearances' sake, and to not give their housekeeper anything to gossip about, he still kept his clothes in their combined closet. He had news for Karen—the housekeeper was smarter than she thought and had figured out long ago that they were living separate lives.

"Yes, I'm back." His response was deliberately as dry as her greeting had been. She hadn't been home when he'd arrived and now he could see why. She was wearing the outfit she usually played tennis in. "Who won the match?" he asked since he really had nothing else to say to her. Just like he knew she truly had nothing else to say to him. How could he have thought he could live this way?

"I won, of course."

He chuckled. "Of course." With all their niceties out of the way, he turned back around to resume unpacking. A part of him truly regretted that he did not feel one iota of guilt about cheating on her. If anything, he felt guilty for not feeling guilty. But in no way did he feel Karen got what she deserved. Regardless of what kind of wife he thought she was, as his wife she had deserved his faithfulness, and for that he knew what he'd done last night with Rita was wrong. But he refused to wish it hadn't happened or regret it. If that made him a bastard then so be it.

He drew in a deep breath when he heard her walk away. He didn't love Karen and she didn't love him. What he should have done years ago was ask for a divorce, but he had thought it would be too complicated. Besides, he felt since he'd put up with things for this long, he might as well continue to put up with them.

But then last night had happened.

He eased down on the bed beside his luggage and stared into space, remembering a night he knew he would never forget. Rita had done more than show him what he'd been missing. She had touched him in a way he hadn't been touched—ever. And the really sad thing about it was that he and Karen hadn't grown apart. They'd always been apart. Even on their wedding night. She'd told him then she would do her duty, give him a child, preferably a son, and that was it.

She had been disappointed that Erica was born a girl because she'd figured he would demand a son, which meant she would have to continue to have sex with him "until the deed was done," as she'd said. He had wanted other children, but listening to her bitch and moan each time they'd shared a bed hadn't been worth it. He could still remember the expression of happiness that shone on her face when he'd finally told her she would not have to be subjected to his lovemaking any longer, because he was satisfied with Erica being their only child.

Wilson moved from the bed and walked over to the window and looked out. He wondered what Rita was doing, what she was thinking. She had no idea what last night had meant to him. It had been an involvement, true enough, but for him it had also been something else. An awakening.

He wished he could call her and tell her not to feel any guilt because his marriage wasn't what she might think it was. Not to feel any guilt because he couldn't make himself feel any. And if given the chance he would do it again.

He sucked in a deep, trembling breath at that realization.

In a way he was pretty damn surprised at how incredibly easy it was to reach such a conclusion with a clear head and not an ounce of scotch in his system. He wanted Rita again but knew her frame of mind wouldn't allow it. If truth be told, he had begun developing feelings for her since the engagement party. He hadn't meant for it to happen, but it had. He needed to talk to her. He needed to see her.

He also needed to finally end his marriage to Karen. Forget about the guilt he didn't feel—he needed to think of the fairness. And to be fair to her, he needed to go his way and let her go hers. He had no problems in providing a generous divorce settlement. Hell, she could have it all.

All he wanted now was his freedom.

"I feel like I'm a part of a soap opera," Rita said softly, glancing out the kitchen window.

When she'd showered and crawled between the covers to take a nap after calling Brian, Lori was there. And when she had awakened three hours later, her friend was still there.

Unfortunately Rita hadn't slept off the guilt. It was still there staring her in the face, right along with an aftermath of luscious sensations that just wouldn't leave her alone. Her breasts were still tender from where Wilson's mouth had been, and the area between her thighs...well, there wasn't much she could say about it. His mouth had been there and also the most hard and thick erection she'd ever seen. When he'd entered her, the invasion had been priceless, right along with the passion they'd fueled and the desire they'd stirred in each other.

"Is that why you cancelled your lunch with Brian and Erica?"

Rita rubbed her hand down her face. "For crying out loud, Lori. How could I look in Erica's face knowing what I've done? What was I supposed to say? Oh, by the way, I ran into your father in Sweden and we had drinks and screwed our brains out."

"Is that how it was?"

Rita threw her head back. "Practically, although what I said almost painted a picture of the two of us being drunk, we were in our right minds, trust me."

"Then why do you think you did it?"

Rita glanced over at Lori. Her friend could ask the damnedest questions at times. It had to be the attorney in her. "Lust, pure and simple."

"So, you weren't operating under the illusion that you've fallen in love?"

"No, although Wilson is a man I think any woman could love. Karen would be a fool if she didn't love him. He's kind, gentle, charismatic, handsome, well built, an extraordinary lover." She paused. "Need I go on?"

"Not unless you want to. You've drawn a pretty damn good picture for me. Now I'm sorry I had that business trip and missed the engagement party and checking out Wilson Sanders for myself."

She knew Lori meant it, although she also knew Wilson would have been much too old for Lori's taste. Her motto these days was "Go young and have much more fun."

"And I would have checked out Karen Sanders," Lori added. "Most men, you know, cheat because of something they're missing at home. I would have been able to tell within seconds if she's putting out."

"It really doesn't matter if she can stand at the head of the line as the Wicked Witch of the West, no woman deserves to be cheated on, Lori. I think you of all people would believe that."

Lori should have believed that. Her ex-husband, Deon, a pilot for one of the major airlines, had cheated on her. Lori had returned to town early from a business trip to find him in their bed with the woman—one of his flight attendants.

"I do, but to be totally honest, Deon and I had begun drifting apart a year before he pulled that stunt. He wasn't getting any from me and with his horny ass, I figured he was probably getting it from somewhere. What pissed me off was the fact that I caught them in our bed. He had money. They could have gotten a hotel room someplace."

Of course Rita knew the entire story. Lori had grabbed the pistol she usually kept in her nightstand and begun shooting. Of course she'd been smart enough to raise the revolver toward the ceiling, but according to Lori it had given her great satisfaction to see her husband and the other woman run butt-naked from the house into the streets. That had given the neighbors, the postman, the garbageman and a UPS man making deliveries in the area something to talk about.

And someone, Lori still didn't know who, had captured the fiasco of the naked couple trying to hide behind bushes—probably on a cell phone—and had mailed the video to her. She had used the pics as leverage to get everything she wanted in the divorce settlement.

Rita had always suspected Deon of being up to no good. On the other hand, she believed Wilson when he'd told her he had never cheated on his wife before. She suspected he was somewhere feeling as bad about what had happened between them as she was. She couldn't help wondering how he would react when he saw her again. How would she react to him?

"So what do you plan to do, Rita? You can't hide from your future daughter-in-law for the rest of your life. Nor from your future in-laws."

Rita began nibbling on her bottom lip. She loved Erica as the daughter she'd never had, but now she had a secret that if ever revealed would destroy that relationship forever. She could just imagine what Erica would think of her. It then flashed through her mind what Brian would think of her. She rubbed her hand down her face when she felt tears threatening to fall.

"Hey, don't you dare cry anymore, Rita Tonette Sparks Lawson. What's done is done and it's time to move on. Time to get prepared."

Rita let out a sigh. "For what?"

"For your body to start craving the very thing you gave it a taste of. All I'm saying, best friend of mine, is don't be surprised if you start feeling the urge to seek out your Mr. Sanders again, married or not."

Chapter Eleven

"Daddy! This is a pleasant surprise."

Wilson smiled as he entered Erica's home after leaning down and kissing her on the cheek. He wished there was some other way to find out the information he wanted but hadn't thought of one, and the need to know about Rita was like a bellyache that wouldn't go away.

"I hadn't seen you in a couple of weeks and missed you," he told her. That was no lie. He had missed her, but he was also hoping for some information during his visit.

"Things were slow at the library so I left for Dallas to start celebrating Brian's promotion early."

"And how is Brian?" he asked as he followed her into the kitchen.

"Brian's fine and we celebrated all four days I was there. On Saturday night I met the other two partners, nice older men who had been friends of Brian's father, and their wives. They took us out to dinner."

"Sounds wonderful." He paused a moment and then asked

the burning question. "What about Brian's family? His grand-parents? His mother? How are they doing?"

He was taking a chance that Rita hadn't mentioned any-thing about them seeing each other in Sweden and being stranded together there. Chances were she was trying hard to forget the entire episode. A part of him knew that if this was the case, he should grant her wish and let her be, but he couldn't.

Erica was standing at the counter making coffee. He was nervous she might suspect something and patted his shirt pocket for cigarettes, but immediately recalled he had broken the nasty habit a year ago. This was the first time he'd forgot-ten he'd done so.

She turned around and smiled. "Everyone is fine. I saw his grandparents and got to spend a little time with them, but I didn't get the chance to see his mother."

A knot settled in his stomach and only deepened the ache there. "Oh? Was she out of town?" he asked, trying to sound as casual about it as possible.

"No, she had just returned from one of her trips the day after I arrived. Seems her flight got delayed somewhere in Europe because of that volcanic ash like yours did. Only thing was she came back with a little bug. She called to cancel our lunch." She paused a moment and then said, "I hate that I didn't get to see Rita this trip. I really like her, Dad."

Wilson drew in a deep breath, tempted to tell his offspring that he really liked the woman as well, but for different reasons.

The time he spent with Rita had shown him that as a man he liked having a woman in his bed, a woman he found desir-able, a woman who had a passion to match his own. A woman he could laugh with, enjoy jazz music with. A woman he could talk about his favorite pieces of art with and who didn't make him feel like a sissy for doing so. A woman who could make his blood race and, yes, a woman who could also give him bellyaches. Like the one he'd been feeling since waking up that morning in Stockholm and finding her gone.

There was only one woman he wanted. She was free to be pursued but he had yet to do any pursuing. However, he planned to remedy that, and soon.

He wanted more than anything to talk to Rita, hear her voice, convince her that what they'd done was no one's fault and that he had no regrets.

And heaven help him, he would do it again in a heartbeat. But only with her.

"Dad?"

It was then he realized that Erica has been talking to him. "Yes, sorry, sweetheart, I missed hearing what you said."

She smiled, reached over and gently patted his hand as if he might be in the first stages of dementia, and if so, that was fine. She understood. "I was saying that I haven't mentioned anything to Mom yet, but I'm thinking about resigning my position at the historical center and moving to Dallas a month early."

He lifted a brow. "Before the wedding?"

"Yes. Brian mentioned the possibility of us looking for a house sooner than we planned. With him making partner it means more money will be coming in."

Wilson couldn't help but smile. His daughter never had to worry about money. Her grandparents on both sides had seen to that by leaving her trust funds. But she had mentioned a few months back, right after she had announced her engagement, that she had no intention to intimidate Brian with all her wealth. For once in her life she wanted to live like a normal human being who had to survive within her means. She had even considered donating all the monies in her trust to various charities.

He had talked her out of doing such a thing and instead

had suggested she keep the trust funds to pass on to her kids, since she and Brian seemed eager to have plenty of them. According to her, they wanted at least four.

He didn't mind being a grandfather, although Karen wasn't looking forward to being a grandmother and was still wailing at the very thought that her daughter would want that many children.

Comments like that often made him wonder about Karen's childhood and what could have possibly gone on at the Delbert house, behind those huge mansion doors. He'd tried to get her to talk about it once and she had refused, saying her parents had given both her and her sister the perfect life, and that she didn't appreciate him insinuating that the Delberts had somehow been a dysfunctional family. Hell, he didn't see why not, when the Sanderses definitely were. His father was a social drunk and his mother a sophisticated and refined nymphomaniac. It was sad but true. His father never wondered, or possibly never cared, why there had been so many gardeners rotating on and off the mansion's grounds. When his mother got tired of one she gave him the boot. Oh, she had been discreet, or tried to be, until the time he and Marshall had stumbled upon her and one of her lovers at the lake house. They'd been kids at the time but old enough to figure out what was going down.

"So, what do you have planned for the rest of the day?" Erica broke into his thoughts to ask him.

He glanced across the table at her and smiled. "Nothing. I decided to take the day off work."

He wanted to blame his malaise on jet lag, but he knew what he really was going through was sexual withdrawal. He had shared something that night with Rita he had never shared before with a woman and his body hadn't adjusted, just refused to accept that it might never get to feel that way again.

Besides, mentioning anything about his time in Europe might get Erica to start asking questions and determine that he and Rita had been stranded in the same city.

"Why are you asking? Is there something you need me to do?" he asked her.

"No, but I was going to do some errands and would love to have you come along. I promise not to bore you and we can take my car. I'll even stay within speed limits."

He chuckled. He knew if she didn't stay within speed limits, she would be the last person that the good sheriff would give a ticket to. That thought made him think of something. "I understand Griffin is thinking about running for mayor."

She smiled brightly. "Yes, I heard. If he does decide to run I think he'll be just what Hattersville needs. He'll get my support."

"You won't be living here then. You'll be in Dallas."

"Yes, but that doesn't mean I can't come back and help in some way with his campaign."

Her father lifted a brow. "And Brian wouldn't have a problem with it, considering Griffin is his rival?"

Erica shook her head, grinning. "Trust me, Griffin was never Brian's rival. Besides, Brian knows all about Mom's planned future for me and Griffin, and doesn't feel threatened by it. He knows I love him and no one else. Just like I know he loves me."

Now it was Wilson who reached across the table and patted his daughter's hand. She sounded confident and he could tell she was happy. It was all over her face, in her voice. And he was happy for her and couldn't wait for the day that he became the father of the bride.

He also couldn't wait for the day he would get to see the mother of the groom again. But he wanted to talk to Rita long before then, and wished there was some way he could ask Erica for her phone number without her wondering why he wanted it.

He would be spending a few more hours with Erica, and hopefully before they parted ways today he would think of something.

Brian glanced around his new office. It was a lot more spacious than the one he'd had before and he had a beautiful view of the new stadium that was still under construction. But what really made it special was knowing this had once been his father's office.

He drew in a deep breath, wondering how he could be so lucky. But then, luck, his grandmother would be quick to say, had nothing to do with it. It was all about blessings. Then in that case he definitely felt blessed.

He reached out and touched the potted plant that was sitting on his new desk. He wasn't into flowers and greenery but he would be into this one. Erica had bought it while they had been out shopping on Saturday and said it would be easy to keep alive with little care. And then when they had come here Sunday night she had placed it on his desk just moments before they had officially christened this office. He couldn't help but smile just remembering it.

He had promised to water the plant every day and to make sure it got plenty of sunlight. He would do all those things and whenever he looked at it, he would think of her.

He turned around when he heard a knock on his door. "Come in."

Donna walked in, smiling. "So this is where you've moved to. I was hoping I would be able to join you in court again this week but I see they've changed your schedule now that you've made partner."

He nodded and returned her smile and leaned against his desk. "Yes, I intend to keep most of my clients, but Roland is filling in for me this week while I attend several important meetings with Talbert and Minor."

"I see." She glanced around the office. "Nice. But you need a pretty plant in here."

He glanced behind him at the plant sitting on his desk, figured she hadn't seen it for him blocking her view and moved out of the way. "I have one already. See?"

She waved her hand in dismissal. "That little plant? I think I could do better."

He frowned. "Excuse me? Erica picked it out for me and I like it just fine. Was there something you wanted?"

Ah hell, Donna thought. Evidently she'd pushed the wrong buttons. The damn ugly plant had sentimental value to him just because his fiancée had given it to him. She needed to leave, regroup and return another time, now that she knew what side of the bread he buttered. He was smitten with his fiancée, that was for sure.

"No, I really didn't want anything, other than to say hello. I jogged by your house for the past couple of days and didn't see you. I thought maybe you'd gone out of town."

She would deliberately time it just right to make sure she jogged by when he was out collecting his morning paper. For the past four days his newspaper had still been in the yard when she'd jogged by.

"I slept later than I usually do. Erica was in town."

She nodded. "Oh. I'm sure you were glad to see her."

His smile widened. "I was."

"Well, I'll let you get back to work. Congratulations again."

"Thanks."

She turned to leave and, pretending that she had just thought of something, she turned back around and smiled brightly. "This is spaghetti night for me and I always seem to make more than I can eat. I'll drop some off later at your place."

He shook his head. "Thanks for the offer, but I'm dining at my mother's place this evening."

"Oh. Well, enjoy."

She then walked out of his office, knowing she had her work cut out for her. But she loved a challenge.

Chapter Twelve

Brian kissed his mother on the cheek and then leaned back to look at her. He might be wrong but it seemed as if she'd lost weight and there were still those bags under her eyes. He frowned, concerned.

"Mom, did you call your doctor?"

Rita glanced up him and smiled. "Yes, and he said I should be fine in a few days. I just need to continue to rest."

Wrapping his arm around her shoulders he walked her over to the sofa. "It's going on a week. You haven't even been back at work and that's not like you. Are you sure you're telling me everything?"

She shot him a surprised look. "Everything like what?" Then she waved him off. "I'm fine and I'll be back to work on Thursday."

"But only if you're feeling well."

She smiled. "Yes, only if I'm feeling well."

"And since I know you're probably not in the mood to cook, I'm here to do it for you."

"You really don't have to bother. Lori dropped off a pot

of soup this morning." She paused and then said, "I'm sorry I didn't get the chance to see Erica while she was here. I really feel bad about that."

"Hey, she understood and like me just wants you to get better. There's a wedding in three months, remember. We definitely want you there."

"Yes, I remember and I will be there." She smiled at him. "You look so happy. But then you've been looking happy since you met Erica. I can remember the day you came back from your trip to South Carolina to tell me about meeting her. I knew then she would be the one."

Brian leaned back against the sofa cushions. "I think I knew she was the one, too. The moment we began talking there was something about her that did it for me. And the more I got to know her, the more in love I fell. And that's saying a lot from a guy who used to think of himself as a bona fide player."

"You just weren't ready to settle down. Your dad was that way, too. He had a reputation around campus. I had heard about it so, of course, I kept my distance."

Brian smiled. "But he kept pursuing you."

"Yes."

"And when did you realize that he was serious?"

"When he began writing poetry just for me." She chuckled. "At first I thought he was merely running a game to break down my defenses, but then he shared other poems he'd written, and then I knew he'd stepped out of his comfort zone of being the macho man around campus for me. We began dating and were together thereafter. By the time he finished law school I was graduating with my bachelor's degree and we married a year later."

Brian nodded. He'd heard the story several times but never tired of hearing it, especially now that he knew how true love really felt. "So, my godmother made some of her heart-winning soup, did she?"

Rita smiled. "Yes. We can eat while you tell me what Erica said when you told her about the trust fund and what a wealthy man you are now," she said, easing off the sofa.

"I didn't tell her."

Rita glanced at him with a lifted brow. "You didn't?"

"No, and I won't tell her before the wedding."

Her brow lifted a bit higher. "Why?"

A huge smile spread across Brian's lips. "I'm telling her on our wedding night. I want to surprise her. What's so special about Erica is that she's willing to marry me, move here, give up a lavish lifestyle and be content to make do on my salary and the paycheck she'll make at the accounting firm that wants to hire her."

"Hey, you're a long way from being a pauper, Brian. You were earning a six-figure salary before making partner, and you've made good investment decisions."

"I know, but she didn't know that." He paused a moment and then said, "She got a call from the accounting firm and they'd like her to start work a month early, and will still give her time off for the wedding."

"She's thinking about doing that?"

"She would love to. Only problem is that she'll be needed in Ohio as we get closer to the wedding date. She has a number of bridal showers planned and luncheons scheduled in her honor. Mrs. Sanders is going all out with our wedding, making it the event of the year."

When his mother got quiet, he glanced up at her. "You okay?"

She met his gaze and smiled. "Yes, I'm fine but I feel hungry. Are you ready for soup?"

He chuckled as he stood to his feet. "Yes, just lead the way."

★ ★ ★

"And how is she today, Ms. Vickers?"

The nurse glanced over at the well-dressed woman and smiled. "Your sister is fine, Mrs. Sanders. For the most part, she's having more good days and when she starts hallucinating, we keep her sedated just like you suggested so she won't harm herself."

Or spill secrets that are better left untold, Karen thought while walking the long dreary halls of Westminster Nursing Home. She hated coming here but knew she had to do so. Most people in Hattersville remembered the young, vibrant and beautiful Blair Delbert. They would shake their heads sadly upon recalling how Karen's younger sister at twenty-two was involved in a near-fatal car accident a week before her wedding to the town's most eligible bachelor, Simon Hayes. She'd lost control of her car and hit a pole. She survived but was left in a coma.

Blair had remained comatose for seven years and then out of the clear blue sky she had emerged into a conscious state. But the brain injury she sustained from the accident had greatly impaired her mental capabilities. Luckily for Karen there were no facilities in Hattersville capable of handling Blair's care so she'd been moved to Westminster, a facility located in Cleveland. Out of sight and out of mind. It had been close to twenty years now.

Most people, including Wilson and Erica, assumed Blair had eventually died because that was the lie Karen had told them. She'd even arranged a private funeral service ten years ago. To this day, no one knew the ashes in the urn that supposedly belonged to Blair were the remains of someone else—a poor soul who'd died without any family. One day her sister would eventually die and take all those sordid secrets they shared to the grave with her.

Karen stood aside as Ms. Vickers unlocked the door. She

had requested that Nurse Vickers, along with Dr. Miller, be the only ones to handle Blair, and since she supplemented their salaries substantially, they always adhered to her wishes.

She walked into the spacious and elegantly furnished room that had few windows, just enough to let the sun come through, and saw Blair sitting in the wheelchair at the table while reading aloud from a book of Mother Goose nursery rhymes. They had been Blair's favorite since the time they were children.

Karen shivered. She didn't want to remember those times but whenever she visited Blair she was forced to do so. "Hello, Blair, you look pretty today."

And she did. That was another stipulation she'd made to Nurse Vickers and Dr. Miller. She wanted her sister to be well taken care of. After all, she *was* a Delbert, no matter what state her mind and body were in.

Instead of answering, Blair slowly lifted her head and glanced over at her. She stared at her for a moment as if trying to remember who she was. Karen knew before her sister opened her mouth that this was not going to be a good visit. Every once in a while seeing Karen would trigger bad memories for Blair. They had never been close and Karen had been the pampered one until Blair was born.

"You let him hurt her."

That single sentence made Karen cringe, although she'd known it was coming. Her sister still blamed her for everything, even for surviving the messy attempt to end her own life.

"And it's a beautiful day outside, Blair," she said, ignoring her sister's outburst. "The sun is shining and there isn't a cloud in the sky. Would you like to go outside today?"

Instead of responding Blair continued to stare as Karen placed her purse on the nightstand and walked over to the fresh flowers. They were picked every morning. Daisies.

Something else that was Blair's favorite. Karen then went and sat in the extra chair in the room. Since Blair seemed in a mood to have nothing positive to say, Karen decided to do all the talking.

She could tell Blair all her secrets because she knew they would go no further. Who would believe her? "Erica thinks she'll be happy with Brian but I know better. It's up to me to make sure a Delbert marries a Hayes like it should have been years ago."

"You let him hurt her."

Blair's words made Karen cringe again. She frowned and her lips began trembling in anger. She leaned in closer and said in a biting tone, "Shut up, damn you. What was I supposed to do? She should have kept her mouth closed and gone along with it like we've always done."

Karen wondered why she was even wasting her breath. Half the time Blair didn't know what day it was, didn't even know her own name. But there were times like these when she remembered far too much to suit Karen. "Keep making those stupid outbursts and I'll make sure Dr. Miller gives you something to calm you down."

She could tell by the fearful look in her sister's eyes that she didn't want that. Good. Maybe now she would behave and act like a Delbert.

Chapter Thirteen

Griffin Hayes wasn't sure what he'd been expecting when the mistress of ceremonies finally called April's name and she began walking across the stage. He had read about the event in the newspaper, and since he hadn't been able to eradicate her from his mind since seeing her that day in New York, he didn't want to miss the opportunity to fly here and see April. Chicago's Daley Civic Center was packed, and not surprisingly there appeared to be more men here than women, at least more who chose to come as single men. There were quite a number of couples who were probably here to do their charitable duty. But he was certain that most were here, like him, to see all the beautiful women scheduled to be auctioned off.

Okay, they weren't being auctioned off. The jewelry they were wearing, compliments of several nationally known jewelers, would be sold. However, each of the women had agreed to at least share a drink later with the highest bidder for her jewelry.

But Griffin knew not one man there was concentrating

on the diamond necklace around April's neck, compliments of Tiffany's. Like him, they were concentrating on the soft curves of a body dressed in an outfit that would bring even the strongest man to his knees.

He'd always thought April was a beautiful woman. Unfortunately, she'd had to leave Hattersville and earn the title of one of the foremost supermodels for others to see what he'd known all along. And tonight that short black dress she wore was exposing her beauty for all to see. Her legs, long and shapely, seemed destined to go on forever.

"Hey, man, she's the reason I'm here tonight," he heard one man whisper to another behind him. "I've had a thing for her ever since she did that *Sports Illustrated* cover. Miss Hot April and I won't just be sharing a drink later," the man continued to whisper rather loudly. "But I'm going to try my best to talk her into something else."

Griffin frowned as he listened to the conversation. He had news for the man if he thought for one minute that he would be the one April would be sharing a drink with. Now that the applause, whistles and catcalls had died down, the MC was talking, asking for everyone's attention. "All right, guys, we have April North, and just take a look at this necklace April is wearing…."

Griffin rolled his eyes. Did the woman really expect any man, including him, especially him, to divert his attention from April's legs to check out her jewelry? Evidently she did, since she went on to describe the jewelry in great detail. He was sure the necklace was nice but he was of the mind that April's legs were nicer.

Even from where he was sitting, halfway back in the auditorium, the bright lights captured her in a way no magazine ad ever could. And he swore he could pick up her scent.

"We have ten thousand. Do I hear fifteen?"

He blinked, realizing the bidding had begun when the

man behind him shouted out a bid. It was apparent he was determined to be the recipient of both the necklace and April. Griffin shrugged. It was all for charity and he'd always had a competitive nature.

It seemed two others had joined the bidding fray, just as determined to share that drink with April. He leaned back comfortably in his seat, deciding to keep his mouth shut for now. He didn't intend to open it until it mattered.

Instead of glancing around to see who the men were, April just stood tall, graceful and poised, while looking over the crowd with a radiant smile on her face. That smile alone would guarantee an arousal out of every man there.

"We have a bid of twenty-five thousand. Do I hear thirty?"

"Fifty!"

A hush fell over the auditorium at the bid from the man behind Griffin.

"We have a bid of fifty thousand! That's wonderful and, remember, it's all for charity. Can we get fifty-five?"

The room remained quiet and Griffin didn't have to turn around to know the man behind him probably had a silly grin on his face.

"Going once, going twice—"

"One hundred thousand dollars," Griffin called out. He didn't have to look around to know people were staring at him as if he'd gone mad, and no doubt the man behind him was fuming. April, he noticed, was still standing there. Curiosity hadn't even made her look over in his direction.

"My goodness," the MC said after the shock wore off. "We have a bid for one hundred thousand dollars for the necklace Ms. North is wearing. Can we get one hundred and five?"

When the room remained quiet the MC then said, "Oh, well. Going once, going twice. Sold to the man in the dark gray suit."

★ ★ ★

April glanced around the reception, certain the man she was looking for was around someplace. He was to approach her with the ticket for his winnings, which she carried in her hand, gift-boxed and ready to deliver. A part of her couldn't wait to meet the person willing to part with a hundred thousand dollars for a ten-thousand-dollar necklace.

She glanced at her watch. She would share the drink with him as agreed and then she would leave. Tomorrow she would fly to Ohio for a few days before heading back out west. She had checked in with Nana today as she did every Saturday and she'd sounded fine, but there was no way she could be this close to Hattersville and not see for herself.

"Would you like a drink, miss?"

She almost told the server yes, but then remembered she was to have her drink with the man who'd won the bid on her jewelry. The event, hosted by Oprah, was to benefit several charities, the purchase of her necklace going to breast cancer awareness.

"No, thank you."

She glanced at her watch again, thinking that surely the man hadn't changed his mind and not taken care of the bill. It was for charity, after all, although he had raised a few eyebrows with the amount of his bid. She was certain he was here; she would just have to look for a man wearing a dark gray suit.

Several people came up, complimenting her on her career and her recent spread in *Vogue.* Although Oprah had made an appearance earlier, she hadn't been seen lately, but this room had an ambience of elegance that only Oprah could exude. She'd overheard earlier that the room had been specially decorated for tonight's affair. She glanced around, admiring the room's high ceiling, crown moldings and rich mahogany windowsills. At that moment she couldn't help but admire the woman's success.

She glanced down at the gift-wrapped box she carried, wondering where the man was, when she felt a presence by her side. She glanced up, expecting to see another server, and her breath immediately got caught in her throat. She was staring up into the eyes of the man who just last night had headlined her naughtiest dream. And now he stood in front of her, with the most mesmerizing smile on his lips that reached the sexiest pair of eyes she'd ever seen.

"Griffin! Hi." The words flowed from her lips in a throaty surprise. "What are you doing here?"

She realized the stupidity of her question the moment she'd asked it. He was in his element here. He'd been born to this type of extravagance. She hadn't.

A smile touched what she'd always thought was a pair of sensual lips. "I heard about the event and thought I'd attend and do my part for charity," he said, sipping the wine he had in his hand.

She felt her heart beating fast and furious in her chest and hoped she didn't melt in a puddle right at his feet. She couldn't believe he was actually here. She tried forcing her heart to calm down. But damn, he looked good in his white shirt and a dark gray suit.

A dark gray suit...

She shook her head, trying to get her senses in check. There was no way Griffin was the man who'd purchased the necklace she'd worn. No way. He gave her another smile that sent everything within her spinning out of control. And then he said, "I think you have something for me."

She swallowed, felt her heart do a triple flip in her chest. "I do?"

"Yes, and you also owe me a drink." He glanced around

and then turned back to her. "But I'd prefer if we share it someplace else."

She fought saying that he could take her to the ends of the earth and she would go, she was just that into him, and had always been. How many years had she gone to bed and dreamed of him, had married others because she'd known he would always be out of her reach?

Had he just suggested they blow this place and go and have a drink somewhere else? Just the two of them? She drew in a deep breath. Could that be considered a date? The thought of her and Griffin sharing a date was way too much. Every part of her responded to the possibility, even her nipples, pressing hard against her dress. They were feeling sensitive, achy, in need of a man's lips and tongue. But not any man's.

"So what do you say, April North?"

Okay, girl, keep your cool. Don't appear too eager and, whatever you do, please keep the drool from falling. He must never know how you feel about him. How you've always felt about him. Besides, he's still out of your reach. He's running for mayor one day. The high-society dames will all have cows if you're ever first lady of Hattersville.

"I assume you're the person who made the bid," she said as calmly as she could, trying to sound like she didn't care one way or the other.

"Yes," he said, handing her the winning ticket that showed he'd taken care of the bill. "I believe I'm supposed to present this to you."

She took it and glanced at it for a second before handing him the gift-wrapped box. "And I believe this is yours."

"Thanks." He looked up at her. "So are you ready to leave here with me and have that drink? I know a café that's only a short cab ride from here."

Knowing how she felt about him, she would be crazy to do it. But then again, knowing how she felt about him, she would be crazy not to do it. Chances were this would never happen again—her participating in an auction and wearing a necklace that he wanted at whatever cost it took him to get it. She wiped the thought from her mind that he would probably give the jewelry to the woman she'd seen him with in New York.

She would dwell on that another day and time.

"Well, what do you say?" he asked, interrupting her thoughts. "Will you share a drink with me elsewhere?"

"Yes."

"Then by all means, let's go." Taking her hand, he led her to the door.

Heat flowed through Griffin's belly at the feel of April's hand in his. Leaving the party was an idea that had popped into his head once he'd seen her mingling at the reception, a number of the men gushing in her wake. For some reason he wanted to have her all to himself. And for her to agree had nearly overwhelmed him.

He kept a firm hold on her hand while hailing a cab, and once one had pulled up at the curb and they'd slid onto the backseat, he turned to her and his body almost melted when she gave him a smile. And then he felt it and wondered if she'd felt it, as well. The air they were sharing seemed charged, pulsating with full sexual awareness. As if captured by a hold he couldn't break, he stared at her, barely breathing while thinking she had to be the most beautiful woman to walk this earth.

It was only when she broke eye contact to glance out the window that he slowly exhaled a deep breath. He didn't have to wonder what that was all about. He knew. It had been that way that day in New York. He had felt the heated sexual chemistry, a mind-blowing awareness from across the room even while he'd been with another woman. Now the question was what did a man do about such a woman.

"Have you been to this café before?"

"Yes," he said. "The food is delicious. I thought that in addition to drinks we can also try out a few of their signature dishes."

A low, throaty chuckle erupted from her throat. "Good, I'm starving."

He was starving, too, he thought to himself. But what his body craved, food could not assuage.

The cab driver interrupted his naughty thoughts. "De-Lonn's Café, sir."

Griffin glanced out the window. "This is the place." He handed the driver more than enough to pay for the short ride. "Keep the change."

The man's face lit up in a huge smile. "Thanks. I hope you enjoy the rest of your evening."

Griffin hoped so, too. "Thanks." When he made a move to open the door, it was then that he realized he was still holding April's hand.

"Would you like something else, April? What about dessert?"

April glanced up and felt the heat of Griffin's gaze connect with hers. When he'd suggested they leave the reception and go somewhere to share their drink, she hadn't a clue where he was taking her and, if truth be known, hadn't really cared. But when she'd walked into DeLonn's she was taken aback. From the outside it looked like a little hole-in-the-wall, but the inside was another matter. Beautifully furnished, the soul food restaurant had various pictures posted of celebrities who'd eaten food prepared by Gramma DeLonn.

April was surprised she'd never heard of the place before.

After biting into Gramma DeLonn's fried chicken, there was no doubt in her mind that she would come back.

"No, I'm full, thank you. But because of you I'm going to have to be on the treadmill for two hours in the morning instead of one."

He chuckled. "So that's one of your activities to stay in shape."

"Yes. I also go swimming every chance I get. You probably don't remember but I was on Hattersville High's swim team back in the day."

"I remember."

She was surprised that he did. "You do?"

"Yes. You made the team in your freshman year. I was a senior."

Oh, yes, she remembered those days when he would walk the halls of the high school and all the girls' panties would get wet. He was hot then and he was still hot now.

"So are you going to tell me how you found out about this place?" Despite the good food, she figured this was not the type of establishment a Hayes would frequent. But she could tell from the way he was familiar with the owner and servers that he'd been here often.

He leaned back in his chair and she watched the movement of his shoulders beneath his jacket when he did so. She was suddenly entrenched in memories of the time she and Erica had come upon him jogging shirtless in the park a few years back when she'd come home for a visit. He had stood there and held a conversation with them for a good twenty minutes, and it had taken all her willpower not to stare at his muscular shoulders and the way his chest hair tapered off toward the waistband of his running shorts.

"Sure, I'll tell you," he said, smiling. "I attended college with Jabar DeLonn, who is Gramma DeLonn's grandson. In fact we were roommates all four years and remain the best of friends today."

"You attended Ohio State, right?"

"Of course."

She rolled her eyes. "That means you're a true-blue Buckeye."

"Is there any other kind? Unlike you, I was loyal to my state. I bet you couldn't wait to get to California."

If you only knew, April thought.

"I couldn't wait to see the Pacific Ocean." She smiled, knowing that hadn't been the only reason.

"You stayed away four years and then some."

She wondered how he knew just how long she'd stayed away. He must have seen the questioning look in her gaze and said, "I returned to Hattersville after college to find it was almost like a ghost town. Everyone I'd grown up with or knew had either left town for good or was doing their own thing. Now I'm glad a number of them got tired of the big city life and are moving back. I talked to Stacie Childress recently. She plans to move back."

She'd heard that. Although Stacie's ancestors hadn't been among the town's founding fathers, because her parents were loaded she had been included in the high-society niche. The one thing April remembered was that Stacie had the hots for Griffin.

April understood that Stacie was a divorcée. She couldn't help but wonder if perhaps Stacie had heard about Erica's marriage plans and figured that meant Griffin was finally free. Was Stacie moving back to Hattersville to try her luck once again? If that was the reason, her timing couldn't have been more perfect. As mayor he would need a wife or fiancée who would be refined and sophisticated.

"I think it's wonderful that Stacie is moving back," she said.

"Do you?"

"Yes. Don't you?"

He shrugged those massive shoulders again. "No reason not to be. At least I figure I'll have her vote."

She didn't say anything for a moment and then decided to ask, "You didn't go to Erica's engagement party. Do you plan to attend the wedding?"

He took a sip of his coffee, then smiled at her. "I haven't decided yet. Erica is a good friend and I think she would expect me to be there. But then I don't want my mother or hers sitting on the edge of their seats thinking I'm going to do something ridiculous like stop the wedding. Knowing them, they'd really expect me to."

Yes, she could imagine that they would. "Did it ever bother you that they tried putting you and Erica together at every twist and turn?"

"Of course it did, but luckily Erica and I formed an alliance to beat them at their own game. Once we knew we could only be friends, we just gave up trying to convince them of that and decided to let them figure it out for themselves."

April shook her head. "I doubt they've figured it out, even now with Erica getting married in a few months. I don't know about your mom, but I think Mrs. Sanders is obsessed with the idea."

"And you know why, don't you?"

"No. Is there a reason?"

Griffin smiled. "She thinks there is. Ever since Hattersville was founded, a Delbert has tried marrying a Hayes and something always happens before the wedding takes place. Some family members say there was a curse placed to keep the families apart."

"A curse?"

"From what I gather, a Hayes was engaged to marry some girl in Canada, and he hauled ass one night a few weeks before the wedding, followed his friends to America and later settled in Ohio where they founded Hattersville. A month later Hayes became engaged to marry someone else, one of the Delbert sisters, and he sent for her to join him and her brother in Ohio. The father of the jilted bride heard about it and considered such an act total disrespect and deliberate humiliation toward his daughter. Some claim he placed a curse that there would never, ever be a Hayes–Delbert union, and so far there hasn't been. Something has happened every time a wedding was to take place."

Griffin took another sip of his coffee and continued. "The last time was over twenty-something years ago when Mrs. Sanders's sister was engaged to marry my uncle Simon. She lost control of the car she was driving a week before the wedding, went into a coma and died."

April nodded. She recalled Erica telling her about the aunt she never got to know.

"Before that, a Delbert was to marry a Hayes and a few weeks before the wedding she ran off with another man and hasn't been heard from since."

"So if you and Erica marry that will supposedly break the curse."

"Yes, but breaking the curse is just one thing. In reversing the curse, untold riches are supposed to be showered upon both families."

She took a sip of her drink. She knew that for Karen Sanders it must have something to do with increasing her wealth. April shook her head. This was the first she'd ever heard about the curse. And it was hard to believe some people actually believed in such stuff. "Does Erica know about this supposed curse?"

"I'm sure she does, but like me she doesn't give a flip. If one of my offspring wants to marry one of Erica's one day, that's fine, but you better believe that it won't be due to any coercion on our parts. She and I have let it be known that if there is a curse it won't be ending in this generation."

He glanced around and saw the busboys breaking down the tables—they were the last couple in the restaurant. "It's time for us to go. Where are you staying tonight?"

"At the Hilton downtown."

He stood and picked up the bill the server had placed on the table earlier. "Come on. Let me make sure you get back to your hotel."

Chapter Fourteen

Griffin had all good intentions of delivering April to her hotel, only sticking around long enough to make sure she got into her room safely. But he hadn't counted on a few things. Like just how aroused he'd gotten sitting across from her and watching her eat. Each and every time she took a sip of her drink or licked her lips he could imagine his tongue easing right into her mouth.

And when they were about to leave the restaurant and he'd pulled the chair out for her, she'd swung her legs around to stand up. He'd gotten flashed by the most gorgeous thighs and wondered just how it would feel to slide right between them.

The cab ride was even worse. He inhaled her scent, that luscious fragrance that he loved so much. Now as he walked beside her into the lobby of her hotel, lust was ripping through him, attacking every cell in his body. He wanted her with a hunger he hadn't ever experienced before.

But then, if he were to be completely honest with himself, he would admit that he'd always wanted April and had deliberately come to Chicago to get her. Oh, he had convinced himself on the flight from Ohio that he was merely here to give a hometown girl support. But he knew that was a lie.

It had nothing to do with support and everything to do with wanting her...as he always had. As he still did. That was the reason he'd come and the reason he'd made a bid for the jewelry she'd worn.

He reached in his pant pocket and pulled out the box she'd given him earlier that night. "I almost forgot to give this back to you."

They'd stopped walking and stood in the lobby. She looked down at the box. "No, it's yours. You paid for it and—"

"I bought it to give to you," he said softly.

Their gazes connected and she looked surprised at such a notion. "You're kidding, right?"

"No, why should I kid about something like that?"

She stared at him, speechless.

"When I read in the paper that you were participating in a charity function here tonight, I decided to come."

"You flew from Ohio to Chicago?"

He chuckled. "You're talking like that's a million miles. Yes, I flew here from Ohio."

"Because of me?"

"Yes, because of you." He held her gaze. "You're a beautiful and desirable woman, April. Is there a reason you don't believe me?"

April felt she could give him a number of reasons, but the one that headed the list was that he was a Hayes. To him that might not mean anything significant, but the importance of such a thing had been drilled into her head so many times she had the puncture wounds to prove it. Besides that, he'd never shown interest in her before, so why now?

She lifted her chin. "Yes, there is a reason."

"And what reason is that?"

"I've done a number of charity gigs and you've never felt the need to attend any before."

He lifted a brow. "How do you know that I haven't?"

She opened her mouth and then firmly shut it. She didn't know, but why would he have?

Instead of allowing her to rethink what he'd said and attempt another response, he took hold of her arm. "Come on, let me walk you to your room. By the way, you will keep the jewelry, April."

She was so taken back by the firmness of his tone that she wasn't aware he'd taken her arm until they were stepping onto the elevator. She glanced up at him while confused emotions ran through her. Had he attended other functions she'd participated in without her knowing about it? If he had, then it didn't make any sense.

"What floor?"

She blinked, realizing he was talking to her. "The twelfth floor."

She felt the elevator beginning to move and glanced up to find him staring at her. "It's not all that complicated, you know," he said softly.

She frowned. "Well, it is to me."

"I don't see why. I'm a man and you're a woman. I'm attracted to you and have been for a while."

She knew for certain *that* was a crock. There was no way he'd been attracted to her. Oh, he might have the hots for her tonight. After all, like he'd said, he was a man and she was a woman and there was definite sexual chemistry boiling over between them. You would have to be dead not to notice it. But to say he'd been attracted to her for a while was spreading a lie a little too thick for her taste.

She decided not to say anything as they continued their

ride up to her floor. Of course the unspoken question looming between them was what would happen once they get
there. Would he expect her to invite him in? Should she? Her
nerves were getting frayed and she needed to do something
to get them smoothed over.

She released a deep sigh and looked down at the floor. And
he really thought it wasn't complicated? If he only knew.

Griffin doubted she realized it but her sigh just now had
been long and deep. She was finding what was between them
complicated and he didn't understand why. She was a single
woman and he was a single man and they clicked. Hell, they
did more than just click. If given the chance they would burn
up the sheets. She was fire and he was kerosene. Together
they would be explosive.

The elevator door swooshed open and he stood back to
let her precede him. Together they began walking down the
long hall. She'd already taken her passkey out of her purse and
held it in her hand along with the gift-wrapped box. He'd
meant what he told her. The necklace was hers to keep.

She stopped in front of her door and released another sigh,
something she'd done quite often tonight. "Well, this is my
room."

He glanced at the room door and smiled. "Funny, it's also
my address."

She lifted a brow. "Excuse me?"

He chuckled. "Room 1234 and I live at 1234 Morgantown
Place. Now, isn't that a coincidence?"

"Yes, rather interesting." She paused for a moment and
then said, "I really appreciate you walking me to my room,
and about this necklace..."

"What about it?"

"It's something we need to talk more about."

"Is it?"

"Yes."

He nodded. "All right, when do you want to discuss it? I have time now if you do."

She eyed him warily while nervously running her tongue across her bottom lip—a gesture that was stirring up heat in his groin. He couldn't help the slow smile that touched the corners of his lips. He'd never considered April to be the nervous kind. She'd always come off as outspoken. He'd heard how she'd given several guys around town a blistering earful when they'd figured that, since she'd lived on what some considered the less desirable side of Hattersville, she would be one of those girls to put out without batting an eye. She'd proven them wrong.

As if she'd made up her mind about something, she straightened and said, "Now is fine. And I have a bottle of wine in my room, compliments of Oprah, if you'd like some."

He gave her another small smile. *Some* was what he wanted and *some* was what he planned on getting. "That sounds great. Thanks."

He stood back to give her room to open the door and seconds later he glanced at her room number as he followed her inside. He didn't believe in curses, so he definitely wasn't a superstitious person, either; but he had a feeling once he walked over the threshold he would get to experience something mind-blowing.

Rita placed the novel on her nightstand, feeling drowsy, and hoped she'd finally be able to get some sleep. She had ended up taking the rest of the week off work. To satisfy Brian she had gone to see her doctor, although she hadn't needed to do so to know what was wrong with her.

She was having withdrawals just like Lori had warned. Withdrawals, right along with the guilt she was carrying around on her shoulders, and that meant a lot of sleepless nights since returning from Sweden.

There wasn't a night that went by that she didn't think about Wilson and what they'd done. The guilt was there, but so were remnants of pleasure. The kind of pleasure her body wanted to experience again.

And that was the root of her problem. She had gone to bed for an entire week dreaming, fantasizing and craving another woman's husband, and as unbelievable as it seemed, she could not help herself.

She stood up to stretch, feeling the tenderness in her breasts and remembering when Wilson's mouth had tasted her there, how his tongue had latched onto her nipples, drawing them into his mouth and sucking in a way that made her pelvic muscles contract. But his mouth hadn't stopped there. He had tasted her all over and when he slid his tongue inside of her, right between her legs...

Gracious!

She eased back in bed and turned off the light knowing the dreams would come again tonight. In them Wilson would be free to give her all the loving she wanted, all she needed, over and over again.

Although the sex between them had been good, there had also been his charisma, his charm, the way he could have a woman eating out of his hands with his appeal. There was such an allure about him that she'd been fascinated, captivated to know it was truly real and not a put-on. If he'd been single he would definitely be a man she would want to get to know...and share a bed with again.

The ringing of her phone almost made her jump and she glanced at the clock on her nightstand. It was late but not too late to get a call from Brian and, assuming it was him, she reached out and picked up the phone.

"Brian, I thought you were going to play cards well into the night with Beau and Charles."

"Hello, Rita. This isn't Brian. It's Wilson."

She drew a deep surprised breath. "Wilson?"

"Yes."

She swallowed deeply. This was the first time they'd ever spoken on the phone and she found his voice to be far sexier than she should have. Her heart began beating fast in her chest and the mere fact he was on the phone had heat stirring a place between her legs he had touched, tasted and taken. "Wilson, how did you get my number and why are you calling me?"

"I got your number from Erica, although I had to make up a lie to get it. I told her I wanted to pass it on to my secretary, since someone I knew might be interested in the services your company provides."

He paused a second and then said, "And as to the reason why I'm calling, I think you know the answer to that, Rita. When I woke up that morning you were gone. Why didn't you wake me to at least say good-bye?"

She lowered her head and closed her eyes. She had wanted to do that and to thank him for a night she'd known she would remember forever. But she hadn't been able to make herself do it. What they'd done was wrong and there was no need to compound that wrong or try finding an excuse.

She opened her eyes and stared into the darkness of her room. "I think we both know the answer to that. What we did was wrong."

He didn't say anything for a moment and then spoke. "I wish I could have regrets, Rita, but I don't. God knows I've tried. If only you knew what you gave me that night, and no, it wasn't just sex. You actually made me feel like a man again.

A man who now knows he has emotions, that he has a sex drive he thought had long ago been destroyed."

She shook her head, not understanding what he was saying but determined not to accept excuses for what they'd done.

"I've been thinking of you," he said huskily. "Maybe I shouldn't, but I have. I need to see you again."

"No, what we did is wrong. The next time you see me will be when my son and your daughter get married. I hope you'll be able to forgive yourself the way I'm trying to forgive myself. Think of how we've betrayed Karen."

"My relationship with Karen is not that way and hasn't been for over twenty years. It was her choice and not mine. Lately, I've been thinking of asking for a divorce."

"No!" she blurted out and felt her heart beating fast. "No, please don't do that because of what we did. I would hate myself more than I do now."

"You shouldn't hate yourself. If only you knew the hell of a marriage I've endured you wouldn't feel guilty."

"No, I don't want to hear it. You are a married man and you should make the most of it. Please leave me out of it."

"That's just it. I can't leave you out of it. Heaven help me but I go to bed every night thinking of you, dreaming of you, wanting you. I want to make love to you again so much that I ache. Hell, I'm fifty-nine, Rita. I shouldn't be having *those* kinds of aches."

Tell me about it, she all but whispered and was glad she hadn't done so. She knew just what kind of aches he was talking about because she was having some of the same kind herself. She couldn't stop her lips from twitching in a smile. Just to think she was the one responsible for his problem made her feel like a woman in a way she hadn't felt in a long while. Not since Patrick died.

And had Wilson truly insinuated that he hadn't been

sexually active in over twenty years? How was that possible when he was a married man? Surely his wife had been seeing to his needs.

"I'm coming to Dallas. I want to see you."

His words snapped her out of her reverie. "You can't come here."

"Yes, I can. I think we need to talk."

"No, we don't."

"Yes, we do. There is no reason for you to feel guilty about anything. Once I tell you everything, then—"

"But I don't need to know everything. Your business is between you and your wife and I don't need to be involved."

"But you are involved, sweetheart. Just hear me out and if afterward you still want to feel guilty, fine, I won't bother you again. The only relationship we'll have is the one our children will give to us. However, that doesn't mean I still won't ask Karen for a divorce after the wedding. I can't live my life this way any longer."

"Wilson, I—"

"Agree to see me when I come to Dallas on Tuesday. Please."

She closed her eyes. She should tell him not to call her again and hang up the phone. Tell him that he and Karen should seek counseling. But she couldn't do any of those things. Heaven help her, she wanted to see him.

She slowly opened her eyes and gripped the phone tighter in her hand. "Okay, I agree to see you when you come to Dallas."

The sigh she heard on the other end of the phone was long and hard. "Thank you. I'll call you Monday with my flight info as well as the hotel where I'm—"

"No! No hotel. We need to meet in a public place."

"All right. I'll make all the arrangements and call you on Monday. Good night, Rita."

"Good night."

She quickly hung up the phone and closed her eyes. How could she have agreed to see him? Deep down in her heart she knew the reason.

Chapter Fifteen

"Nice suite."

April looked over her shoulder while tossing her purse on the sofa. "Thanks."

Now if she could figure out what was going on with the man who was standing in the middle of her suite. She couldn't believe her luck...or her misery. How many times had she dreamed or fantasized of him doing exactly what he was doing now, standing within ten feet of her and looking at her like he could eat her alive, while simmering sexual tension flowed between them. And that tension was getting more heated the longer they stood there staring at each other and saying nothing.

She cleared her throat. "I'll get that wine," she said, thinking a beeline to her kitchenette was in order.

"No, not yet."

She swallowed as she watched him slowly cross the room and come to a stop directly in front of her. Her breath caught at the seductive smile on his lips and she felt her control, the little she had, faltering.

"Why? Was there something you wanted?" When a smile curled his lips she became aware how her question might have sounded.

He reached out and tilted her chin. "Yes, now that you mention it," he murmured in a deep, husky voice that had the area between her legs throbbing. "I was standing over there thinking of just how much I want to get inside of you."

She almost choked on the sensations that suddenly zipped through her. Men had asked to sleep with her before but never quite like that. Griffin hadn't minced words and the way he was looking at her told her he wouldn't waste any time getting what he wanted once she gave him the go-ahead.

And she planned on doing just that. She would be a fool not to. Especially when he was the man she had loved for so long. She shivered at just how long she'd wanted him. How long he had invaded her dreams. How long he had made any man insignificant compared to him.

She could tell from the deep penetrating look he was giving her that he was waiting for her response. "What's stopping you?"

His smile widened. "Nothing. At least not anymore," he whispered. And then he lowered his mouth to hers and began brushing soft kisses across her lips, before taking the hot tip of his tongue and tracing her mouth from side to side.

April felt a moan churning deep in her throat that caused her lips to part at the same time her eyelids fluttered closed. And when he slid his tongue between her parted lips, he immediately began tasting her so deeply and exploring her mouth so thoroughly that she felt her knees weaken.

He opened his mouth fully over hers as if to absorb every single thing about her, and she returned the kiss in the only way she knew how. The way she had done in her dreams so many times, with equal intensity and undiluted pleasure.

Desire flared through her and the pulse in her neck was

beating like crazy as he continued plundering her mouth with a hunger she didn't know could exist in a man. He tilted her head back to get even more of what he was putting down. And what he was so greedily taking. And then with one last, deep lick across her mouth he pulled his lips from hers.

"Griffin…"

His name was a droning ache off her lips and, before she could catch her breath, he bent and swept her off her feet. "I hope you're ready for me, April North," he whispered against her mouth.

If only he knew just how long she'd waited. "I am."

The thought of how ready she was began filtering through her mind as he moved toward the bedroom. Everything was happening so fast that she couldn't think, but then she really didn't want to think. Tonight, all she wanted to do was feel.

Never had the need to make love to any woman been so essential, Griffin thought, placing April on the huge bed. Needing to taste her once more, he leaned down and settled his mouth on hers, as his tongue savored every inch of her mouth with a tenderness he hadn't known he was capable of displaying.

Her scent deluged him with full awareness and he took his time, coaxing her to tangle her tongue with his and then duel with it. His erection pressed hard against his zipper, throbbing mercilessly, and he knew what he needed to do to provide it some relief.

He broke off the kiss and gazed down at her. April was draining him of everything and still demanding more. She lay back against the bed cushions, wearing the same outfit that she'd had when she'd walked across the stage. The same outfit that had driven a number of men tonight nearly out of their minds.

But she was here with him and, before the sun rose in the

morning, he planned on doing the one thing he'd wanted to do for years. Make her his in such a way that she could never belong to anyone else.

Deciding he wouldn't wait any longer, he reached out and, when she took his hand, he tugged her to the center of the bed and began undressing her, removing piece by sensual piece. When she was down to just her thong, he raked his gaze over her, zeroing in on the perfection of her breasts. The nipples were dark, swollen, delicious-looking and he licked his lips as he continued to stare at them, already tasting them, already feeling the way his tongue would wrap around them, draw them in between his lips, suck them into his mouth.

His erection felt hard, even more distended, and it was throbbing with a need to get inside of her. He reached out and lifted her legs and using the tip of his fingers he skimmed what there was of the silky material and slid his fingers beneath.

She let out a pleasurable sigh when he touched her flesh, feeling her moist heat, using the tip of his finger to stir her juices. She moaned when he began easing the thong off her, and when he'd removed it from her body, he slid the scrap of silk beneath his nose to inhale her intimate scent. He tossed the thong aside and then tasted the finger that had been inside of her moments earlier.

In her expression he saw how what he'd just done affected her. How it had increased her breathing, made the dark nipples on her breasts pucker that much harder. And when his gaze shifted downward and he saw the dewy curls between her legs he felt his erection harden that much more.

Her hair was in disarray around her shoulders and she stared at him with dark eyes glazed with desire. She looked like a sexy vixen that needed just what he had in store for her.

Since he had her full attention, he thought he would make

it worth her while. He took a step away from the bed and removed his shoes and socks, his tie and shirt. When his hand went to his zipper, he saw her eyes shift downward and he couldn't help but smile. She reminded him of a kid on Christmas, eager to unwrap her next present.

He began lowering his zipper and heard her sharp intake of breath.

"Need help?" she asked in a voice whose vibrations caressed his skin.

"Think you can?"

She shrugged a pair of gorgeous naked shoulders and her nipples seemed to tighten even more. "We'll never know if I don't try, will we?"

No, they wouldn't. But her attempt just might kill him. He was walking on the edge already and it wouldn't take much to push him over. But he was game if she was. "Yes, come give me some help."

She smiled and scooted across the bed toward him and he had a feeling she was about to give him a lot more than help. She proved him right when she took things over, pushed his hand out of the way and pulled down his zipper to claim what she wanted.

He felt the warmth of her fingers the moment she touched his flesh and when she pulled his erection from his briefs, he drew in his breath at the sensations overtaking him.

"Nice."

He glanced down and saw she was giving his throbbing member one hell of a look-over. But as he watched her lick her lips he had a feeling looking wasn't all she planned to do.

She began massaging him and he threw his head back and closed his eyes. Her hands felt heavenly on him and her fingertips rubbing across the sensitive flesh of his head almost made him come.

When he suddenly felt her mouth on him he snapped open

his eyes and glanced downward. Hell! He moaned loudly when she began working him with her tongue and teeth. It felt better than good. It felt so out of this world he figured he had to be on another planet.

But he knew he was here, in Chicago, at the Hilton Hotel in room 1234, while April, the woman he'd had the hots for most of his life, had his throbbing member in her mouth and having a damn field day with it. The more he moaned the harder she went at it, exerting more pressure, delivering more pleasure and making him groan her name one syllable at a time.

And when he felt himself about ready to explode he tried to pull out of her mouth but her lips clamped down on him and with precise, accurate meticulousness she tightened her hold on him and he felt himself being pulled deeper down her throat.

"April!"

What took place next was like a dream come true. A very, hot enticing dream that he didn't want to end. He shuddered to completion while she maintained possession of his shaft, determined to get the last drop.

When she released him he should have been ready to collapse on the floor but he wasn't. Instead of draining him, what she'd just done sent his testosterone level blasting and the only thing he could think about was returning the favor.

Before she could do any more enjoyable damage, he tumbled her backward in the bed and before she could straighten her position, he was there with his head between her legs, invading her womanly folds with his tongue and lavishing nonstop attention to her clit. He had gotten a sample of her taste earlier, but it couldn't compare to this and he gobbled her up like she was his last meal. She moaned and tried pushing him away, and then within a heartbeat she tried holding him there to her. The more she lifted her hips off the bed, the deeper his greedy tongue went.

"Griffin!"

She screamed his name and tilted her pelvis up and he was there, tangling his tongue inside of her, lapping her up with fervor. When he felt her body go limp, he pulled back to remove his pants and briefs completely.

And then he was back, easing his body between her legs and sliding himself inside of her, groaning in primitive pleasure while doing so. He pressed forward until he reached the hilt and only then did he let his body go still to take pleasure in the feel of her inner muscles convulsing around him while trying to milk him for all he was worth.

Evidently she held his pleasure in high esteem because he felt her making a bold attempt to extract everything out of him, and almost too late he thought of something and looked down at her. "Please tell me you're on the Pill."

He saw the way her lips curled into a heated smile. "Please tell me you're safe."

He chuckled. "Fine time to want to know such things and, yes, I'm safe."

"So am I. And yes, I'm on the Pill."

That's all he needed to know. He began thrusting into her as if he didn't expect to be alive tomorrow and this was his last opportunity to make love with a woman. So he did, with deep, concentrated strokes. He was like a crazy man who couldn't get enough of her. Then he lowered his head to take a nipple in his mouth, and had her whimpering his name when he began sucking on it.

When he felt her explode, heard her cry out his name, felt the way her muscles were pulling everything out of him, he bucked and felt his release as it shot right to her womb.

"April…"

He moaned her name in relentless pleasure while cupping

her hips, raising them to meet his every thrust. A fierce rush of need ripped through him as he continued driving his hardness into her. She didn't know it yet but she belonged to him. And as he continued to explode inside of her he knew if she didn't get that point this time around, she would the next.

April slowly opened her eyes and blinked in amazement. Had she just done four hours of nonstop lovemaking? No, it couldn't be true. But when she shifted and felt the soreness of her body she was convinced that it was.

She turned her head and saw that Griffin's half of the bed was empty. Had he gotten what he wanted from her and hauled ass like a thief in the night? She wasn't sure just how she felt about that. A part of her was elated that she had finally shared a bed with the man she loved, but the thought that it had only been a one-night stand stung. But then, what had she expected? Probably the only emotion that had ruled his mind and body last night was lust. Although she knew it, had known it from the start, she couldn't stop her heart from breaking.

"I was wondering how long you were going to sleep. I apologize for keeping you up most of the night."

She drew in a sharp breath and moved her gaze upward. Griffin was standing beside the bed, looming over her. Where had he come from? She shifted to sit up, felt the tenderness in her thighs, breasts and the juncture of her legs and thought better of it. "I thought you had gone."

He lifted a brow. "Gone where?"

She shrugged her naked shoulders. "Left."

He smiled and sat on the bed to face her. "I was sitting over in the chair, watching you sleep. You actually thought I would make love to you like I did last night and then skip out this morning?"

"Yes."

He reached out and gently caressed the side of her face with the back of his hand. "That tells me that you truly don't know me very well."

I know you well enough to know you've always had my heart, she thought, but she knew they were words she would never get the chance to say. "I guess not."

"Then I'm going to have to remedy that, starting now."

He lowered his mouth over hers, absorbing her gasp of surprise and pleasure. He took the opportunity to slide his tongue inside her mouth and then he began mating his tongue with hers in a way he'd done all through the night. She knew from the past four hours he was a skillful lover and she didn't regret one minute of being in his arms, even if it didn't mean as much to him as it meant to her.

She knew once they parted that this would be nothing more than a shared moment in history. A shared moment she would remember for the rest of her life. She could have her dreams and fantasies, but he had proven to her that there was nothing like the real deal.

He slowed pulled his mouth away and smiled down at her. "Now you see why I didn't want to stay in bed with you? You deserved your rest and as long as you were within reaching distance, I wouldn't let that happen."

He chuckled and then said, "I'm truly not the greedy bastard I came across as last night. It's just that I've wanted you for so long and—"

"What did you just say?" She hated interrupting him but she needed for him to clarify what he meant, especially when he had insinuated something similar yesterday while standing in front of her hotel room door.

He stared at her for a long moment and then he took her hand. "Look, I don't want to come on too heavy and scare you off, but I was only being honest. I've had this thing for you for some time."

Her heart began beating in her chest. "This thing?" She needed more clarification.

A crooked smile touched his lips and she was almost robbed of her breath. "Yeah, you know…"

She nodded. In a way she did know. It was no different from what any man had for a supermodel. Models were some men's fantasy girls. "Oh, a hot thing," she said, trying to keep the sound of disappointment out of her voice and feeling her heart rate slow down.

"Yeah, that, too. But for me it's a lot more than that."

Her heart rate increased again. "In what way?"

"I've always had this thing for you, but I knew since you were Erica's friend that you would never entertain the notion of us dating, although Erica and I are nothing but friends."

Not only was her heart beating faster, it was thumping so loud she thought she could actually hear it beating in her chest. "You wanted to date me?"

"Yes, when you would come home to visit Ms. Connie while in college."

She lifted a brow. "Before I became a model?"

"Yes, before you became a model. Your becoming a model had nothing to do with anything, although I was proud of you. Then you kept meeting guys more in your league and getting engaged and married, and I figured approaching you was out of the question since I never wanted to leave our hometown."

April didn't say anything for the longest time, not knowing what to say and even where to start. He hadn't really said he was in love with her, just that he'd always had this thing for her, and it still could be more sexual than emotional. Because she didn't know what to think, the best thing to do would be to tread lightly to see where this "thing" he had for her would lead.

"You do know I wouldn't feel comfortable dating you openly, don't you, Griffin?"

"Why? Because I'm not in your league?"

She frowned, narrowed her eyes. "No, because I'm not in yours."

Now it was Griffin who narrowed his eyes. "What's that supposed to mean?"

"You know what it means. We've lived in Hattersville all our lives and fully understand their social class system. I'm not in your class."

He released a disgusted sigh. "That's how things used to be."

"That's still how things are."

"They're changing, sweetheart. One of the first things I intend to do as mayor is to bring everyone together. I'm sick and tired of there being separation and a lack of unity."

She tried not to let his term of endearment affect her. "That's how it is, Griffin."

"But it doesn't have to be that way, April, at least not to the extent it is now. You and Erica always got along just fine. The two of you became the best of friends."

"Yes, against her mother's wishes. If Mrs. Sanders had had her way, she would have banished me from the face of the earth. I never understood her problem when it came to me. It was as if she had a personal grudge against me for some reason."

"That's just her way."

April glared. "You can say that, since she's always liked you. You were the chosen one. You still are."

What she didn't add was that, until the day she saw Erica and Brian drive away with a Just Married sign on the back of the car, she would not let her guard down where Mrs. Sanders was concerned. April just didn't believe that Mrs. Sanders had accepted their engagement and thought the woman wasn't above sabotaging the wedding.

"Well, once Erica marries, Mrs. Sanders will think differently."

I doubt it, April thought, but refrained from speaking that thought aloud. She met his gaze. "So what do you want from me, Griffin?"

When his gaze darkened, she rolled her eyes. "Besides that."

He chuckled as he eased down on the bed with her and pulled her into his arms. "I want for us to get to know each other better, and the only way we can do that is to begin dating."

She pulled away from him. "That's out of the question."

"Why?"

"I told you why."

"And you're willing to let a town of closed-minded people keep us from developing a relationship?"

Yes, she was. "You're thinking of running for mayor, for Pete's sake. What on earth will people think?"

"That I refused to let the old ways dictate my life and that my platform actually does stand for change and a new beginning."

She nibbled on her bottom lip and then said, "I hope you know that your parents fall within the category of closed-minded people, right along with Mrs. Sanders."

"I'm very well aware of that. But I've never let my parents or anyone else dictate my life." He paused a moment. "So, will you consider developing a relationship with me?"

"And what about Paulina? The two of you seemed pretty taken with each other in New York, Griff." She hadn't been able to resist calling him that, knowing he would get annoyed by it.

He did and it showed in his expression. "There's nothing

between me and Paulina. The only relationship we had was a sexual one and she's been told more than once how I feel about being called Griff. Some of her antics she thought were cute really weren't. I haven't seen or talked to her since that time in New York."

He then raised a brow. "And what about you and Neil? The two of you seemed rather chummy."

Erica chuckled. "His partner knows I'm no threat."

"Partner?"

"Yes, Neil is gay and Aaron is just as drop-dead gorgeous. They make a beautiful couple."

She studied his features a moment, then asked, "Are you sure there's nothing going on with you and Paulina?"

He smiled. "Positive. I knew my relationship with her was one that wasn't going anywhere, but I don't see that happening with us if given the chance, April. I can definitely see anything that develops between us going places. I think we owe it to ourselves to find out where."

She drew in a deep breath. His offer was making her dream come true, and here she was thinking about turning him down, which would be refusing to take the one thing she'd always wanted. Him. Was she really willing to do that?

"Would you agree for us to date secretly, at least until after Erica marries?" she asked him.

He frowned as if he couldn't fathom why she'd want them to do such a thing. "Is there a reason you wouldn't want anyone to know we're involved?"

"Yes. I couldn't handle Mrs. Sanders's wrath, which she will bring down on my head with a vengeance if she thought for one minute you and I were lovers."

"It doesn't concern her, April."

She heard the irritation in his voice but couldn't let that sway her. "But she'll think it does concern her, and Erica has enough stress keeping her mother under control until the wedding without me doing something that could cause more problems. Let's deal with one thing at a time, and the first thing on the list is Erica's wedding. Until then, I don't want anyone to know about us, Griffin."

She couldn't believe she was actually saying this. She was saying one thing but truly feeling another. She wished she could let everyone know that after all this time there might be a chance for her and Griffin after all. The very thought made her feel downright giddy, but the reality of how many people might be against it kept her feet firmly planted on the ground.

"I don't like the thought of sneaking around with you, April."

The thought that it bothered him touched her deeper than he would ever know. "I don't like the thought of sneaking around, either, but for now it's for the best."

He looked doubtful but said, "Fine, I'll keep things between us for now, but after Erica marries then all bets are off and we won't sneak around again. Understood?"

She nodded, not only understanding but in full agreement.

Chapter Sixteen

"Hello, Rita. Thanks for agreeing to meet with me tonight."

Rita took the chair Wilson slid out for her, not sure agreeing to see him had been the right thing. "Wilson," she responded in a whispered breath. And the moment their eyes connected she felt it. The heat and sizzle belonging to people who had once been intimate.

Her mouth opened to form a word but no sound came out so she closed her lips. It was as if the moment their gazes met and he smiled at her, she'd become lost in his entire presence. What she remembered most about him was his smile. It was so arresting it was causing heat to thrum all through her.

"I'm not sure your coming to Dallas was the right thing to do," she finally found her voice to say.

"And I believe coming here was the only thing I could do, Rita."

"Why?"

"Because I knew you would be feeling guilty about everything."

She leaned closer to him and whispered, "And I shouldn't?"

"No, you shouldn't."

Instead of responding to his statement she sat back and glanced around. At that moment she needed to focus her gaze on anything but Wilson while she allowed her brain to make sense of what he'd said.

The one thing he hadn't come across as was callous, a man who would have no regard for the woman he'd married. From the first she'd read him as being a loyal man, a man who would not hurt anyone. A man who would put others ahead of himself. A man who would love deeply.

But now she didn't know what to think about him. He was sitting here, a married man, telling the woman he'd slept with that she shouldn't feel guilty about the part she'd played in his infidelity. She couldn't help but glance back at him. Their gazes latched together immediately and she felt a pull in the pit of her stomach that she'd never felt before.

"Would you like to order now, sir?"

The waiter's voice had them breaking an intense connection as Wilson responded. "Give us a few more minutes, however, I'd like a scotch and she would like a glass of red wine."

"Yes, sir."

She didn't have to ask how he knew her drink of choice. A part of her wished she could blame her actions that night on the wine she'd drunk. Although she had consumed more glasses than usual, she had been in full control of her senses. What she hadn't been able to control was her body.

And she was having trouble doing that very thing now.

To distract herself, she glanced around the restaurant again. Wilson had chosen a location close to the airport, on the other side of town from where she lived. Glancing at the other patrons she was glad there wasn't a familiar face.

"This is my first time in Dallas in over five years. I can't believe how much things have changed."

She glanced back at Wilson. Why did he appear more handsome than she remembered? More manly? Why did the salt-and-pepper hair around his temples give him such a sexy look? And why was she thinking such things? An even better question was, why was she here?

Knowing he expected a response, she said, "Yes, we're growing by leaps and bounds." She didn't say anything else for a minute, then broached the unspoken subject. "You wanted us to meet and talk, Wilson."

"Yes, but can we enjoy a meal together first?"

She looked away. She didn't know how long she could resist him while in his presence.

"Rita?"

She glanced up at him. "Yes?"

"I don't bite, you know."

She wasn't so sure about that. There had been passion marks left all over her body from their prior encounter. But she didn't want to remember that. She swallowed thickly, feeling anxiety at the back of her throat. "All right, we'll share dinner and then we'll talk, although I doubt there is anything you can say to make me feel better."

"I hope that's not true," he replied. "Let's look at the menu. Hopefully, we can start there."

Wilson knew what he wanted but pretended to study his menu a little longer while Rita was still scanning hers. He glanced up thinking that he liked the way she was wearing her hair tonight. It was styled differently from when they'd been in Sweden. Then it had been shoulder length and now it was cut in a style that to him highlighted her beauty even more.

He tried to push to the back of his mind the thought that

he'd told Karen he was in Boston. He had deliberately lied to her and wasn't feeling guilty about it. He was well aware of lies she'd told him in the past, like the one involving her sister.

It had been by accident last year that he'd discovered Blair was not dead, as he and everyone else thought. He and Karen had separate checking accounts and one day he had come home early from a business trip to find her checkbook open and her records spread across the desk in the study. He had only planned to be there long enough to pour a glass of scotch and had glanced down and noticed an exorbitant amount payable to the nursing home. After looking through the checkbook he'd found several others, all drawn on Karen's trust fund account.

It didn't take long to discover the truth. To this day he hadn't revealed to Karen what he'd uncovered. He knew she had always been ashamed of her sister's physical and mental state and had probably staged the death as a way to deal with it. As long as it appeared she was doing the right thing by properly taking care of her sister—and from the amounts on the checks she'd written out it appeared she was—he'd decided to let her keep her secret since Blair was probably still in a coma anyway.

"I've made up my mind about what I'm having, Wilson."

He glanced up. "Have you?"

"Yes."

He smiled. "Good. I heard everything on the menu is delicious."

"Will there be anything else, sir?"

Jaye Pittman glanced up at the waitress, thinking that she was definitely a looker and hot as hell. He'd noticed her and that cute waitress outfit after the maître d' had escorted him to his table. She had a pair of gorgeous legs, legs he would just love to get between later.

He slid his gaze to her ringless finger and then back up to her face and smiled, deciding he wasn't ready to leave just yet. "Yes. I'd like another glass of wine…and what time do you get off tonight?"

He saw the sultry smile that tilted the corners of her lips. His erection was already hardening against his zipper when she replied, "We close at eleven."

Instead of saying anything, he merely nodded slowly, knowing he would keep that in mind. If he had to be in this town for another week or so, he might as well enjoy himself.

He leaned back in his chair. So far he hadn't been able to find anything incriminating on Brian Lawson and it wasn't for lack of trying. Even the man's former girlfriends were tight-lipped and loyal. And no amount of money could convince them to be otherwise. But he wasn't feeling the weight of failure pressing down on him just yet. If he had to hire someone to fake a few things, then so be it. Karen was paying him a lot of money for the results she wanted.

The waitress returned and refilled his glass. It was only after she'd left that he glanced around the restaurant and his brow lifted. A man resembling Wilson Sanders was having dinner with a woman who he'd been introduced to last month as the mother of Erica's fiancé. Rita Lawson.

Evidently Wilson had flown into town to meet with his future son-in-law and his mother and was taking them out to dinner. He wondered why Karen hadn't mentioned it.

He took another sip and wondered why Brian hadn't yet arrived. It took a few more sips of his wine for him to pick up that Wilson and Ms. Lawson were actually sharing a cozy dinner for two and Brian wouldn't be making an appearance. And he saw how they were looking at each other when each thought the other wasn't noticing. Yes, something was going on between them.

Damn, if that didn't beat all.

Jaye smiled, realizing that Karen, his mother's cousin, would flip if what he was thinking was true. And the more he studied the couple, the more he was convinced that it was. He might not have been able to dig up anything on Karen's future son-in-law, but it seemed Erica's future mother-in-law was another matter.

He leaned back in his chair thinking things were getting rather interesting.

"Will you please just listen to what I have to say, Rita?"

She drew a sigh and shook her head. He could tell she was fighting emotions the same way he was doing. They had enjoyed a meal and had tried talking about topics other than the one they were here to discuss. The conversation had been strained and he regretted that, but more than anything he regretted what she was doing to herself. Guilt was taking a toll on her and it should not have been.

She pursed her lips. "It won't change anything."

"If it doesn't, I will try to accept it."

He paused and took a sip of his scotch. She had preferred coffee and each time she took a sip his stomach knotted in desire. As much as he didn't want to, he wanted her again.

"First, I need to give you a bit of history on Hattersville, Ohio." He told her about the founding families and their pact to join by marriage in order to keep all the wealth in the same families. "So in other words, it was decided that Karen and I would eventually marry even before we were born."

"An arranged marriage?" she asked with disbelief.

"Yes. We'd always known it and accepted it, but at no time did we think we loved each other. It was more like a business arrangement. We treated each other with respect, but after Erica was born our relationship began to change."

She lifted a brow. "In what way?"

"She felt her duty to me was over and that there was no reason for us to continue to sleep together."

Her expression was one of disbelief. "You're joking, right?"

He met her gaze and held it. "Trust me. I would never joke about anything as personal as that."

He took another sip of his drink. "At one time she even suggested that I take a lover, said she could care less as long as I was discreet. But I never did."

She placed her coffee cup in the saucer. "Are you saying that…"

"Yes, that night I made love to you was the first time I'd had sex in over twenty years."

From the shocked look on her face he was fairly certain that she'd been rendered speechless. She opened her mouth to say something and then immediately closed it. She then narrowed her eyes while searching his face for some sign what he'd just told her was a bald-faced lie. But there must have been something in his features that compelled her to believe him.

"How did you survive? Men have needs."

A smile touched his lips. He figured now was not the time to counter that women had needs, as well. "Yes, but I'd convinced myself that I could live without fulfilling those needs. I threw myself into my work, my hobbies and my daughter. And I hoped and prayed that she would never find herself in the kind of loveless marriage her parents are in."

"What about Karen?"

He took another sip of his scotch. "I truly believe she doesn't enjoy the intimacy of marriage. She actually detests being touched."

Rita's eyebrows knitted together and he waited for her to

say something, and when she didn't he continued. "I want you to believe that I tried making a go of my marriage, and once or twice I have come close to asking for a divorce, but the love I have for Erica stopped me. I didn't want her to grow up with divorced parents."

"Do you think she knows that you and her mother…aren't close?"

"It wouldn't surprise me. God knows Karen isn't the easiest person to get along with, for me or for Erica."

Wilson smiled. "But meeting you, Rita, was good for me. I know you probably don't want to hear this, but like I told you that night on the phone, you made me know how it is to be a man with feelings, emotions, wants and desires."

She lifted a brow. "Did I create a monster?"

He saw her lips quirk and knew her question was a teaser. "Not a monster but a man who wants to live again. I'll be sixty in November and I've decided that I don't want to live the rest of my life alone, unhappy and unfulfilled. I want more. I deserve more."

She stared down into her coffee cup and then she glanced at him through hooded lashes. Her voice was torn and deep when she said, "Yes, you deserve more."

He leaned closer to her and whispered, "That night I made love to you awakened feelings I never knew could exist. But they do. Although you didn't create a monster, you did create a man who constantly wants you."

"Don't say that."

"Why not? It's true. I go to bed wanting you and I wake up wanting you. Not just any woman, but you. There is nothing about that night that isn't ingrained into my brain. Nothing I'm convinced I can't remember in full detail. And," he said, holding steadfast to her gaze, "there is nothing about that night that I wouldn't give just about anything to repeat."

He drew in a deep breath and added in a low tone, "More than anything I need you in my life to show me how to love."

She vehemently shook her head. "I can't. I don't have the right."

He reached out and took her hand in his. "You are wrong. You do have that right because I am giving it to you."

She pulled her hand from his. "No. That right can only belong to your wife." She then grabbed her purse and quickly walked out of the restaurant.

Rita got inside her car and locked the door. Instead of starting the ignition she leaned back against the seat and fought the tears that threatened to fall. How unfair life was at times. At least she'd known love and passion with Patrick. The thought that Wilson had never known them at all until he met her, made her heart ache.

She was totally convinced he was a good man. A man who deserved better than what he was getting. Better than what he'd gotten. She didn't want to place blame or pass judgment, but she wondered how Karen Sanders could sleep at night. How could she walk around every day and breathe? Most women would give their right arm for a man like Wilson. It wasn't fair.

All he wanted was to be loved and to love in return.

She buried her face in her hands when sobs began overtaking her. She should not have come here tonight. She should not have listened to what he'd said. And she should not be feeling this way.

She lifted her head, wiped her tears and drew in a deep breath. There was no mistake in what she'd seen in his eyes or the plea she had heard in his voice. He wanted her.

And heaven helped her, but she wanted him, too.

She wanted him so much she ached. All those things he'd

said had been a mirror of her own emotions. She went to sleep wanting him. She woke up wanting him. Not just any man. Only him. To save her soul, to save her sanity, she had to get away from here. She would go back home and drown in her own misery.

Rita was about to turn the key in the ignition to leave when she glanced through her windshield and saw Wilson walking out of the restaurant. His shoulders, those massive shoulders she admired so much, now seemed to slouch in despair and rejection. The sight touched her heart. How could any woman do that to any man? To him? Especially a woman who was his wife.

At that moment she was finally able to see what he had wanted her to see. What he needed her to see and to understand. Karen Sanders was not his wife…at least not a real one. No real wife would do this to her man. No real wife would have denied her husband the love, devotion and companionship he needed and so rightly deserved. She might be his wife on paper but that was all.

But isn't that enough? a voice asked inside her head. And then something inside her snapped with the answer. No, it wasn't enough. He deserved more. He deserved better. He deserved to experience the love he'd never had.

Before she lost her nerve, she got out of the car and crossed the lot to him. When he heard her footsteps he stopped.

"Rita? I thought you had gone."

She drew in a deep breath. "I was in my car about to leave."

"What stopped you?"

"You."

Instead of saying anything, he took the few steps over to her. He looked into her eyes, studied her face. "Will you take a ride with me?"

She swallowed tightly. "Yes."

He took her hand in his and led her to his car. And as she walked beside him, she released a low sigh. Starting tonight she was going to show Wilson Sanders just what love was all about.

Chapter Seventeen

"Can I take the blindfold off now, Brian?"

"No, not yet. Where do you think you are?"

Erica sniffed the air. "The beach, of course."

He laughed. "Of course."

She had arrived at Myrtle Beach a few hours ago. Brian had picked her up from the airport, and had taken her to the private beach house where they would spend the weekend. Walking through the doors was like déjà vu. It was the same beach house where he'd stayed last summer when they'd met. It was his godmother Lori's place. Erica had barely had time to put her luggage down when he'd blindfolded her and walked her back out the door.

"I know we walked through sand because I can feel it in my sandals."

"Yes," he chuckled. "We walked through plenty of sand."

"And we walked up a couple of steps," she added.

"True. So where do you think you are?"

"On a boat. That's it, isn't it, Brian? We're having dinner on a boat."

"Umm, not quite."

He removed her blindfold and she gasped, almost losing her breath at the sight before her. They were standing at the base of the pier, the same one they'd met on last year. Both sides of the pier were lined with beautiful lit candles and there at the very end, overlooking the waters of the Atlantic Ocean, was a candlelit table set for two.

The sun was just setting on the horizon and it was such a romantic sight that it actually brought tears to her eyes. Her gaze swung to Brian. "Oh, Brian, I can't believe you did this. It's so romantic," she said, wrapping her arms around his neck and smothering her face in his chest. She was deeply touched at how he had gone all out to make their weekend together special.

He knew this was the last weekend before the craziness started. She had decided against moving to Dallas a month early after the wedding planner had shown her all she had on the calendar. It was hard to believe this was the Fourth of July weekend. She had begun counting and they had less than five weeks left.

"Hey, sweetheart, I didn't bring you here to cry," he said, gently stroking her back. "It's a time of celebration for the beginning of our life together. It was here on this pier where you captured my heart when you stood in this very spot and told me I was wasting my time since the fish weren't biting."

She tilted her head back and laughed, remembering. "That was my way of hitting on you."

Somehow she'd known he was special even from a distance. And after they began dating he always treated her like she was the most precious thing in the world to him.

She glanced around. "I see the table. Where's the food?"

And then, as if by magic several uniformed servers appeared, seemingly out of nowhere. But as she looked further, she saw the two catering vans parked nearby. She smiled up at Brian. "You've thought of everything."

"For you, always."

Taking her hand they walked the pier toward the table, and Erica couldn't help gazing at the candles and the ocean water surrounding them. Everything was perfect, even the gentle breeze in the air. Her hair was blowing in the wind and she couldn't help but laugh with happiness.

When they reached the table he presented her with two beautiful roses—one red and one white—that were held together by a piece of silken thread. "Together, these roses represent unity and love, and the silken thread holding them together represents the strong bond between us that can never be broken," he told her in a deep, husky voice.

She gazed down at the roses and the thread that held them together. What he'd said was beautiful and touched her deeply. "Yes, it can never be broken."

"And I can't wait for August to get here to make you mine and share my love with you for the rest of my life," he whispered.

She leaned up and captured his jaw gently in her hands. "In my heart I'm already yours, Brian, and I will love you for the rest of my life, as well."

He lowered his head and captured her lips and she knew the countdown had begun. More than anything she looked forward to the day she would become Mrs. Brian Lawson.

Chapter Eighteen

Karen Sanders took a sip of her tea. "It's been almost three months, Jaye. I hope you have something for me that I can use."

Jaye glanced over at her. "I believe I have. However, it's not what you think."

Karen lifted a brow. "As long as it's enough to give Erica a reason to call off this ridiculous wedding."

He nodded. "Unfortunately, I couldn't find anything on Brian Lawson." At her deep frown he smiled. "But I think I have something even more damaging."

She narrowed her gaze. "For your sake, it better be. I've paid you a lot of money and there's more where it came from if you can deliver."

"I believe I can...and I have. It's not Brian you need to worry about, it's his mother."

Karen's gaze reflected surprise. "His mother? Why on earth would I need to be concerned with *her?*"

"Because she's involved in a very heated affair."

Karen shrugged. "So what? She's single. Some women enjoy that sort of thing with a man."

He chuckled. "Yes, some do. But in her case, the man she's enjoying it with happens to be married."

Karen paused with her teacup mere inches from her lips. "Married?" she asked in surprise.

"Yes, and the man is someone you know."

Before she could ask who, Jaye emptied an envelope filled with pictures on the table before her. At her startled gasped, he said, "Yes, Karen. I hate to inform you, but for the past two months Rita Lawson has been having an affair with Wilson."

Jaye watched Karen. Other than picking up the photographs and turning them over and over, one by one, she said nothing. His mother had once said she thought Karen's heart was made of stone and her father had made her that way. He'd wanted sons but his wife had given him daughters. However, Karen could probably be as ruthless as any son Omar Delbert could have sired.

Jaye was beginning to believe his mother knew what she was talking about.

He then watched as a smile curved her lips and she threw the pictures down on the table and laughed. She actually laughed. It was a rich sound. Rich and filled with joy. This was not the reaction he would expect from a woman who'd just been shown proof that her husband was involved with someone else.

While she continued to laugh, he glanced down at the photographs. Once he'd established the fact that Wilson and the woman were involved, all it had taken was following their pattern. Wilson had never returned to Dallas. Instead the two would plan visits in cities and countries where they most traveled on business. Most of the time things had worked out that way for them. On only a few occasions had they made plans themselves.

Jaye had captured them on camera sharing intimate dinners while gazing into each other eyes, holding hands across the table or walking out of restaurants and hotel rooms plastered to each other's side. There were even a few good shots that he'd captured of them sharing a kiss.

"I would not have figured her to be Wilson's type," Karen said, interrupting his thoughts. He wondered what she meant by that, since Rita Lawson wasn't a bad-looking lady. In fact, he could see her as Wilson's type. Although the man was his cousin by marriage, they'd never actually had any dealings with each other. But he always had appreciated Wilson for the times he would stop by and visit with his wheelchair-bound father.

It had been obvious to Jaye when he snapped the photographs that there was more than lust between Wilson and Rita. There was a growing love, and even a cynical bastard like him could see it. Too bad Karen couldn't.

"But since she is Wilson's type, they deserve each other because they will help to destroy what is between her son and our daughter."

Jaye leaned back in his chair. "You think once Erica finds out about the affair she will call off the wedding?"

"Of course. I'm her mother and I'll make sure it appears that I'm so distraught over the affair that—"

"And you're not distraught over the affair?"

She cast him a glance as if she didn't appreciate being interrupted but would let him do so this one time. "Heavens no. I suggested to Wilson years ago that he consider getting a mistress. But as far as I know he's never taken me up on my suggestion until now. Unfortunately, he decided on the wrong woman and I will use his mistake to my benefit."

Jaye saw her eyes light up and could just imagine what

devious plans she had in the works. In a way he didn't want to know. He just wanted to get paid for the work he'd done for her so far.

Feeling the need to escape her presence, he glanced at his watch and stood up. "I have another appointment and need to leave."

"Of course. Let me pay you for your services."

He watched Karen as she moved over to her desk and, using a key, unlocked it. He thought she wasn't a bad-looking woman if she would step down off her high horse every once in a while. He heard about her younger sister and how different the two women had been. There had been an eight-year difference in their ages and, according to his mother, Karen had always been jealous of Blair growing up and hadn't shed a single tear when Blair died.

"Here you are, Jaye."

He glanced down at the check. "Wow! I hadn't expected so much, Karen. Thanks."

"You earned it. Besides, I plan to keep you on retainer. Now that I have a surefire plan to rid Erica of Brian, I can turn my attention to Griffin. I don't believe he's involved with anyone."

"I wouldn't know. But I've heard he's planning to announce his candidacy for mayor soon."

Karen smiled. "Yes, and when he does I plan to have Erica by his side. They'll make a perfect mayor and first lady."

Jaye placed the check in his wallet thinking if she could pull that off then she was definitely a miracle worker. Griffin had said more than once that he and Erica didn't have that sort of relationship. Evidently Karen still wasn't listening.

"Well, you know how to reach me when you need my services again," he said, moving toward the door.

"Yes," she said, smiling. "And I will be calling you."

★ ★ ★

Griffin checked his watch. He had only twelve hours left to spend with April before heading out to the airport. The thought of leaving her tomorrow depressed him already.

Earlier today he had accompanied her on a film shoot on Malibu Beach. Anyone who thought the life of a model was all glitz and glamour and not hard work was completely wrong. April was a professional and handled herself as such but she wasn't standoffish. She had conversed easily with everyone and he could tell the crew liked her a lot. One of the cameramen told him that she didn't give in to immature tempestuousness like some models did.

And, as some of the other crew members had pointed out, she had a heart of gold. Last year she had help organized several charity events. Griffin had to agree with everyone that there was more to April North than her beautiful face and shapely body.

They had officially been dating for a month now and he always looked forward to her phone call in the middle of the week to share her weekend schedule with him. Then he would make plans to join her in some of the most exotic places. There hadn't been a weekend that they hadn't shared together.

He smiled when he thought of last weekend in Orlando when she had talked him into going to Disney World. He'd had more fun that day with April than he'd had at ten years old. And he could definitely say he'd never had more fun with a woman. There was just something about April that made him want to enjoy life in a way he never had before.

"Sorry about that, but I needed to take that call from London," April said, breezing back into the room with her luscious scent following in her wake.

He glanced up and smiled and when she reached the sofa and tumbled playfully into his arms, he caught her as their laughter mingled. And when he adjusted her position in his lap, she turned and lowered her mouth for him to take.

And he took it.

With a hunger that no longer surprised him, he devoured her. He felt his blood rush south when she adjusted her position in his lap and came in blatant contact with his erection. He was hard and was getting harder, more engorged with every little wiggle her sweet behind was making.

"Stop squirming around so much," he warned, pulling his mouth from hers to whisper against her moist lips.

"Why?" she asked, smiling.

"Why you think?" he asked, knowing she had gotten used to his erections by now. It didn't take much to arouse him where she was concerned.

"I like hot sex. I like you. You're beginning to grow on me," she teased.

A smile touched the corners of his lips. "I like hot sex, too, and I like you. And I know all about growing on you. If I expand any more I'm going to do irreparable damage to my zipper."

She glanced down at his lap. "Show me what's growing."

He didn't give her a chance to recant her request as he tumbled her back on the sofa while standing up to quickly remove his jeans, T-shirt and boxer shorts.

"Oh, my, Mr. Hayes, you're truly a Mr. Big," she said, giving his manhood an eyeful.

"So you say."

She chuckled and reached down and caught hold of his shaft. He knew she felt it thickening in her hand. Her smile widened. "So I know."

Not giving him time to say anything else, she covered his mouth with hers and he wrapped his arms around her waist, bringing her closer to him. He pulled back and whispered, "You've got on too many clothes."

"Umm, earlier today you thought I had on too little clothes."

He smiled remembering the bikini she'd worn during her photo shoot. Just thinking about how she looked in it made sensations race through his groin. She felt him grow some more and laughed before pressing the palm of her hand against his chest, sending him tumbling backward.

Moving quickly, she stripped out of her shorts and blouse. He watched her hungrily. "No panties and bra?" he asked when she returned to ease her naked body over his body.

"Around you, why bother?" Without hesitation, she eased her moist heat down on his manhood.

"I like this," she said in a low, husky tone that heated his blood. Made him tingle with all kinds of sensations as he drove deep inside of her. He lifted his hips off the sofa for deeper penetration.

"I like that, too," she then added.

He could feel himself swelling inside of her and when she glanced down and met his gaze he figured it was going to be one of those days that she intended to ride him until he went crazy.

"I like you," she whispered.

He opened his mouth and his voice caught in his throat. The response he had been about to make to her was, "And I love you."

He sucked in a deep breath instead when the truth of his emotions overtook him with a vengeance. He did love her and he might as well tell her. "I don't just like you, April. I've fallen in love with you."

He watched her eyes flicker when she realized what he'd said. Her body went still, but her inner muscles clamping hard on him didn't let up any. And then he saw something form in her eyes he hadn't expected. Tears.

"I didn't mean to make you cry, sweetheart."

"But you told me you loved me," she said as a couple of tears fell down on his chest.

"Would you rather I not tell you? Did you want to think all I want from you is sex? I couldn't do that. To me you're too honest, clean and pure. You're nothing like those other women I've messed around with."

"But I didn't think you would fall in love with me."

He smiled. "Well, I did. And I didn't tell you that to make you express feelings for me that I know you don't feel yet, but I—"

"Don't feel? I've loved you forever, Griffin Hayes!"

Now it was his gaze that flickered. He was totally startled. "What?"

"You heard me. I can't recall a time that I haven't loved you."

He swallowed thickly. "I never knew."

More tears fell. "It wasn't meant for you to know. I wasn't sure how things were between you and Erica and she was my best friend. Besides, Mrs. Sanders would have banished me off the face of the earth if she thought I had fallen for the guy she wanted Erica to marry."

He held her gaze. "But you got married. Three times."

She nodded. "Yes, because I couldn't have you," she said quietly. She drew in a deep breath. "And I still can't."

He frowned. "Why not? You know there's nothing between me and Erica, and you also know I don't give a friggin' damn what Mrs. Sanders thinks."

"Yes, but Hattersville is your home and it will always be. You love it there. It's just the opposite with me. I couldn't wait to finish school and leave there. I hated growing up with people thinking my mother was a tramp because she had me and wasn't married, and that I was beneath them because my grandmother cleaned houses and took care of other people's kids for a living."

He reached out and lifted her chin. "Erica never thought that. Neither did I. In fact, I always admired your accomplishments, was proud of your achievements. Not everybody in our town is as closed-minded as Karen Sanders and my parents."

"Maybe not, but you're thinking of running for mayor and I won't do anything to ruin your chances of winning."

"And how can loving each other ruin my chances?"

She inhaled deeply and then said, "No one would accept me as someone you're interested in."

His eyes narrowed. "I intend to prove you wrong, sweetheart. I've always admitted that there are closed-minded people living in Hattersville, and it won't change overnight. But it will change. I told you my platform. You're going to have to believe in me. Believe that somehow there can and will be an *us,* and that no matter what we will be together."

When she didn't say anything he murmured against her lips, "Tell me that you're willing to believe that, April."

She didn't respond and each second that passed made his heart beat that much faster. "Okay, I'm willing to believe that," she finally whispered. "But you have to promise that you'll still keep our affair a secret until after the wedding. I want to be the one to tell Erica about us, but only after she marries Brian. The less drama before Erica's wedding, the better."

"All right. I promise."

And then he covered her mouth with his, knowing that his top priority was not winning the mayor's race, but showing April that they were meant to be together. When all was said and done, they would be.

Chapter Nineteen

Erica laughed and opened yet another gift. This was her first
bridal shower and she was totally enjoying herself. The past
two weeks had moved by quickly and now she only had three
weeks left...and another half-dozen bridal showers to attend.

This one was being given by a few friends from college
who'd come to town for the weekend. They were using the
patio of the Hattersville Garden Club and the weather had
cooperated nicely.

To her surprise her mother had not put up a fuss about attending. In fact, lately her mother hadn't complained about
anything. When Erica had mentioned it to Brian he'd said
Karen had probably finally resigned herself to the fact that
Erica would be marrying him.

Erica had also noticed a difference in her father. The other
day she had heard him humming the lyrics to Marvin Gaye's
"Distant Lover." And another day she actually heard him
whistle. She couldn't ever recall him walking around the
house whistling before, and the sound had both surprised and
pleased her. And she'd noted he was smiling a lot lately and

wondered if her upcoming wedding had him in such a jo-
vial mood.

She talked to Brian every night and their phone talks were
getting more heated than ever. He'd outlined in full detail
and high definition just what he intended to do to her every
single minute of their two-week honeymoon in Paris. And
likewise, she had outlined with the same noteworthy specifics just what she intended to do to him. Needless to say their
conversations would end with both of them needing cold
showers. Especially since they hadn't made love since their
weekend in Myrtle Beach.

They had decided to abstain from lovemaking to make
their wedding night more special and meaningful. However,
they were now seeing it was making them that much hornier.
There was no doubt in her mind they would leave the reception early, making a mad rush to the airport.

She had driven her mother to the shower and a few hours
later was driving her back home. "You're quiet, Mom," she
said, glancing over at her when the car stopped at a traffic
light.

"I was just thinking about how happy you were at the
shower. You really love him, don't you?"

Erica smiled, grateful her mother was finally getting the
picture. "Yes, I really love Brian. I know you wanted things
to be different but I have to marry for love."

Karen nodded. "If that's what you truly want, Erica, then
I am happy for you."

Erica released a deep sigh. She knew what her mother had
just said was as close to giving her blessings as Erica would
get. "Thanks, Mom."

"Your father tried to tell me but I refused to listen. I wish
he was here now. He would probably get a kick out of hearing me admit at least once that he was right."

Erica laughed. "Yes, I'm sure that would probably make his day. Where is Dad, anyway?"

"He's out of the country on another one of those business trips. He's been taking them a lot lately."

Erica nodded. "Yes, I noticed, but usually they don't extend over the weekend. I guess the office is keeping him busy."

"Yes, I guess so." Karen paused a minute. "When we get to the house I'd like you to come inside for just a moment. I want to show you what I got your father for his birthday."

Erica lifted a brow. "Kind of early, aren't you? His birthday isn't until November."

Karen shrugged. "I went shopping one of those days last month when I needed to take my mind off your wedding. You know, forget it was happening."

Erica shook her head, smiling. At least her mother was being honest.

Karen walked with Erica into the house knowing she had to keep her cool. She needed to convince Erica that, although she still had misgivings about the wedding, she had accepted that her daughter was marrying for love. So far everything was going according to plan. There was no reason for anything to fail at this point. She wouldn't allow it. Even Dr. Cobb had grudgingly agreed to do his part. He didn't have a choice if he wanted her to keep quiet about the affair he'd been having with Aggie for years, every since Lester had been confined to a wheelchair.

"Go on into the study and pour glasses of wine for us. I can certainly use one. I just need to slip out of my heels into more comfortable shoes. I'll be right back."

"Sure, Mom." Erica watched her mother hurry up the stairs before moving toward the study. She had just placed her purse on the coffee table when she heard the text alert sounding. Smiling, she figured it was April calling to see how the bridal shower had gone, and lifted a curious brow at the caption that popped up from an unknown caller.

Pictures for Erica's special day.

She saw the same caption had been sent to the phones of Brian, her mother, his mother and her father, as well. Whoever had sent it knew all of their cell numbers so it had to be someone they knew. She clicked on the text and released a startled gasp at the photo that flashed before her eyes of her father kissing a woman who closely resembled Brian's mother. A closer look showed that it *was* Brian's mother.

It couldn't be. It had to be some sort of trick photography. She kept scrolling to view all eight photos and each was just as damaging. Her head began spinning at the implications of those pictures.

It was then that she heard the loud scream from upstairs and remembered her mother was one of the recipients of the texted photos. Out of curiosity, had she opened the caption as well? With her heart beating fast and furious in her chest Erica took the stairs two at a time and rushed into her mother's bedroom.

And there she found Karen passed out in the center of the room with her cell phone beside her on the floor.

"I swear, Brian, ever since you've gotten engaged, I've yet to beat you at a game of tennis. Erica must be some kind of woman."

Brian couldn't help but grin as he glanced over at Matthew Seacrest, a friend from his high school days and currently CEO of his own P.I. firm. Matt was right on both accounts. He had yet to win a match between them in a while and Erica was some kind of woman. "Stop whining and admit you're not at the top of your game. I think that beer belly I've noticed lately might be slowing you down."

"Hey, you better watch it," Matt warned, pulling the towel

from around his neck and flapping it out to hit Brian's shoulder with it. They were walking off the court and headed into the locker room. The summer's heat had been brutal and although Matt had hinted otherwise, it hadn't been easy for Brian to best his friend today.

Truthfully, he understood that Matt had a lot on his mind. Cassie, Matt's girlfriend, was pregnant and still refused to marry him, saying she wasn't sure she was ready to take such a big step in her life. Brian shook his head. To his way of thinking having a baby was a big step, and if Matt wanted to marry her then what was the holdup? Evidently Matt had begun wondering the same thing.

"I'm taking Cassie to dinner at my folks' tonight. You can join us if you like. They always get a kick out of seeing you."

"Thanks, man, but I have plans for later. Erica is having her first bridal shower today—as we speak—and one of her girlfriends is taping it. I'm going to download it onto my laptop so we can watch it together later."

"Gee, sounds romantic," Matt said, making a kissy face.

Brian smiled, ignoring his friend's gesture and thinking how he and Erica could turn any moment—even long-distance ones—into a romantic time. They could have some heated conversations over the phone, and whenever they added the webcam into the mix it was like exploring a whole new frontier. "Trust me, Matt, it will be romantic."

An hour later Brian had just stepped out of the shower when he heard the alert tone on his phone that meant he'd received a text.

He glanced at the clock and saw the time and figured it was probably Erica sending the video from her bridal shower. He smiled at the caption—*Pictures for Erica's special day*—and immediately clicked it on.

"What the f—!

He sucked in a deep, shocked breath. Whatever he'd been expecting, this wasn't it. He felt blood rush to his head. What the hell was Mr. Sanders doing kissing his mother?

He didn't want to look at the other pictures attached, fearful of what he might find, but felt he had to. Someone had taken several shots of Erica's father and his mother sharing candlelight dinners; walking hand-in-hand through the doors of several five-star hotels; kissing in parking lots, in front of hotel room doors…

He didn't recognize the number that had sent the text, but he did see the other recipients of the pictures and he almost dropped the phone.

He drew in a deep breath and dialed Erica's phone number and the call immediately went to voice mail, which meant she had her phone off.

He ran his hand down his face, waiting on the cue to leave a message. "Erica? Baby, where are you? Call me as soon as you get this message. Please call me."

Blowing out an angry breath he then dialed his mother, who was on a business trip in Japan. As the phone rang he looked at the pictures again, but he refused to believe what he was seeing. Other than his father, he could never recall his mother in a relationship, serious or otherwise, with any man.

But what if this was true? What if his mother and Mr. Sanders were involved? He closed his eyes and sucked in a tormented breath at the thought. What could she have been thinking? What had Mr. Sanders been thinking? Not in a million years would he have expected this. Not in a million years.

On the small idyllic Japanese island of Miyako, Wilson and Rita stood at their hotel window and gazed out at the picturesque beauty of the white sandy beach. They had spent a good portion of the day out there, enjoying the beauty of the island together.

Rita turned in his arms and looked up at him. She could not believe how different her life had been over the past five weeks. Once she had decided to take a bite of the forbidden fruit and teach this tall, handsome and wonderful man what love was about, she'd not given herself time to indulge in any regrets. He kept her too busy to do so.

She looked forward to planning their weekly schedules so they could spend time together during their business travels. So far things had worked out wonderfully for them. Together they had visited the Great Wall of China, attended a polo match in Great Britain and picked coffee beans in Peru. But nothing could surpass her greatest adventures, which were the nights spent in his arms.

Wilson looked down at her and smiled. "What are you thinking about?"

She couldn't help returning his smile and simultaneously she felt a yearning in the pit of her stomach. "How happy I've been these last five weeks."

"Have you really been happy, Rita?"

She nodded. "Considering everything, yes."

And she didn't want to consider everything, had pushed the thought of doing so to the back of her mind. All she'd done was take what was offered and give what she felt was truly deserved.

"What about you, Wilson?"

He chuckled. "Sweetheart, if I can get any happier, I'd burst. And it hasn't been about the sex. Although, I have to admit that's been great, too. Hell, I never knew that there was still so much life in the bedroom after fifty. But it's been about sharing things with you. It's been an awakening for me. One that I didn't expect and I'm so damn grateful for."

He paused and then said, "I know you don't want to talk about it but we need to, Rita."

"Talk about what?"

"My divorce from Karen."

She shook her head. "No, I don't want you to do that, Wilson."

"After spending time with you, loving you the way I do, how can I not?"

She blinked. Her look was one of astonishment. "You love me?"

He threw his head back. "Yes, I love you. You taught me how to love. You gave me love. How else can I feel?"

"Gratitude."

"No, it's not gratitude. It's love. For the first time in my life, months shy of turning sixty, I know how it feels to love a woman. And I don't know how many more years I have left on this earth, Rita. I can't imagine spending any of them without you."

She reached out and pressed her hand to his lips. "No, I won't let you leave your wife for me."

"My marriage was over long ago. After Erica's wedding I'm going to ask Karen for the divorce I should have asked her for years ago."

She eased out of his arms and walked across the room. Over the past five weeks they had shared a bed, true enough, but they'd also shared something else. A friendship. With him she had shared her innermost thoughts and feelings and he'd done likewise with her. A part of her would always love Patrick, but in her heart she knew she loved Wilson, as well. But considering the people they would eventually hurt in the long run, would they ever truly be happy knowing their happiness would cause others pain?

"Rita?"

She turned back to him. "Yes?"

"You do love me, too, don't you?"

She could lie and tell him that, no, she didn't love him, that it was nothing more than needing sex after a fifteen-year drought, and that would be it. But she couldn't hurt him like that, nor could she lie about her feelings for him. "Yes, I do love you, too."

The smile that spread across his face at that moment was priceless and he quickly crossed the room and pulled her into his arms, kissed her deeply. When he finally released her mouth, he whispered against her lips. "It will all work out and in the end, we will be together."

Somehow she believed him. She didn't want to think about all the obstacles they would face. Possibly the loss of love and respect from their children. And the torment of a woman who may not give up her husband so easily.

Rita heard her cell phone ring and glanced around for it, then remembered it had fallen under the bed earlier that day during one of her and Wilson's heated moments. She quickly pulled herself from his arms and scurried across the room to get it. The only two people who'd ever called her while she was on one of her trips were Lori or Brian, and a call from either of them could be important.

"Hello?"

"Mom, where are you?"

She heard the frantic tone in Brian's voice and glanced across the room at Wilson. "I'm in Japan. I told you I would be taking a few extra days and—"

"Did you receive a text message containing photos?"

She frowned. "No, at least not that I'm aware of. I was out of the room earlier, without my phone."

"Mom, check your messages."

She heard the anxiety in his tone. "Brian, what's going on? What's wrong?"

Wilson heard the anxiety in her voice as well and crossed

the room to stand beside her, giving her a questioning glance. She shrugged her shoulders.

"Just check to see if you received the photos."

She removed the BlackBerry from her ear and saw she had one message pending. *Pictures for Erica's special day.* She clicked on the caption and what flashed before her eyes almost made her drop the phone. "Oh, my God!"

"Rita, what's wrong? What's going on?" Wilson all but screamed and caught her when she almost lost her balance.

Instead of answering she covered her mouth with her hands and shoved the phone at him. He took it and saw what she'd seen and nearly gasped. He recovered his voice to ask in a deep, thundering sound, "Who the hell sent these?"

She couldn't find her voice to speak. Instead she dropped down on the bed when her head began spinning. Brian had seen them. She could imagine what he was thinking.

In her frantic state she heard Wilson speak into the phone. "Brian, who sent those pictures?"

Hearing Wilson Sanders's voice was like a knife to Brian's gut. He had wanted to believe a mistake had been made. Someone had used some sort of trick photography. Anything but what the photos conveyed. Now he knew no mistake had been made. Erica's father and his mother were together even now in Japan. Sharing the some hotel room. The thought of what they'd been doing was like a kick to his stomach. The man was married. His mother had allowed herself to be pulled into an adulterous relationship.

"Right now it really doesn't matter who sent them, Mr. Sanders. What matters is that besides me, Mom and you, those photos were also sent to Erica and Mrs. Sanders."

"Damn."

"I tried calling and couldn't reach anyone. I don't know what's going on and whether or not Erica and her mother have seen the photos. They were attending Erica's first bridal shower today."

He drew in a deep breath and then asked, "May I speak to my mom?"

Wilson glanced over at Rita, saw the look of shock and pain in the depths of her gaze. "Brian wants to talk to you." He handed her the phone and she took it.

"Brian?" she said in a shaky voice. "I—"

"No, Mom, please don't say anything now. There's nothing I want to hear you say right now. I'm going to continue to try to reach Erica and if I don't get her tonight, I'm going to catch the next flight out of here to Hattersville."

"I understand. Tell Erica..." She drew in a deep breath and glanced over at Wilson. He was holding her free hand in his. "I guess there's really nothing you can tell her from me, is there?"

"I doubt it. Good-bye, Mom." He then hung up the phone.

Wilson pulled her into his arms and she cried onto his chest. "Shh, everything will be all right."

She pulled out of his arms and glanced up at him. "No, everything won't be all right. Somehow we have to fix this. You need to leave and go home right now. Your family needs you."

"No, I won't leave you this way and—"

"No, please go. You need to be there for them."

"And what about you?"

Rita knew that was a question she could not answer at the moment and wondered if she ever would be able to do so.

Chapter Twenty

"How is she, Dr. Cobb?"

Ralph Cobb looked into Erica Sanders's distraught face. He'd always thought she was a lovely girl, and hated the fact that her mother would stop at nothing to manipulate her life.

Dr. Cobb shook his head. He had reached the conclusion that Karen Sanders had to be one cold and uncaring woman to use her daughter the way she intended to use her to get what she wanted. And Karen was willing to do just about anything to achieve her goal.

He had a good mind to tell Erica the truth but knew he could not. In that sense he was a coward. He knew Karen would make good her threat and he couldn't let that happen. Too much was at risk. He and Aggie had secrets that no one could find out about. They were secrets he would take to the grave with him. Karen didn't know about all of them but she knew enough, and what she knew could not only ruin him but his mistress, his wife and his sons.

"Dr. Cobb?"

He glanced back at the closed bedroom door. The one he'd just walked out of. The one where Karen Sanders was probably in bed smiling already in victory. She had instructed him what to do and what to say. He would lay it on thick. He would have to do so to achieve Karen's purpose.

"Come on, Erica. Let's go downstairs to the study. I've given your mother something to make her rest and we shouldn't disturb her." That was a bald-faced lie as he spoke it. The woman was probably in her room doing a tap dance across the floor.

"All right."

He let Erica lead the way down the stairs and he followed, feeling older than his sixty years. He had been married to his Loretta just as long as Wilson had been married to Karen. All four had been born and raised in Hattersville, all were from well-off families, all were tied to the founding fathers. His great-great-grandfather was the town's first doctor and there had been a Cobb to practice medicine there ever since. He looked forward to retiring next year when his son Sloan would step in and take his place. He smiled when he thought of Sloan. He was proud of him.

"Would you like something to drink, Dr. Cobb?"

Erica's question pulled his thoughts back to the situation at hand. She was fretting, worrying herself to death and really for nothing. Karen was healthy as a horse but he couldn't tell Erica that. He had to support the lie her mother wanted him to weave.

"No, I don't want anything to drink. I'm just glad I was home when you called. Lucky for you I'm right across the street."

Erica nodded. "How is she?"

Dr. Cobb shook his head. "Not good, I'm afraid. She went into shock."

"Is she still in shock?"

"Somewhat. I did get her to talk, though." He went silent, choosing his words carefully, not sure of what he should say and what he could say. "Your mother is a proud woman, Erica. Sometimes a little too proud. Unlike a lot of us whose families help found this town she's always taken that role seriously. If what she mumbled upstairs in her bedroom is true— if your father is having an affair with the mother of the guy you plan to marry—that can destroy her. Most women can walk away from a man and an affair. Your mother can't. Your father is her life. From the time she was born she was bred to believe they would be together forever, regardless."

Erica nodded.

"What your mother needs is to get away for a while. Leave here and go on a trip, a cruise would be nice. Go stay for a while at that place at Lake Tahoe that she and your father own. She can't be bothered by bad news of any kind."

He paused again. "She should have told you and your father this last year. I encouraged her to but she refused to do so."

Panic flared in Erica's eyes. "Told us what?"

"She has a heart condition and too much stress can take her away from here."

Erica's hand flew to her mouth to keep from crying out and her hand began to shake.

"Under normal circumstances I would suggest that your father be the one to take her away from here, but in light of what your mother just confided in me, I don't think that's a good idea."

"That means that I'll have to be there for her."

Dr. Cobb nodded sadly. "Yes, that's what it means. That will be a lot for you to carry on your shoulders, dear, but someone has to be there for her now. Your father's betrayal cut too deep for her. And if word gets out, that will make her a laughingstock of this town. Of course, I won't say anything. But there is the matter of your wedding."

Erica swallowed. "What about my wedding?"

"Considering everything, do you still want one? Having your father and that other woman there together might be too much for your mother, and I suggest you consider postponing it for now. Your mother needs as little stress on her as possible."

Dr. Cobb rubbed his bald head. Karen had wanted him to advise Erica that she should never consider the idea of marrying Brian Lawson and that such a thing could kill her mother. He refused to do that. He would not go that far and destroy all of Erica's dreams of a marriage filled with love. Already he could tell by the look in her eyes that the thought of even calling off her wedding plans was devastating. At that moment he despised Karen even more for being so damn heartless.

He patted Erica's hand as he stood up. "I know you have a lot of decisions to make so I'll leave you for now. Have you contacted your father?"

Erica shook her head as she fought back her tears. "No, I wanted to take care of Mom."

"Well, I think you need to at least let him know what happened here."

"Is Mom on medication for her heart?"

"Yes, I wrote her out a prescription last year. I checked and she needs to get a refill. I'll take care of it and drop them off here later today." They would be nothing more than sugar pills. Karen had pretty much thought of everything.

"Thanks, Dr. Cobb."

A half hour later, after the doctor had left and after checking to make sure her mother was still resting comfortably, Erica went back downstairs to stand at the window in the study to look out. She had awakened that morning the happiest woman on earth and now that happiness had been snatched away from her.

She glanced at her watch and wondered if the others had

gotten their copies of the pictures. She had checked her phone a few minutes ago and seen that both Brian and her father had tried calling her. After receiving those pictures she had turned off both her phone and her mother's phone, just in case there were more pictures where those had come from. She needed to return their calls but wasn't in the right frame of mind to do so. Her mother might prove to be difficult at times but she didn't deserve this. No married woman did. How long had the affair been going on? Was Rita the reason her father had increased his business trips? Brian had mentioned his mother had been going out of town a lot more, too.

She moved away from the window and suddenly went still when a thought struck her. Had Brian known about the affair and not told her? She closed her eyes and shook her head. She had to believe that wasn't true.

And who on earth had sent those photos? Evidently it was someone who wanted to destroy not only her life but her mother's life, as well. There was no doubt in her mind that her mother had rubbed a number of people the wrong way, and there were probably one or two who would like to take her down off her high horse a notch or two. But who would risk her mother's wrath and take the time to bother?

At the moment the identity of the person who sent the pictures wasn't important to her. Making sure her mother was taken care of us was, and she would do whatever she needed to do to make sure that happened.

Lori pulled off her earring as she placed the phone to her ear. "Hello?"

"Everybody knows."

Lori frowned. "Rita? I can barely hear you. What did you say?"

"I said everybody knows now. Someone sent pictures."

"Of you and Wilson?"

"Yes," Rita replied on a choked voice. "I made a mess of things. I was only thinking of my wants and needs and not Brian's. Now there's no telling what's going to happen. Erica probably hates me."

Lori moved to sit down in the nearest chair. "Honey, please calm down. Are you still in Japan?"

"No, I'm in New York at JFK, waiting to come home on my connecting flight. I have a three-hour layover."

Rita nodded. "Start at the beginning and tell me everything."

She did in a trembling voice and had to repeat some parts several times because of crying. "I have to be the most selfish woman on this earth."

"You're not, Karen Sanders is. You can't convince me that woman didn't have something to do with this," Lori said angrily.

"It doesn't matter. What Wilson and I did was wrong and the sad thing about it is that our children might have to pay for it."

Lori didn't say anything for a moment, listening to the heartrending tears through the phone line. Then she asked, "Have you talked to Brian any more?"

"I tried calling him but he's either away from the phone or not answering. I believe it's the latter. I could hear the hurt and disappointment in his voice. I let my son down, Lori. I let him down."

Lori knew there was nothing she could say that would convince Rita otherwise. Her best friend was hurting deeply. "What time does your flight come in?"

"Around ten tonight."

"I'll be at the airport to pick you up."

"No need. My car is parked there," Rita said. Her voice was on the verge of breaking again. She could barely hold back more tears.

"Doesn't matter. I'm picking you up and bringing you here. We can go pick up the car tomorrow."

"Lori, I—"

"No, Rita, we're doing things my way."

"Okay."

"And Rita, about Brian and Erica, there's something I think you and I both know."

"And what is that?"

"He loves her deeply and no matter what, he's not letting her go."

Chapter Twenty-One

Brian jumped the minute his phone rang and he snatched it off the table. "Hello."

"Brian, this is Erica."

He swallowed deeply. Her voice sounded so subdued and held none of the excitement it had that morning when she was looking forward to her first bridal shower. There was no need to ask if she'd opened the text message.

"How are you doing, baby?" he asked softly.

"It's doesn't matter how I'm doing. It's Mom I'm worried about."

"She knows?"

"Yes. She clicked on her text message within seconds of me doing mine. I was at the house with her when she did and she passed out."

"I'm sorry to hear that."

Anger she couldn't keep inside snapped and Erica lashed out. "Are you?"

"Of course I am. I wasn't your mother's favorite person but I wouldn't want anyone to go through pain."

"Too bad my father and *your* mother didn't think of that. Have you spoken to Rita?"

"Briefly." The last thing he would tell her was that her father and his mother were together when he had. "What about you? Have you spoken to your father?"

"No, and in my present mood I'm not looking forward to doing so, either. Mom is my major concern. The doctor said the best thing for her right now is to get away for a few months, go on a cruise or something, or go stay at their place at Lake Tahoe."

"That might be the best thing for your parents right now. For them to go away somewhere together and try to work things out."

"Dad isn't the one who'll be going with her Brian. I am."

"You're going?"

"Yes."

"When?"

"As soon as I can make the arrangements. Hopefully, less than a week from now. The sooner the better."

"But what about your bridal showers? All the activities that are planned before the wedding? Not to mention the wedding itself. It's only three weeks away."

She laughed harshly. "Seriously, Brian, do you honestly think our wedding can go on as planned? Get real. My father and your mother have been involved in an affair. That should give the people a lot to talk about at the wedding, don't you think? A wedding that I doubt my mother will even attend, which will only add to the titillating excitement. I'm sure your mother and my father might prefer things that way, but I don't plan to make them happy, thank you very much."

"What are you saying, Erica?"

"I'm saying until I can decide what I need to do about my mother there's no way I can marry you. The wedding will have to be postponed."

At least she hadn't said there would never be a wedding, he thought quickly, grateful for that at least. But he wasn't happy with any of it. "Fine, we don't have to have a lavish wedding per se, but there is no way you and I won't be getting married in three weeks! What happened is unfortunate, but it does not involve us. It's our parents' mess and we should let them deal with it."

"What! How can you say that?"

"Easily. We can't be held responsible for their behaviors or their issues. I understand you wanting to console your mother and—"

"No, you don't! Don't you think my mother has feelings? My parents have been married for almost thirty years."

And they must not have been all happy years or he wouldn't have cheated on her, he wanted to say but held back. Doing so would only make the situation worse than it was. She was hurt and he could feel her pain even through the phone.

And she was angry. However, he understood her anger more than she did. Her mother had flaws that hadn't been so well hidden. But her father, although not perfect, had always been her knight in shining armor. The one she'd always thought would never let her down. But he had. And he felt the same about his mother. She had let him down, too.

"I want to see you, Erica. I'm coming to Hattersville."

"No, I don't think that's a good idea. I'll call you later and we can talk then."

He felt like she was shutting him out, something she'd never done before. "I want to see you, baby. I *need* to see you."

Something in his voice must have pulled at her heart, a heart he wanted to believe he still had. "I want to see you, but I need to take care of Mom. Her doctor said she even has a heart condition she never told us about and she can't handle too much stress."

She paused and then added, "I'm not sure when Mom and I will be leaving or how long we'll be gone, Brian. I'll call and let you know where we are."

He didn't like the sound of that, but now was not the time to tell her just how he felt. When he talked to her again it would be face-to-face...in a few hours. "I'll talk to you later."

"Fine."

She hung up the phone without telling him good-bye.

Karen smiled as she shifted positions on her bed. She loved the fact that Erica had become the doting daughter. If Karen had known staging a fainting spell would accomplish it, she would have definitely done it sooner. Now if she added her daughter's obedience to the list she would be extremely happy. If she played her cards right, that also would happen soon.

Whatever Ralph told Erica had her daughter worried and that was a good thing. By now all intended parties should have gotten their copies of the pictures. She wished she could have been a fly on the wall in Wilson's hotel room.

She'd known just where he was and whom he was with. The men Jaye had hired to keep tabs on Wilson and his mistress had done a fantastic job. And she had selected eight of the best photos they had taken. Seeing them would have left little doubt in anyone's mind as to the nature of their relationship.

She closed her eyes when she heard Erica coming back up the stairs. A smile touched her lips as she thought about the performance she was about to give, one any soap opera director would be proud of.

She knew the moment Erica opened her bedroom door and slowly moved across the room on soft feet so as not to awaken her. Then she felt her daughter take her hand in hers and hold it as she sat in a chair she'd placed by the bed.

How touching.

She decided to pretend she was coming awake. She opened her eyes slowly, blinked a few times as if to bring everything before her into focus. "Erica?" And then as if she was awakening from a bad dream and couldn't face reality, she forced tears from her eyes. She could just imagine what her daughter thought of that, since she'd probably never seen her cry.

"No, Mom, please don't. Everything is going to be all right."

"How can you say that, Erica? Your father was with *that* woman. And just to think that I had convinced myself it was unfair not to at least try to like her, to get to know her. And all this time, she'd set her sights on Wilson. How could he do this to me? To our marriage?"

"Mom, don't think about it. Don't get yourself upset."

"How can I not think about it? How can I not be upset?"

She could tell by the expression on Erica's face that she had no idea what to say. So she continued on, milking it with everything she had. "Ralph thinks I should get away—take a cruise, go to the cabin on Lake Tahoe. Maybe that's a good idea, since I can't handle being the laughingstock in this town when word gets out."

Karen inwardly laughed. This was one of those rare times she didn't care what the people were going to say. She would have the last laugh after Erica and Griffin were married. She figured that on occasion a person had to make sacrifices now for the things she wanted to have later. Karen would gladly suffer through a scandal rather than risk Erica having children that weren't from the Hayes bloodline.

"I think what he suggested is a good idea, Mom."

"No telling who else received copies of those pictures. I wonder who sent them." *Like she didn't know.*

She was the one who had commandeered the entire thing. While in Cleveland visiting Blair she had gone to one of those places that sold prepaid cell phones. It was the easiest thing to do. No identification had been required. She had programmed the pictures into the card the night before. In just a quick few minutes out of Erica's sight when she had gone upstairs to change her shoes, she had pushed the button and sent the pictures on their way. Modern technology was truly amazing.

"I'll start making plans to leave sometime next week and I won't let your father talk me out of going. Right now I'm not sure I'll ever forgive him. I can't wait to hear what he has to say."

Erica nodded. "Where do you want to go?"

"Anywhere except here for a while. You will have to finalize your wedding plans and the wedding without me."

Erica sat on the side of the bed facing her mother. "Do you honestly think I'll get married now?"

Karen tried not to smile. "What about all those plans?"

"They can wait. I've already talked to Brian and we're going to postpone the wedding for a while."

Postpone the wedding! She almost lost it. *Postponing the wedding wasn't good enough.* "Just so you know, I could never accept him as a son-in-law now, after what his mother and your father did. Every time I see that woman, I will remember, and you can't convince me that Brian didn't know about it. I will never trust either of them again."

"Brian didn't know."

"How can you be so sure of that?" Karen asked in a seemingly disturbed voice. "You could have been betrayed like I was."

"Mom, calm down. Don't get upset."

"Well, I am upset. My marriage has been destroyed and you're still thinking about marrying the man whose mother is responsible."

"Mom…"

She pulled away from Erica. "Go away. Please go away. Marry him if you want, just leave me alone."

And then she began sobbing in earnest while thinking that if this little over-the-top emotional scene didn't get to her daughter, break her down real good, then nothing would.

Erica poured the tea her mother hadn't finished drinking into the sink and leaned against it to get her bearings. Karen had made it pretty clear that she would not accept a marriage between her and Brian in three weeks, or ever. How could her mother expect her to give up the man she loved? Granted, what had happened was serious and she was willing to postpone things for a while...but to give him up totally, cut him completely out of her life, was something she could not do.

She turned and covered her face in her hands, trying to fight back her tears. The thought of not ever having Brian in her life was just too much.

She jumped when she heard her cell phone go off and wondered if it was Brian calling. She wasn't ready to talk to him again just yet. She had enough to deal with. But then, she thought the caller could be her father and she had to talk to him sooner or later. She couldn't dodge his calls forever. Although she wasn't sure what she would say to him. She loved him but resented the hurt and pain he had caused her mother and herself. It was unfair.

She quickly crossed the room, took a deep breath and picked up her phone. "Yes?"

"Hey, what's up?" April asked in a cheery voice.

At the sound of her best friend's voice the tears Erica had fought back came flooding through.

Chapter Twenty-Two

"I smell a rat."

After Erica had explained the whole situation to April, she hadn't expected that reaction from her friend. "What are you saying?" she asked.

"Think about it, Erica. Who benefits the most if you and Brian don't marry?"

"I hope you're not insinuating what I think you are," Erica said in an irritated tone.

"I am," April said boldly. "Your mother never wanted you to marry Brian and would do just about anything to keep the two of you apart. It wouldn't surprise me if she planned the whole thing."

"Oh, yeah, go ahead and blame my mother for everything now," Erica said, almost raising her voice while throwing up her hands. "I'm sure she had a lot of fun forcing my dad and Mrs. Lawson to sleep together. Just like I'm sure she's going to love the embarrassment when word gets out as to why I'm postponing my wedding. You know my mom, April. You know how she prides herself on being above any scandal."

"What I believe and what I know is that she would seize any opportunity to keep you and Brian apart so she can get Griffin back in the picture."

"April, you know as well as I that that won't be happening."

"But you know as well as I that your mother still hasn't gotten that point yet, and she never will until you marry Brian. So yes, Erica, I wouldn't put it past her to do anything to make sure that doesn't happen."

Erica nearly bit the inside of her mouth to keep from screaming out at her friend. She had it all wrong about her mother this time. "Look, I'm ending this conversation now before I say something I might regret."

"All I know is that someone sent those pictures, and until I can come up with someone else who wants you and Brian not to marry then it makes good sense to me for your mother to be the prime suspect," April said, not backing down on her theory.

"But Brian and I are still getting married," Erica broke in to say. "Our wedding will be postponed, not cancelled."

"Not if your mom has anything to do with it."

"Look, I have to go. I have to check on my mother."

"Where's your dad?"

"He's on a business trip and I haven't talked to him. But he did leave a voice message on my phone saying he'll be arriving around midnight."

"You need to let your parents work things out, Erica. It's between them," April said. "It's no different than if you and Brian were married and your parents interfered in one of your arguments with him. What happened is really your parents' business and not yours," she added.

Erica ran her fingers through her hair, a good indication she was getting angrier by the minute. April sounded too much like Brian to suit her. "I happen not to agree with you on that, April. If anything were to happen to my mother I would never forgive myself. Look, I love you, and I'll talk with you later."

"Erica," April called out.

But she had hung up the phone.

"Brian?"

When Brian entered the airport's terminal, he turned at the sound of his name being called, recognizing the voice immediately. "Mom?"

He then glanced at the woman by his mother's side. "Goddy," he greeted, calling his godmother Lori the named he'd called her since he learned to talk.

He then glanced back at his mother as numerous emotions tore into his insides. He loved her as deeply as a son could love a mother and he'd always been proud of the strong, self-assured and confident woman she was. A woman who, after losing her husband, had become a single mother and devoted all her time and attention to her son. But the one thing that was rushing fast and furious through his head at that moment was that his mother's recent actions could cost him the love of his life.

He had tried convincing Erica that their parents' affair didn't concern them, but even he was finding it hard to separate the two while standing here right now and seeing the look of remorse in her gaze. The same question was still ramming through his mind. *What could she and Mr. Sanders have been thinking?*

"You're leaving town?" his mother asked him in a soft tone.

"Yes. I was able to get a last-minute flight to Hattersville." He figured he didn't have to go into any great explanations as to why.

"Will we be able to talk when you get back?"

He drew in a long deep breath. Although he'd rather not, he realized they had to do so. Maybe then she could answer that question presently ramming through his mind. "Yes, I think we should."

She hesitated before asking, "And how is Erica?"

Brian arched a brow. "Shouldn't you be asking how Erica's mother is doing? But that's right. Neither you or Wilson really cared about Karen's feelings, did you?"

"Brian…"

"No, Mom, I'd rather not discuss anything here. Besides, I need to go catch my flight. I need to try to convince Erica not to postpone our wedding. We'll talk when I get back."

Without saying anything else, he turned and moved quickly toward his gate.

For as long as Erica could remember, she'd always gotten filled with excitement at the sound of her father returning home from a day at the office or a business trip. Unfortunately, this was not one of those times. She tossed aside the magazine she was reading when she heard the front door opening and closing.

She had checked on her mother earlier and found her resting. Whether it was peacefully or not, she wasn't sure. Karen's eyes were closed and Erica could only surmise that she was asleep. Her father's last voice mail message said he wouldn't be arriving until after midnight and the clock on the wall indicated he'd been right.

For years she and her mother had suggested that he purchase a private jet for the company, so he could come and go when he pleased without being dependent on commercial airlines. But he'd flatly refused saying it was a luxury he didn't need and that he actually enjoyed spanning the globe like a regular person. Now she couldn't help wondering if perhaps Rita weren't his first affair and not having a private

jet had made things easier for him. Employees had a tendency
to talk.

Moving toward the door, she walked out of the study at the
same time he dropped his luggage in the foyer and glanced
her way. Surprisingly, if he was harboring any guilt she didn't
see it. But then she wasn't sure she would recognize it in him
anyway, since it was something she'd never suspected before.

"Dad," she greeted as calmly as she could.

"Erica."

"Where's your mother?"

"Upstairs sleeping."

He nodded and moved toward her. "Is there somewhere
we can talk privately?"

"At this point, Dad, I'm not sure there is anything you can
say."

She saw a flash of something in the dark depths of his eyes.
It wasn't guilt but hurt. How dare he let what she'd said hurt
him after what he'd done.

"Please. Don't shut me out, Erica."

"What do you expect?"

"Your respect, for starters. And then your ability to be fair
and not judgmental."

She pushed her hair back from her face. "Are you saying
those pictures that were sent aren't real? That you and Rita
are not having an affair?"

He met her eyes and without a waver in his gaze, he said,
"Those pictures are real and yes, Rita and I are having an
affair."

Erica had known all along, but hearing him admit it so
easily without a tinge of regret or remorse in his voice was
like a slap to her face.

"Then what can you honestly say to me, Dad? Besides, it's
not me you need to explain things to, it's Mom. However,
I'm warning you not to upset her any more than she's already

upset. She passed out and I called Dr. Cobb. He's given her something to make her rest. He also told me something— Mom has a heart condition she's been keeping from the two of us and shouldn't get stressed out in any way. He suggested that she go on an extended trip someplace. I've discussed it with her and she wants to do a twelve-day cruise and from there spend a month or so at the cabin in Lake Tahoe. I'm going with her."

Wilson raised a brow. "But what about your wedding?"

"I've called it off. At least for now."

"Erica, please don't let what I did keep you from marrying Brian."

She drew in a deep breath. "How can I not, Dad? Thanks to you and Rita, Mom is more against the wedding than before."

"But what happened is between me and your mother. It doesn't involve you."

She frowned. That was the same thing Brian and April were saying—she disagreed with them and she disagreed with him. "You're wrong, Dad. It does involve me because you and the mother of the man I'm engaged to marry hurt my mother in the worst possible way. Not only did the two of you betray her but you also betrayed me and Brian. At least I assume Brian didn't know. Maybe Mom is right and he knew all along what you and Rita were doing."

Wilson's features hardened. "Don't let you mother intentionally put a wedge between you and Brian by filling your head up with foolishness, Erica."

"Are you saying Brian didn't know?"

"Yes, that's what I'm saying."

Her sigh was one of heartfelt relief. She doubted she would have been able to handle it had Brian known and not shared it with her. "I'm leaving now, but I'll return in the morning to check on Mom. And remember what I said about her heart condition. Dr. Cobb doesn't want her any more upset than she already is."

Before her father could say anything else, she moved past him and slipped out of the front door.

Chapter Twenty-Three

When Brian didn't get an answer, he used his key to unlock the door to Erica's home and immediately entered the security code to shut off the alarm. He then glanced around. Not only did the house look empty, it felt empty, as well.

Deciding to do what he normally did whenever he showed up, which was to make himself at home, he carried his overnight bag into the bedroom and began unpacking.

He had slid off his shoes and was leaving her bedroom in socked feet when he heard Erica's car. His heart began beating fast. She would see the rental car parked out front and know he was here. Would she ask him to leave or would she be glad to see him? He'd never before had to question what her reaction would be to seeing him.

Knowing she would be coming in through her garage, he moved toward the kitchen and was leaning in the doorway that separated the kitchen from the dining room when she turned the key in the lock and walked inside.

She glanced over at him after closing the door behind her, and for a few moments they just stood there, staring at each other across the room. He couldn't stop his gaze from roaming over her and the male in him couldn't help but appreciate what he saw.

His gaze traveled back to her face and he saw she'd been checking him out, too.

As they continued to stare at each other he knew her well enough to know that deep inside she was wrestling with her indecision as to what to do with him. He'd been able to tell by a sudden flash that had appeared her in eyes that she was glad to see him, but was afraid to let herself admit it.

"Why did you come, Brian?" she finally asked.

"I told you I would."

"Yes, but I thought you'd know…" Her words dragged off and she looked past him to the painting on the wall. The one of the pier on Myrtle Beach. Her chest was rising and falling with every breath she took, and it seemed as if her breathing was labored, as if there were knotted muscles in her chest.

"That you preferred I not come because you didn't want me here." He decided to finish for her.

Her gaze snapped back to his as if appalled by his words. "That's not true. And it isn't fair for you to say that."

"Then what is true, Erica?" he asked in a low tone. "And you tell me what's fair? Is it fair for you to decide that a day we've looked forward to for six months is being called off because of something our parents did?"

She stiffened her spine. "You're deliberately making this difficult."

"What I'm really trying to do is make it damn impossible," he said, straightening up his tall frame and slowly moving toward her. "I refuse to allow you to let our parents' behavior come between us."

"You don't understand. I know my mother isn't the easiest person to get along with, but all she has is me."

"Fine, be the daughter she needs but don't be the daughter

she knows she can manipulate," he said, coming to a stop in front of her. "I guess she doesn't like any of the Lawsons about now, and I can respect that. But what I can't and won't accept is you allowing her to poison your mind against me, the man you love and will marry, whether she accepts it or not."

He reached out and cradled her face in the palms of his hands. "I love you, Erica, and I refuse to let your parents or my mother come between us."

Brian then lowered his mouth to hers and knew the exact moment her stiffened spine began to ease and her body melted like pure butter against his. A shudder passed through him and he wrapped his arms around her as their bodies continued to meld together.

He also knew the exact moment she began returning his kiss, mating her mouth ardently with his. Slowly and determinedly he kissed her, letting her know in this sensual exchange just what she meant to him and how much love he had in his heart and in his soul for her.

He wished he could erase the past twelve hours from his mind and from hers, but he knew he couldn't. However, it wasn't in the forefront and that was enough for now. The only thing his thoughts were centered on was the woman in his arms. Fully and completely.

Moments later he pulled his mouth from hers and his gaze automatically drifted downward to the fullness of her lips, still moist from their kiss. And as he watched them, they moved in a soundless appeal. "Make love to me, Brian."

Before she could release her next breath, he swooped her into his arms and headed for the bedroom.

She needed him tonight.

That was the foremost thought on Erica's mind when Brian placed her on the bed and stood back to begin removing his clothes. He would spend hours and hours making love to her first with a tenderness that would bring tears to her eyes and then with a hot, primitive rhythm, that would have her begging for more. It was always that way with them and she knew tonight would not be any different.

He had taken off his shirt, tossed it aside and was now standing there, broad shouldered, heavy muscled and bare chested, fidgeting with the belt on his jeans and looking sexier than any man had a right to look.

A part of her hadn't wanted him to come but then another part was glad that he had. Her mother wanted her not only to postpone the wedding but to give him up completely. She knew it was the pain of all that had happened that was making Karen issue such demands, but the declaration had hurt nonetheless. The thought of never having Brian in her life was too depressing to think about, too mind-boggling to consider.

He was now totally naked and the lamp's light illuminated his dark skin, sculpted muscles and the deep set of his dark eyes, staring at her with a hunger that she felt all the way to the pit of her stomach. Her inner muscles clenched in response and she could feel her panties getting wet just from his intense gaze. It was tantalizingly heated and when he suddenly took a swipe of his bottom lip with the tip of his tongue, she knew that before the night was over, he would lick every inch of her body.

"You want me to take off my clothes?"

The question she asked was a needless one since she knew just how much he enjoyed watching her strip.

He only nodded while watching her with eyes filled with both love and lust.

Pulling up on her haunches she slowly removed her blouse and tossed it aside, then took off her bra. She saw the heated lust flare in his eyes when he lowered his gaze to her chest and saw the fullness of the twin globes before him. He'd always complimented her on her breasts, always said they could make him hard just thinking about all the things he could do to them.

And he was getting hard. His body was responding right before her eyes, as his gaze appeared glued to her breasts. His stare was like a physical caress, a raw and naked hunger that she could actually feel. There seemed to be a strong electrical current in the room, one that was crackling all over her body, making certain areas sensitive and achy.

Her gaze traveled down his body to concentrate on his manhood. Looking down at such an extraordinary male object—one of her most ardent desires—she could distinctly remember the taste of him and the memory literally made the area between her legs throb. Shifting down on her hips, she kicked off her sandals to remove her slacks and her barely-there panties soon followed. And there she was, fully exposed to his hungry eyes and she actually trembled in response to them.

He moved toward the bed, walking toward her with the confidence of a man who not only knew what he wanted but who also intended to get it. She had no problem with that. She was his and would always be so.

And in response to her lover, the man who had her heart, who owned every bit of her soul, her body became a mass of aching need and she lifted her arms to receive him and together they tumbled back onto the bed coverings, mouths connecting and bodies entwined.

Her legs parted automatically and he eased between them, the head of his manhood hungrily seeking out what it wanted and needed; teasing her by sliding back and forth across the slick folds of her labia and driving her to the brink of imminent pleasure.

He kissed her so intensely she moaned deep in her throat,

and he molded his mouth to hers as if it belonged and reminded her without any shame that it did. And his mouth
wasn't the only thing doing the reminding. His hands were
everywhere, probing between her legs, caressing her thighs,
stroking her breasts and sending thrills of pleasure through
every part of her body.

He pulled his mouth from hers and went for her breasts,
devouring the nipples as if the tips were made of his favorite
candy, making her groan with every lick of his tongue. She
leaned into him, made her body even more accessible to his
mouth and he took full advantage.

"Brian!"

With the sound of his name from her lips he slid inside of
her, the head of his penis causing her to shudder as it made
its journey deeper inside of her. Her inner muscles began to
contract, squeezing everything out of him before he could get
started good.

And good was what she knew she would get. She drew in
a deep breath as she felt him enlarge even more, sending an
unbearable need skyrocketing inside of her. She closed her
eyes as sensations began building at the sole of her feet and
moved upward with the force of a tidal wave.

"Look at me, Erica. Look into the face of your mate, your
lover, your future husband, the father of every baby you're
going to have. The man who will die his last breath loving
you."

She opened her eyes and the gaze that snarled hers almost
snatched her breath in the process. He was all those things.
He would be all those things and more. And when his body
began moving, thrusting into her, stroking the pleasure out
of her, she couldn't do anything but hold fast to that gaze and
groan.

They'd made love countless times but never like this.
Never with a hunger, a need, a demand that seemed fueled by

something neither of them could explain. Tonight her mother had tried making her choose between them, which was something she could not and would not do. Brian was her heart and there was no way she could let him go.

But then her mother needed her. How could she turn her back on her?

She pushed the thought to the back of her mind as Brian continued to make love to her, forcing her to savor everything he was giving her and still want more. And then he lifted her hips and shifted his body, hitting a spot inside of her that literally ripped a strangled cry from deep in her throat. His thrusts hardened, his strokes deepened into penetration as profound as any could get, and when she tightened her legs around his waist to lock him inside of her, she felt the moment his body bucked and could feel the hot semen being shot inside of her. Deep into her womb, which she felt to the core.

She screamed as pleasure of the most intense kind overtook her, overtook them, snatched them together and plunged them in the most gratifying waters known to man. As he continued to thrust inside of her, shoot his release inside of her, she could only groan his name over and over, while she begged him not to stop.

And he didn't.

He kept going and going and she could only hold on, clutching his shoulders, wrapping her arms around him, and telling him over and over how much she loved him, how much she needed him. For now. For always. And she knew when it was all said and done, although she didn't want to, she would have to choose, and heaven help her, there was no way she could not choose love.

There was no way she could not choose him.

"Baby, please don't cry anymore. I can't stand to hear you cry like this. Everything is going to be all right." Brian tried whispering soothingly in Erica's ear. After they'd made love and he'd held her in his arms, the dam broke. Tears began coming and they wouldn't seem to stop. So all he could do was hold her, stroke her back and whisper how much he loved her.

She pulled away from his chest. "But I'm going to lose you. I know I am and I couldn't handle it if I did. But Mom needs me now."

He bit down on his lip, trying not to growl out and ask about his needs. He needed her in his life, as his wife, his best friend. He wanted to build a life with her, start making all those babies they wanted to have. It wasn't fair. Life wasn't fair.

"Tell me, sweetheart, what you need me to do and I'll do it. Just don't cry anymore. Please don't. You're making yourself sick. You won't lose me. Ever."

She searched his eyes as if she needed to see in them the truth of his words.

"Tell me, Erica, what do you need from me? If you truly believe postponing the wedding for a while and going away with your mother is what you need to do, then do it. I'll be okay with it."

She swiped at her tears. "You won't like it."

"No, I won't like it but if it's something you think you need to do, I'll give my support. But then I don't want to lose you, either."

She reached up and cradled his face between her open palms. "You could never lose me."

"If your mother has anything to do with it, I will. You do know that she probably is going to try to convince you to move on without me, don't you?"

She nodded. "Yes, but I can't move on without you. I love you. You're my heart."

"And you are mine and I love you, too. So damn much," he said, caressing her cheek with the back of his hand.

For a while, the bedroom was deathly quiet, except for the sound of their breathing. Then he said, "You know we'll have to confront our parents about what they did. We're going to have to be fair to them, Erica."

She lifted her chin. "Fair! We don't owe them anything, Brian. They're the reason I'm not getting married in three weeks. I'm not sure I'll be able to forgive them for that."

He didn't say anything, knowing she felt that way now but eventually would come around. She adored her father just as much as he adored his mother. They'd made mistakes, he could accept that, but still, he wanted to know how it had happened, why it happened. His mother hadn't been involved with a man since his father's death. How and why had she gotten involved with Wilson Sanders?

"There are going to be stipulations regarding us, though," he then spoke up and said.

She wiped away more tears as she glanced up him. "What kind of stipulations?"

A small smile touched his lips although his heart was literally breaking at the thought she was going away on an extended trip with a woman who hated his guts and would probably use every turn to convince Erica she was better off without him. "That you keep in touch regularly. That way I know you're missing me."

She smiled faintly. "I will be missing you and I will marry you when I get back. Not the huge elegant wedding we have planned now, but—"

"Hell, I don't care how it's done as long as it's done," he interrupted. "By Thanksgiving."

She nodded in agreement. "Yes, by Thanksgiving."

"No matter what."

"Yes, no matter what. I promise," she said, wrapping her

arms around him. "Thanks for giving me time to help Mom through this, Brian. It means a lot to me."

He pulled her to him and held her, knowing their separation would be a test of the worst kind. He hoped their love would be strong enough to withstand all the betrayal, deceit and manipulation he had a feeling would be hurled at them.

All he knew was that he loved her and would never give her up.

Chapter Twenty-Four

"Well, well, the whoremonger has returned. Did you bring your slut back with you?"

Wilson turned when Karen entered the kitchen, wincing at her words. She had a right to be angry, but there was no reason for getting down-in-the-gutter nasty. It didn't become her. "Karen. And how are you?"

Her face contorted in more anger. "How am I? How do you think I am after finding out about your affair?"

He crossed his arms over his chest as he leaned back against the kitchen cabinet. "Don't pretend you care about me having an affair when you gave me the go-ahead to indulge in one years ago. When you stopped being a wife to me."

"Is that all you men think about? Getting between a pair of women's legs?"

"No, companionship is nice, too. Having someone to talk to, do things with. Having someone there for you. But you refused to do those things and be those things over twenty years ago and I never was unfaithful to you."

"Then why now?"

He couldn't help but give her a genuine smile. He could answer that question easily. "Because I finally met someone I truly like." He came close to also adding, *Someone I love.*

"Well, your timing on this one was awful, Wilson. And you're right, I really don't give a damn that you're sleeping with another woman. But I refuse to let you behave so deplorably with a woman I will be interacting with on occasion. But then, your thoughtlessness has given me what I wanted. In a way it worked out in my favor."

He lifted a brow, not sure where she was going with this. "What do you mean?"

"There's no way Erica will marry Brian now."

He heard the finality in her voice and couldn't help but smile. "Don't fool yourself on that, Karen. Erica loves Brian and she will not let anything come between them. Not you, me or Rita."

A smile hovered on her lips. "I beg to differ."

It was the sound of her voice at that moment that made him think there was something going on here. He decided to play his hunch. "Who sent those pictures to everyone, Karen?"

"How would I know? Evidently you and your mistress got sloppy."

"No, I don't think so," he said, moving across the room to her. "I hope this isn't something you concocted to—"

"To do what, Wilson? I didn't force you to sleep with Rita Lawson. But you did, without thinking of how it would look to me or your daughter. Rita might have been your first fling, however, I doubt, since you've gotten a taste of a woman after all these years, that she will be your last. That doesn't concern me."

"Because you think you're going to get what you want out of this, don't you?"

She chuckled. "I have no idea what you're talking about

and it doesn't matter. Our lives are what they are. You're not going anywhere and neither am I. The only fool in all of this is Rita Lawson. What did you do? Promise to leave me for her? You and I know that won't be happening."

She was so sure of herself, he thought. So sure of him. "Not this time, Karen."

She lifted a brow. "Not this time, what?"

"I refuse to let you manipulate me in whatever game you're playing. I want a divorce."

She seemed truly shocked. "A divorce?"

"Yes. We haven't had a real marriage in years. I thought I could live with that, but I can't."

"You have no choice."

Now it was he who smiled. "Yes, I do."

She stiffened her spine. "If you leave me for her, Erica will hate you. I'll see to it."

"I'm not going to let your threats keep me from living a happy life, Karen. I met a woman that I can truly enjoy life with and I intend to do just that. And I'm going to believe that our daughter will realize what you're doing. One day she will discover just what a mean, hateful, vindictive and manipulating person you are. When she does, then she will hate you. Is that what you want?"

Karen flinched. "That won't happen."

"For your sake, you better hope that it doesn't. I won't waste my time telling Erica my suspicions because she probably won't believe me, considering everything. But eventually, she will find out the truth about you. There are some secrets that can't be hidden forever."

Without having anything else to say, he walked out of the kitchen.

April glanced across the table at Griffin. Surprising her, he had shown up a few hours ago and she was glad to see him.

He had whisked her off to her favorite L.A. restaurant and
she hadn't wasted time before telling him that Erica was postponing the wedding and the reason she was doing so. Considering the ice queen—*Griffin's words, not hers*—that Wilson
was married to, he wasn't taken aback to learn the man was
involved in an affair.

Griffin had shaken his head sadly and said his own father
was still holding the lead as the man to have the most affairs
in Hattersville, and that there was no telling how many illegitimate children his old man could rightfully claim but
chose not to do so. April hadn't wanted to admit that she'd
heard Herbert Hayes had had a problem keeping his pants
zipped over the years.

"I think Erica is pretty upset with me," she said after taking
a sip of her tea.

Griffin glanced over at her. "That was coming down hard
to accuse her mother of setting the whole thing up."

"But who else would have benefited from it? I'm not saying
she did it herself, but I bet she arranged it all. Everything is
too pat. She's my prime suspect because for her everything
will fall perfectly into place."

Griffin met her gaze. "I disagree. They will only fall into
place if Erica allows herself to be manipulated."

"And you."

He lifted a brow. "Me?"

"Yes. I still think her sole purpose is to get you and Erica
together."

He chuckled. "It's not happening. And I think you might
be wrong about Karen Sanders this time. I wouldn't put some
things past her but I'm just not sure about this one. Mainly
because when word gets out that Mr. Sanders had an affair, it
will evolve into a scandal, which is something she wouldn't
want to deal with. She's not *that* desperate to get me and Erica
together."

"But what if she is?" April implored.

"Even if she does believe in that Hayes–Delbert curse and is convinced the only way to break it is for me and Erica to marry, it takes two to tango. That's one dance neither of us is willing to do, so it would be a waste of time on her part."

"I don't know, Griffin. I just have a funny feeling about the whole thing."

He reached across the table and captured her hand in his. "Hey, don't worry about it. Even if she managed to manipulate Erica, which I doubt she can do, she still has to try her wiles on me and she can't do it. I'm not in love with Erica. I love you, baby."

A myriad of sensations raced through April's stomach. She had needed to hear him say those words while looking in her eyes. She needed to see the intensity in the dark depths, the passion, the desire and more than anything, the love. And she saw all of it and was tempted to pinch herself to make sure she wasn't dreaming.

"And I love you, Griffin."

He squeezed her hand before releasing it and gave her one hell of a sexy smile. "So, now that Erica's wedding has been postponed, when are you going to tell her about us?"

Nerves skittered through her. "I'm not sure."

He glanced at her over the rim of his coffee cup. "Is there a reason you want to continue to wait? And please don't tell me it has something to do with your theory about Mrs. Sanders. If you truly believe that, then the sooner we let her and everyone else know about us, the better off we'll be. Then she'll know for certain that my future is set...with you."

"Yes, but..."

"But what?"

"Erica is going through a lot right now."

"And what does that have to do with us, April?"

She drew in a deep breath, not knowing what she could

tell him. It really didn't have anything to do with them and, knowing Erica, she would be happy for them. However, that crazy feeling she had just wouldn't go away.

"Nothing, really, but I prefer not telling her until she gets back. She's going on an extended trip with her mother. Dr. Cobb feels she needs to get away for a while."

"How long will she be gone?"

"Not sure. First they're doing a twelve-day cruise and then they plan to stay at their place on Lake Tahoe. Erica said something about being gone for almost six weeks."

"That's a long time."

"Yes, but I think they're hoping the scandal will have died down by then."

He took a sip of his coffee. "And they're sure there will be one? What if the only persons getting those texted pictures are the four of them? I wouldn't think anyone would want to spread that story."

"Yes, but once word gets out that Erica has put off her wedding everyone will wonder why."

"Then don't put it off."

April rolled her eyes. "Can you honestly see Mr. and Mrs. Sanders standing alongside of Brian's mother in a receiving line?"

"It would be rather strained," he said.

"To say the least."

Griffin checked his watch. "Do you want to take a walk on the beach before we head back to your place?"

She gave him a huge smile. "That's a wonderful idea. Let's do it."

"All right."

He always made even the simplest things such a joy whenever he came to town. She appreciated every single thing about him and he liked telling her every chance he got that he was hers. Other than Nana, and her friendship with Erica, she'd never felt anyone or anything was truly hers before. He was making her believe that dreams did come true and that she deserved love and happiness in her life like everyone else. And that she didn't have to settle for less.

Now if she could get rid of this nagging fear that it was all a dream and one day she would wake up and he would be gone, that she had only imagined the whole thing, or even worse, that someone would come between them and tear them apart.

Her prayer every night was that it wouldn't happen but her nagging fear just wouldn't go away.

Chapter Twenty-Five

Erica opened the door to find her father standing there. "Dad? What are you doing here?"

"You've been avoiding me. May I come in?"

It was on the tip of her tongue to tell him that she didn't want him to come in, but for some reason she couldn't do that. And he was right. She had been avoiding him.

It had been five days since those pictures had been sent, and all the arrangements had been made. She and her mother would be leaving in the morning to fly to Barcelona for a twelve-day Mediterranean cruise. Then they would spend an entire month at Lake Tahoe.

She and Brian talked every night and, now that they had officially postponed their wedding and sent notices informing family and friends of their decision, phone calls had begun coming in. Everyone wanted to know the reason but she had refused to go into any details.

She let her father in, closing the door behind him. "I really don't know why you came, Dad. You've admitted to the affair and as far as I'm concerned there is no excuse for what you and Ms. Lawson have done," she said. "And now to think she is breaking up your marriage. Mom told me you've asked her for a divorce and—"

"Oh, come on, Erica, you've known the state of our marriage for years. Your mother and I were existing in a loveless marriage. I had made up in my mind to ask Karen for a divorce even before meeting Rita, but decided to wait until after your wedding."

Erica crossed her arms over her chest. "And that's supposed to make what you did right?"

"No, but for once I wanted to know how it felt to love and be loved in return."

She dropped her arms and her mouth practically fell open. "Are you saying you love Rita and she supposedly loves you?"

"Yes. Although she's willing to end things between us. She figures you and Brian will never accept us being together and that we've caused you and him too much pain."

"What about the pain you've caused Mom?"

"Your mother has been aware of the state of our marriage for years and—"

"Of course you want me to believe she gave you her blessings to go ahead and indulge in affairs. She said you would probably try to convince me of something so ridiculous. She also told me she suspected you of other affairs in the past, but she didn't want to believe it. What do you have to say about that?"

"Your mother is filling your head with lies."

"Then what's the truth?"

"In all my thirty years I've never been unfaithful to your mother."

"Until now?"

"Yes, until now. I'm not going to divulge the personal business between your mother and me because it really doesn't concern you, Erica. All I'm asking is that you believe that this affair with Rita was my first and it wasn't just a fling. I love Rita and, yes, if she will have me and I hope that she will, I want to spend the rest of my days with her. And yes, I am divorcing your mother to make that happen. I know it all looks bad, but there's nothing I can really do about it because I don't intend to give Rita up."

He paused for a moment and then said in a softer tone. "For once I am happy. Truly happy. You'll never know how it was to wake up in the morning knowing my sixtieth birthday was around the corner and realizing that I didn't know the meaning of love. Now I wake up every morning with a reason to be happy. And if that makes me a terrible person, I'm sorry. I endured a loveless marriage for thirty years and I don't plan to continue doing so."

He moved to the door and before reaching it, he turned around. "Your mother has already started manipulating you, Erica. I regret that you can't see what she's doing."

Erica narrowed her gaze. "No one is manipulating me, Dad. And what I see, which you so clearly explained yourself, is that you want to divorce my mother to marry another woman."

Silence followed and then without saying anything else, her father opened the door and walked out.

Rita moved around her home wondering how she would approach her son and what she would say when she finally spoke to him. She had called his office and he'd been in meetings. She had left her name but he had yet to return her calls. In the past, a day hadn't gone by without him checking on her, calling to talk to her, but now...

She drew in a deep breath and was heading toward the kitchen when her phone rang. Hoping it was Brian she quickly moved across the room and picked it up without noticing the caller ID.

"Hello?"

"Rita, baby, I need to see you."

She almost dropped the phone and hearing the sound of Wilson's voice made emotions she'd tried keeping at bay come rushing to the forefront. She covered her face with her hand and fought back the sob that erupted in the back of her throat. He was the last person she needed to talk to now. Wilson Sanders was her weakness. He was the one man, after all these years, that she had fallen in love with. But he belonged to someone else. Why had it been so easy for her to forget that?

"I can't talk to you, Wilson. We can't continue what we started. And we can't see each other. Brian is hurting because Erica has called off the wedding and he blames me. And he has every right to do so."

"No he doesn't, and stop blaming yourself, Rita. And I refuse to let anyone take away the happiness I am just discovering I can feel with you. Brian and Erica will get married eventually. You and I both know that."

"Will they? Can we be so sure of that? Your wife hates anyone with the last name of Lawson and I have a feeling she will do anything to make sure a wedding doesn't take place, just to spite me. To spite us."

"Then we need to make sure that doesn't happen. I asked Karen for a divorce and—"

"No!" The hand flew from her face and she nearly dropped the phone again. "You should not have done that."

"You're wrong, sweetheart. I should have done it years ago."

"But our children, Wilson."

"They will eventually come around and accept our love

for each other, Rita. I don't want you to regret falling in love with me."

Rita dropped down on the sofa. His words tore at her heart. "I don't regret it."

"And never start regretting it, no matter what. We're in this together, sweetheart. And I refuse to let you go."

Rita shook her head. He had no choice but to let her go. "I can't believe this has happened. I thought we were being discreet. How on earth did someone take those pictures? Who took them?"

"I have a feeling about those pictures. Personally, I think Karen was behind them and made sure they were sent to expose us. Right now I don't put anything past her and that's why I need to talk to Brian."

"No, please don't. At least not now. He's going through some things and prefers not being bothered and—"

"He hasn't talked to you about this?"

Tears Rita tried holding back fell down her cheek. "No, but that's okay. I understand and—"

"Well, hell, I don't understand. This should not involve our kids, but Karen went out of her way to make sure that it did. Erica and Karen left today for a six-week trip. I see what she's doing, if no one else does—especially Erica, who refuses to question her mother's motives right now."

"And what do you think Karen is doing?"

"Trying to keep Erica and Brian apart and Brian can't let that happen."

"If she thinks she can do that then she really doesn't know my son."

"Yes, but still, I need to talk to him."

"Please, not now, Wilson. Give him some time, which is what I'm doing. I have to believe that he'll come around. I have to believe that."

"And he will, just like I believe the same thing of Erica.

Karen thinks she has everything well planned but there's something she has overlooked and sadly knows nothing about."

"What?"

"Love and the power behind it. I think in the end she's going to be in for a rude awakening."

Rita drew in a deep breath when she glanced out her living room window and saw Brian's car pull into the driveway. As glad as she was that he had finally come to see her, she wasn't sure how the meeting between them would pan out. Both Wilson and Lori thought she was making a mistake to put his happiness above her own, but that's exactly what she would do. There was no way she would let her behavior with Wilson cause him more misery.

She moved toward the door when the doorbell sounded, willing to do whatever it took to repair her relationship with her son. "Brian," she said, opening the door and then stepping back to let him in.

"Mom."

"I was just about to eat dinner. You're welcome to join me if you like."

"No, thanks. I just came to talk. I promise not to take up much of your time."

He could never take up her time, she thought, and her heart ached that he assumed that he could. "All right, let's sit in the living room."

She kept her eyes on him as they walked to the sofa. He looked like he hadn't gotten much sleep, and he'd lost weight, as well. Not much, but enough where a mother would notice. They'd always had a close relationship, even when Patrick was alive, and then when they'd lost the man they'd considered their rock, the bond between them had thickened even more.

The thought that that bond had broken caused a pain to swell within her chest.

She decided to cut to the chase. "How's Erica?" she asked.

He drew in a deep breath. "I assume she's fine. She and her mother left on a trip today." He paused a moment. "I'm sure you know by now that the wedding has been postponed."

"Yes, Wilson told me."

Brian's brow lifted. "So you and Mr. Sanders are still communicating with each other?"

She heard the accusing tone whether he intended for her to or not. And she would not lie to him about her relationship with Wilson. "Yes."

Brian stared at her for a long moment and she wished she could read his thoughts. He then leaned forward in his chair, resting his elbows on his thighs while pinning her with his deep gaze. "Will you tell me something, Mom?"

"Yes, anything you want to know." And she meant it. Although the conversation may end up being painful and embarrassing, she would be forthcoming. He deserved that.

"Why Mr. Sanders? You hadn't dated anyone since Dad died. So why him? Especially when you knew he's a married man and it was no secret how Mrs. Sanders felt about Erica marrying me."

She clasped her hands in her lap and stared down at them for a moment wondering how she would answer his question. She didn't expect him to accept her behavior but she needed him to understand it.

She raised her head and met his gaze. There was only one answer she could give him. "Because I fell in love with him."

He looked shocked, as if her answer was out of left field, beyond the scope of his comprehension at the moment. He simply sat there and stared at her.

She cleared her throat. "I know it's probably hard for you

to understand how such a thing could happen, and it's not that I wanted it to happen. Like you said he is a married man and I wanted to respect that."

"But you didn't."

She flinched at his mocking tone. He was right, she didn't. "No, but I tried. However, I saw something in Wilson besides the warm, caring person that he is. I saw a man who deserved to be loved and who deserved to know how it felt to love."

She paused a moment before continuing. "I know that's no excuse for what I did, for what we did, but it happened. And now…it's over between us."

Brian shifted in his chair again. "But you said you loved him."

"I do and I won't take that back. But loving him is causing others pain and I can't let that happen."

"Are you aware that he's asked Karen for a divorce?"

She nodded. "Yes, but he had planned to do that anyway, before he even met me. However, he wanted to wait until after the wedding. I am not the cause of their divorce."

"She's saying that you are."

"Then she is wrong."

Brian looked at her with dark eyes that were so much like Patrick's. "You say you love him, yet you're giving him up," he said. "Because of me and Erica?"

She smiled slightly when she felt a single tear fall from her eye. "Yes, but then I never should have had him in the first place. What I did was wrong and I admit that. What I should have done was wait until he was a free man."

"And had he come to you a 'free' man you would have gotten involved with him?"

"Yes, because I'd fallen in love with him."

When Brian didn't say anything but sat there for a long while, she finally asked, "Is there anything else you want to ask me about the situation?"

"Yes, do you believe that he loves you?"

She lifted her chin and met his direct, penetrating gaze. She saw no point in telling him that Wilson had told her several times that he did, and she believed him every time he'd whispered the words to her. She knew in her heart that Wilson loved her as much as she loved him. But this was one time love wouldn't be enough.

"Mom?"

She swallowed hard. "It doesn't matter if he does or not."

Brian stood up and she tilted her head to look up at him. When he reached out his hand to her, she took it and he gently tugged her to her feet, as well. She felt the strength in the hands that held hers and she appreciated it at that moment.

"I think it will matter, Mom, especially if what you believe about his feelings for you are true. I've told Erica that what happened between Wilson and you doesn't concern us, and eventually she'll see that it doesn't. You and Wilson have to live your lives, like Erica and I have to live ours. You're my mother and I will always love you, no matter what."

His words caused a rush of breath from Rita's lungs and she leaned warily against him, lowering her head to his chest when she felt more tears fall from her eyes. Her son was a man she was proud of. He loved her no matter what and she couldn't ask for more than that.

When he wrapped his arms around her, she couldn't help but let even more tears fall. Right now she needed his strength and he was unselfishly giving it.

She lifted her head and gazed up at him through wet lashes. "I'm sorry for hurting you and for letting you down," she whispered brokenly.

He shook his head. "Something I've realized since meeting Erica is that love makes no demands, it provides no ultimatums and it refuses to accept any regrets. What it does is embrace life and promise happiness even when you're going through the worst part of a storm. There will be better and brighter days at the end."

She swiped at her eyes. "You actually believe that?"

He smiled as he tucked a loose strand of hair behind her ear. "Yes, Mom, I actually believe that."

She couldn't decide if her son was a romantic, a realist or a revolutionist. And at that particular moment, for her it truly didn't matter. She wanted to believe what he said and decided that she would.

Chapter Twenty-Six

"Are you all right, Erica?

Erica forced a smile on her lips as she placed her book down in her lap. "I'm fine, Mom, why do you ask?"

Karen shrugged her shoulders. "You seem annoyed about something."

Erica shook her head. "No, I'm fine."

She resumed reading her book while thinking what she'd told her mother just now was a bald-faced lie if ever there was one. She wasn't fine. It had been three days and she had yet to talk to Brian. For some reason she couldn't get a connection on the ship and a message said his phone was blocked from receiving international calls. Why would he place such a restriction on his phone when he knew she was out of the country? That didn't make sense.

"I feel bad that you're stuck here with me. I can tell you're not enjoying yourself."

Erica glanced over the top of the book to her mother again. They were relaxing on deck, stretched out in loungers. The ocean was beautiful and the weather perfect. But her mother was right. She was not enjoying herself. This was supposed to have been the week before her wedding.

"I'm fine, Mom."

"No, you're not. It was selfish of me to suggest that you come along. If anything, I could have suggested you bring one of your friends. Verne Gamble probably would have loved to join us."

Erica all but rolled her eyes. Verne was not her friend anymore. As kids they might have been buddies, but that changed when they reached high school and Verne ran neck and neck with her mother in the snobbery department. At least Erica would have thought that a few days ago, but she could see the changes in her mother. She hadn't said anything unkind about anyone so far on this trip and seemed to be relaxed, calm and enjoying herself. In fact, neither her father's, Rita's nor Brian's names had been mentioned. It was as if they had been completely obliterated from her mother's mind. Maybe for now that was a good thing.

And Erica went out of her way not to bring them up, fearing a relapse.

"I think I'm going to the cabin to lie down for a while," her mother said. "We have a full day tomorrow when we pull into port in Alexandria. I can't wait. I would think you'd be excited, too."

"I am excited, Mom. I just want to finish my book."

"Well, don't stay out here too much longer, sweetie."

"I won't." Erica forced another smile as her mother left for her cabin. Erica was grateful to be alone.

"Excuse me, is this lounger taken?"

Erica glanced up and smiled at a woman who appeared to be her age. She'd seen her a number of times on ship over the past week with a handsome man. And since she was wearing a wedding ring, she assumed the man was her husband. "Not anymore. Help yourself."

"Thanks."

Erica went back to reading her book and a short while later she couldn't help overhearing the woman's conversation on her mobile. She was talking to someone in Oregon. How was she able to phone the States on her mobile phone when Erica could not?

She placed her book down and pulled her mobile phone from her tote bag and dialed Brian's number, not caring that it was probably the middle of the night in Texas. When she still couldn't get a signal, she breathed out her frustration in a heavy sigh.

"Are you okay?"

Erica glanced over at the woman. "Yes, and sorry, I didn't mean to disturb you just now."

"Oh, you didn't."

"Have you been having trouble calling the States on your cell phone?"

The woman smiled. "No, thank goodness. I left my little boy with my parents and I usually call them two and three times a day." She chuckled. "They're probably tired of me checking in with them so often and wish I would have trouble calling. Why? Are you having problems?"

"Yes. I haven't been able to place a single call off this ship with my cell phone."

The woman frowned. "That's odd. If there's someone you need to call you can use mine."

Erica shook her head. "I can't do that."

"Sure you can. My husband, Pete, works for an internet provider and all my calls are free. Here, go ahead and use it. And I'm Summer, by the way."

"And I'm Erica."

Erica stared at the phone Summer was holding out to her like it was a big juicy steak that she was trying to decide if she should really have. Knowing she probably couldn't last another day without at least hearing Brian's voice, she quickly took the phone out of Summer's hand. A huge smile spread across her lips. "Thanks."

She then punched in Brian's number and held her breath hoping that her call would go through.

Brian leaned against his kitchen counter at two in the morning nursing a cold beer while gazing into space. Most people who woke up in the middle of the night went for a glass of milk. He'd needed something a hell of a lot stronger and was glad he'd decided to work at home tomorrow. If another person tried finding out why he was postponing his wedding he was liable to throw something. Hell, maybe throwing something wasn't such a bad idea. And on top of that, this was the third day in a row that he hadn't been able to sleep and blamed Erica.

Why hadn't she called him?

His mind was conjuring up many reasons and none of them were any good right now. Had Mrs. Sanders convinced her not to marry him after all? He shook his head, refusing to believe Erica would let her mother manipulate her to that point. But he couldn't underestimate Karen Sanders. He had agreed to give Erica time to deal with her mother, but she had agreed to keep in touch. So why hadn't she?

Hell, he'd gotten used to hearing her voice every night and the sex talks they would share. He'd even gotten used to them using a webcam in ways few people probably thought about. He couldn't help but smile at the memories that began floating around in his mind.

Damn, he missed her.

He was about to take another swig of beer when his phone rang.

"Hello."

"Brian!"

"Erica! Why haven't you called, baby?" he asked, so glad to hear her voice.

"I've tried. Every day," Erica said. "For some reason my calls won't go through and you have an international block on your phone. I'm using someone else's phone now."

He frowned. "I don't have an international block on my phone. Why would I when I knew you would be calling?"

"I wondered the same thing. You might want to check with your phone company tomorrow."

"I will. When will you be in port?"

"Tomorrow. We dock in Alexandria in the morning and we'll be there for two days."

"Buy another cell phone while you're there. There has to be something wrong with yours. God, I miss you baby."

"I miss you, too."

"How's your mother?"

"Fine. She hasn't said anything about anyone and in a way that's a good thing. Hopefully she's been thinking."

"We can only hope good thoughts."

"Lay off my mom, Brian. She's going through a rough time right now. The next thing you know, you'll be blaming her for us not being able to reach each other."

He chuckled. "That hadn't crossed my mind."

She grinned. "Yeah, right. Look, I have to go. Like I said, I'm using someone else's phone but I'll buy a spare in Alexandria and call you tomorrow."

"Okay, and I love you."

"I love you, too. We'll talk tomorrow."

"I'm looking forward to it, baby."

When the call ended Brian felt a deep ache in his heart. He wouldn't be satisfied until Erica was finally his wife.

Karen clicked on her phone. "You have some news for me, Jaye?"

"Yes, I do," Jaye said. "Some good and some bad."

Karen sat on the side of the bed. "Tell me the bad first. I left Erica out on deck and she might come in any second. She can't figure out why she can't make outside calls from the ship."

"It wasn't easy working that out by putting those blocks in place. I had inside help at the phone company," he said.

"Whatever works. Now, tell me the bad news."

"Griffin Hayes is involved with someone."

Karen made a sound of disgust. "How serious is it?"

"I'm not sure. It seems they're keeping the affair hush-hush for now, but he goes out of his way to spend a lot of time with her, every chance he gets, and if I were to guess, I'd think things were pretty serious."

Karen stood and began pacing the room. This wasn't good. In order for her plan to work both Erica and Griffin couldn't be involved with others. "Do whatever you need to do to break them up."

"That's not going to be easy. He seems taken with her. Besides, it might raise suspicions if we messed up both Erica's and Griffin's relationships. It would need to look coincidental and not planned."

Karen tapped her sandaled foot on the floor, annoyed. "Who is she?"

"A hometown girl who happens to be Erica's close friend. April North."

Karen nearly dropped the phone. "April North!"

"Yes. Do you think Erica is aware they're dating?"

"Who knows? Even if she knew she would probably give them her blessings. How dare that poor, worthless slut think she's suitable for Griffin Hayes. I gave Griffin better sense than that. He wants a political career. Doesn't he know messing around with someone from the Fifth Ward is political suicide?"

For a moment Karen didn't say anything as she thought of

a plan. She smiled before saying, "I'll take care of it. Now, what's the good news?"

"I might be able to get to Brian by using one of the female attorneys in his office who I hear has the hots for him anyway. I'll give you the lowdown after I work out all the details."

Karen nodded. "I'm counting on you."

"Trust me, Karen. For the money you're paying me I won't let you down."

Chapter Twenty-Seven

"You seem to be in a good mood today, Erica."

Erica glanced over at her mother and smiled. "It's a beautiful day and we're visiting a beautiful country. Why wouldn't I be in a good mood?"

Karen shrugged. "I don't know. You acted so down in the dumps yesterday."

Erica knew that was true, but talking to Brian yesterday had definitely brightened her spirits, though there was no way she would tell her mother that. She would probably freak out at the mere mention of Brian's name. "I was, but now I'm fine." That's all she intended to say on the matter.

They had shopped at several stores before Erica noticed a phone store across the street. "I need to go into that shop over there."

Karen lifted a brow. "Why?"

"Because I haven't been able to make calls on my phone for some reason. I met a lady whose phone is working fine so I figured there must be something wrong with mine."

"Is that really necessary?"

Erica glanced over at her mom. "Is what really necessary?"

"That you communicate with the outside world. I'm trying to forget anyone on the other side of the ocean exists right now."

Erica understood her wanting to do that, considering everything. "That might be fine for you, but it's not for me, Mom. There are people I need to communicate with."

There. She would let her mother draw her own conclusions from that.

"And how is April these days?"

Erica lifted a surprised brow. Her mother was asking about April? This was a first. "Last time I talked to her she was fine."

"She's not on husband number four yet?"

Erica couldn't help but smile. "No. In fact she's not seriously involved with anyone." Her mother didn't know that April liked to joke about having male friends with benefits.

When her mother didn't say anything, Erica glanced over at her. "Why the interest in April?"

Karen shrugged. "Umm, maybe I was too hard on her all those years. She has become someone famous."

Erica nodded, surprised with her mother's admission. "Yes, she has." She then drew in a deep breath. Was her mother changing her ways and perceptions about people? If so, it was long overdue.

Rita walked off the elevator and toward her office. She had met Lori for lunch at one of the cafés downtown and they'd talked about Brian's visit.

That her son supported her was a load off her back, especially in light of the nightly phone calls she received from Wilson. He was still determined to divorce Karen and had consulted an attorney. However, his attorney had warned him that Karen could make things ugly and probably wouldn't hesitate to name Rita as the reason for the divorce.

"Rita!"

She glanced around and met one of her coworker's smiling faces. "Yes, Janet?"

"Have you been to your office yet?" Janet asked in an excited tone.

Rita lifted a brow. "Not since this morning. Why?"

Janet's smile widened even more. "Well, prepare yourself, honey."

"For what?"

"You'll see."

Rita increased her pace as she moved toward her office. The pleasant scent of flowers eased through her nostrils the moment she opened the door. She couldn't help but gasp in surprise at the beautiful arrangement of roses on her desk. There had to be over a hundred and all in various colors just like a rainbow.

She closed the door and wondered who else had seen them being delivered. News traveled fast on this floor.

She moved toward her desk and pulled off the card and silently read it:

Rita, you have become the sunshine of my life. If I could bottle it and present it to you, then I would. I hope you accept these instead. Flowers of the rainbow. They represent the love I know in my heart. I will love you forever.
—W.S.

Rita stood there and reread the card over and over again while tears filled her eyes. During every conversation she had with Wilson she would tell him to just forget about her. And during each of these talks he would tell her that he could not and would not. They had agreed to keep their distance until his divorce was final, but she knew that he'd made plans to move out of his house by the time Karen returned.

She held the card tight to her chest. She didn't like the thought of being a home wrecker, the other woman, but she did love him so much. Moving around her desk, she slipped the card into her purse. She would have it close to read it when she felt so alone and was missing him like crazy. At night was the hardest, when she would remember their stolen hours together. At least that was something Karen could never take away from them.

She had sat down in her chair when her phone rang. She quickly reached out and picked it up. "Rita Lawson."

"How would you like to go out to dinner with me to-night?"

She smiled upon hearing Brian's voice. "I'd love to."

Donna Hardy looked up when the mailroom guy dropped an envelope addressed to her on her desk. She unfolded the crisp white letter and gasped after reading the typewritten note.

I know about your scandalous affair with Judge Mead-ows. If you don't want this information sent to your boss, then meet me tonight at Stella's Bar and Grill, six o'clock sharp.
—A friend

Fuming, Donna stood and walked over to the window. Who knew about her relationship with Judge Meadows? She always made sure she was discreet when visiting his office. A friend wouldn't do this her, so who had sent her the letter? Who would want to ruin her?

She had a good mind to call the authorities but knew she couldn't do so. News of her affair with Judge Meadows could destroy her career. Fine, she would meet with this person tonight to see what he or she wanted with her and why she was being targeted.

Chapter Twenty-Eight

Donna decided to arrive at Stella's early and sit in the back to check out the place and see if she recognized anyone who entered.

She glanced at her watch before looking around the establishment once again. Two women sat at the bar, several couples at tables, and a man at a corner table was pecking away on his laptop. She recognized none of them.

She got the waitress's attention for a refill on her drink and continued to wait. She had cancelled her sex session with Judge Meadows and he hadn't been at all pleased about it. He was beginning to get on her last nerve with his horny self.

"May I join you?"

She nearly jumped out of her skin. She had been so busy staring at the entrance that she hadn't noticed that the man with the laptop had gotten up. At that moment a knot tightened in her stomach.

She swallowed thickly. "Why would you want to join me?" she asked coolly, not liking the vibes she was getting from him.

The smile he then gave her nearly made her flesh crawl. "We have a meeting planned. Let me introduce myself. I'm your friend."

Jaye pulled out a chair and sat down. He thought Donna Hardy was even prettier up close, but there was no doubt in his mind that this was one lady he had to watch. Lethal. At no time could he ever let her assume she had the upper hand. Any man who did so was a fool. He would tell her what he wanted and give her no choice in the matter.

"Who are you?"

He smiled over at her and the dark angry eyes staring back didn't bother him one bit. She was at his mercy and not the opposite. "I told you. I'm your friend."

"What is this about?"

"It's about you and Brian Lawson."

He saw surprise flicker in her eyes. "Brian Lawson? You must have me mistaken for someone else. The only thing between me and Brian is that he's my boss and, if you don't already know, he's getting married."

"Not if you have anything to do with it."

She lifted a brow. "What do you mean?"

He leaned back in his chair. "What I mean is that although the wedding has now been postponed, I want to make sure there will never be a wedding."

Her gaze widened with curiosity. "Why?"

"I have my reasons and you shouldn't concern yourself with them. All you need to do is deliver what I want."

"And if I don't?"

He chuckled as he took a sip of the drink he'd brought to the table with him. "And if you don't, then everyone at the office will know what a slut you are. And I wouldn't hesitate to post your secrets all over the internet."

She sat up straight in her chair, her face flaming in anger.

"I would not only sue you but I'd handle your case and win."

He shook his head and laughed. "Sweetheart, there's no way you could win with the amount of dirt I've got on you." At her surprised blink he said, "Just do what you're told." He stood. "I'll be in touch." He then walked off, whistling as he exited the bar.

Later that night Jaye contacted Karen. Once again he had some good news and he had some bad news. The good news was the update he had to give her on his meeting with Donna Hardy. He was convinced the woman would do whatever they needed her to do.

However, the bad news was that his sources had reported that Griffin had purchased an engagement ring and the likely recipient was April North. Of course Karen was furious and said they would need to move up their timetable.

The more Jaye talked to Karen the more he was convinced that she would do anything to make sure both Griffin and Erica were free to eventually marry each other.

As he undressed for bed that night he shrugged, deciding if there was something else driving her obsession he was better off not knowing. Over the past three months he'd determined that his mother's cousin wasn't playing with a full deck…but she was paying him a lot of money and that meant he would do whatever she wanted him to do.

Little did she know he would do her dirty work, but in the long run it would cost her for him to keep quiet.

He smiled, thinking that in a few years he would be able to retire, and not only that, with the videos and photographs he had of Donna Hardy, she would want to keep him pretty happy, as well.

He chuckled. Life was good.

Chapter Twenty-Nine

"Guess who I talked to today?"

Erica glanced over at her mother. They had returned to the States and were now at the Sanders's cabin on Lake Tahoe. As a child she'd always liked it here and this had always been one of her favorite pastimes, sitting in the backyard watching all the beautiful boats that went by.

"Who did you hear from today, Mom?" Erica figured it probably was too much to hope for that her father had called. Neither she nor her mother had heard from him since they'd left home and that had been almost two weeks ago. She figured he was probably too busy getting the divorce off the ground.

"Marnita. Surely you remember her."

Erica searched her brain for a few moments before finally remembering. "Your friend from college who lives in Wyoming?"

"Yes, that's the one. Her husband died a few years ago and she's invited me to come visit her for a few days. I figured that would give you a break from me for a while. You might want to go visit April in California while I'm gone."

She glanced over at her mother, trying to keep the happiness out of her face. Was she really suggesting she visit with April? Umm, at that moment an idea popped into her head. She would let her mother assume she was visiting April in L.A. but instead she would catch a plane to Dallas and see Brian.

God, she missed him. Although after purchasing another phone in Alexandria she had been able to talk to him more, she needed to see him.

"Well, what do you think?"

She smiled. "I think that's a wonderful idea, Mom, and I appreciate your thinking of it."

"It's the least I can do. You have been spending a lot of time with me and all. I feel bad you're doing it."

"I've enjoyed our time together," she said. The only thing she regretted was that she hadn't mentioned Brian to her mother at all. In a way she felt bad that her mother hadn't suggested she go visit Brian instead of April. It was as if Karen intended to wipe Brian from her memory and refused to acknowledge that he still existed.

"Then it's settled. I'm going to leave day after tomorrow to visit Marnita for a few days and you're going to visit with April. This should be fun and is probably something we both need."

Erica couldn't help but smile. Yes, seeing Brian was definitely something she needed.

"Are you sure of your plan, Karen?"

Karen stood at the window and watched Erica standing near the water. Every so often she would stick her toe in and then snatch it back out. Erica was in a good mood, and had been ever since she'd suggested she go visit with April. But

Karen knew her daughter well enough to know where she would be going instead.

"Yes, Jaye, I deliberately eavesdropped on her conversation with April a little while ago when she thought I was taking a nap. April is in Los Angeles like you said, but Erica has already purchased a ticket to Dallas. She's going to surprise Brian and show up on Wednesday. And while she's headed for Texas, my flight is taking me to L.A. to deal with April."

"Are you sure you want to meet with April yourself? You've been letting me handle everything so that no one would know about your involvement. What if April goes back and tells Erica about your visit? She might put two and two together and—"

"It won't happen, trust me," Karen said, smiling. "I know something about April that she will want kept a secret and I will do so if she gives me what I want."

"Which is for her to get out of Griffin's life," Jaye said.

"Precisely."

"And are you sure you won't run into Griffin while you're visiting with April?"

Karen eased down in the chair. "Positive. I talked to his mother earlier today, and she mentioned that Griffin is home this weekend."

She unfolded a sheet of paper. "I have Erica's flight information for Wednesday. I'm depending on you to make sure when she returns here that there's nothing left of the relationship between her and Brian that can be salvaged."

Donna was silent as she listened to the male voice on the other end of the phone.

"Erica Sanders will be arriving at Brian Lawson's house around two o'clock that day. It's my guess since it's a surprise that she will come straight from the airport and let herself in."

"It's a gated community. They won't let her in," Donna said, trying to get out of whatever she was being forced to do.

"According to my sources, her name is approved on security's registry and she has a key to let herself in. I need you to arrive before she gets there and do your thing. By the time Brian arrives I want you to have painted a picture so condemning she won't believe a thing he says."

Donna nibbled at her bottom lip. She didn't want to do it but she had no choice. "And you sure there's nothing that will link anything back to me?"

"Not unless you get sloppy with what you need to do and I suggest that you don't. Do we understand each other, Donna?"

She drew in a deep breath, again wondering who didn't want Brian to marry his fiancée to the point they would go through all this trouble to make sure they were kept apart. "Yes, we understand each other."

The phone then clicked dead in her ear.

"Hello."

A chagrined look touched Griffin's features at the sound of the sleepy voice. "Oops. Sorry, I assumed you would still be up. Did I wake you up, sweetheart?" California was two hours behind Ohio, which meant it was only eight o'clock there.

"I would have been up had it not been such a grueling day. But I always love hearing from you, just like I love you."

Griffin couldn't help but smile. Now that he and April had declared their love for each other, these were the happiest days of his life. He only wished she would give in and let him be open about their relationship. But he figured next weekend would change that. He intended to ask her to marry him. And if she said yes, there was no way he would continue to keep her a secret.

"And I love you," he said. "I wish I was there with you this week."

"You had things to do, I understand," she said. "Besides, with this new makeup campaign, I've been getting up at the crack of dawn for shoots. We're still on for next weekend, right?"

"Definitely." He wouldn't spoil his surprise by telling her just how *on* they were. The game plan was for him to arrive in L.A., spend the night and then whisk her off to a bungalow in Australia's outback that was owned by a business associate of his.

"Get some rest, baby. You're going to need it for next week," he said and chuckled.

"I think I'll give you the same warning."

"Warning taken."

When he hung up the phone half an hour later, he snuggled beneath the bedcovers thinking that one day he wouldn't sleep each night alone in this bed anymore. He couldn't wait.

Chapter Thirty

Erica felt elated as she entered Brian's home. She couldn't wait to see the look on his face when he came home from work. She had thought about telling him she was coming and then decided to surprise him, although he would probably figure out she was here when he saw the rental car in his driveway.

She and her mother had two more weeks at Lake Tahoe and then there would be no reason she and Brian couldn't reschedule their wedding. They needed to talk about it while she was here for a few days.

And she had decided to meet with Rita while she was here, too, and get a grip on the other woman's relationship with her father. Angry that her father hadn't at least tried to contact them, she had called him from the airport to tell him exactly what she'd thought of his insensitive behavior, only to be told by him that he had indeed tried calling both her and her mother several times. Her mother had outright refused to talk to him, told him not to call back, and he'd said for some reason he couldn't get through on her line.

She really wasn't surprised her mother hadn't mentioned that her father had tried calling them on the cruise. Karen had been perfectly happy letting Erica assume he had basically written them off.

Pulling her carry-on luggage behind her, she moved up the stairs. The first thing she was going to do was unpack and then she would start preparing Brian's favorite meal. Unless he worked late at the office she could expect him home in a few hours and she wanted everything ready. She smiled, thinking she would greet him at the door wearing the sexy nightie she'd purchased at an airport shop. Brian would definitely like that.

She couldn't help but envision how her night with Brian would pan out. She intended to stay until Sunday night, returning to Lake Tahoe before her mother did on Monday evening. Hopefully the glow would have worn off her face by then.

The scent of Allure met her nostrils the moment she opened Brian's bedroom door. She glanced around the room and felt a sickening lump in her stomach. Brian's bed was unmade, which for him was not uncommon, but she knew he stayed on his side of the bed—unless he was sharing it with someone. It was plain to see the way bedcovers were strewn all over the place that there had been two bodies in this bed.

She pulled in a deep breath, refusing to jump to any conclusions, but the heavy scent of Allure that swept through her nostrils was making that hard to do. Whoever had been in this room wore that fragrance. Leaving her carry-on by the door, like a person in shock she slowly moved to the center of the room. There had to be a reason why his clothes were tossed carelessly on the floor.

She picked up his dress shirt and blinked back tears at the red lipstick stain she saw on the collar. A strangled sound of pain caught in her throat. He hadn't known she was coming. Had he been playing her for a fool all this time?

She closed her eyes and shook her head not wanting to believe what was so clearly in front of her. A man and a woman had shared that bed, and the woman wore Allure. She then recalled the last time she had come into contact with that particular fragrance.

The jogger, the woman who was another lawyer at Brian's firm, wore it. Her name was Donna Hardy. Erica had warned Brian about her. Had the woman played on Brian's moment of weakness? Her blood began boiling at the mere thought, the very possibility.

She closed her eyes and placed her hands over her ears as if to shut out all the damaging evidence that was going through her mind, but the moment she opened her eyes and uncovered her ears, she saw that nothing that was wrong had changed. She refused to believe that Brian had been playing her from the beginning. He had loved her. He did love her. The mere thought that he didn't was too much to bear.

She wanted to go back to her earlier assumptions that that Donna woman had gotten to him in a weak moment, but even if that was true Erica doubted she could forgive him for what he'd done. He had destroyed her faith and her trust totally.

She stood and wrapped her arms around herself, feeling pain in every part of her body. Knowing she needed to leave, that she couldn't remain in the perfume-drenched bedroom a moment longer, she went to the door and, taking hold of her carry-on luggage, she beat a hasty retreat down the stairs, with anger raging out of every single pore.

She headed for the door and something made her stop. Maybe it was her love for him, and that part of her that refused to believe what she'd seen and wanted to believe there had to be a reason for it. Maybe he hadn't slept here last night. What if he had loaned his house to one of his friends? More than one woman could wear Allure. She just refused to believe the worst of the man she intended to marry one day. The man who had promised to love her forever and she thought would never be unfaithful to her.

Deciding he deserved a day in court no matter how damaging things might look, she parked her carry-on at the foot of the stairs and moved toward the sofa. She would wait for Brian to come home as she'd originally planned and then she would ask him to explain.

She moved toward the sofa and stopped when she saw a piece of red cloth sticking out between the cushions. She quickly strode over to the sofa and snatched up the panties that had almost gotten buried between the cushions. Panties monogrammed with the initial *D*.

She threw the panties down and then dropped on the sofa. Feeling the pain of a broken heart, not only in her chest but in every part of her body, she buried her face in her hands and cried.

With an inward sigh April kicked off her shoes as she walked out of her bedroom. She appreciated the fact that the makeup shoot had ended early today and she would spend the rest of the day relaxing. A soak in her Jacuzzi sounded nice for later, but first she needed to go into the kitchen and find something to eat.

Moments later she was in the middle of preparing a salad when her intercom went off. She wiped her hands on a kitchen towel and she moved across the room to answer it. "Yes, Denny?" she greeted her doorman.

"There's someone to see you. A Ms. Sanders."

April blinked. Why was Erica in Los Angeles when she should be in Dallas by now? What could have happened to make her change her plans? "Yes, please let her come up."

April placed the salad in the refrigerator and quickly moved to the door when she heard the doorbell. She hurriedly snatched it opened and gasped in disbelief, almost losing her balance in shock. "Mrs. Sanders! What are you doing here?"

Without waiting for an invitation to come inside, the woman walked past April then turned around with a cold look on her face. "It's time that we have a talk, April."

The minute Brian opened the door to his condo, he found it hard to believe his eyes. Erica had consumed his mind and thoughts all day, and now she was here. But instead of the sexy greeting he expected, she crossed the room and pounced on him.

"How could you do this to me? To us? I loved you! I trusted you!"

A shocked Brian reached out to grab Erica's hand before it could make contact with his face. "Erica, what are you doing here? What's wrong? Why are you upset?"

She snatched his hand from hers. "Like you don't know. I arrived today to surprise you and I found out about your little tryst. How could you do this to us, Brian? How could you?"

"What are you talking about?" he demanded furiously, not knowing what the hell she was talking about.

"This!" she said, hurling a piece of fabric in his face. "Remember these?"

The item fell to the floor and he reached down and picked them up. Ladies panties? He glanced back at her, confused. "What are you accusing me of, Erica?"

She placed her hands on her hips. Fire was blazing in her eyes. He had never seen her this angry before. "You tell me, Brian. I found them sticking out of your sofa cushions. Do you want to tell me who they belong to?"

He stiffened visibly. "If they were stuffed under my sofa

then I would assume they are yours, Erica. The last time you were here we made love on that sofa several times, or have you forgotten?"

"They aren't mine," she almost screamed. "I would not wear panties monogrammed with the initial *D*. So tell me, Brian. Who do they belong to? And as you're trying to come up with a name, you might as well tell me why a woman's perfume is all over your room, who slept in the bed with you last night and whose red lipstick is on your shirt collar on the floor in your bedroom."

He looked at her like she'd lost her mind. "No one slept in my bed last night and there is no fragrance in my room other than my aftershave and there is no red lipstick on my shirt in my room." He hadn't made his bed this morning, but there definitely hadn't been any perfume on anything and his white shirt had gotten tossed in the laundry bin as usual. What the hell was she talking about?

"Come on, Erica, let's go up to my bedroom and you can show me what you think you saw."

"What I *think* I saw? Oh, so now you want me to believe I'm crazy and that I'm imagining things?"

"No, that's not it at all, but if things are like you say then there has to be a reason for it. One I don't know about, like those panties. If they aren't yours then I truly don't know who they belong to."

"I don't believe you!"

He stared at her incredulously and then anger seeped into his body. "How in hell can you say that you don't believe me when I've never given you reason to doubt my love or my honesty? What kind of crazy thoughts has your mother been feeding you these past three weeks?"

"My mother has nothing to do with this. She hasn't mentioned you and she thinks I'm visiting April in L.A. I lied to her to come here."

He crossed his arms over his chest. "Why would you have to lie to your mother to come see me? You're a grown woman who doesn't need permission to come see the man you're supposed to love."

She glared thunderously at him. "Please don't try shifting the blame from you to me. My mother had nothing to do with me finding out the man I'd planned to marry is screwing around on me. I know what I found here today, Brian. And you can have this back because there won't be a wedding!"

She pulled off her engagement ring and threw it at him, hitting him on the cheek before it fell to the floor. He grabbed her before she could get out of his reach and jerked her to him.

"I don't know what the hell is going on here, Erica, but don't end things like this. If things are as you say then something is going on that I know nothing about. I love you, baby," he whispered gently, close to her ear. "Please believe that I would not destroy our love or cheapen it in any way."

For a moment he thought he had gotten through to her, but then she twisted out of his arms. "No," she said, with tears streaming down his face. "You couldn't love me and hurt me this way. I warned you about *that* woman who works at your office, but you evidently didn't heed my warning."

"What are you talking about?"

"That day I was here and she was jogging by wearing red lipstick and Allure perfume. And the panties had the initial D. Didn't you tell me her name was Donna?"

He clenched his jaw. "I have not been having an affair with Donna, Erica. How could you think that of me?"

"Why shouldn't I? Like mother, like son."

He flinched as if he'd been slapped. "You're wrong for that, Erica," he said, as hurt filled his lungs to a bursting point. His body ached and he felt wounded all over.

"And you're wrong for what you did," she replied. "Just stay the hell away from me. I don't ever want to see you again."

She grabbed her carry-on and stormed out of the house.

Chapter Thirty-One

April crossed her arms over her chest. "I doubt there is anything we have to talk about, Mrs. Sanders. And why are you here in L.A. and not Wyoming?"

Karen sneered. "Maybe I should be asking why Erica is in Dallas and not here. The two of you thought you were smart to pull something on me, but me being here shows I'm a lot smarter than either of you."

April shook her head. She could so clearly remember the day Erica had brought her home from school for dinner. Mrs. Sanders had acted as if April was no better than the mess on the bottom of someone's shoes. She hadn't even pretended to like her and, in fact, she would go out of her way to let April know just how much she detested her. Erica always said it was just the way her mother was and not to take it personally, but for some reason April had always taken it that way.

"My visit won't take up much of your time," Karen said, placing her purse on the coffee table and sitting down.

She glanced around. "Nice place you have here. You have certainly come up in the world, April."

"I would say thank-you if I thought for one minute you meant it."

Karen smiled. "You and I are more alike than you think. You see something you want and you go after it. You've always wanted Griffin, haven't you?"

April saw no reason to lie about it. This woman couldn't hurt her and she most certainly would not let her intimidate her any longer. "Yes, that's right."

Karen shook her head with a sad expression on her face. "I wished I had known before now. I could have saved you a lot of pain."

"Could you have?"

"Yes. You can't have Griffin."

April glared. "Why? Because you refused to give up your obsession that he and Erica get together?" The woman had a smug look on her face and April could feel her flesh beginning to crawl.

"Yes, but that's not the only reason."

"Is there another?"

Karen smiled. "Yes. Have you ever wondered about the identity of your father?"

April shrugged. Even if she had she would never admit it to this woman. "Not really."

"Then maybe you should have. It would have spared you a lot of grief now."

"I don't know what you're talking about."

Karen threw her head back and chuckled. "That doesn't surprise me. You were never very bright, and your mother had even less intelligence."

April filled with rage. "How dare you say such a thing about my mother. I want you to leave."

"Not until I have my say. You can hear the truth from me or you can read about it in the Hattersville newspaper when I tell everyone, which will ruin any chance of Griffin becoming a politician."

"What truth?"

The smile that appeared on Karen's face was so cold that April felt chilled to the bone. "The fact that the two of you share the same daddy. In other words, April, Griffin is your biological brother."

The woman's words were like a hard blow and April felt her head spinning. She lost her balance and sank into the chair beside her.

She closed her eyes, thinking this was all a bad dream and when she reopened her eyes Karen Sanders wouldn't be sitting across from her with a smug look on her face, looking as if she had finally delivered the fatal blow to destroy her forever. A question rang through her head—one that had always been there, where Mrs. Sanders was concerned. Why did she hate her so much?

April had once mentioned it to her grandmother, who'd merely shrugged and said the woman had issues, always had and always would. Nana had told her to ignore her and her ways, and most of all to pray for her. For a while April had done just that, asking God to somehow change the woman's heart. But so far he hadn't.

"That's not true," April heard herself say over the rush of blood in her head. "There's no way Herbert Hayes is my father."

"Oh, but it is true and I have everything I need to prove it. You are just another of his bastards, trust me. He's got them spread all over town. Imagine what the people of Hattersville will think when they find out you and Griffin have been engaging in incestuous activities. It will destroy any chances he has for ever becoming mayor. As for you, well, the tabloids will have a field day with it."

April fought back the bile coming up in her throat. She needed to make it to the bathroom. She needed to get the woman out of her home.

She stood on wobbly legs. "Get out, Mrs. Sanders."

Karen stood. "Oh, I'll leave as long as we understand each other. I want you out of Griffin's life. I also want you out of my daughter's life. You are not and never were fit to be her friend. I don't care how you do it, but do it. Because if you don't, I will make good on my threat."

"You are crazy. You are a demon. You are——"

"A woman who intends to get what she wants, which is a marriage between Griffin and Erica."

April was at that moment convinced the woman was crazy. "But Griffin and Erica don't love each other. Why can't you see and accept that? Erica loves Brian."

Karen waved off April's words like they meant nothing. "Love doesn't do anything but cause heartbreak. Erica will soon find that out. And as far as Griffin is concerned, I can see how he could be infatuated with you since you are a pretty girl, but beneath that covering you are still the slut your mother was. You know what they say—the apple doesn't fall far from the tree."

"My mother was not a slut!"

"Oh, but she was. Everyone figured she was hopelessly and foolishly in love with Ivan Witherspoon, when she was really sleeping around with old man Hayes, so he would buy her the little pretty things that your grandmother could not," Karen said snidely.

April knew about her mother's love for Ivan Witherspoon only because of the one or two love letters she'd found while going through her belongings after she died. That's why, although she'd never known the identity of her father, she'd always assumed he had been Witherspoon.

According to what she had been able to find out, Ivan and

his family had packed up and moved away from Hattersville a short time after her mother got pregnant. April had heard some town people figured he was trying to escape his responsibility after having knocked up a girl from the Fifth Ward.

"I hope we understand each other, April. I want you to end things with Griffin and stay away from Erica or everyone will know the truth. And it will behoove you to keep my visit and our secret to yourself. If you tell anyone I've been here, I will have to tell them why and, trust me, that's something I'd think you would want no one else to know, especially Griffin."

Without saying anything else, Karen gathered her purse and strutted out the door with the same air of confidence and determination she'd had when she'd strutted in.

Brian stood at the window and watched Erica drive away, not believing what had happened here in this very house between them just moments ago. He closed his eyes wanting to believe it had been an out-of-body experience, a nightmare, and that all he needed was a stiff drink to come back to reality.

But when he reopened his eyes his gaze lit on the pair or red panties lying on his living room floor. If they weren't Erica's then where the hell had they come from? He crossed the room to pick them up and sure enough, they were monogrammed with the initial *D*.

He then moved quickly, taking the stairs two at a time, to take a look at his bedroom. Just like she'd claimed, perfume blasted his nostrils the moment he walked into the room. He glanced around, not believing what he was seeing. It looked like two people had had a sexual marathon in his bed. He saw his white shirt on the floor—a shirt he knew for certain he'd put in the laundry hamper yesterday.

Brian picked up the shirt and saw the red lipstick stain, not believing his eyes. At that moment something snapped inside of him and he let out a deep bellow of rage that erupted in the pit of his stomach and traveled through all parts of him, transporting fury in its wake.

None of this made any sense. Who would set him up this way? Did Donna have anything to do with this? But the woman had never gotten out of line with him. They barely communicated, and he couldn't remember the last time she'd jogged past his house.

But if not Donna, then who? And why? The only person he knew who'd want friction between him and Erica was her mother. But he wouldn't accuse the woman of going that far. Besides, Karen couldn't be in two places at the same time and she was too emotionally torn with her own troubles to cook up something like this.

One thing was certain. Whoever had had the nerve to set him up this way had definitely underestimated him. If it took every penny he had, he would find the person responsible and when he did, there would be hell to pay.

April wasn't sure how long she sat on her sofa curled up in a ball of pain so intense she'd never feel whole again. Anger and agony consumed her.

Somehow, she had known the one person she could never protect herself from in life was Karen Sanders. She had known it since that first day Erica had taken her home and the woman had looked at her with such loathing. At the age of thirteen, she hadn't known or understood why. She still didn't, but today showed just how deep the hatred went. Karen wouldn't hesitate to lash out at anyone who she thought was a threat to what she considered a dream match between Erica and Griffin.

Griffin.

The thought of him made more tears fill her eyes. They

were sister and brother! The very thought sickened her. How had she gone through life and not known, not even suspected? Surely someone would have let the cat out of the bag by now. What about Colleen Wingate, the biggest gossip in Hattersville? Although Colleen lived in the Fifth Ward, she had connections since she had cleaned every house on Wellington Road.

And then what about Mr. Carroll, who owned the deli? For years he'd hinted at the possibility that Ivan Witherspoon could be her father like she'd always assumed...but never Herbert Hayes. It was no secret Mr. Hayes used to be a rolling stone in his day and had a number of illegitimate kids all over the place, but most favored him in some way. It had been easy to tell that Griffin and Marcus Stratlet, Paul Ringard and Omar Gates were siblings, although they never claimed to be.

She nearly jumped when her phone rang again and didn't have to look to know the caller was either Griffin or Erica. From the tearful message Erica had left earlier asking her to call her as soon as possible, April could only imagine what was going on with her. Whatever had happened when Erica had arrived in Dallas had been Karen Sanders's doing.

The woman was playing her game well, making sure everything she wanted fell right into place, and this was one time April couldn't stop her or tell anyone what a cruel and heartless bitch she was, one who would stop at nothing to get what she wanted.

"Sweetheart, I guess you're still not home yet. Call me when you get this message. I love you."

Griffin's voice cut her deep and she knew the first thing she had to do was end things between them. The sad thing about it was that she couldn't tell him why. Something he would demand to know. She knew one way to end things was to all of a sudden become romantically linked to another man. That would hurt him deeply and he would never for-give her.

The thought of hurting him that way was too much to think about now, but she knew that it was needed for a clean break. For now she needed time and space to deal with it all. She would send him a message letting him know she was fine but needed time alone. Then she would be able to come up with a plan for how to get the only man she had ever loved out of her life for good.

Chapter Thirty-Two

Brian still not could not believe everything that had transpired over the past hour. He rubbed his hand across his face and closed his eyes as he leaned against the closed door. If he was not a rational man with his senses fully intact, he would think he was passing through the Twilight Zone.

He was now furious, madder than hell at Erica for so easily believing the worst of him. How could she accuse him of being unfaithful when since meeting her he hadn't looked twice at another woman? No woman consumed his thoughts but Erica. No matter how damaging the evidence she had found at his house, she should have believed in him.

But then considering what she had arrived at his house to find, a part of him couldn't very well blame her for the way she'd reacted and the accusations she'd hurled at him.

He hadn't known Erica was visiting him today but someone else had, and that person had deliberately set him up.

He pulled the phone off his belt and, deciding to give Matt a call, punched in a few numbers. He needed help in unraveling this mess and he needed it fast.

When his friend answered, Brian drew in a deep breath. "Someone set me up, man."

"What are you talking about?"

"Erica came to town unexpectedly and she thinks I'm involved in an affair."

"Why would she think that?"

"Someone entered my house to deliberately make it look that way. She's calling off the wedding and doesn't want to see me ever again. I'm no longer paranoid," he said, remembering how Matt has once accused him of such a thing where Karen Sanders was concerned. "What I am is madder than hell. I want to find the person responsible. And I need your help."

Without a pause, Matt said, "I'll be right over."

Griffin checked his watch. It was close to two in the morning in Hattersville, which meant it was midnight in L.A., so where the hell was April and why hadn't she returned his calls?

He stopped his pacing to stare out of his bedroom window and, from where he stood on the third floor of his home, he could see that most of the residents were asleep. He truly loved this town, faults and all, and wanted to make it into the thriving city that he knew it could be. There was so much undeveloped land, and with the right plans in place there was no doubt in his mind the town could double its size in no time.

Over the past year he had spoken to a lot of his former classmates who'd moved away to live in the big cities. They'd wanted to raise their families in a small town, yet all of them had said Hattersville would be their last choice. That bothered him but he of all people understood their sentiments. Many of them like him had been considered the upper echelon of the community, but a number of those families over the years had fallen on hard times, and a decline in status was considered unforgivable in the eyes of those still prospering. They had been treated worse than those who'd been born in the Fifth Ward.

He intended to change things when he became mayor and with April by his side he believed he could do the impossible. But first he needed to convince her to be the woman by his side.

He wanted her to continue her career but he also wanted her to know that a positive change was about to happen. He intended to make it that way not only for her, but for so many others who felt the town had let them down.

He moved away from the window to his nightstand to pick up his phone. He would try reaching April again. When he had talked to her last night she hadn't mentioned any function she would be attending tonight.

Moments later he hung up the phone. Her condo was pretty secure but he knew he wouldn't be totally satisfied until he heard her voice.

Matt Seacrest leaned back against the sofa cushion and made a steeple with his fingers while glancing over at Brian. His friend was in a bad way and he couldn't recall ever seeing him this broken.

"And you really think it's the old lady's doing?" he asked his friend.

Brian stopped pacing and instinctively Matt glanced down at the floor, curious to see if his best friend had worn a hole in the carpet. He had been here for over an hour and this was the first time Brian had stood still.

"Yes, but a part of me doesn't know how."

"Easily, if she has help."

Brian lifted a brow. "So now you don't think I'm paranoid after all?"

A smile touched Matt's lips. "Let's just say after finally getting Cassie to marry me, I can't imagine Erica not marrying you, especially when I know how much you love her and that your loyalty to her is sincere. You have evidence—the panties, lipstick on your shirt and the fragrance of that perfume that even I can smell. Yes, bro, someone set you up and if the old lady is the only one who would be happy if you and Erica didn't get married, then she would be my first suspect. Although, one would think that doing what she's done, just to get Erica to not marry you, is a little overboard."

Brian shrugged. "She wants her to marry this guy named Griffin Hayes."

"Yes, but why? What would she get out of it if Erica and Hayes were to marry? Would it double, triple or quadruple the size of the family's wealth or something? She has to have an ulterior motive to go to this extreme to keep you apart."

"With what happened between my mother and her husband, don't you think for her that would be reason enough?"

"Honestly, no. I could see her being spiteful and even a little vengeful. But not outright manipulative to this degree, this cold and heartless. A woman who would deliberately destroy her daughter's chance at happiness sounds like someone who isn't emotionally stable, someone who is obsessed with her daughter marrying someone else. Why?"

"There is this nonsense of a family curse she believes in."

That got Matt's attention and he sat up. "What family curse?"

Brian took the chair across from the sofa and for the next twenty minutes retold what Erica had once shared with him. At the time he, like her, had found the whole idea of the Hayes–Delbert curse rather out there and not worth very much thought. Evidently her mother was determined to destroy this so-called curse.

"And what about Donna?"

Brian lifted a brow. "Donna?"

"Yes. Erica is convinced she set you up, so how is she connected to Karen Sanders?"

Brian shook his head. "I don't know if she is." He blew out a frustrated breath. "This whole thing sounds far-fetched, but I want answers, Matt. Maybe Mrs. Sanders had nothing to do with it, and maybe things played out to her advantage coincidentally. But I have to know that for sure. And I want to know who entered my home today and intentionally left all those things behind so Erica could find them."

Matt tapped his fingers on the coffee table. "And you're sure, at least as far as you know, Donna Hardy doesn't have the hots for you and set out to deliberately sabotage your relationship with Erica."

"As far as I know she doesn't have a thing for me. Even if she did, how could she have known Erica was coming to town today?"

"I'm not sure," Matt said, standing. "But you better believe I'm going to find out."

Brian knew Matt well enough to know that he would. In fact, there was no doubt in Brian's mind that, when it was all over, Matt would not only put an end to this madness, but he would have the names of the person or persons responsible.

Griffin got out of bed the next morning after a sleepless night, mainly because he still hadn't been able to reach April. It was so unlike her not to touch base with him every day.

He was about to go take his shower when the doorbell rang. Grabbing his bathrobe he nearly flew down the stairs, hoping it was April and that she had decided to surprise him with a visit.

He opened the door, disappointed to find a FedEx deliveryman standing there instead of April. "Yes?"

"Overnight delivery for you, sir. Please sign this."

Griffin signed the document and was then handed an envelope. It was from April. He frowned wondering what the hell was going on and, after closing the door, he swiftly opened the envelope and pulled out the single piece of paper and began reading.

Griffin,
I know this is the coward's way out but this is the way it has to be. I am ending things between us. It was fun while it lasted but I decided that I can't corner myself into a relationship right now with anyone. I should not have led you to believe there could be more when I know there can't be. You would think after three failed marriages I would learn my lesson. Bottom line is I prefer we don't see each other again. I have my life and you have yours. I need a break from work and I'm taking a few weeks off to be by myself. Don't try calling me because I prefer no contact from you. It's over between us.
April

Griffin reread the letter twice to make sure he wasn't mistaken. And then rage consumed him. How dare she play with his heart. And what about all those times she'd told him that she loved him? They had been nothing more than lies?

He closed his eyes and could envision how she'd looked the last time they'd been together. After making love they had held each other, stared into each other's eyes and poured out their love. His hand shook with anger as he placed the letter back into the envelope. She was right. She had taken the coward's way out and he didn't intend to let her off that easily.

April had captured his heart and if he had to tear through America and Europe to find her, he would.

Chapter Thirty-Three

"And how was your visit with April?"

Erica glanced across the dinner table at her mother. Surprisingly, she didn't detect the normally sarcastic tone in her voice whenever she mentioned April. Erica had been asleep when her mother had arrived in Lake Tahoe late last night and Erica had deliberately pretended exhaustion to sleep late this morning. She needed to give her body time to heal from pain and hoped her mother couldn't look at her and tell she'd been crying the last two days. Her eyes were no longer as red as they had been but her heart was still aching inside.

She had checked her messages and saw Brian had tried calling her several times but she didn't want to hear anything he had to say at the moment. The evidence she'd seen spoke for itself and, as far as she was concerned, there was really nothing he could say. And knowing there was no way he could redeem himself made it that much harder, because she loved him so much.

"Erica?"

Remembering that her mother had asked a question, she

plastered a smile on her face. "My visit was great. It was good seeing her again," she lied. No matter what, she refused to let her mother know what had happened between her and Brian. Karen had enough garbage of her own to sort through. Besides, the thought of her and her mother sharing a pity party only made her pain that much worse.

"And what about your trip, Mom? How was it?"

A huge smile touched her mother's mouth from corner to corner. "It was simply wonderful. I wasn't sure how things would turn out before I left but I think it was worth the trip."

Erica continued to eat her food while her mother chatted away about people Erica didn't know. But she could tell by the sound of her mother's voice that getting away had been good for her. She was glad and hoped her mother's attitude stayed intact when she made the request she was about to make.

"Mom, can we go home?"

The smile on Karen's face left instantly. "Why? Aren't you enjoying spending time with me?"

Erica breathed deeply. Good grief! The last thing she wanted was for her mother to assume that she was disloyal. But she needed to be alone to wallow in her own grief. "That's not it, Mom, but I just want to go home now. I think we've been gone long enough, don't you think?"

Karen nodded slowly. "Yes, I guess you're right." She hesitated for a moment, fidgeting with her napkin in a nervous gesture before saying, "I didn't want to mention this to you. In fact I put it out of my mind until I was ready to deal with it."

Erica had a sinking feeling in the pit of her stomach. "Deal with what?"

Karen held her gaze. "I talked to your father a couple of weeks ago while we were still on the cruise."

"Yes, he mentioned it when I spoke with him a few days ago. Why didn't you tell me he called? Why did you have me believing that he hadn't cared enough to do so, Mom?"

She saw fire flare into her mother's eyes. "Because there was no way I could tell you he called without telling you why he called. And the reason was too upsetting." She placed her fork down beside her plate to make sure she had Erica's attention. "He has filed for the divorce and is in the process of moving out of our home."

Erica's mouth dropped open from the news.

"And he plans to divorce me and marry her," her mother added.

Erica frowned. "Is that what he said?"

"No, that's what I've prepared myself for and that's fine. I'll just live my life alone until I die."

Erica's heart took a nosedive and a part of her wished she hadn't asked to go home now.

"So I hope you understand why I didn't mention his call," Karen said. "It was just too devastating to think about and I was determined to put him and that tramp he's been messing with out of my mind."

"I can understand that." She reached across the table to take her mother's hand in hers. "Mom, I'm truly sorry."

Her mother nodded. "So am I. Maybe you've been right all along. Your father and I had an arranged marriage and things didn't work out. I guess marrying for love is the only way to assure your heart won't get broken."

Those words were too much for Erica to hear. She wanted to tell her that marrying for love wasn't what she thought it would be. On the verge of tears, she pushed back from the table. "Excuse me, Mom, I need some time alone for a minute."

Karen watched as Erica quickly left the room. Poor baby. The smile that formed on her lips couldn't be withheld. She lifted her glass to take a sip of her wine. Things were going as planned, and yes, she was ready to go home, as well. The sooner she could get Griffin and Erica together, the better.

If two people were drawn together to console each other's broken hearts, then so be it.

Rita nibbled on her bottom lip as she waited for Wilson to answer the phone. "It's Rita," she said as he picked up.

"Rita, how are you, love?"

She hung her head and took a deep breath. Such words coming from him should not make her heart beat so fast. Should not cause goose bumps to break out over her arms. But they did because no matter how their relationship had begun or how wrong it was to have started in the first place, she loved him. He was her love, like she knew she was his.

It had been over a month since they'd been together and she knew if given the word he would hop the first plane to Dallas to see her. But they had agreed they would not be together, could not be together, until he was no longer a married man.

"There's a problem between Erica and Brian," she said, her heart almost breaking just thinking about it.

"What problem? I talked to Erica a few days ago. She called me from the airport on her way to Dallas to see Brian."

"Yes, and someone set him up, Wilson."

"Set him up? How?"

She spent the next thirty minutes going over in detail what Brian had shared with her a few days ago. He had appeared on her doorstep on the brink of exhaustion. He'd barely been able to eat and had taken time off work to try and pull himself together.

It had been totally heartbreaking for a mother to see her child in such pain but know there was nothing she could do about it. Even now she was worried about him, although he had returned to work today and claimed he was doing better. He had tried calling Erica but she refused his calls.

"There is no way Brian would cheat on Erica, Wilson," she said, almost in tears.

"I know, sweetheart. To be honest with you, it wouldn't at all surprise me if Karen didn't have something to do with it."

Rita's breath caught. That had crossed her mind originally, but there were so many things that had happened that were so out of Karen's reach. "How is that possible when she was at Lake Tahoe?" His suspicions were beginning to sound like a demented soap opera.

"I know, but over the years my wife has kept secrets of her own."

"Really?"

"Nothing involving an affair or anything, as far as I know, but a secret I discovered last year regarding her sister."

"Her sister? Erica once mentioned her mother had one sister who'd been in a car accident and went into a coma and later died."

"Yes, that's what we all thought."

"What do you mean?"

"I know for a fact that her sister Blair is alive, although Karen fabricated the funeral years ago to make us think otherwise."

Rita nearly dropped the phone out of her hands. "What?"

"Yes, I only found out because I came across the checks Karen has been writing for her care in a private exclusive nursing home. She makes sure Blair is getting the best of care, but just to think Karen went so far as to fabricate her sister's death and funeral lets me know she is capable of doing just about anything."

"Yet you stayed with her?"

"Yes, only because I figured, with the way Karen thinks, if

people knew Blair had finally come out of her coma it would be embarrassing for Karen. Blair was her younger sister, beautiful and vibrant. The car accident took place a week before she was to get married."

"How awful."

"Yes, it was. But if Karen has managed to keep Blair a secret all these years then it wouldn't surprise me what else she can manage to do."

The thought of that sent chills down Rita's spine. "Brian has hired a private detective, his best friend, and Matt is good and feels he has a personal stake in this. Someone is out to ruin Brian's happiness and Matt's not going to be satisfied until he finds out who it is."

Chapter Thirty-Four

Over the next couple of weeks Brian tried to continue to hold his life together, going to work and coming home while hoping Matt would have something for him that would explain the madness he was going through.

Erica still refused his calls and he'd even thought about flying to Hattersville to confront her again but followed Matt's advice not to do so. They both needed time to think and Brian was hoping, praying, that eventually she would realize what a mistake she'd made in not believing in him, in not trusting him completely. More than anything that is what hurt him the most.

He might be wrong but it seemed Donna was deliberately keeping her distance. Matt had decided he would check her out first, verify she was not involved in any way.

Brian stood and walked over to the office window to glance out. Basically he was a man operating on autopilot. He went home every day, ate dinner and went to bed. He tried getting absorbed in his court cases and would admit they helped tremendously. But it was late at night, when he thought of Erica the most, that the pain tore through him.

He turned when the phone rang and moved to his desk to pick it up. "Yes, Jessie?"

"Matt Seacrest is on the line for you, Mr. Lawson."

"Please put him through." He hadn't heard from Matt since last week and hoped he was calling because he'd found out something. "Matt?"

"I found out some things that might interest you, man. When can we meet?"

Erica was glad to be home but even within these walls she felt only bone-deep loneliness. She had returned to find her father had moved out and was living in one of those exclusive apartments near the lake. And now most everyone in town knew her parents were getting a divorce and the reason for it. This was a small town and news, good or bad, traveled fast. Her mother had had a lot of messages waiting for her when she returned. Erica was sure they were from her mother's country club buddies, who were eager to give her a shoulder to cry on while getting their ears filled with what they thought would be some juicy gossip.

Erica hadn't seen her father since she and her mother had returned a couple of weeks ago. He had wanted to meet with her but the pain of his betrayal was still raw and, now that he was actually going through with the divorce and had moved out, she was more torn than ever. A part of her wanted to understand what had driven him to such madness. Was this nothing but a middle-age crisis?

And she would have to admit that more than once over the past few weeks she had questioned herself, wondering if she'd jumped to conclusions, been too quick in accusing Brian. Her mother was worried about her and had tried getting Erica to stay a few days with her. But she had needed the privacy of her own place. She had needed her space.

She was about to go into the kitchen and prepare something for lunch when her doorbell rang. She moved to the door and glanced out the peephole and saw her visitor was none other than Griffin Hayes.

She opened the door and smiled. "Griffin, how are you?"

"I'm fine, Erica. May I come in?"

"Sure."

She stood back and let him in and then she saw the strain surrounding his eyes. He appeared deeply worried about something. "Griffin? Is everything all right?"

He drew in a deep breath. "No. I'm trying to find April. Do you know where she is?"

"April?"

"Yes."

Erica fell silent for a few moments as she contemplated his response. Of course she knew April and Griffin were acquainted but had never considered them as even friends. She did know April had had a crush on Griffin for years, although she was certain April wasn't aware she had figured that out years ago.

Why was Griffin looking for April? She decided the only way to find out was to ask him. "Why are you trying to find April?"

He rubbed the back of his neck with his hand and then said, "April and I have been involved for about four months, and a few weeks ago she sent me a letter saying she needed space and didn't want to see me."

Of all the things Erica had expected to hear, that wasn't it. "You and April have been involved?"

"Yes."

She shook her head. "This is news to me."

"She didn't want to tell you until after your wedding."

Erica was confused. "Why?"

"She was obsessed with not letting your mother find out. She figured as long as you weren't married Mrs. Sanders would still harbor hope that something would develop between you and me. She thought once you were happily married then it would be okay to let everyone know."

Erica nodded. She could see April thinking that way. For some reason April had always been afraid of her mother's wrath. It was sad. "April should not have let my mom affect her happiness. Gosh, she's loved you forever."

The tightness around his mouth eased into a smile. "She said she has."

"She's not lying, although again because of my mother, she never wanted me to know. I figured things out on my own years ago, while we were still in high school. That's the reason I made sure we called things off in your senior year before you left for college, in case you would be bold enough to let April know you were interested in her, as well."

This time Griffin threw his head back and laughed. "You figured that out, too?"

"Yes, and to be honest with you, I really don't know where April is, which is unusual. She hasn't contacted me in a few weeks, and I'm concerned. In fact, I'm going to pay Ms. Connie a visit. Now your visit explains some things."

"Like what?"

"Why April doesn't want to be found. In her mind she's probably thinking that since I didn't marry I'll pose a threat to your relationship with her, which isn't true."

Griffin nodded. "Yes, she actually thinks your mother can wield that much power."

Erica shook her head. "Trust me, my mother has enough of her own problems to deal with at the moment."

Griffin nodded again. "I heard about your parents. I'm sorry, Erica."

"Me, too, but someone told me I had to realize their problems aren't mine," she said. "In fact I was told it really wasn't any of my business."

He gave a slight smile. "And I can just imagine who told you that."

Erica smiled, as well. Yes, April had been the one to tell her that. So had Brian. Thoughts of him made her heart ache.

"I love her, Erica, and I've got to find her and convince her that no one is a threat to us. Do you know where she might be?"

Erica nibbled on her bottom lip. Yes, she had an idea. A few years ago she and April had purchased a house together in Hawaii. It was their "girlcave." Under normal circumstances she wouldn't divulge her friend's whereabouts to anyone. But Erica had a gut feeling that this time was different.

"Erica?"

She looked up at Griffin and made a quick decision.

"April and I bought this place in Maui a few years ago and I have a feeling that's probably where she is."

An appreciative smile lit up Griffin's face and he leaned over to place a kiss on Erica's cheek. "Thank you."

"So what do you have to tell me?"

The minute Brian spotted Matt seated at a table in Larry's Sandwich Shop, he grabbed a seat and cut right to the chase. He knew his friend would understand.

Without preamble, Matt replied, "It seems your girl Donna is the one who set you up."

Over the past week Brian hadn't wanted to consider the possibility that Donna had a part in what happened, and to know that she had made his blood boil. "You sound certain."

"I am. Rule number one. Don't set a brother up unless you intend to cover your tracks."

"And she didn't?"

"Not completely." Matt then took a sip of his beer. "First there were those infamous red panties with the letter *D*. Turns out they're made to order. Some designer in Chicago. I was able to track down the identity of the person who ordered them. A professor at the same law school Donna graduated from."

Brian nodded slowly. "Circumstantial evidence."

Matt chuckled. "Yes, but what if I told you she was known around campus as the 'blow-job queen' and it was rumored that she and this professor had something going on and that their secret affair is what helped her graduate from law school at the top of her class?"

"Still circumstantial," Brian said after the waiter had placed a beer in front of him and he had taken a sip.

"And what if I were to tell you that she is presently blowing Judge Meadows?"

Brian almost choked on the sip he'd taken. "Are you sure?"

"Yes. I put a tail on her and my man reported that, not only does she have a standing time each week in the judge's chambers, but they also schedule clandestine meetings at the Ritz-Carlton twice a week. And we have pictures to prove it." Matt paused for a moment. "She was also placed at your home the day of Erica's visit."

Brian set his glass aside. "She was?"

"Yes. You live in a gated community. She has access because she lives there as well, so no one had to check when she came in and when she left. But what she didn't think about was the security cameras. I obtained a video."

Anger was radiating from every pore in Brian's body. "But why did she do it?"

"I guess she wanted to make sure there wasn't a snowball's chance in hell that you and Erica would marry, and I can only assume she figured once she got Erica out of the picture, she would go after you for herself."

Brian leaned back in the chair. "Well, I guess you solved that one."

Matt shook his head. "No, it only opens more questions up in my mind and there is one sticking out further than the others."

"Which one?""

"How did she know Erica was surprising you and coming to town, in order to time things so perfectly?"

Brian lifted a brow. "That's a good question and there's only one way to find out."

Matt chuckled. "Yes, we'll be paying Ms. Hardy a visit after we leave here."

Less than an hour later both Matt and Brian were knocking on Donna Hardy's front door. When she opened it Brian could tell that she was surprised to see him.

"Brian? How nice to see you."

"Donna, this is a good friend of mine, Matthew Seacrest. He's a private investigator and I hired him to find out who broke into my house and set me up." He saw something flash in the depths of her eyes. It happened so quickly that if he hadn't been observant he would have missed it.

She crossed her arms over her chest. "Oh, really? I wasn't aware someone burglarized your home. But what does that have to do with me?"

"Give us a few moments of your time," Matt said, "and we'll certainly tell you."

"I was on my way out," Donna said.

"That may be, but I think it would behoove you to let us come in and discuss a few things," Matt said.

She shrugged and took a step back. "Mr. Lawson is my boss so I can't refuse to meet with him, can I?"

A smile touched Matt's lips. "You can, but I think regarding this matter I'd think twice about it."

She paused slightly and then said, "Then please come in."

They entered her home and the smell of Allure greeted them, just like it had that day in his bedroom. "I would offer the two of you something to drink, but like I said I'm on my way out. I have a date."

"With Judge Meadows?" Matt threw out.

Brian watched her spine stiffen and knew what Matt was doing. He was already going in for the kill before he did any disabling of the defenses. It was a tactic Brian had used in court a lot when he was certain that the accused was guilty as sin.

"I see Judge Meadows in court once a week and that's enough," she said.

"No, you see him more than that, but that's not why we're here," Matt said. "Not only am I a private investigator, Ms. Hardy, I also consider myself one of Brian's closest friends. When someone does something to him they might as well do it to me."

"How touching." She then glanced over at Brian. "What's this about? Or are you letting him be your spokesman, Counselor?"

Brian frowned. In a few moments she would probably regret what she'd just said. Matt might be a pain in the ass but a pissed off Brian Lawson could be one hundred degrees worse than him.

"Why did you do it, Donna?" he asked her.

He could tell before she even opened her mouth that she intended to play dumb. "I have no idea what you're talking about."

"You set me up to guarantee a breakup with my fiancée. Why?"

She threw her hair over her shoulder. "Look, Brian, if you've got problems in your relationship—"

"I have proof you were in my apartment."

"You don't have proof because I wasn't there."

"Yes, we do," Matt interjected. "First of all, there are your panties that were purchased for you, as a gift I presume, from one of your professors in law school."

"You can't prove that."

"Yes, we can. And your alibi with Judge Meadows won't hold much water, when we have security footage that shows you at Brian's condo." He held up a copy for effect. "As an attorney you know it's admissible in court."

"In court?" she asked, turning her attention to Brian. "With something like that in addition to the panties you would get laughed out of the courtroom."

Brian had heard enough. "We're not talking about a court of law, Donna. We are talking about your livelihood. Your career and your future. The one you had with my firm is over and I will make sure you never use your law degree again if you don't tell us what we want to know."

"You can't come in here and threaten me."

"Yes, I can. You deliberately entered my home without my permission and sabotaged my relationship with my fiancée."

"If she was a true fiancée she wouldn't have believed the worst about you."

"Maybe, but then if you had any decency, you would not have done what you did, so why?"

"I have nothing to say."

"Fine, but don't think this is going away. You either tell me now who put you up to this and why, or I will take you to court and expose you for being the lying manipulator that you are. Breaking and entering is a crime and, trust me, you won't get any help from Judge Meadows. He will be using all his time and energy to save his own career when word gets out as to what the two of you have been doing in his chambers and twice a week at the Ritz-Carlton."

Matt wasted no time. "What we want to know is how you knew Erica was coming to town."

At first Donna didn't say anything and Brian wondered if she would continue to pretend innocence. It took a few moments and then she dropped down on a sofa and said, "I was told she was coming."

Brian swallowed a lump in his throat before asking, "By whom?"

"Don't know."

Matt chuckled. "You really want us to believe that?"

She frowned up at him. "It's true. This man contacted me and threatened to expose something I did if I didn't meet with him. I did. He told me what he wanted done, but didn't give any specifics as to why. He said he would call when he was ready. He did and without telling me how to achieve what he wanted done he just told me to do it. He didn't give me much time to come up with a plan and that was the best I could do. I really didn't think you would be so damn thorough in checking things out."

Brian nodded. "And who is this man, Donna?"

"I told you I don't know. He didn't give a name and whenever I asked he referred to himself only as a friend."

"When was the last time you heard from him?" Matt asked.

"A few days afterward when he called to compliment me on a job well done. He said his client was pleased."

Matt and Brian exchanged glances at that last piece of information. "Describe this man to us," Matt said.

No one Brian knew fit the description she proceeded to give. "Where did the two of you make connections?" he then asked.

"We met at Stella's."

"When?"

She provided him with the date.

"What time?" Matt asked.

"Our meeting was at six but he was already there when I arrived."

Brian knew Matt would try and trace the identity of the person through the use of the man's credit card.

A short while later as he and Matt were leaving, Brian paused at the door and suggested she put in her resignation. Donna agreed that would be the best thing under the circumstances. She apologized and said what she'd done hadn't been personal and hoped he and his girlfriend got back together. *Now, how ironic is that?* Brian thought.

"So what do you think?" he asked Matt when they were back in the car.

"I think you might have an idea just who that 'client' might be, don't you?"

Yes, Brian had a real good idea, but it floored him that Karen Sanders not only hated him that much but was willing to sacrifice her daughter's happiness to get what she wanted. That proved just how manipulating, deceitful and uncaring she was. But he still couldn't understand why getting him out of the picture was so important to her. Why was Erica's marrying Griffin Hayes an obsession with her?

"Yes," he finally responded. "I have a pretty good idea."

Chapter Thirty-Five

Griffin didn't care how many times he visited Hawaii, he would always appreciate the island's beauty. After talking to Erica yesterday, he hadn't wasted any time booking a flight to California and then, after an overnight stay at a hotel in San Francisco, he had flown from there to Maui.

He rented a car at the airport and, using his GPS, it didn't take long for him to find the villa, which seemed to be situated right in paradise, amidst lush greenery, flowering plants and foliage. He didn't intend to leave until he found out the real reason April had decided to end things between them.

It was late-evening when he arrived but he pulled into the driveway, already lit by tiki torches. It was a huge two-story contemporary-style home with slate roofing, set against the ocean and mountains. His heart began beating faster at the mere thought that somewhere inside was the woman he loved. She had come here to escape him and he was determined to find out why.

After getting out of the car he took a moment to stretch his legs. Maybe he was a fool for running after a woman as if he didn't have a damn ounce of pride. But at the moment his heart was his main concern and it didn't take much to be reminded that she had his heart wrapped real tight.

There was one thing he couldn't shake from his mind and that was what Erica had shared with him. She was not getting married. The wedding was not just postponed but had now been called off completely. Although she hadn't gone into any details as to why, he felt it had to do with something more than finding out her father was having an affair with her future mother-in-law. And whatever happened had occurred rather recently. He could tell the pain of her decision was still raw.

He hadn't questioned her about it, but if the reason she was no longer getting married was due to something other than her father's alleged affair, then Griffin could only wonder at the timing of the demise of both his relationship with April and Erica's relationship with her fiancé. It might be just co-incidental, a cruel twist of fate...or was it something else entirely? But what?

He thought about April's fears regarding Karen Sanders and shrugged them off. Like Erica had said, her mother had too many of her own problems to deal with to worry about his or anyone else's. Besides, what sort of trouble could one woman cause to two affairs? You would have to be a twenty-four-hour manipulator to accomplish that, and like he'd said, Karen didn't wield that much power.

He heard the sound of music when he made it to the door and couldn't resist the temptation of looking through the open curtains. His breath almost caught when he saw April sitting at the table in the kitchen with her reading glasses on and a book in her hand. She seemed totally absorbed in what she was reading. Now that he'd found her he was more determined than ever to make her tell him what he wanted to know.

With that single-minded resolution, he raised his hand to knock on her door.

April was so absorbed in the book she had purchased online a few days ago, *Forbidden World of Incest,* that she hardly heard the knock at the door. She reluctantly closed the book but not before inserting her bookmark to pick up where she'd left off later.

Now she was wondering if she was normal. All it should take was the realization that Griffin was her brother to stop her heart from being filled with so much love for him. No such luck. She had just finished reading the story of a couple who had married only to discover they were twins who'd been separated at birth. They had to have the marriage annulled. It was heartbreaking to read about and she could just imagine how the two must have felt once they found out. At least she had found out the truth, even if Griffin didn't have a clue.

As she made it toward the door she wondered who could be calling on her and hoped to God it wasn't her neighbor again. The woman was determined to be her new best friend and April just wasn't feeling it.

"I'm coming. I'm coming," she yelled out when the knock at her door became even more persistent.

She snatched open the door. "Look, lady, I—"

Any other words she was about to say died on her lips when she looked into Griffin's face. She blinked, certain she was seeing things. When the image of him didn't go away she tried to jump back and slam the door shut. But it was too late. He reached out to stop the door from slamming on him and quickly moved inside.

"I didn't invite you in, Griffin," she snarled out at him. She couldn't help it. It was either be angry at him or throw herself into his arms and she knew there was no way she could do the latter. She knew then that she should have gone through with her first plan to fly to England and make him think she had picked up her affair with Green. The tabloids would have had a field day with that and she would have accomplished just what she wanted by putting an end to her relationship with Griffin. There was no way he would ever forgive her if he thought she was sleeping with him and another man. But a part of her just couldn't hurt him that way. Now she wished she had if it had kept him from tracking her down this way.

"Doesn't matter if you invited me or not, April. I want to know what's wrong, baby."

"Don't call me that. I am not your baby," she almost screamed. Then a voice inside her said, *I'm your sister. I am your friggin' sister who is still feelings things for you that she shouldn't.*

"What's wrong with you?" he asked, looking at her like she'd lost her mind.

"Nothing is wrong with me. Now please leave."

"Why do you want me to leave? I love you, baby. Let's talk this out."

"But you don't understand," she said in a choked tone, fighting back tears and anger as well as monumental heartbreak.

"Then make me understand why you don't want me anymore. Why you are willing to throw away everything. And you can't convince me that you don't love me because deep in my heart I believe you do. You've convinced me over the past six weeks that you do."

"But don't you see that I can't?" she said, with tears starting to stream down her face. "I can't."

"Why do you think you can't?"

She drew in a sob. Why wouldn't he just take her words at face value and be done with it? Why was he breaking down her defenses, her common sense, tenderness and kindness? She wiped tears from her eyes. "Because we can't."

"You're not making any sense, April."

She knew the only way to get through to him would be to tell him the truth, but she remembered Karen Sanders's threat and had no doubt in her mind what the outcome would be if she did tell him. She knew Griffin. He would not let her go. He would not release her so the two of them could heal from this unless he knew the truth. But first, he had to promise not to tell anyone—not a living soul. And he couldn't get mad at Karen Sanders for interfering in their lives. Although she might have had the worst intentions for doing so, in a way April was glad it had been exposed to her. She didn't want to think about what might have happened later if they'd been left clueless.

"Tell me, April."

Making her decision, she glanced up at him. "Fine. You want to know then I'll tell you, but you have to promise me that you won't tell anyone and, no matter what, you can't confront Karen Sanders about it."

He lifted a brow. "What does Karen Sanders have to do with it?"

"I told you that she would stop at nothing to break us apart. Well, she succeeded. Only sad thing is that we should appreciate that she did, or things could have been worse in the end."

An irritated look touched his features. "Baby, what are you talking about?"

Instead of answering him she walked off and went to the table to pick up the book she'd been reading and, squaring her shoulders, she returned to where he stood in the middle of her living room.

She handed him the book. "Here."

He took the book from her, read the title and then glanced

up at her with an even more confused look. *"Forbidden World of Incest?* What does that have to do with us?"

She fought back the sob that threatened to tear through her throat, but she couldn't help the tears that were determined to fall anyway. A part of her knew before it was over there would be even more tears. Tears she would shed for the rest of her life.

"April, what does this have to do with us?" he asked again.

She drew in a deep breath and said, "I'm your sister."

Griffin could only stare at her for a few moments and when she burst into tears and began crying uncontrollably he couldn't help but pull her into his arms, ignoring her attempt to resist him. A part of him was shocked by what she'd said, but another part of him was angry beyond belief. He was fighting hard to contain his rage, especially when he felt the wetness of her tears through his shirt.

"Did you hear me?" She pulled back to look up at him.

He reached up to tenderly sweep a strand of hair back from her face. "Yes, sweetheart, I heard you. Now, I want you to hear me. You are not my sister."

She jerked away from him. "Denying the truth won't help the situation, Griffin."

"Only because there isn't a situation. You are not my sister and Karen Sanders will pay dearly for lying to you this way. And the sad thing about it is that it almost worked. Trust me, we don't share the same father."

She stared at him for a moment and he saw the look of hope in her eyes. "How can you be so sure? Everybody knew your dad fathered outside children," she said softly.

"Yes, but he is not your father. And the reason I'm certain is because I know who your father is and he isn't mine. I promise you."

★ ★ ★

April's heart nearly stopped breathing. Could Griffin be telling the truth or was he refusing to accept the reality of what she had revealed to him? "How do you know who my father is when I don't even know?"

"I never knew that you didn't know the identity of your father, April. I overheard your father telling mine what happened one night while he'd been drinking, how he forced himself on your mother and how she'd gotten pregnant as a result of it. He admitted to my father that you were his daughter, but that no one was supposed to know. He'd offered your mother money for an abortion but she refused to take it. He was pretty pissed about that. And he had forced her to tell no one what happened and that he was the father of her child."

April didn't say anything. She just sat there and stared at Griffin. Was he telling the truth? As if that question shone in her eyes, he said, "I'm telling the truth, April. Honest. I was sixteen and the two men thought I was outside but I had been hiding out in the wine cellar so I wouldn't get caught sampling some of my father's wine. I was there hiding behind a few crates when they came down there to drink and talk. All these years I kept what I heard to myself, seeing no reason to mention it to anyone...until now. I was more than a little disappointed by what I heard because I'd always respected the man. But not anymore from that day on."

Her heart began beating. Had Karen Sanders intentionally lied, figuring April would never learn the truth because she was too afraid and ashamed to ask anyone for verification? However, if what Griffin said was true...

Anger flooded through her and she was consumed with rage. "Who is it, Griffin? Who is the man who forced himself on my mother, got her pregnant and didn't give one red cent about claiming me as his?"

Griffin reached out and pulled her into his arms. She could tell he was just as mad as she was. "I'm not sure you're ready for that information."

She looked up at him, clearly upset. "Don't play with me, Griffin. I want to know who he is."

"Isn't it enough to know it's not my father? If you want proof that we aren't related we can go get our DNA tested on Monday."

"Who is he, Griffin?"

It had become quite obvious that he was trying hard not to tell her.

"Tell me."

"Baby, I—"

She twisted out of his arms. "No, tell me now!"

He reached out and drew her back to him. "Okay. I'll tell you."

She felt his tight grip on her arm as if he was fearful she might collapse on her feet once he told her. He looked deeply into her eyes as he spoke. "Your father was Omar Delbert."

Her knees weakened and she all but crumbled in his arms. "That means…"

"Yes, baby. It means Karen Sanders is your sister and Erica is your niece."

"Here, baby, drink this." Griffin handed a glass of watered-down vodka to April.

"Thanks."

He then sat on the sofa beside her and took her hand in his. They didn't say anything for long moments and that was fine with him. He needed to chill a while and dwell on what had taken place and what had been revealed here tonight. What he'd said earlier was true. He'd had no idea she hadn't known the identity of her father and, since the subject had never come up between them, he'd felt no reason to bring it up himself.

He had lived in Hattersville long enough to know that a lot of the people, especially those living in the Wellington Road area—the ones who had all the money and thought they ran the town—had all kinds of secrets and skeletons in their closets. He cringed at the thought of what some of those secrets might be and knew some were best left untold.

April broke into his thoughts. "Do you think that Mrs. Sanders knows, and that's why she has hated me so much all these years and resented my friendship with Erica?"

He glanced over at her. "I'm not sure, April. But what I do know is the lie she told you about us being siblings was cruel and heartless. Even if she thought it was true, to use it to blackmail you, force you to end a relationship with me, is as manipulative as she could get. And just like I lost respect for her father that day, I've now lost respect for her."

April shook her head. "I just don't get it, Griffin. Why would she lie like that? Why is she so obsessed with you marrying Erica that she would go to such extremes? I haven't talked to Erica since her mother's visit, since she threatened to reveal our biological connections if I did, but from some of the things Karen said, I know she is doing something to break Erica and Brian up, as well."

"She might have succeeded. Erica told me her wedding is not postponed but officially off. I didn't ask why."

Clearly angry, April let her voice grow louder. "Brian loves Erica, Griffin, and she loves him. What Mrs. Sanders has done is so wrong and she needs to be stopped once and for all. The woman is destroying lives."

Griffin reached out and pulled April into his arms. He knew what she said was true. Hadn't Mrs. Sanders tried destroying his and April's lives? "There has to be a reason for this obsession of hers," he said, feeling his own anger igniting once again when he thought about all he'd almost lost. What if April hadn't shared with him the reason she was ending things? What if they never got the opportunity to reconcile their issues? Ever? Sad thing was, Karen Sanders had been counting on that.

"Karen Sanders thought she had it all worked out," Griffin said. "She would get you out of my life, get Brian out of Erica's and then she would go to work on me and Erica and try to get us together...although, Erica and I have told her countless times that we don't feel that way about each other."

"It would not have mattered to her," April replied. "She figured with your and Erica's broken hearts, the two of you would have been glad to settle into a loveless marriage. Like hers. You would think with Mr. Sanders's affair she would have learned her lesson."

Griffin tenderly stroked her shoulder. "A normal person would have but not one obsessed with getting what she wanted, which brings me back to my earlier question. Why such an obsession?"

"Maybe she believes strongly in that curse that Erica told me about."

"My family knows about that curse but hasn't ever given it a second thought...except when Mrs. Sanders convinced my mother that my marrying Erica was crucial to our way of life. My mother has pretty much accepted my decision and got off my back about it years ago."

"Then I don't know what to tell you, Griffin, and I don't want to think about what she will do or the lies she will tell when she finds out we're back together."

He heard the trembling in her voice and knew Karen Sanders's visit had done a number on April, sent her into an emotional spin. And he doubted he would ever be able to forgive the old woman for doing that.

"I need to talk to Erica," he said deeply. "Once I tell her what her mother has done—"

"She won't believe you until you have solid proof. She thinks her mother is going through an emotional trauma and is protective of her right now. Besides, once Mrs. Sanders get wind that you're on to her she will probably try covering her tracks. It's going to take all Karen Sanders's intended victims to work together to bring all her lies to light and end her manipulations once and for all."

Griffin was silent as he thought about what April had said. Then an idea came into his head, one that would definitely set Karen Sanders back a notch, and he smiled at the thought of how it could be executed.

"What are you smiling about?" April asked.

He glanced over at her and then pulled her into his arms. It felt so good having her there. He reached out and ran his fingers through her hair, pushing a few loose strands away from her face. "I'll tell you later. But first I think some making-up time is in order," he said, before lowering his mouth to hers.

Chapter Thirty-Six

Wilson Sanders shook his head in disbelief as he stared at Griffin. "Karen actually threatened April with that kind of foolishness?"

"Yes, sir, so I hope you can understand why I intend to end this once and for all. She has gone too far," Griffin said.

"Yes, she has and to think she might have been responsible for Erica and Brian's breakup makes me furious. I had my suspicions and even told Brian's mother I believed Karen was capable of doing such a thing. However, it would be hard for anyone to believe she would actually go that far."

Griffin nodded. "Well, I think she did go that far and I'm hoping you can explain to me why she's so obsessed with me and Erica marrying."

Wilson leaned forward. "I wish I knew but I don't have a clue. She was close to her father while growing up, and I'm thinking that since he really believed in that Hayes–Delbert curse he might have brainwashed her into believing that there was a valid reason for the curse to be revoked. That wouldn't surprise me, considering her sister Blair was supposed to marry your uncle Simon. The Delberts were depending on a union between them and according to what Simon told me later, they put both him and Blair under a lot of pressure."

"So they weren't in love?"

"No. They were getting married because everyone expected them to do so. But when the wedding didn't take place the families decided you and Erica were the next likely couple for a Hayes–Delbert union."

Frustration lined Griffin's features. "But why? Why is such a union so important?"

"The only person who can answer that is Karen, and maybe Blair, depending on what condition her mind is in."

Griffin stared at him. "Blair? But Blair's dead."

Wilson shook his head. "No, she's not. Karen fabricated the story of Blair's death, but as far as I know she's alive and living in some exclusive private rest home."

He could tell that bit of news had shocked the younger man.

"Blair's alive and Mrs. Sanders has kept that information hidden all these years?"

"Yes. Karen's not even aware that I know. I haven't told her because knowing how her mind works, I figure she's doing it so Blair doesn't embarrass her in a comatose condition. Most people wouldn't think that way, but Karen has an unusual way of seeing things. Besides, she and Blair were never close. Karen was always jealous of her sister. But at least I know that she is taking care of her. The place she has her in isn't cheap."

Griffin inhaled a deep breath. "I take it Erica doesn't know."

Wilson shook his head. "Erica has no idea what her mother is capable of, which is why I agree with what April told you. Before approaching Erica I would have my ducks in a row. She sees her mother as the victim and not the perpetrator. It's going to hurt her deeply to discover all the stuff Karen has done, especially how she intentionally ruined her relationship with Brian."

"What exactly happened, if you don't mind me asking?"

"No, I don't mind." Wilson then told Griffin what Rita had relayed to him. He felt bad that Griffin was being overloaded with all his wife's heartless antics and ended by saying, "That's the gist of it. Brian has hired a private investigator and intends to find out who set him up. He is just as determined as you to find out the truth."

"That's good to hear, since I plan to fly to Dallas to meet with Brian. I believe at this stage that it would be wise for us to get together and compare notes."

Wilson nodded. "Considering everything, I think that's a good idea. A real good one."

"I'm leaving for the day now, Mr. Lawson. Will you need anything else before I go?"

Brian glanced up at his secretary. "No, I'm fine. Have a good evening and I'll see you in the morning." He leaned back in his chair the moment the door was closed and thought about the call he'd gotten that morning from Griffin Hayes. The man had requested a meeting with him, preferring not to discuss things over the phone. Brian couldn't help wondering why Hayes of all people would fly all the way to Dallas to meet with him.

Brian glanced at his watch. He had instructed security to notify him when the man arrived and then escort him up to his office. He stood and walked over to the window, thinking of the latest developments. Earlier today Matt had called with the name of the person who'd met with Donna Hardy that day at Stella's. He was a private investigator from New York by the name of Jaye Pittman.

Brian drew in a deep breath. At least he didn't have to put

up with seeing Donna Hardy around the office any longer. The woman had turned in her resignation.

Brian had given her fair warning that she might be hearing from him again if he decided to take legal action, depending on what else Matt uncovered. He could tell she had been bothered by that, knowing she wasn't getting a clean break. And he'd read in the paper today that Judge Meadows had officially submitted his resignation. No doubt Donna had told him about all the pictures and information Matt had collected.

The buzzer sounded on his desk and he moved across the room. It was security calling. "Yes?"

"That gentleman you were expecting is here, sir. We're about to escort him up."

"Thanks." Brian was more than ready for this meeting and figured he would find out soon enough what it was about.

Timing the arrival perfectly, he was standing in front of his door when a knock sounded and he opened it. He had never met Griffin Hayes but Erica had pretty much told him the man's whole story.

"Griffin Hayes? I'm Brian Lawson," he said, extending his hand and getting what he expected. A firm handshake.

"Glad to meet you, Brian. I think we have a few things we need to discuss," Griffin said as he preceded Brian into his office.

"Do we?"

"Yes. What I'm about to tell you will change your life, believe me."

It didn't take Griffin long to determine he liked Brian. Not only had he taken the news of Karen Sanders's sabotage well, he was able to add some further details, thanks to his own investigation.

"So to answer your question, Griffin," Brian was saying,

"there is no doubt in my mind Karen Sanders is behind it and I think Matt figured out how it was done. She has someone working behind the scenes for her, a P.I. from New York by the name of Jaye Pittman."

"Jaye?"

Brian raised a brow. "I take it you know him?"

"Yes. He was born and raised in Hattersville and in fact he's related to Karen. He was an attorney at one time but after a few years decided to become a private investigator. I went to school with him and he always seemed rather strange then."

"Well, it seems he's the one behind the setup at my place and he used Donna Hardy to carry out his plan, which ultimately was orchestrated by Karen."

Griffin nodded. "According to April, Karen led Erica to believe she was visiting a friend in Wyoming, and Erica told her mother she was going to visit with April in L.A. Karen was so sure that was a lie and Erica was coming to see you that she caught a plane to L.A. and then met with April and convinced her we were siblings."

At that moment the buzzer on Brian's desk sounded and he answered. It was security again. "Yes?"

"Mr. Matt Seacrest is here to see you, sir."

"Send him on up."

Brian then glanced over at Griffin. "Matt has been out of town checking up on some lead. I wasn't expecting him back for a day or so."

At the knock on the door, Brian called out, "Come on in, Matt."

Moments later introductions had been made and Brian could tell from Matt's expression that whatever he'd discovered wasn't good. "What did you find out, Matt?"

Matt looked first at Brian, then at Griffin and again back

at Brian. "I think this thing with Karen Sanders goes deeper than either of you can imagine."

"In what way?" Griffin asked.

"I ran into Stacy Barnes while in Houston and she mentioned that someone contacted her trying to get some smut on you, Brian. She had the man's number still in her phone, so I traced it back to Jaye Pittman. But that was back in June, a few weeks after her engagement party and before the shit hit the fan with your mother and Mr. Sanders."

He paused a moment and drew in a deep breath. "This might seem crazy to you, but hear me out as to what I think, okay?"

Brian nodded. "Okay."

Matt leaned forward in the chair. "I think that somehow this Jaye guy found out about your mother and Sanders's affair and told Karen about it. I'm convinced she knew about it long before those pictures were sent through the phone."

Brian stared at him for a moment and then said, "If what you're saying is true, then all her so-called emotional trauma was nothing more than an act."

Matt nodded. "I have every reason to believe that it was. And I even think she sent the pictures to herself and Erica, you and Wilson."

At the shocked look on both Brian's and Griffin's faces he held up his hand. "Hear me out for a second and I'll tell you why I think she did it. In fact I probably can prove it.

"Using the same procedures manufacturers use to recall a product, after I was able to determine the kind of phone those pictures were sent from, I did a search to find out what outlet stores were selling them. It's one of those prepay models you can buy from just about anywhere, but most stores only sell particular brands."

He paused to take something out of his jacket. "This is a list of all the ones purchased in Hattersville or surrounding areas thirty days before those pictures were sent. I was able to trace one purchased a mere week before, and guess who bought it?"

"Jaye Pittman?"

He nodded. "I was able to trace the satellite signal. Jaye was in New York that week and the signal came from Hattersville. It's my guess Karen used it and sent those pictures to the four phones."

Brian exhaled a deep breath. "But we don't have concrete proof of that."

"If you find the phone then you will. I bet it's still somewhere in her possession."

The room got quiet as they processed Matt's new information. Griffin spoke first. "Considering what we know so far I think we need to tell Erica. She might not think she can trust you anymore, Brian, but she trusts April. If we're all there, collaborating each other's story, then she has to at least believe we're on to something, and maybe she can come up with a reason for her mother's obsession."

Brian frowned. "I think we all know the reason. That damn curse."

Griffin shook his head. "It might be, but personally, I think there's more to it."

Brian lifted a brow. "More to it, like what?"

Griffin shrugged. "I don't know. Maybe her sister knows."

"Her sister? Erica said her mother's sister died years ago."

"Everyone thought she died, just the way Karen wanted them to," Griffin said, shaking his head as if the entire thought was too unbelievable to share. "But Wilson discovered last year she hadn't died. Karen had fabricated her death and faked her funeral. Blair is still alive in some nursing home in Cleveland."

"You got to be kidding," Matt said, as if he refused to believe one word of what Griffin had said.

"I kid you not. It's an exclusive place, and I'm sure to have kept a secret like that for this long, Karen is paying good money to the medical staff to keep her hidden," Griffin said.

"Then if money is what we need to see her, let's see if we can arrange a visit. Find out what we can about the place, but we don't want to do anything to tip our hand to Karen that we're on to her," Brian cautioned.

"I still say it's time we let Erica know at least what we've found out without raising her mother's suspicions that something is going on," Griffin said. He smiled. "And I know just the way to do it. Hear me out and let me know what you guys think."

Chapter Thirty-Seven

Karen was in the dining room sitting at the table with Erica when she heard the doorbell ring. "I wonder who that can be this time of the day," she said, taking a sip of her tea. She looked up moments later when her housekeeper appeared. "Who is it, Cretia?"

"Mr. Griffin is here to see Ms. Erica."

"He is?" Karen said, a smile beaming off her face as she quickly got to her feet. "Then please show him in."

Surprise flickered in Erica's eyes as she stood, too. Why did Griffin want to see her? Although she hadn't yet spoken to April, she had gotten a text message from Griffin a few days ago saying he and April were trying to work things out and not to mention anything to her mother about them. His request had been odd but she had done what he'd asked.

She stood by the table as Cretia escorted Griffin into the kitchen. "Hello, Mrs. Sanders."

And then he flashed a smile over at Erica. "I thought that was your car I saw parked in the driveway. I was passing by

on my way to my parents' house and thought I'd drop in since
I haven't seen you in months."

He was apparently up to something, Erica realized, since
he had just seen her last week. She tried to play along. "It's
always good seeing you, Griffin. Did you need me for something?" Her mother was hanging on their every word while
she continued to beam.

"Yes, that new Tyler Perry movie starts today in Cleveland
and I wondered if you'd be interested in going to a matinee
to avoid the mad rush that will probably be there tonight."

Before she could reply, her mother spoke for her. "A day
at the movies sounds like fun. You two should go and enjoy
yourselves. Have a good time."

Griffin grinned. "I agree with Mrs. Sanders. Come on,
Erica. I need to get away for a while and I would love to take
you to the movies with me."

Erica shook her head and smiled. "I never said I wouldn't
go. What time do you want to pick me up later from my
place?"

"What about around two?" he said.

"Fine. I'll be ready." And then she gave him a look that
clearly said, *And you, Griffin Hayes, better be ready to explain
what this little stunt is all about.*

Griffin was on time and Erica was dressed and ready to
walk out the door. "Okay, Griffin, what's going on and where
is April?"

He waited for her to close and lock the door behind her.
"I'm taking you to her now."

"I figured you would be, but why so secretive? And why
on earth did you pull that stunt earlier in front of Mom? You
deliberately gave her the wrong impression. Now she thinks
something is developing between us."

"April will explain everything."

Moments later when they were seated in his car, he glanced over at her. "Promise me you'll keep an open mind."

"About what?"

"About anything and everything."

The look she gave him told him that she was more confused than ever. A half hour later he could tell her confusion increased when he took a turnoff for the interstate and headed for the lake house his parents had once owned but sold to him a few years back. But she didn't ask any questions and he was glad of that.

He was also glad to see April standing outside when they pulled into the lake house drive. Erica, he noticed, had seen April, too, and a huge smile spread across her lips.

Griffin thought it was actually kind of strange the way things had started out between them all those years ago. There had always been a closeness between April and Erica, a deep friendship that even Karen Sanders hadn't been able to destroy. And the sad thing about it was that the older woman truly thought she had destroyed it.

Karen's visit to April should have accomplished that. It was sad, Griffin thought, that she didn't know anything about love—the kind between true friends as well as the undying love between a man and a woman. That had been Karen Sanders's downfall.

Erica had opened the car door to get out before he brought the vehicle to a complete stop. And as he unhooked his seat belt he saw the two women run toward each other and embrace.

"Girl, where have you been? Don't you dare let me worry about you like that again. No matter what is happening with you, I should have been there for you," Erica said, looking her friend over to make sure she was okay.

"I know. It was something I couldn't share with you at the time but now I can," April said, smiling.

"And this had better be a good reason for shutting me out."

"I think it will be. And I understand you've been going through your own hell without me," April said.

The smile left Erica lips when she was reminded why she cried herself to sleep every night and had lost weight. Heartbreak could do that to you.

She tried not thinking about Brian but would find herself doing so anyway, anytime and anyplace. All the time. Whenever she thought about her love for him and the pain caused by his betrayal, her heart would start breaking all over again.

Beside her, April ushered her up the steps. "Come on inside so we can talk."

Erica sensed something was going on the moment her feet touched the porch and she glanced over at April, who gave her a funny look. Griffin had a similar look on his face. "Okay, you guys, what's going on?"

Instead of responding, Griffin opened the door and then they stepped aside to let her enter first. She frowned as she walked over the threshold. She was vaguely aware of someone closing the door behind her when she caught a movement across the room out of her peripheral vision.

She knew even before turning who was in the room with her; she picked up his warm, subtle scent. And when he moved out of the shadows her breath caught in her throat. She looked into his face and her heart jumped at the sight of him. His features taut, serious and as handsome as she remembered, Brian stood there looking so overwhelmingly sexy. It had been almost four weeks since she'd seen him, but she had thought of him every day.

"Hello, Erica. It's good seeing you again," he said, his gaze focused on her shocked face.

From the first time they'd met his voice had been what had captured her. It was a deep, rich timbre that had made blood rush all the way to her head, as it was doing now. She came close to running over to him, throwing herself in his arms, when she remembered the pain he'd caused her. Then she took a step back before swinging around to face Griffin and April.

"Why did you bring me here? Why is he here?"

April reached out and captured her hand. "Because it's time you heard the truth, Erica."

She pulled her hand away. "What are you talking about? I know the truth, April," she said, fighting back tears. "I haven't had a chance to tell you what happened, what I found when I arrived in Dallas."

"You don't have to," April said softly. "Both you and Brian were played just like Griffin and I were played, and I think it's time for us to compare notes."

Erica frowned. "What are you talking about?"

April crossed her arms over her chest. "I'm talking about the fact that your mother lied to you, Erica. That day you told her you were going to visit me in L.A., she knew you were lying and had every intention of going to see Brian."

"No, there was no way she could have known."

"Yes, she figured just where you would go the first chance you got and it wouldn't be to spend time with me. She knew you were going to Dallas, just like she'd never planned to go to Wyoming to visit that friend."

"What are you saying?"

"I'm saying that I know for a fact that your mother never went to Wyoming because she came to see me in Los Angeles."

Erica shook her head, confused. "That's not possible."

"It is possible. She did."

"But why would Mom come to see you?"

April leaned against Griffin as if she needed him for support. She glanced up at him before looking back at Erica. "The reason she came to see me was to make sure I ended things between me and Griffin. She threatened me with dire consequences if I didn't."

"She did what!"

"She said she had proof I was fathered by Herbert Hayes and she would tell everyone that Griffin and I were involved in an incestuous relationship if I didn't end things with him, as well as walk away from my friendship with you. That's why I didn't call you. I was too afraid to. And that's why I ended things with Griffin."

Erica placed her hand to her mouth in disbelief. "No."

"Yes. Thankfully you told Griffin where I was and he assured me Herbert Hayes was not my father and we aren't related. Your mother had lied. And she mentioned while she was in L.A. that she was also making sure you ended your relationship with Brian, as well. That way you and Griffin could be free for each other. She figured heartbreak would bring the two of you together, if nothing else would."

Erica's head began spinning and she closed her eyes. "No, no. None of that can be true."

"It is true, Erica. Everything you saw at Brian's house that day was exactly what she wanted you to see. What she paid someone to do to make it seem like he had betrayed you. She planned it all. She knew you were on your way to Dallas and made sure things were ready when you got there. She hired Jaye Pittman to help her get what she wanted."

"Jaye?"

"Yes, your good old cousin Jaye. He did whatever your mother paid him to do. But that's not all. We have proof she is the one who texted those pictures of your father's affair and then pretended she was so torn up about it. I'm sure if you searched her room you'll find the prepaid phone she used, if she hasn't thrown it away yet. Even if she did, we got the receipt showing Jaye purchased it for her. She used your father's affair with Brian's mother to her advantage, playing on your sympathy, getting your support and turning you against Brian. In her mind she had everything to gain by doing so.

"Think about how perfect the timing was," April continued. "And those prescriptions she'd been taking for a heart problem are nothing more than sugar pills. I had Margie Graham who works for Dr. Cobb check for me. Margie owed me a favor from years ago when I loaned her money for her divorce. I figured someone who was doing as much devilment as your mother didn't necessarily have a bad heart...just an evil one."

Erica took it all in, and only one thought was able to form in her brain. She swung around to gaze at Brian. Looked into the depths of his dark eyes, saw the pain and hurt she'd caused by not believing in him and not trusting him. He had tried telling her he was innocent but she hadn't believed him. She had seen the worst and she had believed it.

"Brian—"

She took a step toward him and he took a step back. Then he turned and walked off toward the kitchen. She flinched when she heard the kitchen door slam shut behind him.

A flood of remorse tore into her and she felt the weight of everything April had told her on her shoulders. Tears she couldn't stop racked her body and she began shaking.

"It's okay, Erica." She heard April's voice and knew as always her friend was there.

Somehow April helped her over to the sofa and she dropped down on it and hid her face in her hands as her tears continued to fall. Ashamed. She was so ashamed for everything her mother had done. Everything she had believed because of her mother. She dropped her hands down in her lap. "How could she do this to me, April? To Brian? How could she do what she did to anyone? To you and Griffin. How could any one person be so evil, so vindictive and so manipulating."

"That's the one thing we can't figure out," April said softly. "Why she did it."

Erica turned to her, filled with anger. "I know why she did it. It has everything to do with that damn curse. She's always been obsessed with it."

"Then we need to know why." April shifted in her seat. "There are two other things I need to tell you about."

Erica shook her head. "I don't think I can handle any more." She looked toward the door through which Brian had left. "He hates me. I should have believed in him, April. I should not have thought the worst."

"Yes, but from what I heard the evidence against him was pretty damaging. I think even he understands that. However, he can't help but feel a little down right now. I think he needs a little time to himself."

"How did you get him to come?" Erica asked, staring at April through her tears.

"He asked to come. To be here for you, Erica. He had hired a private investigator to prove his innocence. They had already figured out your mother's duplicity by the time Griffin flew to Dallas to pay Brian a visit."

Erica drew in a deep breath. "And I thought he was having an affair with that attorney at his firm. Donna Hardy."

"Evidently, Jaye was able to get something on Hardy to make her do whatever he wanted. He told her to set up the scene and make it seem like Brian was unfaithful to you."

Erica threw her head back and inhaled deeply. "It worked. I didn't want to hear anything he said. Our love was based on trust and I let him down."

She then glanced around. "Where is Griffin?"

"He went outside. He's still shaken by what your mother

tried doing, as well. He and Brian were determined to get to the truth. They loved us that much."

Erica shook her head. "Griffin might love you, but I've lost Brian's love and I doubt that I'll ever be able to get it back."

"Don't do this to yourself, Erica. Brian still loves you or else he wouldn't be here for you now."

Erica wiped her eyes. "You think so?"

"Yes. Go to him. Talk to him. Tell him how you feel. Everyone is entitled to at least one mistake."

Erica stood slowly on wobbly knees as she drew in a calming breath. She did owe him an apology, but she wouldn't blame him if he didn't accept it. She'd started to walk away when she thought of something. "What are the two other things that I need to know?"

A small smile touched April's lips as she waved her hand. "Go on. It can wait. Just go to your man."

Erica ran to the kitchen to go out the same door where Brian had exited earlier.

Chapter Thirty-Eight

Brian heard the sound of the screen door closing but didn't need to turn around to see who it was. He hadn't figured seeing Erica again would have such an effect on him, but it had.

"I owe you an apology, Brian."

He was tempted to turn around but didn't. He would let her have her say and then he would have his.

"I said mean and hateful things to you that day and I doubted you when I should have believed in you. Our love, our trust was put to the test for the first time and I failed. I am so sorry."

He heard the choke in her voice and couldn't help but turn around. But he wasn't ready to give up his anger and pain yet. He had gone without her for four weeks. For four weeks he had walked around like a dead man, a man emotionally crippled in just about every way. But now seeing her again brought it all home to him. He loved her and nothing would ever change that. While love filled his heart, the hurt still lingered there.

Before he could tell her, she said, "I wish I could take back all the cruel things I said to you that day, but I can't. Things seemed so black-and-white and it nearly destroyed me to think that I wasn't enough for you.

"And to think my mother was behind it. That she is capable of doing such evil things, that she put her own selfish wants and needs above my happiness, hurts deeply."

He gazed intensely into her eyes and saw the pain there, the hurt, the shame and the regrets. He hadn't been looking for love that day in Myrtle Beach, but it had found him anyway and more than once over the past four weeks a part of him had regretted ever meeting her, had resented falling in love so boundlessly. But now as he looked at her he knew it couldn't be helped. He was made to love her, which was the main reason he was here. He had wanted to be here when she heard the truth. Not to gloat or shove it in her face that she was wrong and should have been more trusting of him, but to be here to shoulder her pain, help her through this. Help them through this. And to be the man he would always be. The man who loved her.

"Now you know the truth," he said. "She can't hurt us anymore."

She wiped a tear away from her eye. "Us?"

He smiled softly. "Yes, us. There will always be an us, Erica. We just finished traveling a pretty rocky road. There were times it appeared we wouldn't make it, but we did. Nothing has changed. I love you. You love me. Besides," he said with a little catch in his voice, "do you honestly think I'd give you up that easily?"

Erica began nibbling on her bottom lip, too afraid to hope. "Are you saying, considering everything, including what an evil mother I have, you still want me?"

"I'll always want you and I'm marrying you and not your mother."

Their gazes held and then Erica rushed toward him and threw herself into his arms. He held her tight and whispered how much he loved her. In turn she told him how much she loved him and apologized again for not trusting him, for almost throwing away the best thing to ever come into her life.

"I've missed you so much, baby," he whispered against her hair. "I've been like a dying man and every day I was afraid I was about to take my last breath without you in my life."

"And I've missed you, as well," Erica said, tilting her head back and looking up into his eyes while keeping her arms wrapped tightly around him. "And to think of how much I almost lost because of my mother. I can't—"

He placed a finger to her lips. "Shh. I don't want to talk about your mother now. We can do that again later. This is what I want. What I need."

And then he captured her lips. The moment contact was made, every bone in his body seemed to pulverize. Blood rushed through his veins and he felt more love for her at that moment than ever before. He wanted to do more than just kiss her and knew that would all come later. They still had a lot to discuss regarding her mother, but for now he was happy to have her in his arms and kiss her like there were no tomorrows.

Long moments later their mouths separated but he still had his arms wrapped around her, as though fearful if he removed them she would vanish into thin air. He smiled down at her. "As much as I'd like to finish this—and I truly do intend to do so later—there are still more things we need to discuss and additional plans we need to make. Come on."

He then placed her hand in his and led her into the house.

Erica, sitting in Brian's lap on the sofa, glanced across the room at April, who likewise was sitting on the love seat in

Griffin's lap. She could tell from the look on her friend's face she was happy and the thought that her mother almost ruined that happiness was unforgivable. She couldn't wait to confront her mother about this. No wonder her father had been so eager to grab love when he'd gotten the chance to do so.

She cleared her throat, deciding if she didn't get April and Griffin's attention they would be headed back to the bedroom. She smiled when she thought of how when she and Brian had come back inside the house, April and Griffin had been behind closed doors. It hadn't taken much to figure out what was going on so they had gone back outside to take a walk and to talk some more. They had stayed away from the topic of her mother. The conversation had been about them and how they intended to reschedule their wedding as soon as possible.

"Okay, April," she said, deciding now was the time. "You indicated earlier that you had two additional things to cover. Tell me now because I intend to head back home." And Brian would be coming with her. They had decided to confront her mother together.

She noticed the room suddenly got quiet, too quiet, and she studied April, who looked down as if she was nervous about what she had to say.

The tightening of Brian's arms around her waist was a good sign that whatever April would be sharing with her would be more of her mother's evil shenanigans, and Erica didn't want to think what they could possibly be.

"April?"

April looked up at her. Erica could tell she was nervous. But why? "Tell me."

April nodded. "You recall earlier when I told you that your mother tried breaking me and Griffin up by claiming Herbert Hayes was my daddy?"

"Yes, and you said you knew that he wasn't, so that's all good, right?"

"Yes, that's all good. But what I didn't tell you is that I know who my real father is."

Erica lifted a brow. "Who told you? You've never known before."

"Griffin told me. He overheard my real father talking to his father one day in the wine cellar when he was only sixteen, so he's known all this time. He never had a reason to tell me because he figured I knew."

"So, who is he? Was it Ivan Witherspoon like we thought?"

April shook her head. "No, it wasn't him."

"Who was it then?" she asked, noticing April evasiveness.

When April didn't respond Erica glanced over at Brian and from the look on his face she could tell that he knew. She looked back over to April. "Okay, girlfriend, what's going on? Who is your daddy?" she tried asking in a lighthearted way.

"Omar Delbert was my father."

Erica's eyes widened. "My grandfather?"

"Yes. And I have reason to believe he raped my mother when she was fifteen."

Brian pulled Erica into his arms and held her while she cried. As soon as she had comprehended what April had said she burst into tears that she hadn't been able to stop. He had felt her anger. Her pain. Her shame. To know that her grandfather had abused a fifteen-year-old girl had shaken her to the core. And when it had hit her that April was her mother's sister and her own aunt, she had raced across the room and hugged April, welcomed her to the family and apologized for the shameful way both her and her mother had been treated by the Delberts over the years.

She had started shaking then. And she was still shaking.

Trembling and crying. Brian continued to rub her back while whispering soothing words to her. Letting her know that above all else, he loved her and would be there for her.

April still had one other thing to tell her and, after the way Erica had broken down earlier, he figured it would probably be best if he went ahead and told her himself.

"There is one other thing we need to tell you, Erica. Something we think you need to know, sweetheart."

She slowly pulled her face from his chest where she'd wet his shirt with her tears. She looked up at him. "I don't think I can handle any more bad deeds from my mother and her side of the family, Brian. Please tell me what you're about to say isn't about them."

He wished he could but he couldn't. In one afternoon she had discovered that not only was her mother a manipulating and heartless person, so was her grandfather. Brian's heart ached for her.

"I can't, baby." When she flinched he wrapped his arms around her. "But when it's all over and we learn the truth about everything, we will deal with it together. Okay?"

"Yes, okay. So tell me."

He hesitated for a moment. "It's about your aunt Blair."

Her brows lifted. "Aunt Blair? She's been dead for a long time. Remember, I told you about her being in a car accident a week before her wedding to Griffin's uncle. She was in a coma for a while and then she died."

He shook his head. "No, that's not true."

She blinked. "What's not true? Are you saying she wasn't in a car accident?"

"Yes, she was in a car accident and, yes, she was in a coma. What she didn't do was die. Your aunt is alive, Erica. Your father only found out last year. Your mother fabricated her death, and all this time your aunt has been alive and kept at this exclusive nursing home in Cleveland."

Erica just stared at him as if what he'd told her was the most ridiculous thing she'd ever heard. But then, as if his expression indicated the truth of his words, she shook her head. "Please tell me it isn't true. That Mom didn't lie to us about that, as well."

"I'm sorry but she did," Brian said softly. "And your aunt Blair might hold the key to why your mother is so obsessed with this curse. Matt has made arrangements for us to visit the nursing home tonight when the head administrator and the private nurse leave. It seems they are on your mother's bankroll and will do whatever she wants them to do regarding her sister's care. We don't know what we might find. She still might be in a coma and not able to shed light on anything, I don't know. But we felt it would be worth a shot before we confront your mother to expose all her lies."

"When will all the lies and deceit end?" Erica asked softly before snuggling her face in his shirt again.

Later that evening the two couples and Matt were escorted through the back door of the Westminster Nursing Home. The male nurse who was being paid to sneak them in was very cautious as he moved them from one empty corridor to the next.

"I don't know a lot about the patient you want to see. But I can tell you from what I was able to find out after checking the charts, she isn't comatose. But her nurse, Ms. Vickers, is required to keep her drugged up if she has too many outbursts."

"That doesn't surprise me," Matt said. He had met them here in Cleveland where, for the past two days, he'd been working out the intricate details of making sure they had a way into the nursing home after hours.

The nurse beckoned them to walk quickly as he moved

them to another part of the building. "This is where she is being kept as per her caretaker's orders."

April glanced around. This part of the building looked spacious, elegant, and it was obvious anyone who was put in this wing was connected to money. Goose bumps ran down her arm as she realized she was about to meet her half sister.

The nurse ushered them into a huge room and the door was closed behind them. April glanced around the same time everyone else did and their gazes lit on a woman sitting in a wheelchair at a table reading softly to herself. She glanced up when she saw them and smiled, and April's knees almost buckled beneath her.

She was beautiful. Her hair was elegantly styled and her skin shone. Karen Sanders might have kept her sister well hidden from the world, but at least she had kept her in Delbert fashion.

"Did you come to read to me?" Blair asked them. She then added, "No one has read to me about the cat and the fiddle. I used to have a cat once."

Following Erica's lead, April moved closer. The three men hung back.

"I would love to read to you, Aunt Blair," Erica said, sliding into the chair across from her. "You like hearing nursery rhymes?"

"Yes. It makes me forget."

Erica looked at April and nodded. "What does it make you forget?" she asked softly, using the approach Matt had suggested they use if they found her able to talk.

Blair's gaze then moved from Erica to April and the smile slowly left her face. "What my daddy did to her." She pointed at April. "That's Connie's child. Latonia."

Though taken aback, April followed the older woman's thoughts. Blair thought she was her mother. Nana had always told her she looked like a younger version of her mother.

"What did your daddy do to her?" Erica asked softly.

"He hurt her. I saw him. Karen saw him. We should have stopped him, but we didn't. I pleaded with Karen to stop him but she wouldn't. She never liked Connie's daughter and said she was getting what she deserved. It was ugly."

Blair seemed to be staring into space as if she was remembering. "I couldn't take it anymore so I ran away. I was driving too fast and couldn't slow down. I lost control. I—I..."

She placed her hands over her face and Erica reached out and gently pulled them back down. "It's okay, Aunt Blair. It's okay."

Blair then looked at April. "Will you forgive me, Latonia? I should have stopped him, but no one can stop him when he gets that way."

An hour later after taking turns reading nursery rhymes to Blair, April and Erica followed the men out the door. Brian pulled Erica gently to him. "Don't worry. I have a feeling that between you and April she will continue to be taken care of."

Erica nodded. Yes, between her and April, Blair Delbert would always be taken care of.

Chapter Thirty-Nine

Erica knew everyone was watching her when she picked up the phone to call her mother. It was time to bring the lies and deceit to an end and it would start with this phone call.

What she was about to do had been Matt's idea and it seemed like the perfect way to bring Karen Sanders's years of manipulations, evil and control to an end. Erica had no qualms about what she was to do and felt it was totally justified. Her mother needed help and she would make sure she got it.

She had returned to the lake house with everyone to find her father there, waiting for her. In tears she had walked out of Brian's arms into his and, just as she'd done when she was a child, she had cried on him. The main question that had been on her mind when she'd met her father's gaze was how he had endured living with her mother all those years.

He had taken her outside to sit on the porch to explain it to her. "At first it didn't matter. I never knew love, and you can't miss what you never had. I knew just what kind of marriage

I would have before I wedded your mother. I wasn't looking for love and neither was she."

He'd reached out and taken her hand in his. "Then you were born and any thoughts of getting a divorce dissolved from my mind. I just wanted to be the best dad I could be to you. To be there whenever you needed me."

Erica had nodded. "And you were." She hugged her dad, feeling sorry for ever doubting him.

"You're ready to do it, Erica?" April asked softly, pulling her out of her reverie.

She nodded her head. "Yes, I'm ready."

She glanced at her watch. It was close to eleven o'clock as she began dialing her mother's phone number. Her mother was probably still up, working crossword puzzles or playing a game of solitaire.

"Hello."

Erica swallowed. The sound of her mother's voice sent cold chills through her body at the thought of all the things her mother had done, the lies she had told. The people she had hurt.

"Hi, Mom, this is Erica."

"Erica, I'm glad you called. How was your date today with Griffin? You have to tell me all about it. How long have you been home?"

"I'm not home yet, Mom. In fact, Griffin and I are still to-gether." She glanced across the room at Griffin, who had his arm around April. "Griffin and I have made a few decisions about our lives."

"Really? Have you?"

"Yes. And we've decided to fly to Vegas tonight and do something we should have done long ago."

"Oh, my goodness!" Erica could hear the excitement in her mother's voice. Since she was on speakerphone, everyone in the room could hear it.

"We'll be there for a few days," Erica added. "Don't expect us back to town for a while."

"Of course, I do understand," Karen said, bubbling over. "It's about time the two of you act responsibly and do the right thing."

"Yes, we think so, too. I'll contact you when we get back."

"Okay, and don't rush back. Have fun and don't have any regrets."

Erica couldn't help but smile when she glanced over at Brian. "Trust me, Mom, I don't plan on having any regrets. Good-bye."

After Erica clicked off the phone she crossed the room and walked straight into Brian's arms. He held her a minute before Matt spoke up. "Okay, everyone, it's time to get to the airport. This is the first time I've ever coordinated a double wedding. Hell, this is the first time I've coordinated a wedding, period."

Everyone, including Erica's father, was ushered out of the lake house. Brian had called his mother and she had agreed to catch a flight and join them in Vegas. Erica couldn't help but smile, thinking that this time her mother was right. She and Griffin were doing the right thing.

Less than twenty-four hours later, the two couples, surrounded by family and close friends, pledged their love for each other and committed their lives together.

Rita dabbed the tears from her eyes as she stood next to Lori and looked on. Once she'd heard of her godson's wedding, Lori had packed her bag for Vegas, too. Rita couldn't help glancing across the room every chance she got to meet Wilson's gaze. She was glad the truth had come out but nothing between them had changed. He was still a married man.

Although seeing him again made her realize just how much she loved him and missed him.

"He's so good-looking," Lori leaned over close to whisper. "If you don't jump his bones tonight, I might be tempted to."

Rita couldn't help but smile at her friend's flirty comment. "I told you what we had decided to do...or should I say not to do. He's still married."

"But he is separated from his wife. Didn't you say he'd moved out and is in the process of getting a divorce?" At Rita's nod, she said, "Well, then... And trust me, girl, you don't owe anything to Karen Sanders anymore. That woman is as evil as evil could get. The thought of what she did to those two couples to keep them apart makes my blood boil."

Rita thought it made her blood boil, as well.

"Besides," Lori said, lowering her voice further still. "It's okay to be naughty and break rules here. It's Vegas. And what happens in Vegas stays in Vegas. You might want to remember that."

Rita glanced over at Wilson again. Judging by the look in his eyes, there was no way she could forget it. Just as she knew there was no way she was going to leave Vegas without sharing her bed with him.

Four days later, walking side by side, Griffin and Erica entered her mother's home. They had called her from the airport to let her know they were on their way home.

Her mother was there waiting for them in the living room with a huge, expectant smile on her face. "Well, well," she said, beaming even more when she saw the wedding rings on their fingers. "Welcome home!"

Erica had enjoyed her time away, spending all four days in Vegas wrapped in her husband's arms. The moment the plane had landed in Cleveland, however, all that happiness had fled.

She'd gotten depressed at the thought of what she and Griffin had to do. But there was no stopping it.

"Griffin and I need to make an announcement, Mom," she said after taking a deep breath. "We got married."

Karen glowed so bright it was almost blinding. "I know. And I am totally happy for you."

"Are you really, Mom? That's good to hear because there is one little glitch with us marrying."

Karen looked confused. "I don't understand. What kind of glitch can there be?"

It was Griffin who crossed his arms over his chest, smiled and said, "We didn't marry each other. Erica married Brian and I married April. We did the one thing you never wanted to see happen. We both married the persons we love."

Karen's face became all but distorted. "How dare the two of you mess with the Delbert legacy?"

Griffin chuckled. "Excuse me, ma'am, but I don't give a royal damn about any legacy. Erica and I have been telling you for years we weren't in love but you wouldn't listen. What you tried doing to April and Brian was unforgivable."

"Unforgivable?" she snarled before bursting into tears. "Do you know what the two of you have done? That curse needed to be broken or else..."

"Or else what, Mom? Why are you so obsessed with that curse? Why does Aunt Blair think it's linked to what Granddaddy did to April's mother?"

At the shocked look on her mother's face, Erica said, "Yes, I know all about Aunt Blair being alive and what she saw that day to make her get into a car accident. I also know about the lies you told April to keep her and Griffin apart and what you paid Jaye to do to Brian. He was set up by your orders and I doubt I can ever forgive you."

"But do you realize what the two of you have done? I was trying to protect your daughters."

"Protect our daughters how?"

Karen was rubbing her hands together. "Until that curse is broken any Delbert male that is born will have a hunger to lust after his daughter, his own flesh and blood. I know about it, trust me."

Erica went speechless at the implications of her mother's words. "Granddaddy abused you?" she asked her mom softly, hoping against hope that assumption was wrong.

"Yes. Both Blair and me. When I got older and realized what he was doing was wrong, he explained things to me. He said it was all because of that curse and until it was broken he couldn't stop it. Blair was to marry Simon to stop it, but she didn't. She freaked out when she walked in on what he was doing to Latonia. That caused her accident. Blair had threatened to tell Simon what he was doing to her so Dad turned his attentions to others like Latonia. Blair blamed herself for it happening."

Erica thought she was going to be sick and dropped down in the armchair. How could her grandfather use the curse as an excuse for his demented behavior, and how could her mother have believed him?

"The curse had nothing to do with your father's behavior, Mrs. Sanders," Griffin told her. "He was a sick man to do that to you, Blair, Latonia or any other young girl that he touched. He lied to you to cover up his actions. He was nothing but a bona fide pedophile, who should have been locked up with the key thrown away."

Karen turned on him, her eyes flashing fire. "How dare you! He was an outstanding member of this community. One of this town's forefathers. I understood why he was coming into my room and so did Blair, until Latonia came into the picture working as the laundry girl. She messed up everything."

Erica could only stare at her mother. She had been truly

brainwashed by Omar Delbert. "Griffin is right, Mom. There is no excuse for what he did to you, Blair or Latonia, and no telling how many other young girls. He was a sick man and I'm glad I never got a chance to know him."

Her mother ignored her words as she continued to rant and rave. "It will be your fault, mark my word," she screamed, pointing at them. "You should have married each other. Now it will take another generation for the curse to be broken."

"No, it won't," Griffin said angrily. "If you really believe in the curse then you know it officially ended four days ago when a Hayes married a Delbert. April has just as much Delbert blood running through her veins as you and Erica."

He then turned and walked out of the house. Erica glanced back at her mother. "He's right, so your curse is now broken."

She turned to leave and her mother called out, "Erica, don't go. My heart. You know what the doctor said about my heart."

Erica rolled her eyes as she turned around. "Then I suggest you take your sugar pills and yes, I know about that lie, too." She didn't wait to hear her mother's denial. "Oh, and over the next couple of weeks, I'm putting my house on the market and moving to Dallas to be with my husband."

She had thought about taking her aunt Blair and putting her in a facility close to her in Dallas but decided her mother would need her sister more now than ever. She doubted her mother knew just how alone she would be.

"Good-bye, Mom." She walked out the door, only glancing up when she'd closed it behind her. Griffin was waiting and together they walked toward the car that pulled up at that moment.

April got out of the car and ran into her husband's arms, while Erica went to Brian. It didn't seem to bother him that he'd left his mother and her father together in Vegas. The two weren't quite ready to leave Sin City and no one had to wonder why.

"Ready to go?" Brian asked, taking her hand in his.

"Yes, with you always." She glanced back at the huge house that had always been her home, a house she'd loved. But she was ready to move on. She had been ready.

On their wedding night Brian had told her about his surprise, the money his father had placed in trust for him. He'd known with her it had never been about money, but he had talked his godmother into selling them the house in Myrtle Beach. Lori had said she couldn't think of a couple who deserved it more.

Moments later as they drove down Wellington Road she knew in her heart that despite all the emotional drama, everything had ended well for her and April.

Epilogue

Six months later

Erica looked up from the book she was reading when she heard her name called. She smiled as she glanced out at the pier and waved. Seeing Brian sitting out there with a fishing rod in his hand reminded her of the day they first met.

She glanced down at her ring and smiled. She was truly happy. When Brian called her name again she looked up and saw him coming toward her. That morning she had awakened to a red rose and a white rose tied together with a silken thread on her nightstand. It had been a reminder of the love they had almost lost. And he had sat on the edge of the bed and whispered to her the same words he had spoken that day he had surprised her with dinner on this very same pier.

"Together, these roses represent unity and love, and the silken thread holding them together represents the strong bond between us that can never be broken."

The last six months had been special, even with her mother's refusal to acknowledge her marriage to Brian. Karen lived in the big house alone, shut away from family and friends. Her parents' divorce had become final last month, and she knew that her father and Rita were now an item, a very hot one. He was thinking about selling his company and moving to Dallas. But then she heard he and Rita might decide to move to Florida. They weren't making any final decisions about anything. Erica knew the older couple was enjoying their time together and she could truly say she was happy for them.

"Is that book any good?" Brian asked when he'd finally reached her.

"I wouldn't be reading it if it wasn't," she said, and grinned when he pulled her hair. "I talked to April today. She's happy being back in Hattersville and kicking off Griffin's mayoral campaign."

Of course some of the snobbish citizens were taken aback by Griffin's surprise marriage to April, but surprisingly there were others who were genuinely happy for them.

She kept in close contact with her aunt and flew to Cleveland to see her at least three times a month. She enjoyed reading the nursery rhymes to Blair, and on a few occasions April had gone with her.

It was during one of those times she had run into her mother while she was there. When Karen had seen her and April, she'd acted like she didn't know them. It was Erica's hope that one day her mother would come to realize all the wrongs she had done and all the people her actions had hurt.

"Whoa!" Before she'd realized what he was doing Brian had swept her off her feet, making the book fall from her hand.

"What do you think you're doing, Brian Lawson?"

He smiled down at her. "Taking you inside the house. I need a shower."

"So, what does that have to do with me?"

"You get to take one, too."

She smiled, thinking she had no complaints. She loved taking showers with him. She loved doing everything with him, even making babies. They wanted a lot of them and she couldn't wait to tell him tonight the first of the Lawson babies was on its way. The pregnancy test she had taken that morning had confirmed it.

She wrapped her arms around his neck. "I love you," she whispered.

"And I love you back," was his automatic response.

She smiled, knowing he did and that just like he'd said that morning, their bond could never be broken.

★ ★ ★ ★ ★

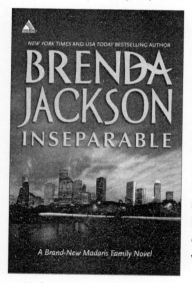